W9-CAZ-712

2020

EMERALD BLAZE

By Ilona Andrews

Hidden Legacy series
BURN FOR ME
WHITE HOT
WILDFIRE
DIAMOND FIRE (novella)
SAPPHIRE FLAMES
EMERALD BLAZE

Kate Daniels series
MAGIC BITES
MAGIC BURNS
MAGIC STRIKES
MAGIC BLEEDS
MAGIC SLAYS
MAGIC RISES
MAGIC BREAKS
MAGIC GIFTS (novella)
MAGIC SHIFTS
MAGIC BINDS
MAGIC TRIUMPHS

The Edge series
ON THE EDGE
BAYOU MOON
FATE'S EDGE
STEEL'S EDGE

ILONA ANDREWS

EMERALD BLAZE

A Hidden Legacy Novel

Fiction
Andrews

AVONBOOKS

An Imprint of HarperCollins*Publishers*

EMERALD BLAZE. Copyright © 2020 by Ilona Gordon and Andrew Gordon. All rights reserved. Printed in the United States of America. No part of this book may be used or reproduced in any manner whatsoever without written permission except in the case of brief quotations embodied in critical articles and reviews. For information, address HarperCollins Publishers, 195 Broadway, New York, NY 10007.

First Avon Books mass market printing: September 2020
First Avon Books hardcover printing: August 2020

Print Edition ISBN: 978-0-06-303547-8
Digital Edition ISBN: 978-0-06-287837-3

Avon, Avon & logo, and Avon Books & logo are registered trademarks of HarperCollins Publishers in the United States of America and other countries. HarperCollins is a registered trademark of HarperCollins Publishers in the United States of America and other countries.

FIRST EDITION

20 21 22 23 24   LSC   10 9 8 7 6 5 4 3 2 1

To the essential workers and medical personnel on the front lines of the COVID-19 pandemic.
We are alive because of you.
Thank you.

 # Acknowledgments

We would like to thank our wonderful editor, Erika Tsang, for making a mess into a book and "having faith" in us. We also would like to thank all the people we tortured at Avon: Nicole Fischer, Christine Langone, Brittani DiMare, and Pamela Jaffee. You thought you would escape unharmed, Pam. Ha-ha.

We are incredibly grateful to Nancy Yost, our agent, and the amazing and long-suffering crew at Nancy Yost Literary Agency: Sarah Younger, Natanya Wheeler, and Cheryl Pientka. Yay, we finished another book, somehow, against all odds.

A special thank you to Stephanie Mowery, who helped us to make our copyedits even more thorough, and Jessie Mihalik, Jill Smith, and RJ Blain for their advice and friendship. Huge thank you to poor Jeaniene Frost, who put aside her own novel to critique chunks of unfinished manuscript and endured our endless whining about it.

We also would like to thank all the people who kindly lent us their expertise. All mistakes in the manuscript are ours alone. Thank you to Chiara Prato, Harriet Chow, Jing Ting, Sherene Neo, and Nina Z. Javan, Esq.

Last but not least, we would love to thank all of our beta readers, who have read the working version of the manuscript and somehow survived: Hasna Saadani, Kate Small, Jeanine Rachau, Julie Heckert, Scott Drummond, Tori Benson, Robyn Huffman, Kristi DeCourcy, and Debra J. Murray. If we forgot someone, we are so sorry.

 # Prologue

*T*he wolf was coming.

Lander Morton knew this because he'd invited the wolf into his home. His body man, Sheldon, had come to tell him the wolf was at the door and had gone to fetch him. Now the two of them were coming back, but Lander only heard one set of footsteps echo through the house.

He shifted in his wheelchair and took a long swallow of his bourbon. Fire rolled down his throat. His old guts would make him pay for it later, but he didn't care. Some men were men, and others were wolves in human skin. He needed a human wolf for this job, and he would get one.

For the first time in the last three days he felt something other than crushing grief. This new emotion cut through the thick fog of despair, and he recognized it as anticipation. No, it was more than that. It was a heady mix of expectation, apprehension, and excitement tinged with fear. He used to feel like this years ago, when he was on the verge of closing a huge deal. It had been decades since he'd experienced this splash of adrenaline, and for a moment, he felt young again.

Sheldon appeared in the doorway of the study and stood aside, letting the other man enter. The guest took three steps inside and stopped, letting himself be seen. He was young, so young, and he moved with an easy grace that made Lander feel ancient. Strong, tall, handsome in that Mediterranean way, shaped by sun and salt water. When Felix's boy grew up, he might look like that.

Pain lashed him, and Lander struggled with it.

His guest waited.

Lander looked at his face. There it was, in the eyes, the wolf looking back at him. Cold. *Hungry.*

About time he got here. No, he couldn't say that. He had to be civil. He couldn't fuck this up. "Thank you for coming to see me on such short notice."

Sheldon stepped back into the hall and closed the doors. He would wait by them to make sure they wouldn't be interrupted.

"Please think nothing of it," the guest said. "My condolences."

Lander nodded to the bottle of Blood Oath Pact bourbon waiting on a corner of the desk. "A drink?"

The guest shook his head. "I don't drink on the job."

"Smart." Lander splashed another inch of bourbon into his glass. He wasn't sure if he was drowning his grief or building up liquid courage. If he failed to state his case and the man walked away . . . He couldn't let him walk away.

"I knew your father," Lander said. "I met him and your mother while I was over there making a deal for Carrara marble for the Castle Hotel. It was expensive as hell, but I wanted the best."

The man shrugged.

Panic squirmed through Lander. Words came tumbling out. "They killed my son. They took his money, they used his knowledge and connections, and then they murdered him, and I don't know why."

"Do you care why?"

"Yes, but I've already hired someone for that."

"So, what do you want from me?"

"I loved my son. He was smart, sharp, sharper than I ever was, and honest. People hate my guts, but everyone liked him because he was a good man. His wife, Sofia, died three years ago, and he took care of their kids by himself. A son and two daughters. The boy is the oldest, fourteen years old. I've had a stroke, and there's cancer eating at me, but now I can't croak for four more years. I've got to hold on until the boy is old enough to take over. I want those bastards to die!"

Lander clenched his fists. His voice had gone hoarse and some part of him warned him he sounded unhinged. But the hurt was too raw, and it bled out of him.

"I want them to suffer, and I want them to know why. They took my son from me and from his children. They've ruined my boy, my handsome, smart boy. Everything I built, everything he built, they think they can just rip it all away from me." His voice dropped barely above a whisper, rough and dripping pain. "Kill them. Kill them for me."

Silence filled the study.

Worry drowned Lander. Had he said too much? Did he sound too crazy?

"My mother remembers meeting you," the guest said. "There is a photo of the three of you on the yacht. She was pregnant with me at the time. She said her morning sickness was unbearable and you told her that ginger ale was the best for upset stomachs. There was no ginger ale to be had so you ordered a case of it from Milan by courier."

The guest stepped up to the desk, splashed a finger of bourbon into the second glass, and raised it. "To your son."

He drained the glass in one swallow and Lander saw the wolf again, staring at him from within the man's soul.

"Does this mean you'll take the job?"

"Yes."

The relief was almost overwhelming. Lander slumped in his chair.

"I reviewed your situation prior to my visit," the guest said. "It will take time and money. It will be complicated, because it has to be done right."

"Whatever it takes," Lander said. He felt so tired. He'd done it. He could look at Felix's gravestone now and he could promise his son that revenge was coming.

"The proof of their guilt must be irrefutable."

"Don't worry about that," Lander said. "You'll have your proof. I only hire the best."

 Chapter 1

"House Baylor Investigative Agency," I shouted. "Holster your weapons and step away from the monkey!"

The orange tamarin monkey, about the size of a large squirrel, stared at me from the top of the lamppost, silhouetted against the bright blue sky of a late afternoon. The two men and a woman under the post continued to grip their guns.

All three wore casual clothes, the men in khakis and T-shirts, the woman in white capris and a pale blue blouse. All three were in good shape, and they held their guns in nearly identical positions, with their barrels pointing slightly down, which marked them as professionals who didn't want to accidentally shoot us. Given that none of us had drawn weapons yet, they must have felt they had the upper hand. Sadly for them, their assessment of their personal safety was wildly off the mark.

Next to me, Leon bared his teeth. "Catalina, I really don't like it when people point guns at me."

Neither did I, but unlike Leon, I would be highly unlikely to shoot each of them through the left eye "for symmetry reasons."

"Montgomery International Investigations," the older of the men announced. "Pack it in and head back to the mystery machine, kids."

Usually Augustine's people wore suits, but chasing monkeys through the sweltering inferno of Houston's July called for a more casual attire.

Leon and I had opted for casual as well. My face was dirty, my dark hair was piled in a messy bun on top of my head, and my clothes wouldn't impress anyone. Of the three of us, only Cornelius looked decent, and even he was drenched in sweat.

"You're interfering with our lawful recovery," I announced. "Step aside."

The female agent stepped forward. She was in her thirties, fit, with light brown skin and glossy dark hair pulled into a ponytail.

"You seem like a nice girl."

You have no idea.

She kept going. "Let's be reasonable about this before the testosterone starts flying. This monkey is the property of House Thom. It's a part of a very important pharmaceutical trial. I don't know what you've been told, but we have a certificate identifying the ownership of the monkey. I'll be happy to let you verify it for yourself. You're still young, so a word of advice, always get the proper paperwork to cover your ass."

"Oh no she didn't," Leon muttered under his breath.

At twenty-one, most of my peers were either in college, working for their House, or enjoying the luxury carefree lifestyle the powerful magic of their families provided. Being underestimated worked in my favor. However, we'd been looking for the monkey for several days. I was hot, tired, and hungry and my patience was in short supply. Besides, she'd insulted my paperwork skills. Paperwork was my middle name.

"This monkey is a helper monkey, a highly trained service animal, certified to assist individuals with spinal cord injuries. She was snatched from her rightful owner during a trip to the doctor and illegally sold to your client. I have her pedigree report, immunization records, vet records, certificate from the Faces, Paws, and Tails nonprofit that trained her, a signed affidavit from her owner, a copy of the police report, and her DNA profile. Also, I'm not a nice girl. I *am* the Head of my House conducting a lawful recovery of stolen property. Do not impede me again."

On my left Cornelius frowned. "Could we hurry this along? Rosebud is experiencing a lot of stress."

"You heard the animal mage," Leon called out. "Don't we all want what's best for the stressed-out monkey?"

The shorter of the men squinted at us. "Head of the House, huh? How do you even know this is the same monkey?"

How many golden lion tamarin monkeys did he expect to be running around in Eleanor Tinsley Park? "Rosebud, sing."

The monkey raised her adorable head, opened her mouth, and trilled like a little bird.

The three MII employees stared at her. Here's hoping for logic and reason . . .

"This proves nothing," the woman announced.

As it happened so often with our species, logical reasoning was discarded in favor of the overpowering need to be right, facts and consequences be damned.

"What about now?" Leon asked. "Can I kill one? Just one. Please."

Leon was extremely selective about shooting people, but the MII agents drew on me and Cornelius, and his protective instinct kicked into overdrive. If they raised their guns another two inches, they would die, and my cousin was doing his best deranged rattlesnake act to keep that from happening.

Leon wagged his eyebrows at me.

"No," I told him.

"I said please. What about the kneecaps? I can shoot them in the kneecaps, and they won't die. They won't be happy, but they won't die."

"No." I turned to Cornelius. "Is there any way to retrieve her without hurting them?"

He smiled and looked to the sky.

Cornelius Maddox Harrison didn't look particularly threatening. He was white and thirty-one years old, of average build and below average height. His dark blond hair was trimmed by a professional stylist into a short but flattering cut. His features were attractive, his jaw clean shaven, and his blue eyes were always quiet, calm, and just a little distant. The three MII agents took one look at his face and his badass ensemble of light khaki pants and white dress shirt with rolled-up sleeves and decided they had nothing to worry about. Next to him, dark haired, tan, and lean, Leon radiated menace and kept making threats, so they judged him to be the bigger risk.

"This has been fun and all," the older MII agent said. "But playtime is over, and we have an actual job to do."

A reddish-brown hawk plummeted from the sky, plucked the monkey from the pole, swooped over the agents, and dropped Rosebud into Cornelius' waiting hand. The monkey scampered up Cornelius' arm and onto his shoulder, hugged his neck, and trilled into his ear. The chicken hawk flew to our left and perched on the limb of a red myrtle growing by the sidewalk.

"Well, shit," the woman said.

"Feel free to report this to Augustine," I told them. "He has my number."

And if he had a problem with it, I would smooth it over. Augustine Montgomery and our family had a complicated relationship. I'd studied him with the same dedication I used to study complex equations, so if he ever became a threat, I could neutralize him.

The older of the men gave us a hard stare. His firearm crept up an inch. "Where do you think you're going?"

I snapped my Prime face on. "Leon, if he targets us, cripple him."

Leon's lips stretched into a soft, dreamy smile.

People in the violence business quickly learned to recognize other professionals. The MII agents were well trained and experienced, because Augustine prided himself on quality. They looked into my cousin's eyes and knew that Leon was all in. There was no fear or apprehension there. He enjoyed what he did, and given permission, he wouldn't hesitate.

Then they looked at me. Over the past six months I'd become adept at assuming my Head of the House persona. My eyes told them that I didn't care about their lives or their survival. If they made themselves into an obstacle, I would have them removed. It didn't matter what I wore, how old I was, or what words I said. That look would tell them everything they needed to know.

The tense silence stretched.

The woman whipped out her cell phone and turned away, dialing a number. The two men lowered their guns.

Oh good. Everyone would get to go home.

Augustine's people marched toward the river, the shorter man in the lead, and turned right, heading for the small parking lot where I had parked Rhino, the custom armored SUV Grandma Frida had made for me. They gave us a wide berth. We watched them go. No reason to force another confrontation in the parking lot.

We'd been looking for Rosebud for five days straight, ever since Cornelius took the case. Her owner, a twelve-year-old girl, was so traumatized by the theft, she'd had to be sedated. Finding the little monkey had trumped the rest of our caseload. We had accepted this job pro bono, because snatching a service animal from a child in a wheelchair was a heinous act and someone had to make it right.

Scouring Houston in hundred-degree heat looking for a tiny monkey took a lot of effort. I had barely managed five hours of sleep in the last forty-eight, but every bit of my sweat would be worth it if I could see Maya hug her monkey. My Monday was looking up.

Cornelius smiled again. "I do so love happy endings."

"Happy ending for you, maybe," Leon grumbled. "I didn't get to shoot anybody."

First, we would deliver Rosebud to Maya, and then I would go home, take a shower, and then a long, happy nap.

Cornelius shook his head. "Your reliance on violence is quite disturbing. What happens when you meet someone faster than you?"

My cousin pondered it. "I'll be dead, and it won't matter?"

Talon suddenly took to the air with a shriek, swooping over Buffalo Bayou River. Leon and Cornelius stopped at the same time. Cornelius frowned, looking at the murky waters to the left of a large tree.

Directly in front of us, a narrow strip of mowed lawn hugged the sidewalk. Past the grass, the ground sloped sharply, hidden by tall weeds all the way to the river that stretched to Memorial Parkway Bridge in the distance.

The river lay placid. Not even a ripple troubled the surface.

I glanced at Leon. A second ago his hands were empty. Now he held a SIG P226 in one hand and a Glock 17 in the other. It gave him thirty-two rounds of 9 mm ammunition. He only needed one round to make a kill.

"What is it?" I asked quietly.

"I don't know," Leon said.

"The hawk is scared," Cornelius said.

The surface of the river was still and shining slightly, reflecting the sunlight like a tarnished dime.

The distance in Cornelius' eyes grew deeper. "Something's coming," he whispered.

We had no reason to hang around and wait for it. "Let's go."

I turned right and sped up toward our vehicles. Leon and Cornelius followed.

Ahead the shorter of the MII agents was almost to the lot. The woman trailed him, while the taller agent brought up the rear.

A green body burst through the weeds. Eight feet long and four feet tall, it scrambled forward on two big muscular legs, dragging a long scaly tail fringed with bright carmine fins. Another fin—this one bloodred and crested with foot-long spikes—thrust from its spine. Its head could have belonged to an aquatic dinosaur or a prehistoric crocodile—huge pincher-like jaws that opened like giant scissors studded with conical fangs designed to grab and hold struggling prey while the beast pulled them under. Two pairs of small eyes, sunken deep into its skull, glowed with violet.

This didn't look like anything our planet had birthed. It was either some magic experiment gone haywire or a summon from the arcane realm.

We would need bigger guns.

The beast rushed across the grass. The taller MII agent was directly in its path.

"Run!" Leon and I screamed at the same time.

The man whipped around. For a frantic half second he froze, then jerked his gun up, and fired at the creature. Bullets bit into the beast and glanced off its thick scales.

The two other MII agents pivoted to the beast and opened fire. I sprinted to Rhino and the combat shotgun inside it. Leon dashed after me, trying to get a better angle on the creature. Cornelius followed.

Augustine's people emptied their magazines into the beast. It plowed through them, knocking them aside. Purple blood stained its sides, but the wounds barely bled, as if the bullets had merely chipped its scales.

The beast's gaze locked on me. It ignored the agents and hauled itself toward me, two massive paws gouging the turf with red claws.

Leon fired a two-bullet burst from each gun. Four bloody holes gaped where the creature's beady eyes used to be. It roared, stumbled, and crashed to the ground.

I halted. Cornelius ran past me to the lot.

The female MII agent rose slowly. Her tall friend stared at a bright red gash in his bare thigh. His left pant leg hung in bloody shreds around his ankle. He shifted his weight. Blood poured from the wound and I saw a glimpse of bone inside. The agent gaped at it, wide-eyed, clearly in shock.

"Holy shit," the shorter MII agent muttered and snapped a new magazine into his HK45.

At the edge of the parking lot, Cornelius spun around and waved his arms toward the river. "Don't stop! There's more! More are coming!"

Green beasts poured through the weeds, a mass of scaled bodies, finned tails, and fanged jaws, and in the center of their pack, buried under the creatures, a dense knot of magic pulsated like an invisible beacon. The knot's magic splayed out, touched me, and broke around my power, like a wave against a breaker. A sea of violet eyes focused on me.

The pack turned toward me and charged.

Whatever was emanating magic in the center of the pack was also controlling them. If I had a second, I could've fought it with my magic, but the cluster of bodies was too thick, and the beasts came too fast.

I turned and sprinted toward Rhino. The thing's magic followed me, pinging from my mind like radar. I didn't need to look back to know the entire pack chased me.

Ahead Cornelius jerked a car remote from his pocket. The lights of his BMW hybrid flashed. The hatchback rose and a massive blue beast tore out, a tiger on steroids, with glossy indigo fur splattered with black and pale blue rosettes.

Zeus landed, roared, flashing fangs the size of steak knives, and bounded across the parking lot. The fringe of tentacles around his neck snapped open, individual tendrils writhing. We passed each other, him sprinting at the creatures and me running in the opposite direction to Rhino.

Gunfire popped behind me like firecrackers going off—Leon, thinning the pack. He'd run out of bullets before they ran out of bodies.

I jumped into Rhino, mashed the brake, and pushed the ignition switch. The engine roared. Cornelius flung the passenger door open and landed in the seat. I stepped on it. Rhino's custom engine kicked into gear. We shot forward and jumped the curb onto the grass.

In front of us the lawn churned with bodies. A trail of scaled corpses stretched to the left, piling up at the curb of Allen Parkway. Across the street, Leon methodically sank bullets into the creatures in short bursts, using traffic as cover. Zeus snarled next to him. A corpse of a scaled beast lay nearby and Zeus raked it with his claws to underscore his point.

On our right the female agent and the leader had put their arms under the injured man's shoulders and staggered toward the parking lot. He hung limp, dragging his bleeding leg behind him. The leading beasts on the left snapped their jaws only feet behind them.

No more people would be mauled by these things today if I could help it.

I steered right, cutting the creatures off from the MII agents at a sharp angle. The enormously heavy bulk of Rhino smashed into the closest creature with a wet crunch. The armored vehicle careened as we rolled over a body. We burst through the edge of the pack into the clear. I put my foot down on the accelerator, tearing down the lawn. Behind me the pack thinned out as the creatures got in each other's way trying to turn to follow us. For a moment, the cluster of bodies dispersed. Something spun in their center, something metal, round, and glowing. The strange magic knot.

"You see it?"

"I see it." Cornelius pulled the tactical shotgun from the floorboards and pumped it.

"Can you reach their minds?"

"No. They're too preoccupied."

Asking him what that meant now would distract him. I made a hard left, clipping what was once the back of the pack, knocking the stragglers out of the way.

"Ready," Cornelius said, his voice calm.

I hit the button to lower the front windows and cut straight through the pack, mowing a diagonal line to the left. The churning rolling thing spun on our right, drawing tight circles on the grass. Cornelius stuck the barrel of the shotgun out the window and fired at the metal object.

BOOM.

My ears rang.

BOOM.

"One more time," Cornelius said, as if asking for another cup of tea.

We flashed by the pack, smashed head-on into a beast, and I veered right and jumped the curb back into the parking lot. In front of us, the MII vehicle, a silver Jeep Grand Cherokee, peeled out onto Allen Parkway with a squeal of tires. The stench of burning rubber blew into the cabin.

"You're welcome," Cornelius called after them and reloaded.

I made a hard right onto the parkway. The pack of beasts streaked by on our right.

BOOM.

BOOM.

"Didn't get it," Cornelius said. "The slugs bounced off the metal. There's something alive inside that spinning shell."

"Animal?"

"Not exactly."

If it was alive, we could kill it.

We could drive around until the pack tired enough to slow down, grab Leon and Zeus, and drive off, but then these things would rampage through Houston. There was a group of kids playing baseball just a quarter of a mile down the road. We had passed them and the adults who were watching them on our way in to retrieve Rosebud.

Rosebud!

"Where's the monkey?"

"Safe in the BMW."

Oh good. Good, good, good.

I pulled a sharp U-turn and sped down the street back toward the parking lot. The beasts scrambled to follow. The gaps between the bodies widened to several feet and I saw clearly the source of the magic. Two metal rings, spinning one inside the other, like a gyroscope. A small blue glow hovered between them.

We passed Leon. He pointed to the glowing thing with his SIG and pretended to smash the two guns in his hands together. *Ram it.* Thank you, Captain Strategy, I got it. That thing had survived the river. If I hit it with Rhino, it might just bounce aside, and if it was arcane, there was no telling what sort of damage it would do to the car. No, this would require precision.

"Rapier?" I asked.

"One moment." Cornelius turned and hit the switch on the console between our seats. Most SUV vehicles had two front seats and a wide backseat designed to seat three. Rhino's backseat was split into two, with a long, custom-built console storage space running lengthwise between them. The console popped open, and a weapon shelf sprang up, offering a choice of two blades and two guns secured by prongs.

I pulled another U-turn. A white truck screeched to a stop in front of me. The driver laid on the horn, saw the beasts, and reversed down the street at breakneck speed.

"Got it." Cornelius turned back in his seat, my rapier in his hand.

I aimed Rhino at the gyroscope. Bodies slammed against the car.

"This is foolhardy," Cornelius advised. "What if it explodes?"

"Then I'll be dead, and it won't matter," I quoted.

"Using Leon as inspiration is a doubtful survival strategy."

I slammed on the brakes. Rhino slid across the lawn and stopped. I grabbed the rapier from Cornelius and jumped out of the SUV. The rotating thing spun only fifty feet away from me. I sprinted to it.

A beast lunged at me. I jumped aside and kept running.

Behind me Rhino thundered as Cornelius revved the engine to distract them.

The air turned to fire in my lungs. I dodged a beast, another . . .

Thirty feet.

The shining object pinged me with its magic.

Twenty.

Ten.

The metal rings spun in front of me, a foot wide, splattered with slime and algae. Inside a flower bud glowed, a brilliant electric blue lotus woven of pure magic and just about to bloom.

My family's magic coursed through me, guiding my thrust. I stabbed it.

The bud burst, sending a cloud of luminescent sparks into the air. Its glow vanished. The rings spun one last time and collapsed.

The beasts around me froze.

For a torturous moment nothing moved.

The creatures stared at me. I stared back.

The pack turned and made a break for the river.

It was over.

Relief washed over me. A steady rhythmic noise came into focus, and I realized it was my heart racing in my chest. My knees shook. A bitter metallic patina coated my tongue. My body couldn't figure out if it was hot or cold. The world felt wrong, as if I had been poisoned.

The ruins of the device lay in front of me. I tried to take a step. My leg folded under me, the ground decided to spontaneously tilt to the side, and I almost wiped out on a perfectly level lawn. Too much adrenaline. Nothing to do but wait it out. Some people were born for the knife-edge intensity of combat. I wasn't one of them.

Focusing on something to distract myself usually helped. I crouched and scrutinized the rings. The metal didn't look exactly like steel, but it might have been some sort of iron alloy. A string of glyphs ran the circumference of each ring.

I pulled my phone out of my pocket and snapped a pic.

The rings fit inside each other, the inner about three inches smaller than the outer one. The flower stalk was attached to the bottom of the inner ring. No, not attached. It grew from the inner ring, seamlessly protruding from the metal.

How?

I picked up the ring and tugged on the stalk. It held. I ran my fingers along the flower. Toward the severed end, where the flower bud had been, the texture felt like a typical plant. But the lower I moved my fingers, the more metallic the texture became. A true biomechanical meld. To my knowledge, no mage had yet achieved it.

Rhino rolled up next to me and Cornelius jumped out. Pale purple blood splattered the armored vehicle's custom grille guard. Bits and pieces of alien flesh hung from the metal.

"Are you all right?" Cornelius asked.

No. "Yes. I'm so sorry," I told him. "I know this was very unpleasant for you."

Animal mages formed a special bond with a few chosen animals, but they cared about all of them, and we had just mowed down at least a dozen, maybe more.

Cornelius nodded. "Thank you for your concern. They weren't true animals in the native sense of the word. It helped some."

"Is this a summon?" I asked.

Cornelius shook his head. "I don't think so. They feel slightly similar to Zeus. Not of Earth but not completely of the arcane realm either."

"Earlier you said they were too 'preoccupied' to reach?"

Cornelius frowned and nodded at the rings and the bud within. "This object emitted magic."

"I felt it."

"The emissions were so dense, they effectively deafened the creatures. They couldn't feel me. I tried to contact the object itself, but the biological component of it is so primitive, it was like trying to communicate with a sea sponge."

The House lab scenario looked more and more likely. If these proto-crocodiles had come out of the arcane realm, we would have seen a summoner and a portal. Massive holes in reality were kind of hard to miss.

Linus would just love this.

I pulled out my phone and dialed his number. One beep, two, three . . .

At the other end of the lawn Leon jogged across the road, Zeus in tow.

The phone kept ringing. Officially Linus Duncan was retired. In reality, he still served the state of Texas in a new, more frightening capacity, and I was his Deputy. He always answered my calls.

Beep. Another.

Linus' voice came on the line. "Yes?"

"I was attacked by magic monsters in Eleanor Tinsley Park. They were controlled by a biomechanical device powered with magic."

Leon ran up and halted next to me.

"Do you require assistance?" Linus asked.

"Not anymore."

"Show me."

I activated FaceTime, switched the camera, and panned the phone, capturing the device, the corpses, and the fleeing creatures. On the screen, Linus stared into the phone. In his sixties, still fit, with thick salt-and-pepper hair, he always had the Texas tan. His features were handsome and bold, a square jaw framed by a short beard, prominent nose, thick dark eyebrows, and dark eyes that looked either hazel or brown, depending on the light. He smiled easily, and when he paid attention to you, you felt special. If you asked ten people who just met him to describe him, they would all say one word—*charming*.

The man looking back at me from the phone was the real Linus Duncan, a Prime, former Speaker of the Texas Assembly, focused, sharp, his eyes merciless. He looked like an old tiger who spotted an intruder in his domain and was sharpening his claws for the kill. A dry staccato came through the phone, a rhythmic *thud-thud-thud*, followed by a mechanical whine. Linus' turrets. He was under attack.

Who in the world would assault Linus Duncan in his home? He was a Hephaestus mage. He made lethal firearms out of discarded paperclips and duct tape and his house packed enough firepower to wipe out an elite battalion in minutes.

They attacked me and Linus simultaneously. The thought burned a trail through my mind like a comet. Was someone targeting the Office of the Warden?

"Disengage," Linus said. "Go straight to MII and take over the Morton case, use the badge. Repeat."

"Go straight to MII, show the badge, take over the Morton case."

Usually Linus brought me in after jurisdiction had been established. In the last six months, I'd had to use my badge exactly once, to take over an FBI investigation. To say they had been unhappy about it would be a gross understatement.

"I'll send the files." Linus hung up.

"That was turret fire," Leon said.

"It sure was."

My cousin grinned, no doubt anticipating another fight. "What are we doing?"

"You're driving me to MII."

"I'll follow." Cornelius sprinted to the parking lot, Zeus on his heels, bounding like an overly enthusiastic kitten.

I grabbed the device. The metal rings were slick with mud and slime. I walked to Rhino, threw the device into the bin in the back, and jumped into the passenger seat.

In the distance, police sirens wailed, getting closer.

Leon peeled out onto the street. In the rearview mirror, Cornelius' BMW glided out of the parking lot. We'd likely lose him before long. Cornelius' top driving speed usually stayed four miles over the posted limit. MII was roughly thirty minutes away but knowing Leon we would get there much faster if the traffic let us.

"Call Bern."

My cousin answered on the second ring, his voice coming from Rhino's speakers as the phone synced with the car's control panel.

"I was just attacked by some magical monsters. So was Linus."

"Was he with you?"

"No. He was at his mansion. Lock us down, please."

"Done. Do you need help?"

"No. Is everything okay there?"

"Everything is fine."

"I'm fine too, Bern!" Leon yelled.

"That's debatable," his older brother said.

"I'll call you in a bit," I told him and hung up.

My phone chimed, announcing a new email. I clicked my inbox. A message from Linus with a video file attached. The file was huge. Linus didn't optimize the video. I tapped it to download. This would take a while.

"Let me get this straight. Linus is attacked. You don't ask him if he needs help. You just drop everything and go to MII to take over some case you never heard about before." Leon shook his head.

"Yes. If Linus required my help, he would tell me." The Morton case was likely connected to the attacks somehow.

"One day you'll have to tell me what you do for Linus Duncan," Leon said.

"But then I'd have to kill you, and, as you often point out, you're my favorite cousin."

Leon snorted.

Most of my family had no problem with secrecy. Grandma Frida and Mom both served in the military, Bern naturally kept things to himself, and Nevada was a truthseeker. She could fill her and Rogan's mansion with other people's secrets and kept them to herself. But Leon and Arabella thrived on gossip. They knew I was doing something confidential for Linus Duncan, but they had no idea what exactly, and it was driving them both up the wall.

I dialed Augustine's direct number. Voice mail. Getting to see the head of MII on short notice could prove to be a problem. He was busy. But like Leon and Arabella, he loved to collect information—the more exclusive, the better. I had to bait my hook and dangle it in front of him just out of reach.

"This is Catalina Baylor. I have critical information regarding the Morton case. I must see you in person. I'll be at your office in twenty minutes."

I hung up.

"Who is Morton?" Leon asked, taking a corner too fast.

"Most likely Lander Morton. A Prime geokinetic, very old, very rich, one of the prominent developers in the state."

"How do you know that?"

I knew that because I did my homework. Linus Duncan had had a long and eventful career and he made no effort to conceal the close relationship between our two Houses. I wasn't sure if we would inherit his friends, but we would definitely inherit his enemies, which was why I had built a biographical database around Linus complete with charts profiling his relationships with various Houses.

"After Linus retired from the Army, he went into politics. Lander Morton used to be Linus' political rival. The first bill Linus tried to bring to the floor of the Assembly involved zoning restrictions for various Houses. Lander Morton opposed it. A lot of people owed him favors, and he called them in to kill the bill. It got ugly. Morton gave an interview to *Houston Chronicle* and told them that he would trust Linus with governance as soon as he took 'his mama's titty out of his mouth.'"

Leon choked on air. "How old was Linus, exactly?"

"Forty-two."

"And he let that slide?"

"He got Morton back three years later. They both tried to buy the same building, and Linus won. As soon as the ink dried on the closing papers, Linus bought earthquake insurance."

And he got it dirt cheap too. The last time a natural earthquake occurred around Houston was in 1910, near Hempstead. It was so weak, the city didn't even feel it.

"Two months after Linus moved his company in, a very small yet surprisingly powerful earthquake destroyed the building. Nobody died. The Assembly and the insurance company investigated, and Morton was slapped with a huge fine and barred from voting in the Assembly for three years. What he really lost was political power."

Leon frowned. "Is this Linus settling an old score?"

"I doubt it."

While it wasn't out of the realm of possibility, it was highly unlikely. Linus dedicated himself to service, first military, then civil. Using his official position in a petty political squabble went against everything I knew about him.

The video file finally downloaded. I opened it.

Someone was flying a drone above a swamp. Bright algae islands, emerald green, electric blue, and neon orange floated on the surface. Here and there an abandoned husk of a building thrust through the bog, wrapped in vines and sheathed in moss. Lilies bloomed on the dark water, but rather than the usual white or pink, they were bloodred, so vivid, they almost glowed. Strange trees spread their branches over the mire, their limbs contorted and knotted.

Where was this? It looked like some alien world.

The drone ducked under a tree tinseled with long strands of bizarre moss and emerged into a clearing. Four rickety wooden bridges met at a small island supporting the remnants of what once must have been an office building. Someone had jury-rigged power lines and several long cables converged at a small power pole on top of the structure. One of them supported a body.

It hung above the water, its neck caught in a loop of the cable stretching from the nearby building. The drone turned, getting a better view of the corpse. A man in his late thirties, white, dark haired, wearing pants from a business suit, a torn blue dress shirt, and black dress shoes.

The drone's camera dipped down, closed in, then panned up, capturing the body from bottom to the top.

No, he wasn't wearing shoes. His feet had been burned to charred blackness. Ragged gaps marked his trousers over the knees, their edges stained with blood. A melon-sized chunk of his right side was missing, the wound red and jagged, dripping blood from where it had pooled in the body cavity. Prickly heat stabbed at my spine. He'd suffered before he died.

Breathe. This is your job. Do your job.

His face was an awful mess of blood and broken bone. His left eye had swollen shut. The bridge of his nose jutted to the side. His mouth gaped open and a green slimy trail had leaked from his busted lips, staining the front of his shirt.

The sheer brutality of it was nauseating. I wanted to cover my eyes so I wouldn't have to look at him.

How could anyone do this to another human being?

"Catalina?" Leon asked, concern in his voice. "Are you okay? What is it?"

"It's not Lander Morton." Lander was eighty-three. The dead man had the build and dark hair of someone much younger.

What was this? Where was this?

A silver Alfa Romeo Spider flew past us down the street.

Alessandro.

The thought sliced through me, hot and sharp. I yanked myself back from it. Alessandro left six months ago. He was never coming back.

"It wasn't him," Leon said. "In the car."

"I know."

"If it was that jackass, I would've shot him by now." His voice was cold and measured. He meant it.

"Why would you want to shoot him?"

"He broke your heart. You were miserable for weeks."

"I broke my own heart, Leon. He was just the hammer I hit it with."

Leon raised his eyebrows. "That's deep, Catalina. Small problem though. I was there. He took advantage of your feelings, used you to help him, and then he split. You were depressed for months. You know that saying 'I'll make him wish he was never born'? If he shows his face here again, I'll actually do that."

Leon's face had that particular calm, focused look that came over him when he locked on to his target.

If I detached enough to look at what happened between me and Alessandro, it made perfect sense. My magic had isolated me since I was born. If I liked someone or wanted them to notice me, they fell in love with me, completely and absolutely. Soon magic-fueled love progressed into obsession that turned violent. I was homeschooled until high school, because every time I thought I had my magic under control and tried to enroll in public school, disaster followed.

My attempts at relationships had been hesitant and always ended badly. A boy in middle school had built a shrine out of my used tissues and chewed-up pencils in his room and cut his wrists open to keep his parents from confiscating it. His family moved out of state to escape his obsession and I had to go back to being homeschooled. A high school football hero who all of a sudden noticed me panicked at the end of our perfectly nice date because I was leaving, grabbed me by the hair, and tried to force me into his car. There were others. Some escaped with their lives relatively unscathed, but others didn't. I didn't make a true friend outside the family until a few months ago. By that point, I had learned to control my power but lived in a constant state of paranoia, afraid that I would slip up and ruin someone's life and endanger mine.

There was a time somewhere between fifteen and twenty when I desperately wanted friends. I had wanted a boyfriend, someone who was amazing, and handsome, and smart, who could carry on a conversation with me and get my jokes. Someone who would take off his jacket and drape it over my shoulders if we were caught in the rain. I wanted a connection, that simple human feeling of having someone to share things with. Handsome witty princes were in short supply, so I invented one, woven from book-inspired fantasies and naive little dreams. And then, one day I stumbled over Alessandro Sagredo's Instagram account.

He was everything I had imagined my prince to be. Smart, handsome, charming. He lived in Italy, he was a Prime, an heir to an old noble family, and he sailed on the Mediterranean and rode horses in Spain. He was safe to dream about because he and I would never meet, and so I did.

Then, when I was eighteen, our family was forced to become a House, and I had to face off against Alessandro in the trials to prove that I was a Prime. He was everything his Instagram promised, and he noticed me. I was so terrified I had cooked him with my magic that when he came to ask me on a date, I did everything I could to push him away and then called the cops to keep him safe from me.

Six months ago, he crashed into my life again. The carefree playboy turned out to be a front. Alessandro was a ruthless, lethal killer. He tried to protect me, he flirted with me, he ate dinner with my family. He was immune to my magic, which meant that when he said he was obsessed with me, he actually meant it. He liked me for me.

The enormity of all that had short-circuited what little sense I had left. I never had a chance. I wanted to save him from the life of a contract killer and set him free. I wanted him to be happy.

And then the investigation ended and his fascination with me did as well. I had come to confess my love to him and found him packing. He was moving on to the next target on his hit list. When I asked him if he would ever come back, he told me he didn't want to lie. It felt like someone pushed me off the top of a tall building and I hit the ground hard.

The rough landing woke me up. He had chosen the life he had for a reason and he wasn't planning on giving it up. And whatever he felt for me, it sure wasn't love. If you're obsessed with someone, you don't leave. You stay and try your hardest to make it work. I had been a fun diversion on his way to someplace else.

The obsession was now over. It hurt, but according to Sergeant Heart, who supervised my martial arts training, pain was the best teacher. Alessandro had people to kill, and I had a House to run and MII cases to take over. Leon was right. I had been depressed for months, but I wasn't mourning Alessandro abandoning me. I was mourning the old me. For the new me to emerge, the old me had to disappear, and killing her bit by bit hurt.

Alessandro was a catalyst for that change. Eventually I'd scrounge up some gratitude for the lesson. No matter how agonizing, it was a necessary transformation. The old me would have gotten the lot of us killed. For now, I had to settle for determination. I would never again let myself sink that deep. And I wouldn't allow my cousin to be hurt for my sake.

"Leon, if you shoot Alessandro, he will know he hurt me. I don't want him to."

Leon glanced at me.

I met his gaze.

"You have a point," he said and pulled into the parking lot.

In front of us the MII building rose, a sharp triangular blade of cobalt glass and steel. It was time to earn my pay.

 # Chapter 2

I marched through the gleaming lobby of Montgomery International Investigations at full speed. Cornelius and Leon walked a couple of steps behind me. Rosebud still perched on Cornelius' shoulder, her tiny arms around his neck.

The guard by the metal detector focused on me. Recognition sparked in his eyes.

"Good afternoon, Ms. Baylor."

"Good afternoon."

I walked through the metal detector and kept going to the stainless-steel elevator doors. Cornelius and Leon followed me. We took the elevator to the 17th floor. The double doors whispered open to glossy indigo floors and white walls. To the left lay a waiting area, tinted by the light spilling through the floor-to-ceiling wall of blue glass. Directly in front of us Lina sat at the reception desk. Today her hair was a rich purple and twisted into a conservative slick bun, contrasting nicely with her deep bronze skin and blue eyes. She wore an impeccably tailored olive-green sheath dress, which, combined with her hair, made her look like a stalk of flowering lavender.

"He's expecting you," she said.

I nodded and turned right at her desk, trailing the curving white wall. Behind me Lina asked, "Can I get you some refreshments, gentlemen?"

"Could I trouble you for some grapes?" Cornelius asked. "For the monkey."

"We can get her all the grapes ever, because she is so adorable, yes, she is," Lina cooed.

Walking through Augustine's domain was like swimming under-water. The entire left wall was cobalt glass, two floors high, the city distant and remote behind it. The blue light colored the pale floor and walls, the pattern within the glass creating a perfect illusion of sunlight fracturing on the surface of water. It was its own little world, away from everything, soothing and calm, and I treasured the few moments I had to enjoy it.

I was about to expose my official status to Augustine. There would be no turning back from it.

Ahead a wall of frosted glass blocked the way. When Augustine wanted to impress, he projected his magic onto it, painting it with shifting patterns like frost growing on a window. But I had been to his office before and he felt no need to impress me. The wall remained beautiful but mundane. And solid. Augustine must've been wrapping up some business. I had to wait.

I crossed the floor to the wall of cobalt glass and looked at the city below, a great big sea of people. Towers of glass, steel, and concrete were its islands and icebergs, the currents of cars through the streets were the schools of its fish, and within its depths, hidden in luxurious offices, human sharks ran their magic empires.

The world didn't always have magic. Oh, there were rumors and legends, but nothing obvious. Then, a century and a half ago, half a dozen countries were looking for the cure for the influenza pandemic ravaging the globe. They shared their research and discovered the Osiris serum, almost simultaneously. Those who took the serum could expect one of the three equally likely outcomes: they would die, they would turn into a monster and die after living for a couple of years, or they would gain magic powers. The quality of magic varied: one could have a minor talent, or one could become a Prime, able to unleash devastating power.

At first, the serum was given to anyone brave enough to chance the consequences. Nobody stopped to think that randomly handing people the power to incinerate entire city blocks and spew deadly plagues could be a terrible idea. Then the World War broke out. The eight years that followed were known as the Time of Horrors.

Lord Acton, a 19th century historian, once wrote that power tended to corrupt. According to him, great men were almost always bad men. Great mages of the Time of Horrors proved him right. They were abominations who slaughtered their fellow human beings like cattle because they felt like it. People died by the thousands. Revolts and riots sparked all over the planet. The world caught on fire, and when the blaze finally died down, humanity learned three lessons.

First, the use of Osiris serum had to be banned by an international decree.

Second, the magic powers turned out to be hereditary. Primes beget Primes, leading to the formation of magic families referred to as Houses.

Third, the magic community had to find a way to stabilize itself. During the Time of Horrors people without magic weren't the only ones who died. Stronger magic users had preyed on the weaker mages, and those who committed atrocities eventually met mob justice. No matter how powerful an individual mage was, they were always vastly outnumbered. Nobody wanted the repeat of riots and mass executions. They were bad for business, and having achieved power, the Houses now wanted order and safety to reap its benefits.

The Houses came together and instituted state Assemblies, where each Prime had voting power. The state Assemblies answered to the National Assembly, the ultimate authority on all things magic. The National Assembly required someone to investigate breaches of its laws. That's where the Office of the Warden came in. The Texas Rangers' official motto was "One riot, One Ranger." The National Assembly subscribed to that philosophy. There was only one Warden per state, a mage of outstanding power whose identity remained confidential. Each Warden was allowed one apprentice.

Linus Duncan was the Warden of Texas and six months ago I became his Deputy. It happened almost by accident. If you had asked me a year ago who Linus Duncan was, I would've said that he was a family friend. He'd been one of the two official witnesses at the formation of our House and had taken an interest in us from that point. He invited us to his backyard barbecues. He'd been to our home multiple times. He was like a rich uncle everyone liked.

Now I knew better. Linus Duncan was the last line of defense between humanity and the horrors spawned by people with too much magic and consumed by lust for money and power. In the past six months, I had seen things that made me wake up in a cold sweat in the middle of the night. Between that and the crucible of Victoria Tremaine, they forged me from a shy person who stammered when an older adult gave her a critical look into this new version of me.

I became the Deputy to keep the people I loved safe. No matter how many family dinners Linus attended, how much he doted on us, and how often he invited the entire House Baylor to his ranch and his mansion, if I breached the boundaries he laid out for me, he would eliminate us without hesitation. So no matter how many cute comments my cousin made, I would tell him nothing. I would follow my orders and do my job.

A section of the glass slid aside. Prime Montgomery was finally ready for me.

I strode into the ultramodern office. Augustine looked at me from behind his desk. An illusion Prime, he could look like anyone, including me. He chose to look like a demigod. His pale skin all but glowed. His face was masculine but heartbreaking in its beauty. His nearly white hair framed his features with impossible perfection. If it wasn't for the sharp awareness in his green eyes and wire-thin glasses, people would worship him when they saw him on the street.

The demigod in a three-thousand-dollar suit spoke. "Ms. Baylor. To what do I owe the pleasure?"

Augustine hoarded information. Keeping my Deputy status confidential was in my best interest, but he would never give me the case without it. I had walked into his place of business and was about to strong-arm him. That would infuriate any Prime, and I would need his cooperation throughout this investigation.

I had to soften the blow. The only way to do that was to make him think he was forcing me to do something I didn't want to. It would give him the illusion of having the upper hand.

"I would like you to give me the Morton case."

Augustine leaned back in his chair, his eyes amused. "And why would I do that?"

"I would consider it a personal favor."

"No. Even if I were inclined to pass on this lucrative opportunity, I wouldn't be doing you any favors. This case is a nightmare, which explains its commensurate price tag."

"Please reconsider."

Augustine studied me. "You haven't given me a reason to do so. The answer is still no."

Good enough.

I raised my arm, bending it at the elbow so he could see my forearm, and concentrated. Magic twisted through my bone and muscle. It was like trying to squeeze a rubber ring with my fingers. A circle braided from a stylized vine shone through my skin with an amber glow, enclosing the five-point star inside.

Augustine blinked. For a shocked moment, he just stared. Then a slow smile curved his lips. "This explains so much."

"Should we skip the formalities?"

"No, by all means, continue. I would like the full treatment."

I sighed. "Prime Augustine Montgomery, by the authority vested in me by the National Assembly, I, Catalina Baylor, Deputy Warden of the State of Texas, hereby claim ownership of all matters pertaining to House Morton. You are commanded to provide all information and render all necessary aid to me in my pursuance of this matter. You will present me to the involved parties as a representative of MII and you will maintain the highest level of secrecy regarding my true affiliation. The National Assembly appreciates your compliance."

I let the badge fade.

Augustine looked like a hungry kid in a candy store. "Is Duncan the Warden?"

There was no point in lying. "Yes."

"Does Connor know?"

The rivalry between Augustine and my brother-in-law stretched all the way back to their college days. Was he asking if Connor knew that

Linus was the Warden or that I was his Deputy? The less information I gave him, the better.

"Please be more specific."

Augustine snapped his fingers. "He doesn't know about you, but he knows about Duncan. Did Duncan try to recruit him?"

"You would have to ask him."

"He did, and Connor must've turned him down, and now you took his place. This is wonderful. I love it."

"If you're done gloating . . ."

"I can gloat and cooperate at the same time." Augustine pushed a key on his desk phone and said, "See me. Catalina, what do you know about the Morton case?"

"Nothing."

"Lander Morton's only son, Felix, was murdered three days ago. He was involved in a reclamation project with representatives of four other Houses."

"What are they reclaiming?"

"The Pit."

Jersey Village? The little city, a part of Houston metro, had been flooded years ago during a harebrained attempt to build a subway system. Now the alien swamp in the video sort of made sense. But the last time I had gone to the Pit, over three years ago, it looked just like a typical flood zone with stagnant water and half-burst buildings where drug addicts, the homeless, and the magic-warped hid among the moldy garbage. It hadn't looked like the arcane realm had thrown up in it.

"The five Houses had signed a contract specifying that they would submit to an investigation in case one of them died under suspicious circumstances. Each of the principles carries a vital personal insurance policy that won't be paid out until such an investigation is concluded. The four surviving partners are currently suspects. They and Lander Morton are coming here today to meet with my chief investigator."

Five Primes expecting a top-of-the-line professional investigator, Montgomery's best. "Today when?"

He smiled.

The wall opened and Lina walked through the door.

"Ms. Baylor is about to meet with five Primes," Augustine said. "I need you to fix . . ." He waved his hand at me. "That."

Lina pursed her lips.

I wore athletic sandals, jean shorts, and a sleeveless T-shirt with spaghetti straps, stained with sweat. My bun had fallen, my hair was a tangled mess, and I was pretty sure there were twigs in it, since two hours ago I had climbed a giant pecan tree because I thought I spotted Rosebud in it and my hair got caught in the branches. I had also climbed onto a roof of a building to peer into a chimney, and the dust and soot had combined with sweat to give my face a swirly sheen of grime. Minor scrapes covered my arms and legs. Purple blood splattered my clothes. And the star of the show—a three-claw-shaped scrape on my left thigh, which I must have gotten sprinting to the device. It wasn't deep, but it had bled, adding dried blood to my award-winning fashion ensemble.

"How much time do I have?" Lina asked.

"The meeting is in forty-three minutes," Augustine said. "I still need to brief her."

"Could you glamour her?" Lina asked.

"No. She's meeting with her grieving client and a room full of Primes, who know they are suspects. They would recognize illusion. She needs to inspire trust and be a beacon of integrity."

Lina rolled her eyes and grabbed my hand. "Come with me."

Twenty minutes later I sat in Augustine's office trying not to move while Lina attempted to brush my hair. The shower in the executive bathroom was truly lovely but scrubbing all the blood off my skin took longer than I expected. I wore light grey slacks with a white blouse and a towel draped over my back, so my half-dried hair wouldn't stain the satin top.

"Over the years, the Pit became the go-to place to dump magical hazmat," Augustine said. "Currently the amount of arcane matter within the Pit has reached critical levels. Summoned creatures that escape control of their summoners seem to be drawn to it and now they are breeding in the bog. The city council offered a lucrative contract to whoever could fix it. If reclaimed, the Pit would become an area of prized real estate, to which the reclamation crew would hold certain rights."

That made sense. The former Jersey Village was close enough to Houston's downtown to be valuable as both residential and commercial property and since nobody lived there, aside from the homeless and junkies, there would be no relocation costs associated with it. Whoever claimed it could build whatever they wanted and make a fortune.

"The contract went to the alliance of five Houses." Augustine clicked a remote. A section of the frosted wall turned into a large digital screen. On it, five people sat, obviously posing for a publicity picture.

"How can you have so much hair?" Lina growled. "And it's so long too."

"Seventeen minutes," Augustine told her. "First from the left, our victim, Felix Morton. Forty-two years old, widower, three young children, a geokinetic like his father."

The athletic white man in the picture, dark haired, handsome, with an easy, genuine smile, looked nothing like the mutilated corpse hanging from the electric cable.

"Publicly, Lander and Felix were estranged. Privately, Lander adored his son. Like his father, Felix was smart and had a talent for making money. Unlike his father, he was amiable and likeable. Lander realizes that even his close associates detest him. He didn't want his son to inherit his enemies, so they concocted this feud and took pains to keep it up, but privately Lander and Felix were a team. Lander was consulted on all major decisions Felix made."

Lina finished brushing and moved on to braiding.

"Did you do the preliminaries?"

Augustine gave me a look reserved for someone with half a brain and passed me a zippered leather folder. I unzipped it. The coroner's report, police report, notes from the detectives on the scene, timeline, a set of keys . . .

I held out the keys.

"Lander took the grandchildren to his house. You have full access to Felix's home and his computer. The passwords are on a card in the left pocket."

"Thank you."

"These are Felix's business partners," Augustine said, turning back to the publicity picture.

"You said that these four Primes are the primary suspects. Why them? Felix's death threatens the project. Don't they have an interest in keeping the reclamation going?"

Augustine nodded. "Indeed. The Pit is a chain of islands, connected by bridges and accessible by a single road. At night, the Pit is shut down. All personnel withdraw except for the guard at the gate that blocks that road. The main island with the project's HQ is protected by a fence and a gate. The gate requires an after-hours code that is known only by the five members of the board. The night Felix died the code was used twice. First time by an unknown member of the board or their agent, who then proceeded to destroy the surveillance footage from the hidden camera feed, and second by Felix himself."

"He walked into a trap."

"Yes." Augustine turned back to the publicity shot. "From left to right. Next to Felix is Marat Kazarian, Prime, Summoner."

Marat was in his midthirties with tanned skin and curly dark hair, dark eyes, a prominent nose, and a short dark beard. He wore a wine-colored suit, an unusual choice, but it fit him. The last name pointed to Armenian roots. I didn't immediately recognize the House. There was something dangerous about Marat. He would look at home in a black outfit atop a dark horse brandishing a sword. He stared at the camera as if it was challenging him.

"Cheryl Castellano, Prime, Animator."

Cheryl could have been anywhere from twenty-five to forty-five. She had olive skin and a beautiful full face with a wide mouth and big grey eyes under artfully shaped eyebrows. Her brown hair with caramel high-lights was pulled back into a loose, effortless updo. Her expression was kind and slightly tired, as if she fully understood the artificial nature of the picture but had resigned herself to playing her part. I hadn't come across her House either, although I'd heard her name before, associated with some charitable work.

"Stephen Jiang, Prime, Aquakinetic."

Stephen was ridiculously handsome. If I didn't know better, I would have taken him for an illusion Prime. In his early twenties or possibly thirties, he sat on a stool wearing a navy suit with a white shirt and dark blue tie. His dark hair was cut in a fashionable style and brushed back, exposing a broad high forehead. His cheekbones were perfect, his cheeks slightly concave above a square jaw with a strong chin. His nose was narrow, his lips full, and his eyes, dark and piercing, looked at the world with surprising intensity.

He also looked vaguely familiar. For the life of me I couldn't remember where I'd seen him before. We hadn't met. I would remember that.

"Yummy," Lina volunteered, twisting the braid in the back of my head.

"Yes, he's handsome." Augustine looked at me. "Almost as handsome as Alessandro Sagredo."

Grabbing a pen off the desk and stabbing Augustine Montgomery with it wasn't in the best interest of my House and would significantly hamper my investigation. But I would have enjoyed it.

"And finally . . ."

"Tatyana Pierce," I finished. "Prime, Pyrokinetic."

About four years ago, Adam Pierce, the youngest son of House Pierce, handsome and spoiled by his family, involved himself in a political conspiracy, which was now known as the Sturm-Charles conspiracy, and tried to burn down Houston. My older sister, Nevada, and my brother-in-law were the reason the city was still standing, and Adam was now rotting in a high security prison in Alaska. Tatyana Pierce was his sister.

I looked at Tatyana. She was thirty-six years old, with chestnut hair pulled into a loose braid and tossed over one shoulder. Both Adam and Peter, her older brother, were lean, but she was softer, with a rounded face and a generous figure. A beautiful woman, the kind who would turn heads and reduce stainless-steel beams to puddles of glowing metal in seconds. And she hated Connor, Nevada, and our entire family.

This was less than ideal. Much, much less.

"Time's up." Augustine rose. "Remember, every participant contributed money to the Pit but the bulk of the investment came from House Morton. The project was plagued with issues from the start. If the flow of that cash stops today, tomorrow the site will become a construction equipment graveyard."

I pulled the towel off my shoulders. The section of the frosted wall turned into a mirror in front of me. I looked exactly the way I would have chosen to look for this meeting. Well put together, professional, with subtle makeup and my hair out of the way in a complex plait on my neck. Lina's expertise with cosmetics made me look older. I had let Victoria Tremaine's granddaughter out of the cage.

"Whoa," Lina murmured.

"I believe we're ready." Augustine waved his hand and the section of the frosted wall slid aside. He invited me to go through. "Please."

We walked down the underwater hallway side by side.

"Any words of wisdom?" I asked. Augustine enjoyed a mentor role.

"Life is full of surprises," he said. "Try to cope with grace."

We entered a small room. Inside two MII employees waited by an elderly white man sitting in a wheelchair. Gaunt, his grey hair cut very short, he stared through me with dark eyes, like an old buzzard defending its carrion. If I showed any weakness at all, he would claw me bloody. Lander Morton. My new employer.

Lander peered at Augustine. "About time. I thought you said it would be a man."

Augustine shrugged. "She's better."

"She looks young. How old are you?"

"Old enough. I'm here because I deliver. Do you want results, or do you want someone who looks the part?"

Lander squinted at me. "She'll do. Let's get on with this."

Augustine nodded. The female employee opened the double doors, revealing a luxury conference room. The four Primes from the publicity photo sat at the table, each with an assistant standing behind them.

Lander motioned me over with a wave of his bony fingers. I stepped closer and bent down.

"One of these fuckers killed my boy," he told me in a hoarse whisper loud enough for everyone in the room to hear. "You find which one of them did it."

I nodded and straightened.

Lander touched the controls on his chair, and it rolled forward into the room. Augustine and I followed, he on the left and I on the right.

Nobody rose. Clearly, manners were in short supply.

Lander stopped his chair a few feet from the table, peering at the group. Augustine smoothly stepped to the side, out of the way, leaving me and Lander on our own.

"Our deepest condolences," Cheryl said. She sounded like she meant it.

"Save it," Lander snapped at her. "You all know why we're here. My son is dead and the contract you signed obligates you to cooperate with the inquest into his death. Montgomery will handle the investigation. This is his girl. She'll be doing the grunt work. I expect you to talk to her or I'll haul you before the Assembly so fast, you'll piss yourselves."

Marat began to rise. "Who do you think—"

"Also," Lander's voice cracked like a whip. "If you give the girl any trouble, you won't get another dime out of my House. In case you forgot, my House is bankrolling most of this project."

Tatyana put her hand on Marat's forearm. He sat back down.

"House Jiang extends its deepest regrets for the loss of the heir," Stephen said. "Should you take some time to mourn and make the necessary arrangements, we will extend you every courtesy."

Lander swiveled toward him. "Fuck your regrets."

Stephen blinked.

"I have more money than all of you put together," Lander announced. "I can tie this up in court for years. It will give me something to live for."

Cheryl cleared her throat. "Of course we will cooperate fully. The sooner the cause of this tragedy is discovered, the better. As much as it pains me, I must point out that Felix was involved in every aspect of the project and often served as tiebreaker during our votes. Will you be taking over for him?"

"I'm old," Lander said. "My health isn't good. I have doctors and grandchildren to keep happy. This project needs someone young with a good head on his shoulders. Someone none of you can influence."

Marat opened his mouth. Lander glared at him, and Marat clamped it shut.

"You'll appoint a proxy?" Tatyana asked.

"Yes. It's my right."

The sound of quick steps echoed through the open doors.

"That would be him now," Lander said.

A dark-haired man walked through the doorway, gliding as if his joints were liquid. All the air went out of the room. I tried to take a breath but there was none to be had.

"My apologies," Alessandro Sagredo said with a charming Italian accent. "So sorry to be late."

Augustine Montgomery was a dead man. He just didn't know it yet.

Alessandro looked straight at me. Our stares connected and for a split second my brain ground to a halt. I couldn't think, I could only feel, and what I felt was intense, searing rage.

I couldn't afford to react.

Tiny orange flames sparked in his irises and vanished. Nobody else saw it. His expression remained perfectly neutral.

Why? He had the entire world at his disposal. He could have gone anywhere, but he came back here, to my city. It hurt to look at him. It hurt to remember him holding me, because when he wrapped his arms around me, he made me feel safe, and loved, and wanted. All that and he left, without apology, without explanation. He'd made it absolutely clear that I didn't matter and now he was back, the son of a bitch, as if nothing had happened.

Alessandro walked to Lander's left side and bent to him, an expression of utmost concern on his handsome face. "How are you feeling today, *Zio*?"

I had to snap out of it. There would be time to feel later. Right now, I had to think, because the equivalent of a hungry raptor just casually strolled into the room and nobody besides me, Morton, and possibly Augustine knew it. Alessandro called Lander his uncle. They weren't related. I knew the genealogy of House Sagredo like the back of my hand. I could recite them down to the fourth generation in my sleep.

Lander patted Alessandro's hand with his, affectionately, as you would to a nephew.

"I didn't know House Morton and House Sagredo were on such good terms," Tatyana commented.

"Why would you know? When his father and I were friends, you were just a twitch in your daddy's dick," Lander said.

Lander Morton, the very soul of courtesy.

Marat rolled his eyes.

Alessandro straightened. Not a hint of magic. He'd pulled his power so deep inside himself, he felt inert. Harmless. Most of his targets kept on thinking he was harmless, right up until he killed them. That's why they called him the Artisan. He'd elevated murder for hire to an art.

Why are you here? Was this work or really a family obligation?

He wore a pewter-colored suit, impeccably tailored, Neapolitan-style, cut close to the body to accentuate his narrow waist. The suit shimmered slightly, probably a summer wool-and-silk blend. *Spalla camicia*, the "shirt shoulder," without any padding and wide lapels with a convex curve that drew the eye, all of which minimized the shoulder line. Alessandro had shoulders like a gymnast; if you put any padding on him, he would resemble a linebacker. He was here to work, and he was trying to disguise his build to appear less of a threat.

It might work on the four Primes. It might even work on Augustine. They would look at his suntanned skin, his artfully disheveled brown hair, the expensive suit, the tailored trousers ending at a perfect shivering break—the hem meeting the shoes' vamps as closely as was possible without rumpling—and they would see a young Italian Prime, an heir to an old family, indulged, confident, carefree, handling a bit of business as a favor.

It didn't work on me. I'd seen him fight. Once you witnessed the way he moved—flawless, spare, each strike landing with unattainable precision—you never forgot it. Alessandro dedicated himself to killing.

Under that shimmering suit, his body was corded with powerful flexible muscle. He was shockingly strong and abnormally fast. His face wasn't just handsome, it was the face of a fighter, chiseled, masculine—strong jaw, full lips, straight Roman nose, carved cheekbones. His amber eyes scanned the room, and I watched him assess the threats and measure the distance to them in a split second. They saw a playboy. I saw a gladiator.

Alessandro unleashed a smile. The two women shifted slightly.

"I have arrived here on short notice and under painful circumstances."

Usually he had almost no accent. Right now, he was layering it in. If he sounded any more Italian, the conference table might sprout grape-vines and olive branches while the strains of "*Inno di Mameli*" spilled from the speakers.

"I am not familiar with this project, so I ask for your patience and guidance as I find my footing. Let us move forward through this time of grief and ensure the continued success and prosperity of our families."

"Mr. Sagredo," Marat said, "I think you give yourself too little credit. You'll get up to speed in no time."

"Yes," Tatyana said. "Any of us would be happy to answer any questions you have."

The mood around the conference table lightened. He looked like them, he spoke their language, and he was pleasant. They had no idea he could slit their throats before they realized what was happening.

How shrewd. Lander showed up, insulted them, threatened them, and then presented them with an attractive, urbane alternative. Given a choice between Alessandro and the basket of joy that was Lander Morton, they fell over themselves in a rush to choose Alessandro, accept-ing him without scrutiny or questions.

This was the major leagues of House society: every word mattered, and every action had a hidden meaning.

"There," Lander croaked. "It's settled. Alessandro will look after my business interests, and the girl will find out which one of you killed my son."

"None of us killed Felix," Tatyana growled.

Lander sneered at her. "We'll know who did it soon enough. I'm done here."

He turned his wheelchair and rolled out of the room.

"It's pointless to argue with him," Cheryl said. "In his mind, he's already convicted the four of us."

"This is ridiculous," Marat said.

Stephen watched Lander exit. His gaze slid to me, then to Alessandro.

There was only one reason Lander would've brought Alessandro in. He counted on me to find the murderer of his son, so Alessandro could kill him.

Tatyana locked on me. "You're Catalina Baylor."

"Yes."

"Your sister is a truthseeker."

The other three Primes focused on me.

Well, that didn't take long. I leveled my stare at Tatyana. She didn't flinch, but some of the confidence faded from her eyes. However, she'd started the assault and now she had to follow through.

"Your magic is sealed. How do we know you are not a truthseeker?" Tatyana asked.

"Would it be important if I was?"

"I won't submit to an interrogation by a truthseeker," Marat stated, his voice flat. "I like my mind intact."

"As a representative of House Jiang, I have nothing to hide," Stephen said. "However, House Jiang has varied business interests and I'm privy to a great deal of confidential information. As stewards of our business, we have obligations, not only to our House and all within it, but to our employees, our business associates, and our clients, all of whom trust us and count on our discretion. What my partner is trying to say in his direct way is that submitting to an interrogation by a truthseeker would mean breaking that confidence. Therefore we must regretfully decline."

Marat glowered at him.

They did not present a united front. It wouldn't be me against an alliance; it would be me against four individuals.

"I'm waiting for a response," Tatyana said.

She felt comfortable picking on me and none of the others warned her off. I failed to impress. Good.

I could slap Tatyana down, but being cagey and evasive would make me seem vulnerable. Let them think I was unsure. If one of them decided I was easy pickings and attacked me shortly after this meeting, I could put a nice bow on this nightmare and get on with my life.

I faced Tatyana. "Prime Pierce, are you planning on lying to me?"

"I have nothing to hide," Tatyana said.

"Then whether or not I am a truthseeker shouldn't matter, should it?"

"On the contrary," Cheryl said. "It matters very much. We all have secrets we don't wish to disclose."

Marat slapped his palm on the table. "You're not rummaging in my head."

Stephen remained calm and pleasant. He had clearly said everything he felt needed to be said and was perfectly content to let others babble and argue. He would be difficult.

"I can assure you Ms. Baylor isn't Magus Elenchus," Alessandro declared.

What was he doing?

"Oh?" Cheryl asked.

"I was at her trials."

Stop helping me.

"In what capacity?" Stephen asked.

"I was the control."

Shut up.

"While Ms. Baylor isn't a truthseeker, her powers are quite formidable."

"Really?" Stephen raised his eyebrows. "You were impressed?"

Do not answer that.

"It gave me pause," Alessandro confessed, his face suitably grave.

I would strangle him. My carefully woven cloak of helplessness exploded and dramatically fell to the floor in burning pieces. Instead of being vulnerable and alone, I turned into a mysterious Prime who gave Alessandro, the most powerful antistasi on record, "pause." Now they would do their homework and find pictures of us attending opera together with Linus Duncan.

Alessandro nodded. "I would characterize it as an unforgettable experience."

I pivoted to him. I couldn't help myself. "Really? Was that you? So that's where I know you from. I couldn't quite recall."

Alessandro opened his eyes wide and put his hand on his chest. "I'm crushed. Am I that forgettable?"

"You know what they say, out of sight, out of mind. Perhaps you should work more on making a memorable first impression."

Surprise flickered in his eyes.

Baiting him was dumb and dangerous, and it felt amazing.

"While the exact nature of Ms. Baylor's magic remains sealed, should you have any doubts, the Keeper of Records will confirm that she isn't a truthseeker," Augustine said. He'd stayed so quiet, I'd almost forgotten he was there. "House Baylor and MII have a long history of professional cooperation. She has my complete confidence."

"She accused me of lying." Tatyana stared at me.

There was no point in playing games now. "Prime Pierce, I understand your animosity toward me due to my House's role in the apprehension and incarceration of your brother."

Tatyana's eyes narrowed. Yes, I went there.

"However, right now I would like everyone to find time in their schedule to be interviewed by me individually. The more you stall and attempt to avoid me, the more money and resources it will cost you. Allow me to eliminate you from the pool of suspects." I turned back to Tatyana. "If Prime Pierce would like to indulge in further antagonism, you'll have ample opportunity to do so during our personal meeting."

"She's right," Cheryl said. "We're wasting time."

She motioned to her assistant, a young slender woman in a pale red dress.

"I'll need to examine the murder site as well," I said.

"You can do that tomorrow," Marat said. "I'm on-site most of the time. If I have to waste time on this ridiculous interview, I might as well get everything out of the way. Tomorrow at ten?"

"That will be fine."

The other three Primes followed suit. In five minutes, I had appointments for four interviews over the next two days. I would see Marat tomorrow at ten, followed by Cheryl at four, and Tatyana the next day at nine. Stephen would be my last stop, at two in the afternoon.

"Thank you all for your cooperation. I'm sure you must have many things to discuss with Mr. Sagredo. I'll leave you to it. Good afternoon."

I turned and walked out.

 # Chapter 3

I walked quickly, the pristine white wall on my right, the cobalt windows on my left. My heart hammered against my ribs. My throat closed up, squeezing itself too tight to swallow.

The wall ended abruptly, giving way to a short hallway that branched off, two doors on the left and an arched niche on the right, inlaid with a sea glass mosaic. I stepped into the hallway and leaned against the wall, letting it bear the brunt of my weight. Alessandro's voice surfaced from my memory.

Look at me. Look me in the eyes. Your witchery doesn't work on me. I'm already obsessed with you.

I breathed in slow and deep.

Beyond the glass, the horizon ignited with the yellow and orange of a Texas sunset, the sky enormous and deep above the city. The blue lights playing on the white walls turned aqua and green. The short hallway turned dark.

If I closed my eyes, I could conjure him right here next to me. I remembered his voice, his face, his scent . . . He was engraved in my memory. The relationship might have meant nothing to him, but it was my first. I hadn't known it was necessary to guard myself against committing completely. I didn't realize it was doomed from the start. I just fell in love.

I'd spent the last few months gluing my heart together shard by shard and seeing him stabbed me again, right in the still-raw wound. It was so easy to just rage about it, because the alternative would be to hurt. Anger was better than pain, but I couldn't afford either. I had to be sharp.

Someone was coming down the hallway. I heard nothing, but I sensed someone moving closer. I sank into the wall niche, my back flat against the glass tiles, found the phone in my pocket, and turned it off.

Alessandro stalked into view. He moved silently; a jaguar, sleek, stealthy, an ambush predator capable of explosive power. I was being hunted.

He stopped.

The tiny hairs on the back of my neck rose. I sank deeper into the shadowy niche. The trick to staying invisible was to think of nothing at all.

Alessandro turned. A focused expression claimed his face. None of the charismatic, urbane son-of-wealth-and-privilege persona remained. He looked predatory and slightly vicious. Bright orange flames curled in his eyes, his magic smoldering just under the surface.

I breathed quietly through a barely open mouth and pulled my magic to me. It built inside me like a geyser ready to erupt.

Alessandro took a step toward the hallway.

That's it. Come closer. Make my day. This won't go the way you think it will.

"Prime Sagredo!" Marat called.

The orange fire vanished. Alessandro's expression rearranged itself. His brow relaxed, his mouth curved, and his eyes lost their lethal concentration, softening. He turned around with a dazzling smile.

"Are you looking for something?" Marat asked.

"A bathroom," Alessandro confessed, looking helpless. If I hadn't witnessed it, I wouldn't have believed the two were the same man.

"It's the other way," Marat said. "I'll walk with you."

"You're too kind."

"I want to make sure you don't get the wrong idea about this project," Marat started. "The profits could be sky-high, but we must play this just right."

Alessandro opened his eyes a bit wider. "Not to worry. As we say in Italy, profit *è il mio cavallo di battaglia.*"

"What does that mean?"

It meant that profit was his battle horse.

"It's my forte," Alessandro said. "Making money is what I do."

"Fantastic."

The sound of their voices and steps receded.

I waited another full minute and slipped out of the niche. He would come looking for me. I would bet our family's entire annual budget on it.

I turned left and hurried down the hallway, turning my phone on. It pinged. A text message from Linus.

I sent a car.

I walked into the waiting area. Cornelius stood by the windows, looking at the city below. Tension radiated from his posture. His shoulders were stiff, his arms crossed on his chest, and a guarded expression hardened his face. It would've been a grave sight, except that Rosebud perched on his head, clutching his blond hair in her adorable little hands.

I raised my phone and snapped a picture.

"Where's Leon?" I asked.

"Calling 911."

I almost groaned. "Audrey?"

Cornelius nodded.

"What is it this time?"

"There's an intruder in her house," Cornelius said. "Leon has to come and save her."

For some reason, our family had the worst luck with women named Audrey. On the first day of kindergarten, blond Audrey, whose last name I couldn't remember, didn't like my backpack so she spat in my hair. In high school, Audrey Swan got together with the guy Arabella liked and the two of them posted a video mocking her on Snapchat. Grandma Frida had a nemesis, a nasty old lady with a shrill voice, who used to be her next-door neighbor. Her name was Audri Burns. The worst officer my mother ever served with was named Jenna Audreigh. Leon's Audrey was no exception.

Audrey Duarte was an influencer. She specialized in "total look" tutorials, combining trendy fashion with the right makeup and hair, and made a lot of money promoting cosmetics and clothes labels. Her 1.2 million followers thought she walked on water.

About two months ago, she contacted our firm. She'd been receiving threatening letters promising to disfigure her. Leon had taken the case, because its "noir nature" appealed to him. Somewhere in his head a 1930s soundtrack must've been playing while a rich baritone announced, "A beautiful dame walked into my office. She was trouble. Dames always are." He quickly determined that the threatening mail had come from her competitor, which was fortunate since real stalking cases were difficult to resolve. Convincing someone to let go of the object of their affection took a long time and often ended badly.

Leon closed the case and moved on. Audrey didn't. Leon was attractive and dangerous, and she decided he should belong to her. She was used to being adored for things like curling her hair and she couldn't understand why he wasn't falling at her feet and promising her the world. In an ironic twist, she developed stalker tendencies. She sent him hundreds of texts a week. He blocked her number, so she went on a disposable phone spree. She showed up at our place, but security blocked her. We watched her try to charm, then pout, then scream at our guards, until they threatened to call the cops. She bought him a motorcycle and had it delivered to us, and we refused the delivery.

Her latest strategy was to bombard Leon with emergencies from her numerous burner cells. The last time it was a fire. The time before that, she heard strange noises in the garage. No matter what the emergency was, the request was always the same—her life was in danger, and Leon had to come and save her.

With the emergencies, Audrey graduated to threats of harm, in her case, to herself. Once was an isolated occurrence, twice could be coincidence, but the third time constituted "a pattern of behavior." Stalking was a third-degree felony in the state of Texas, and she had just given us enough ammunition. Tomorrow I would authorize Sabrian Turner, our

House counsel, to contact Audrey's family and arrange for a heart-to-heart.

Cornelius looked at me. "I saw Tatyana Pierce."

Ah. That explained his expression. House Harrison and House Pierce didn't get along. Nevada knew more about it than I did, but she told me before that both Cornelius and his older sister Diana detested the Pierce family.

"Is she involved in this matter?" Cornelius asked.

"She is. I'll understand if you choose to avoid this one." Cornelius had full discretion when it came to our cases. Some he claimed, others he passed on.

Cornelius locked his jaw. "Oh no. Quite the opposite."

Rosebud pulled on his hair and trilled at me for emphasis, clearly ready to do battle.

Well, we had a pint-size battle monkey on our side. This case was as good as solved.

Leon strode around the bend of the wall, his face annoyed. He saw me and grimaced. "I handled it."

"Are you okay?"

"Yeah. She sounded really freaked out. If I didn't know better, I'd believe her."

"But you do know better. You called 911. They'll take it from here."

He puffed his cheeks and blew the air out slowly. "What's next?"

"I have to go see Linus."

"Do you want me to take you?" Leon asked.

"No, he sent a car. Could the two of you take Rosebud to Maya?"

"Linus will wait," Leon said. "Come be a hero with us."

"You barely slept for three days," Cornelius added. "You worked really hard on this. You deserve to be there when Maya gets her back."

I wanted to. So much. "I can't. Take a video for me. Please?"

"This sucks," Leon said.

Cornelius shook his head. "Video is not the same. Happy moments like these don't happen very often. You should be there."

I should, but Linus couldn't wait. "I would if I could. I'll see you tomorrow, Cornelius."

I started down the hallway. A stray thought made me turn and I walked backward. "Leon, don't go over there. Don't go to Audrey's."

"Give me some credit."

"I mean it."

He waved me off. "Stop worrying."

I turned and headed for the elevator.

It was so simple to say. Stop worrying about this. Stop worrying about that. It will be fine. But often it wasn't fine. Sometimes I felt like a spider who'd spun a web across a bottomless drop. My family was walking across, balancing on hair-thin strands, and it was my job to keep them from falling.

Of all the ritzy neighborhoods in Houston, River Oaks was the most exclusive and the most expensive. The minimum home price ran upward of three million, and yard space was worth its weight in gold. Common wisdom said one should never own the nicest house in the neighborhood. Linus Duncan didn't give a damn.

The ostentatious mansions rolled past the armored window as the Rolls Royce Cullinan glided up the picturesque road. In the driver's seat, Pete checked the rearview mirror for the seventh time since I started counting. Six feet three inches tall, with pale skin and light hair cropped short, he was in his late forties. He could throw me over his shoulder, run eight hundred meters at full speed in under three minutes, set me down, do forty pull-ups, then drop and do fifty push-ups. He also fired a gun with deadly accuracy and could kill a skilled opponent with his hands, which was why he was one of two people Duncan trusted with his personal safety. And now Pete was cautious.

I didn't ask why. The home defense turrets Linus made emitted a specific sound, a magic twang, followed by the crack of a bullet leaving the barrel. Once you heard it, you never forgot it. I hadn't imagined hearing it during our phone call. Whatever had happened wasn't good. Pete had to concentrate on keeping me safe, and nobody won if I made his job harder by asking questions. I texted Runa Etterson instead.

Six months ago, we had helped Runa find her kidnapped sister
and avenge her mother's murder. Runa had been working on her post-
graduate degree at UCLA. But now both her sister and her brother
needed a lot of support, and therapy, and reassurance. Their life was
here in Houston, and she'd decided not to force them to abandon everything by dragging them to California. A great deal of paperwork later,
she walked away from her research at UCLA and ended up starting
over at Rice. I saw her every week and her siblings, Ragnar and Halle,
every other week or so. For the first time in my life, I had a best friend.
It was weird as hell.

I need a favor.

The phone chimed back. *Shoot.*

**Do you know anybody doing work on merging of organic matter and
metal? I need something assessed and I have to keep it quiet.**

Linus?

Yes.

Runa had been at the center of the investigation into her mother's
death. She'd very quickly figured out that Linus and I were connected;
she'd watched me stumble, shell-shocked, through my first couple of
cases, and she'd grown more and more worried. Eventually I broke down
and told her about the Deputy Warden thing. I shouldn't have, but I had
to tell someone and it made things so much easier.

I know someone, Runa texted back. *Do you want me to take the thing
to her?*

Thank you. I'll ask Cornelius to drop it off at your place.

Are you okay?

I was pretty damn far from okay, but I didn't want to do this over text. **I'll live. Thanks for asking.**

Pete steered the Rolls Royce around the bend and Linus' house came into view.

The sturdy wrought-iron gates hung askew, wrenched from their mounts by some powerful force. Behind them, unnaturally bright blood smeared the paver stones of a wide circular driveway. Normally, in the center of the driveway a white fountain rose from the middle of an artfully landscaped flower bed, water cascading out of its top and spilling into the triple basin. Right now, the fountain was dry, its top scattered in pieces across the driveway. A broken turret jutted on the right between the decorative shrubs, knocked off its retractable mount. Ahead a palatial mansion waited like a castle from an animated fairy tale. The blood smears stopped ten yards short of the door. No assailants had reached the front steps.

Pete parked, exited the car, and held my door open. I stepped out and he led me to the front door. There was a momentary pause as the security system recognized my face, then the locks clicked, and Pete opened the door and ushered me into a three-story foyer.

The interior of the house was as grand as the outside promised it would be. The polished white marble floor gleamed like a mirror, reflecting walls of Venetian plaster in white and cream decorated with acanthus-leaf molding. Another ornate fountain rose in the middle of the foyer, cradled by a double grand staircase twisting to the second floor on both sides. Above it, a stained-glass dome offered white clouds floating over the blue sky. An enormous chandelier dripped long strands of crystal from the center of the dome, illuminating the fountain, and the entire place glowed, white and elegant despite its opulence.

"He's waiting in the study," Pete said.

"Thank you." I turned right and crossed the foyer to the side doorway, then walked through a small sitting room, through another hallway, and entered the study.

The Venetian plaster here was beige rather than cream and trimmed with light brown. Bookshelves filled the arched alcoves—Linus embraced technology, but he loved the texture of paper. Like the foyer, the study was elegant and uncluttered—two padded chairs, a love seat in the corner, a black-and-gold desk that would have been at home in Versailles, and a single ficus tree to the left of the fireplace that somehow thrived despite Linus' neglect. The air smelled of aromatic tobacco and coffee. He kept loose tobacco on hand because he liked the scent and either Pete or Hera, his other bodyguard, replaced it every few weeks when it lost its aroma.

Linus Duncan sat behind the desk, engrossed in his tablet. A heavy crystal glass with about a finger of whiskey waited forgotten on his right.

I sat in the nearest chair.

Linus leaned back and looked at me. "How did it go with Montgomery?"

Apparently we were going to ignore me being attacked in the park and him being attacked in his house.

"I'm in." I would have to phrase this next bit carefully. "There are complications."

He pinned me with his gaze. "What complications?"

"Lander Morton and Alessandro Sagredo are a package deal."

He rested his elbows on the arms of his chair and steepled his fingers, thinking. "Is that a problem?"

"No," I lied. "It's not a problem. It just makes things slightly more complicated, because I have to account for an overpowered assassin with an unknown motive."

"Don't we all."

"I'd like permission to run a Warden Network search on Sagredo." The Warden Network included access to several law enforcement databases that were off-limits to civilians.

"Why?"

"I don't like to be surprised."

"Denied," Linus said. "You know his capabilities and his temperament. In some ways, you know him better than almost anyone else. Anything the Warden Network would tell you would be a guess at best. How are things progressing with Albert Ravenscroft?"

"They're not."

Albert Ravenscroft, the heir to House Ravenscroft, was a Prime psionic, twenty-six years old, handsome, and very persistent. He operated on the assumption that if he just put in enough time and effort, I would recognize his beauty and wit. Even if his efforts had managed to wear me down, our relationship would be doomed. Albert was interested in marriage.

Six months ago, when a psychotic mind ripper mage had trapped Alessandro, I made a deal with my evil grandmother. She gave me what I needed to save him. In return, I swore to dedicate myself to House Baylor. I would never become a part of another House. The man who married me would have to join mine. He would have to take my name and abandon all claims on his previous family. I hadn't shared this bit with Linus because he didn't need to know. Albert was looking to strengthen his House, not to run away from it.

Linus mulled it over. "His choice or yours?"

"Mine."

He watched me carefully. "Albert would be easy to manage."

"I have no interest in managing him. Besides, I'm busy. Why are we interested in House Morton?"

Linus' tablet chimed. He glanced at it. "It appears I have a guest. I think he's here for you."

He turned the tablet toward me. On it Alessandro drove a silver Alfa Romeo Spider through the broken gates and parked in front of the door.

We waited in silence. Five seconds. Ten . . .

Alessandro walked into the study carrying an unconscious Pete over his shoulder, deposited him on the love seat in the corner, and sat in the other chair.

Linus looked at Pete and sighed. "Please join us, won't you, Prime Sagredo?"

No. Don't join us. Turn around and go away as far and as fast as you can.

Linus looked at me, then at Alessandro. Neither of us said anything.

"Well." Linus spread his arms. "Let's start with you, Alessandro. Why are you here?"

Alessandro threw one long leg over the other and leaned back. "Officially I'm here because Lander Morton hired me to kill the person or persons who murdered his son."

Linus raised his eyebrows. "Do you think I'm hiding them here in my house?"

"Unofficially I'm here because she is in danger." Alessandro looked at Linus. "Does the name Ignat Orlov mean anything to you?"

He pronounced Ignat with an *uh*, so it sounded almost like *ignite*.

Linus grimaced, as if he'd bitten something sour.

"It doesn't to me," I said.

"Former officer of the Russian Imperial Defense," Alessandro said.

"An Imperium-sanctioned assassin," Linus supplied. "Trained, experienced, and very good, since he managed to survive all these years."

"Goes by the name Arkan," Alessandro added. "It means *lasso*."

The nicknames professional killers gave themselves never failed to make me roll my eyes. "Because he snares his enemies?"

"Yes," Alessandro and Linus said at the same time.

"Why is he important?"

"Excellent question," Linus said.

Alessandro gave us a short, humorless smile. "Because he stole your serum."

The Office of the Warden had a primary directive: to safeguard the Osiris serum. In unscrupulous hands, the serum had the potential to wipe out our civilization. A couple of years ago, someone broke into the Northern Vault and stole five samples of it, labeled 161-165AC. Six months ago, we had gone against an assassin firm, Diatheke, to get one of the samples back. They'd used it to turn humans into magic-wielding monsters. We'd managed to recover sample 164AC and its derivatives, and destroyed Diatheke along with Benedict De Lacy, the assassin who ran it, in the process. Four other samples were still missing.

How was that connected to the Pit? I looked at Linus.

Linus pondered Alessandro, his eyes calculating. He was trying to decide how much Alessandro knew and how difficult it would be to dispose of him, if things came to that.

"Felix Morton ran into me at the last Assembly session," Linus said finally. "Quite literally. He collided with me in the elevator, apologized, then told me that 'it's been ages since we last talked.' I found it curious, because we'd never spoken. Also because he passed me this envelope."

Linus took out a white envelope from his desk drawer and slid it toward me across the desk.

I picked it up. A plain unmarked envelope, generic, the kind you can buy in any office store. It was unsealed. I opened it and pulled out a photograph. A shot of the swamp, probably the Pit, taken early in the morning or late in the evening. The photographer must have been aiming at the derelict building on the other side of the bog—it was in focus—and if I hadn't looked closely, I would have missed it. Two spinning rings, half-submerged and churning water about ten feet from the shore, with a blue light glowing under the surface.

The hair on the back of my neck rose.

I flipped the photograph. On the back in a hurried cursive someone had written "Jane Saurage, my appraiser, disappeared in the Pit 07/09. This was the last image uploaded to her cloud. I need to speak with you ASAP."

Alessandro held out his hand for the envelope.

I put the picture on the desk instead and tapped the spinning rings. "One of these controlled the creatures that attacked us."

"I now have one in my basement." Linus frowned. "And I have no idea how it was made. It's biomechanical in nature, but on a level I don't understand. I have an expert coming, but it may take some time."

Alessandro rose, picked up the envelope and the photograph, and sat back in his chair.

Linus continued. "Four hours after he handed this to me, Felix was murdered in the Pit. His body wasn't found until the next morning. Do you remember Agent Wahl?"

"Yes." I tried to keep a groan from my voice and failed.

Agent Wahl had spearheaded an investigation into the trafficking of the magic-warped—people so transformed by magic, they were no longer human. Some of them had come from the Diatheke's assassin lab which Linus, Alessandro, and our family had destroyed. I had taken that case away from Agent Wahl at Linus' direction and his wail of outrage could have been heard all the way in Amarillo. He made it plain that he didn't respect me, didn't recognize my authority, and generally felt that a two-year-old could have done a much better job in my place. He had to cooperate with me, but he spent the entire time convinced that I would screw everything up beyond all hope, so he'd bugged my car, tried to clone my phone, and had me tailed in case I failed and he would have to ride in on a white steed, or possibly a black SUV, to save the day.

"He came to see me today," Linus said.

"Has his leg healed?"

"Yes, although he's still using the cane. Apparently, Felix contacted him about some workers disappearing and mentioned 162AC."

Shit.

"Agent Wahl, in a rare fit of common sense, gave your name, and mine, to Felix. He left town on assignment shortly after and didn't return until this morning. He didn't know if Felix got ahold of me, but once he learned about the funeral, he wanted to be sure."

And of course, Wahl would have recognized the formula. When we pulled the corpses of the magic-warped people out of a mass grave, they had been tattooed with 164AC followed by the number of the serum variant. I didn't know what Linus told him, but at some point, Agent Wahl stopped asking inconvenient questions.

"We were having our chat when a swarm of giant arcane snakes with moth wings attacked my home."

Snakes with moth wings? "How did Agent Wahl take it?"

"Oh, he had a grand time. He also shared with me that any time the Office of the Warden becomes involved in something, the 'world falls down.' He finds this fact very exciting. Interesting fellow."

Linus turned to Alessandro and made a your-turn gesture.

"Sixteen years ago, Arkan went private," Alessandro said.

"That's debatable," Linus said, "but go on."

"Right now, Arkan stays at his estate in Canada. I've secured means of surveilling him."

"Why?" I asked.

"Because I have a personal interest in killing him."

Ask a stupid question . . .

"When Arkan broke into the Northern Vault and stole the serum you've been trying to recover, he didn't do it because someone paid him. He was the driving force behind the theft, but the operation was complex and expensive, and he did have investors. The serum was divided between the participants."

"Was Diatheke one of these investors?" I asked.

"Diatheke was run by a board of shareholders," Alessandro answered. "Arkan owned the controlling interest. It was his firm and Benedict De Lacy answered directly to him."

The memory of Alessandro's assassin database flashed before me. At the time I thought he was simply studying the competition. However, if Arkan was his target all along, the database took on a new meaning.

"Three days ago, one of these investors called him," Alessandro said. "I don't know who it was. I only heard his end of the conversation."

"What was said?" Linus asked.

"The person on the other line had killed Felix Morton and panicked. They must've mentioned your name"—Alessandro looked at Linus—"because Arkan told them that he would handle Duncan and there was nothing to worry about."

Linus raised his eyebrows. "Did he now?"

"He did."

This lined up with Augustine's theory that Felix's killer was one of the board members. Only a well-connected, powerful Prime would be brazen enough to become involved in the theft of the Osiris serum.

"Arkan assured them that he would be sending help," Alessandro continued. "After the conversation, he called in someone and instructed them to go to Houston. He mentioned you by name." Alessandro nodded to Linus and turned to me. "And then he mentioned you. Arkan knows that Linus is the Warden and that you are his Deputy."

Great.

"The plan is simple. Linus is too hard of a target. Killing a Warden would unleash a meteor shower, and Arkan wants to avoid the attention of the National Assembly. His people will go after you instead. You're easier to kill. Arkan's banking that once Linus discovers that his apprentice is in danger, he will move to protect you, all of which will disrupt the investigation. I don't know if he's buying time to clean it up or if his plans are more complex, but I know you're his primary target."

"Do you have any proof?" Linus asked.

Alessandro brushed a speck of lint off his knee. "Proof is your problem. I don't plan on taking him to court. I know and that's enough. I reached out to Lander Morton through an intermediary and offered my condolences. Lander is a vindictive old buzzard. The most important person in his life had just been murdered. I knew he would jump on the chance to get revenge. He hired me."

"I imagine he's paying quite well," I said.

Alessandro didn't rise to the bait. "Money is of no consequence. I'm here to make sure you don't die."

"I'm touched, Prime Sagredo, but your protection is not necessary." Or welcome.

Alessandro turned to Linus. "The contract you had me sign has no expiration date. I'll abide by its provisions. Let me keep her safe."

Linus pondered it.

No. Absolutely not.

"Work with him," Linus said.

The betrayal stung. I had three seconds to pick an emotion. I could storm off angry, which would be childish; I could refuse and show everyone just how deep Alessandro had hurt me; or I could swallow my feelings, act like it didn't matter, and be professional about it.

"Is that an order?" I kept my voice casual.

"Does it have to be?" Linus asked.

"He shares no information unless his arm is twisted, which makes him unpredictable, and he's driven by self-interest, which makes him a liability. He has no loyalty, he can't be counted on, and his principles are murky. I have no problem working with him, but I want my objection noted, so when he cuts and runs at the worst moment, I can tell you 'I told you so.'" And I would really rub it in.

"I told you before that I would see things through," Alessandro said. "I kept my promise and I'll do it again. When I sign on the dotted line, I always deliver."

I shrugged.

"You do remember what betraying the trust of the National Assembly of the United States means?" Linus said. "There is no place on this planet where we won't find you."

"I haven't forgotten," Alessandro said.

Linus smiled again, showing even white teeth. "See? He knows the consequences." He clapped his hands together. "It's settled. You will investigate, he will protect you, and everything will come up roses. Moving on."

This was some kind of nightmare. Not only did Alessandro reappear in my life, now I had to work with him. He would insist on following me everywhere. We would be around each other all the time. I would rather walk on broken glass all day than spend fifteen minutes talking to him.

I had picked my path. I swore an oath to the Wardens. Like Mom said, it was time to put up or shut up.

I wrestled my mind back to the problem at hand. There would be time to vent all of this later. "You don't know who Arkan sent?"

"No," Alessandro said.

"Do you think he is behind the two attacks?"

"Unlikely. Arkan's people are precise and fast. This was stupid."

As much as I hated to admit it, he was right. "Agreed. First, they attacked Linus in his home where he is the strongest. Second, they attacked both of us and simultaneously. It wasn't just an assault on two Primes, it was an assault on the Office of the Warden. All of this guarantees that we will drop everything and investigate. Why?"

"That's what you'll need to find out." Linus leaned forward. "The recovery of the serum is your first priority. Get in and shake them up until it falls out. Get me the evidence I need to force my way in. Don't die."

He looked at me and said, enunciating every word, "Do me this favor, Catalina."

"Of course, Mr. Duncan."

We went through this ritual with every assignment. I called it "Victoria Tremaine's insurance."

Linus nodded at Alessandro. "Wait outside. She'll be along shortly."

Alessandro rose from the chair with that liquid grace and walked out.

I waited until he'd had time to reach the front door. "How could you?"

"I know it hurts. I know you're angry. He's an arrogant jackass, but he is very, very good at what he does. Your survival matters to me a great deal more than your feelings."

"Anybody but him. I could have taken Pete."

Linus raised his eyebrows and pointed at the unconscious Pete with his thumb. "He would be difficult to carry."

My feelings must have shown on my face, because Linus sat back.

"Do you understand why I can't take this over now?"

"You have no justification. The Office of the Warden can't just run over the private affairs of Primes. The Houses would scream bloody murder."

Linus nodded. "I have a lot of things to verify. If what that hotshot said is true, I have to cover a lot of ground. I may not be available to provide assistance."

"I'm not sure I can count on Alessandro to provide it either."

Linus steepled his fingers. "You've had a chance to observe him here. Tell me what's different about him from the Alessandro you remember."

I ran through the last twenty minutes in my head. "He didn't challenge you. You gave him multiple chances to mouth off, but he didn't take them." No, Alessandro was in full Artisan mode. Ice cold, calculating, resolute.

"What else?"

"He offered information without being prompted." That was new as well. The last time we met, I had to pull every bit of intelligence out of him with tweezers even when our lives depended on it.

"Something must've happened to him," Linus said. "I suspect it was extremely unpleasant. I like his determination. It's a welcome change."

I gave up. "How dangerous is Arkan?"

"Dangerous enough that the Imperial Department of Defense let him go rather than kill him, which is their usual procedure. It was judged to be more cost-effective."

"Wow. He gave the Russian Imperium pause?"

"Yes. The man is a mass murderer, Catalina. He has a black tag. Just him alone."

In the Warden Network, potential threats were tagged with different colors, from low to high. Black indicated the highest level, critical. It was usually reserved for criminal organizations and small governments rather than individuals. Even my brother-in-law, who could level an entire city once he got going, was marked as brown.

"One wonders how much easier our lives would be if the Russian Imperium had collapsed during the farmer revolt." Linus opened a drawer of his desk, took out a large box, and held it out to me. "I'm throwing you into a den of wolves. The least I can do is give you a stick to hold them at bay."

"Thank you."

I took my present. Made of polished cedar, it was about two and a half feet long. A stylized tree branch with five leaves was carved into the lid, wrapped in a ribbon of Norse runes.

"It's beautiful."

"This is a prototype, with all the issues that entails. I planned to refine it, but we have no time."

I opened the box. Inside on turquoise velvet lay a short sword. It was a straightforward weapon, almost plain: about fourteen inches overall, with a ten-inch double-edged blade, and a wooden grip wrapped in a leather cord. Both the simple cross guard and the round pommel shimmered with blued steel, catching the light. The blade seemed unusually wide for the length, about forty-eight millimeters, at least.

Aww. He made me a sword. He never made swords. He specialized in projectile weapons.

I set the box on his desk and plucked the weapon out. Heavy. And weighted oddly, most of the mass at the hilt. This wasn't a functional sword, more like a decorative sword-shaped object you would hang on the wall.

It didn't matter. It wasn't a very good sword, but he'd made it specially for me.

"I love it," I said. Nobody had ever made me a sword before.

Linus sighed. "Flick it."

"What?"

"Stand up and wave it around."

I got up and sliced through the air. The blade unfolded like a telescopic pole and I almost dropped it. The new sword was thirty inches long.

Um . . . I raised the sword and studied the blade. Logic said there should have been lines between the segments, but I couldn't find any. I spun, swinging in a quick combination of slashes. The blade held. Still, the structural integrity of it had to be crap. A good sword was essentially a somewhat flexible length of sharpened steel designed to slash and stab through objects with high resistance and would be sturdy enough to block a strike. A segmented sword, by definition, was hollow. If I tried to cut something, it would snap at the joints. If I tried to block, it might snap at the hilt.

I manufactured some enthusiasm. "Awesome."

Linus shook his head. "You are a terrible liar. Sink some magic into it."

I relaxed my hold on my power and let it flow into the hilt. Faint dark lines formed on the blade, growing into an intricate pattern of tiny arcane circles. What was this? Mages used arcane circles to supplement and channel their magic. Some circles amplified magic; others contained or shaped it. The most prominent families developed House spells, which unleashed catastrophic power and required circles of dazzling complexity. But all circles had to be drawn fresh with chalk or other organic substances like soap or wax. That's why I redrew the trap circles in our house every couple of weeks.

I looked at Linus.

He pointed at the box. "Hit it."

A sword wasn't an axe, and since this one was hollow, it would break. But he ordered me to hit it. I raised the blade and chopped down.

The sword cut through the box like it was butter and sank into the desk. Crap. I reversed the swing, expecting resistance. There was none. The weapon came free, and if I hadn't gripped it tight, I would've flung it into the air. The momentum pitched me back, and I spun, bringing the sword in a wide arc around me, shut off the flow of magic, and stopped, blinking.

Linus slow clapped.

Holy shit.

"How?"

Linus chuckled. "Null space."

Some arcane circles required so much magic that their boundary ceased to exist in our physical realm. It was a place where our reality touched the arcane. Nothing could penetrate it. A mage inside such a circle was invincible until his magic ran out, which would happen quite quickly. The very nature of such circles made them unsustainable long-term.

"I don't understand."

"I used an organometallic compound to embed the arcane lines. It contains a bond between metal and carbon atoms, which makes this particular substance suitable for magic channeling. Unfortunately, it's also sensitive to moisture and air and you wouldn't believe the hoops I jumped through to modify it."

Oh my God. He'd just revolutionized the entire science of arcane metallurgy. If it ever got out, the line of people trying to kill me for this sword would stretch down the I-10 all the way to San Antonio.

"Every time you feed it magic, the compound reacts, so in effect, you are redrawing the circles with every application. It remains to be seen how durable it is. Like I said, it's not perfect, but I'm not *unhappy* with it."

I choked on air.

"This is an emergency blade," Linus said. "Swing it long enough and it will drain you dry. You know what happens then."

First, I would see glowing dots, then the world would shrink, and if I kept going, I'd either pass out or die. I nodded.

Linus Duncan fixed me with his hazel eyes. "Be careful, Catalina. The night is dark, and the wolves have vicious teeth. Guard yourself."

"I will," I promised.

 # Chapter 4

Outside the sunset burned across the sky, orange and red against the encroaching darkness. The air had cooled enough to breathe, and the first bats streaked back and forth above the oaks bordering Linus' property. Alessandro was leaning against the Spider, arms crossed, slouching slightly, a tired prince, waiting.

Yeah, that didn't work on me anymore.

I walked down the stairs to the driveway. He peeled himself from the car.

"Let me take you home."

Pete, who would have been my ride, was still unconscious. I could call my family, but that would mean pulling them out of a secure base, and after today's fight, I couldn't bring myself to do it. My imagination painted Grandma Frida trying to drive Brick, her special armored monster of a vehicle, through a cloud of snakes with moth wings. No, thank you. I could call an Uber, but there was no telling who would respond to that request.

The memory of Alessandro stalking me through MII popped into my head. It was a sad day when your safest way home was a rabid killer who broke your heart and you were getting into his car to prove to yourself that you weren't a coward.

"I need to go to Felix's house first."

"I'll take you."

"Thank you, Mr. Sagredo."

He opened the front passenger door for me and I got in. The last time I was in this car, he had jumped over a gap in an overpass. On second thought, this was probably a different car. That Spider had barely limped to our warehouse. He must have replaced it. He was wealthy enough to buy one of these every month in a different color.

Alessandro slid behind the wheel and the engine came to life with a growl. I plugged the address into my phone. Same neighborhood as Linus, but it would take several minutes to get there.

"Make a left out of the driveway."

The Spider glided forward and we were off.

I pulled out my phone and texted Bern. **Safe. Coming home soon.**

The next text message went to Patricia Taft, our head of security. **ETA 45 min w/ Count. Not hostile.**

Understood.

I'm being targeted in connection with a case. Let's stay on lockdown.

Got it.

I didn't expect Alessandro to ever come back, but when we hired Patricia, she did a threat assessment based on past acquaintances, and Alessandro was at the top of her list. He and Augustine, whose moniker was Pancakes.

After Alessandro left, I had spent some time researching the Artisan. Partially because Patricia requested all of the information I had so she could build his threat profile and partially because I wanted to shut the lid on the pain of him leaving. I wanted to know all the terrible crap he had done, so I could move on.

I found out very little and what I did find was surprising. Alessandro was expensive and elusive. Hiring him required going through a specific intermediary. No other broker had access to him. Alessandro was the intermediary's only client, which suggested a trusted friend or a family member. Alessandro declined most jobs offered to him. I found one would-be client who unwisely left a comment on the wrong forum thinking he would be anonymous. Bern traced him and broke into his email server. The client had been a Prime of a wealthy Brazilian House. He ranted to a family member about Alessandro's refusal to take the job because it didn't meet his criteria.

I thought I would find a trail of blood and it would be easier to hate him. Instead I found questions.

I pulled up my email and began going through my inbox. Riding in a car with him was a mistake. It reminded me of things I had desperately wanted. They had been in reach, so, so close, and then they were ripped away. I wasn't even angry anymore. I was just sad and tired.

Alessandro glanced over at me again. He had been looking at me every minute or two.

I looked directly at him. "Yes?"

He kept his eyes on the road. "Just making sure you're really there."

Aha. "Do you think I learned to teleport?"

"No. It's just for the first time in the last six months I know exactly where you are."

He did not just go there. "No need to worry. I won't jump out of the car. Make a right at the next crossroads, please."

I went back to my phone. Seconds stretched. I had read this stupid email three times and I still didn't know what it said.

"I'm sorry," he said.

If I could buy the power to teleport with ten years of my life, I would do it in a heartbeat.

"I'm sorry I treated you as an amateur. I'm sorry I tried to force you to abandon the investigation into the death of your friend's mother. I'm sorry for the things I said. I'm sorry I left. I'm sorry I didn't call."

An apology from Alessandro Sagredo. No dancing around, no excuses, no shifting the blame onto anyone else. A direct and firm admission of guilt. If I wasn't so busy trying to wrangle my emotions under control, I might die from shock.

"No need. What's done is done. Now we must work together, so let's clear the air. You were my first serious relationship. I had unrealistic expectations. It must have been very awkward for you."

A muscle in his cheek jerked.

"I've moved on, so don't worry, things won't become unpleasant."

And I'd just lied through my teeth. Things were unpleasant as hell.

"I never thought things were unpleasant."

"Good. I'm glad it wasn't a total torture for you." Okay, that was petty, but he deserved it.

"Catalina . . ."

"Ms. Baylor," I corrected.

"Catalina," he repeated. His voice told me he wasn't going to budge on that point. "I'm sorry I hurt you."

I shut up. Nothing he said should've mattered, but it did, and I didn't know if I was mad at him or at myself.

The Spider whispered to a stop before a large Tudor. I keyed the code from Augustine's folder into the electronic lock, the gate slid aside, and Alessandro guided the Spider down the long driveway to the door.

Alessandro shut off the engine. We sat quietly in front of the dark building.

"What are you thinking?" he asked.

"This is a dead man's house. Nobody's home."

I dreaded this part. I had done it several times now, and it always left me hollow.

"Let me help you," he said.

"My objection to your presence was on purely professional grounds. You don't share information, Alessandro. I don't trust you."

He didn't just not share, he actively hid information.

"What do you want to know?"

Let me make you a list . . .

I went for the jugular. "Why did you become the Artisan?"

Silence.

As expected. Mr. Ask Me Anything lost his tongue. Alessandro didn't answer any questions about himself, his family, or anything having to do with what he did or why he did it, and this was the most important one. He probably wasn't even capable of that kind of honesty. Telling people about yourself made you vulnerable and he avoided vulnerabilities at all costs.

"When I was ten years old, a stranger murdered my father in front of me."

What?

"I thought my father was the strongest man in the world. I'd watched him fight bigger men, scarier men, and he won every time. Important people came to the house and gave my father respect. He was invincible."

His face was completely flat, his voice devoid of any emotion, but his eyes boiled with magic. It splayed out of him, filling the vehicle, a violent, dangerous current.

"I watched him die. The stranger had stabbed him. My father sagged on the ground by the killer's feet. He was trying to breathe, and bloody foam bubbled up from his mouth. I remember the fear in his eyes. I think he must have wondered if my mother and I would survive. My invincible father was dying, he was afraid, and I couldn't do anything."

There was an awful, raw sincerity in his voice, and it cut me like a knife.

"There were hundreds of people around us, and none of them tried to help. They just watched. Like me."

"Where did it happen?" I asked softly.

"At a wedding. My father was the best man."

My research into the family said his father had died, but no amount of online prying told me how. Now I knew. How horrifying it must've been for a young boy to stand there and watch his father bleed to death surrounded by people, none of whom moved to help. How did they manage to hide it?

"After the stranger killed my father, he walked by me, patted my shoulder, and said, 'Sorry, kid. It's business.'"

Oh my God.

"My grandfather explained it to me later. The groom was the intended target. My father had jumped in to save his best friend and died for it. And my grandfather spent years expounding on what an idiot my father was for putting his childhood friend's safety before the needs of his family. A man provides for his family first; nothing else matters."

He turned to look at me. All of the rage against the killer and against his grandfather flooded his eyes. That's what people must have imagined Lucifer looked like—beautiful, frightening, and full of fury. His magic twisted and convulsed through the car, sparking with deep amber.

"Every person I ever eliminated was a murderer or worked for one. I've spent the last ten years trying to find the man who killed my father." His voice was a ragged growl. "I found him. Now he wants to kill you."

Arkan had murdered Alessandro's father.

It explained so much. When he spoke of assassins, he barely managed to keep his hate under control, and I had never understood why. The database of professional killers who I thought were his rivals? They were his targets. That's why Runa's mother, an assassin, had hired him when she knew her life was in danger. It must've been known in their circles that the Artisan was an assassin who killed other killers. He was their boogeyman.

The silence lay heavy between us.

"Is that why you left six months ago?" I asked him. "To track Arkan down?"

The rage in his eyes subsided. He seemed almost relaxed now. He'd ripped his biggest secret out and offered it to me. The effort must've drained him to nothing.

"Yes."

They fought and Alessandro lost. I sensed it the same way I sensed that his failure had seared him, tempering him like fire tempered a sword. He'd survived, but whatever he'd been through had burned off the veneer of playboy and Instagram idol. The Artisan was in the driver's seat now.

"I didn't get him," he said. "I fucked that up too."

Oh Alessandro. There was so much pain in those two sentences.

"I won't let him hurt you." His voice, so suffused with rage a moment ago, was ice cold now, measured and calm, and the determination in his eyes scared me more than his anger. "I'll kill anyone who tries to end your life. I'll answer any question you ask. I'll pay any price to keep you alive. Let me protect you."

His magic coiled around me, a current of warm sparks.

"Say yes, Catalina."

"My permission isn't necessary. Linus ordered me to work with you."

"I don't care what Linus said. I know you. If you don't want to work with me, you'll find a way to . . . not. I will protect you anyway, but if you're always trying to lose me, it will make things harder. We're so much stronger when we work together."

If only it was that easy. Six months ago, just a glimpse of his grief and pain, and I would have fallen over myself to throw my arms around his neck and kiss him until the hurt inside him melted away. But I had learned that life was a vicious bitch and people were complicated. They lied to themselves.

"Do you want to protect me because of me or because it would throw a wrench into Arkan's plans?"

He opened his mouth.

"Please, don't answer," I told him. "I have work to do now."

I got out of the car. He followed. I walked up the brick steps, keyed the code into the lock, and opened the front door. The house stretched before us, cavernous and dark.

Alessandro stepped around me, moving in that stalking smooth way, raised his hand to the wall, and the lights came on. The house was white: white walls, white ceiling, white piano in the foyer on the ashy pine floor. It had a classic Texas layout, particular to "executive-style" homes—a grand foyer with vaulted ceilings that opened into the formal living room. A wall of windows directly opposite the front door offered the view of an infinity pool and a cabana bar illuminated by solar lights. On the right lay a formal dining room. On the left an office waited.

I turned left. The office was furnished in the traditional English-study style. Ornate mahogany shelves that stretched from floor to ceiling, wood paneling on the walls between two oversize windows, a large baroque desk, and a fireplace with a mantel of carved mahogany. An oil portrait of Lander Morton and a plump blond woman, both in their fifties, hung above the mantel. The only modern touches were electronic. A thoroughly modern computer with a huge screen, a printer, and several digital frames displaying pictures of the kids. A teenage boy, around fourteen or so, already echoing Felix in the build but not in his face, and two younger girls with long dark hair. Kids riding horses. Kids tubing on the river. Kids fishing in the ocean from a boat.

I walked around the desk and sat in the chair. Two picture frames flanked the monitor. On the right, the kids again, looking crestfallen and wearing brand-new school uniforms. On the left, a woman in her early thirties, slim, dark haired, with olive skin and big brown eyes. Felix's wife and the children's mother. According to Augustine's dossier, she'd died three years ago. Rich or poor, mage or a dud, cancer didn't discriminate.

I hated this part. Walking into someone else's life, cut so abruptly short. The signs of things left undone everywhere. Notes scribbled on a pad of paper. A cup of half-finished coffee that nobody remembered to take to wash in the torrent of shock and grief. We were trespassing. Intruding on someone's private existence without their permission.

I pushed the power button on the tower and the computer came to life with a soft whir. I pulled a USB stick I had taken from Rhino before I got into the car with Pete out of my pocket, plugged it in, and accessed the new drive. An icon of a heraldic shield with a styled *B* and *S* on it popped up. I clicked it and watched the program install.

Alessandro drifted through the office, looking at the pictures, studying the book spines on the shelves, and eventually came to stand beside me.

The installer finished. I pressed Windows and R. A Run window popped up and I typed "recent" into it. A new window opened, presenting me with a list of recently accessed files.

"What are you looking for?" he asked.

"Anything that has to do with the Pit. Felix was trying to keep what he found secret, so he likely saved it under some mundane name."

I found the image from the file on the fourth try, saved as Sofia's Dance Recital. There were two others, one from a different angle, and a close-up, zooming in on the churning ring with the glowing bulb in it, all saved under innocuous names. I copied all three to the USB, right clicked them one by one, selecting Add to Scrubber, and combed the computer for anything else related to the Pit. There were three folders and a few dozen documents. I copied them to the USB, added them to the Scrubber as well, clicked the shield icon on the desktop, and watched the list populate in the window.

"What is this?" Alessandro asked.

"Bern's Scrubber. It deletes the files and overwrites the disk space with random data over and over, making the files unrecoverable."

He drifted to the other side of the desk and leaned against the bookshelves.

"Why are you doing this?"

"When your father died, did you search the Internet for the man who killed him?"

"I did." His expression turned grimmer.

I nodded at the picture of the three teenagers. "If my father was murdered, I would get on his computer and I would try to find out everything I could. What he was doing, where, why, with whom. The theft of the Osiris serum is a huge failure for the US Assembly. They will do anything to erase the evidence of that failure."

"Including killing children?" he asked.

"I would like to think not, but I don't trust them enough to take that chance."

The Scrubber chewed through the files one by one. The silence was almost unbearable. He tore himself open for me and I couldn't just ignore it. I had to clear the air.

"Why do you care what happens to me, Alessandro?"

"Do you remember what you told me when I came to see you after the trials?" he asked.

No, I didn't. I had rambled, because I thought my magic had affected him and I'd panicked.

"You said, 'I want you to have a happy life. I want you to get to do all the things you want to do.' And then you went on about how your powers had scrambled my brain and you were so sorry, but 'it will wear off, I promise.'"

"All that?"

"Those were the highlights."

His magic coiled around him, a focused dense current flashing with orange like a lethal serpent whose scales shimmered, catching some hidden light. Suddenly the office seemed too small and the distance between us nonexistent.

"I want you to have a happy life, Catalina. I want you to get to do all the things you want to do. It's not everything I want but it will have to be enough."

"Why?"

"Because you're the person I care about the most."

He had no idea how much that meant to me. Maybe . . .

No. He left before, he would leave again. It had been so hard when he left. If I let myself care about him now, the next time he walked away would shatter me. I couldn't afford to be that hurt. I had to be sharp and capable. My family counted on me. Linus counted on me. I had to guard the people I loved from Victoria. I could never allow a repeat of what happened eighteen months ago.

And even if he meant every word he said, I wasn't free. Victoria Tremaine made sure of that. There would be no future for me and Alessandro.

I had to pull myself together.

The Scrubber finished. I ordered it to uninstall itself and looked at him.

"What do you think your 'uncle' Lander wants?" My voice was even. Grandma Victoria's lessons paying off.

"Punishment."

I nodded. "Lander wants to punish, Linus wants the serum, the National Assembly wants to keep it all quiet, Augustine wants his fee, and the Pit Primes want their project reopened." I reached out and brushed the frame with the three children. "I want to help them."

"Noble. And foolish."

"Says the man who ran into the building full of assassins to save a teenage kid. Ragnar Etterson still talks about how awesome you are. You have to be careful. If you show up unannounced when he is over at the house, he might faint."

He didn't say anything.

"I'm not naive, Alessandro. Since you left, I've seen and done things I never thought myself capable of. I know what my role is now. When

I take on a case, I do my best to make sure that people devastated by whatever fucked-up mess I'm walking into can salvage some small part of their lives. I'm the mitigating factor."

"The buffer." His voice sounded bitter.

"Yes. What I do makes the world a little safer for my family. It makes a difference, and while it may not seem like much, to the people affected by it, my help is everything. These are the cards I was dealt, and I choose to play the game this way. I don't need a rescue or your protection."

I took the USB, shut down the computer, and walked to the door. Behind me, Alessandro turned off the lights. We left the house as we found it, dark and devoid of warmth.

We didn't speak on the way out of the subdivision.

I should've never started this conversation. When I got into the car, I was okay. My emotions had taken a beating, but I was functional. Now . . .

"Ask me something else," he said. "Ask me any question. I'll answer."

He must have realized that information about himself was the only currency he had, and he was desperately trying to spend it. For some unknown reason, I was that important to him.

He was waiting for my answer.

Stab him, Victoria's voice said in my head. *Stab him now, right into his soul, while he's vulnerable, and slam this door shut forever. Do it before he hurts you again.*

Victoria Tremaine's granddaughter would've done it. Should have done it. But I was Catalina Baylor.

I couldn't hurt him. I felt like crying from the sheer strain of it.

The truck in front of us slammed on the brakes. Alessandro braked hard, throwing an arm in front of me.

I would treat this as a professional partnership. Linus ordered me to work with Alessandro, after all. I would do what I had to do, and I would never let Alessandro or anyone else know what it cost me.

"Marat's expecting me tomorrow at ten. Would you like to join me?"

"Yes," he said.

"My family hates you. If they try to provoke you, don't injure them."

"I won't," he said.

"They don't know I am a Deputy. They do know that I work for Linus, and that my assignments are government-related and confidential. They know I can't refuse the jobs he gives me. They accept it, they help me, and they don't ask questions. Please don't put them in danger by saying too much."

It didn't hurt that being a Deputy Warden paid exceptionally well. Linus had failed to mention that part when he deputized me. When the first wire had landed in our account, I'd almost had a heart attack.

"I promise," he said.

"Give me your number."

He rattled it off and I added it to my contact list.

He turned the corner. Our guardhouse swung into view, lit up by floodlights. Alessandro brought the Spider to a smooth stop. He parked and moved to get out of the car.

"No need. I can open my own door."

"Tomorrow," he said.

"Yes. See you tomorrow."

I got out of the car and headed to the guardhouse. I felt like I was bruised from the inside out.

Things would be so easy if it wasn't for feelings.

Chapter 5

I walked to the window of the security booth and pressed my hand against the glass in the designated circle where small round holes had been drilled in the bulletproof glass. The tinted windows hid the two guards inside, and I felt slightly vulnerable.

"Password?" a clipped male voice demanded through the speaker.

"Manhunters from Venus." Leon was in charge of the daily pass-phrases and he'd been working his way through the masters of sword and planet science fiction.

"Welcome home, Ms. Baylor."

"Thank you, Samir."

Metal clanged and a section of the barrier slid down. I walked through the gap and up the street, to the three-story brick building that served as our temporary base.

When my father was dying of cancer, Mom sold our house to pay for his medical bills. Grandma Frida did the same, and we moved into a warehouse together, which we had split into an office, living space, and a motor pool for Grandma Frida's armored car and mobile artillery business.

The warehouse was no more. Six months ago, an assassin attacked us and I caught him in an arcane circle. The spell failed to contain our combined magic, and the overflow exploded our home. If I craned my neck, I could see the empty lot where it had stood, and the guilt bit at me every time.

We had to stay somewhere, so Connor, who had bought up roughly two miles of real estate around the warehouse to keep Nevada and us safe when they were investigating the Sturm-Charles conspiracy, sold us one of the larger buildings and the three structures around it for the princely sum of one dollar. We tried to reason with him, but he refused to name a reasonable price, and we needed a place to stay, so I said thank you and took it. It allowed us to concentrate on hiring a new security force and banking money for a new house.

It also established a strong public link between our Houses. When I had become the official Head of the House after turning twenty-one, I'd fought tooth and nail to keep our two Houses separate in public view. I didn't want us to be seen as a vassal House to House Rogan. Now my priorities had changed. Once Victoria Tremaine took an interest in your life, nothing was the same.

Leon's Shelby was in his parking space. The other three family cars occupied their spots as well, and a big silver Range Rover took up the visitor's spot. June, a compact white woman, leaned against the wall by the door. My older sister was in residence.

June nodded at me. She was short, with broad shoulders and muscular arms that showed definition even when she relaxed. Her caramel hair was pulled back from her face into a short braid. She was Nevada's personal aegis, a shield mage. If someone shot at my sister, June's magic would block the projectiles. Asking her to come inside was pointless. She would guard the door no matter what anybody said. I nodded back at her, punched the code into the lock, and stepped inside.

In its past life, this building served as an office, which worked for us on a business level, but wasn't great for our living arrangements. I walked past the receptionist counter, made a left, and headed down a long hallway to what was once the cafeteria and now was our kitchen. Ahead, bright electric lights and loud voices told me the family was up. Kind of late for dinner . . .

A little black shadow padded out of the kitchen and streaked to me, her tail wagging so hard, she nearly went airborne.

I scooped my dog up. Shadow licked my face, her whole body wiggling. My chest tightened. Suddenly heat warmed the backs of my eyes.

Noises drifted from the kitchen, excited chatter, the sound of forks and knives on plates, the clatter of glasses being picked up and set back down. The air smelled of spicy meat and baked taco shells.

I hugged Shadow to me and stuck my face into her fur, trying to get myself under control. I couldn't walk in there crying.

Leon said something I didn't catch. Grandma Frida laughed.

It was fine. It had been a long day with many sharp turns, that was all. I was just tired.

Shadow twisted around in my arms. Hot tongue brushed my cheek. The tight knot in my chest dissolved. I squeezed her to me and set her down on the floor. She wagged her tail. I didn't have to do anything to make my little black dog happy. I just had to come home.

The urge to cry passed, and my brain woke up. I had things to do and the first on that list was to verify what Alessandro had told me. He didn't lie to me. That kind of emotional storm would be impossible to fake. But I wanted to see things for myself.

His father died at a wedding less than twenty years ago. Any wedding attended by a Prime would be special enough to be filmed.

I pulled out my phone and stepped into one of the front rooms that served as our office. Shadow bounded in after me. I shut the door and texted Bug.

Are you busy?

Bug worked as Connor and Nevada's surveillance specialist. A swarmer implanted with arcane magic, he processed visual information at superhuman speed.

The phone chimed. *Not particularly.*

I need a quick search and I don't want anyone to know.

Shoot.

I paused, trying to organize my thoughts. Shadow made circles around my feet, sniffing at my borrowed shoes.

I need to know about a wedding. It took place fifteen years ago, probably in Italy. The best man was Marcello Sagredo. I need to confirm he was murdered during this wedding. There might be a recording.

My phone rang. I answered.

"Is he right there next to you?" Bug roared into the phone. "Is that spoiled moneyfucker in the room with you now, Catalina?"

"No, because he died fifteen years ago."

"That's not who I mean, and you know it. He came back, didn't he? Let me guess, he's in trouble and he needs you to save him."

"No. He isn't in trouble, but I'm forced to work with him."

"Shit on a stick!"

"Bug, I don't have a choice. Can you do this for me or not?"

"Of course I'll do it. Here is my price. Next time you see him, I want you to tell him, 'Hey dickfucker, Bug is watching you.' Because I am."

He hung up.

Well, that went well.

Shadow stood up on her hind legs and leaned on my leg, looking up at me with big brown eyes. I petted her. "Let's go."

I walked into the kitchen. The whole family had gathered around the oversized dining room table. Bern, my oldest cousin, big, broad-shouldered, with tousled hair that couldn't decide if it was light brown or dark blond. Leon next to him, a sharp grin on his face. Arabella, looking surly, her long blond hair curled into ringlets.

On the other side of Bern, at the head of the table, Grandma Frida loaded her taco. Thin, bird-boned, with a halo of platinum curls and a hint of machine grease at her hairline, she saw me and winked. On her left, Mom scooped mango salsa onto her plate. Dark haired and bronze skinned, the only person in the family with darker skin than me, Mom used to be athletic and hard. During her last tour in the Balkans, she'd ended up as a POW. The experience robbed her of the full use of one of her legs. Even after two surgeries, her knee still hurt.

Nevada sat next to Mom. She wore a pristine white dress with a boat neckline, three-quarter sleeves, and a knee-length paneled skirt that draped gracefully over her bump. Her hair framed her face in a sophisticated updo and her makeup was perfectly done. She must've come from a business meeting.

Nevada picked up a pickle, dipped it into honey, and stuck half of it into her mouth.

"Eww," Arabella said. "Someone take that away from her."

Nevada squinted at her. Most of the pregnancy books I read warned to expect mood swings in the last trimester. Nevada was forty weeks pregnant and cool as a cucumber. She claimed she'd put on forty pounds, which didn't slow her down any, and if she had mood swings, we sure as hell hadn't seen them. She was her calm, sometimes scary, self, and the look she gave Arabella would have given the five Primes I'd met today serious pause.

"Touch my pickles and die."

I took the chair next to Nevada. She reached over and patted my back. Leon must have brought everyone up to speed on our monster adventure and race to MII.

Arabella squinted back. "You're almost nine months pregnant. Shouldn't you be soft, and happy, and glowing? When are we gonna see some glow?"

Arabella clearly had a death wish.

Nevada finished her pickle spear and licked honey off of her fingertips. "My back hurts, the kid inside me keeps kicking me in the kidneys, I have to pee every five minutes, my legs cramp, and I can't get out of bed by myself. I have to roll to the side, which is harder right now since my husband is somewhere in the Russian Imperium and he isn't there to steady me. And how was your day of being young, beautiful, skinny, and carefree? Why aren't you glowing?"

Arabella stuck her tongue out and turned back to her plate. Something was wrong.

"What happened?" I asked her.

"Nothing happened."

"Something did."

Arabella rolled her eyes. "I can't get any privacy in this family."

No, you can't. "What happened?"

"Some guy rear-ended me with his Tahoe on Wilcrest Drive."

The collective chewing stopped.

"Are you okay?" Nevada asked.

"I'm okay, Baby is okay; he just bounced off my bumper."

"Damn right he did," Grandma Frida said between bites. "That's 7.5 mm ballistic steel."

Arabella loved her red Mercedes. We bought it for her used, and she had been in three accidents since getting her license. This made four. After our warehouse was attacked by an elite mercenary team, Grandma Frida tried to convince her to switch to something more "sensible," but my sister refused, since Grandma Frida's idea of sensible was a tank. Grandma settled for upgrading the Mercedes to VPAM 7 armor. She souped up the engine to compensate for the added weight and now the Mercedes sounded like a pack of hungry lions.

"What were you doing out on Wilcrest?" Mom asked.

"I wanted oyster nachos from Cajun Kitchen."

Nevada's eyes glazed over for a second. "Oh, that does sound good."

"I'll get you some next time," Arabella said.

Leon dropped his fork on the table and shook his hands. "What happened with the accident?"

"Nothing happened. He got out of the car. I got out too. I was in a really good mood because I'd curled my hair and had a sundress on."

And that was my younger sister in a nutshell. Curling her hair and putting on a sundress meant the world was hers.

"He came out, looked at his grille, and then he grabbed his hair and started screaming that it was an aftermarket grille. He accused me of driving my mom's car, not knowing how to drive, called me the C-word. And his friends in the car laughed and pointed at me."

"So he just screamed at you?" Nevada leaned forward, her expression focused.

"Pretty much."

"And what did you do?" Nevada asked.

Arabella sighed. "You want to know what I did? Nothing. I stood there like a moron and let him scream at me. I don't even know why I did that. I'm not a pushover."

Three years ago, Arabella would have exploded. She would have changed shape right there in front of the Cajun Kitchen, stomped on that Tahoe, and rode it like a skateboard up and down the street. We had dodged a giant bullet.

"What did the driver look like?" I asked.

"I don't know. I didn't look at him that well. Blond, well-built, jock type, probably twenty-five, twenty-eight, between one hundred and sixty and one hundred and eighty pounds, about five foot ten, clean shaven, black T-shirt with a grey outline of Texas on it, khaki cargo shorts, carrot-red Nikes with white laces, a fake Rolex. And not a good fake Rolex either. He was driving a black Chevy Tahoe, maybe 2012 or so, with a small dent in the bumper on the driver's side. There were three other people in the car."

"Did you take a pic?" I asked.

"No," Arabella squeezed out through clenched teeth. "Like I said, I stood there and let him yell at me. He didn't even give me his insurance. Since he kept screaming about his grille, I told him he could sell the knock-off Rolex he was wearing to pay for a new one. He started cussing, and I said that we needed to get the cops involved. Then he just drove off. It was a random thing. I don't want to talk about it anymore. We were talking about Nevada. When is Connor coming home?"

Really? That was a low blow.

A week ago, Connor got word that one of the soldiers he served with got himself entangled in a kidnapping in Russia. He was part of the rescue team, which hadn't come back to base. Alan was one of the sixteen soldiers who made it out of the Belize jungle with Connor. My brother-in-law would do anything for them, but Nevada could be due any day, so he'd hesitated. And my pregnant sister practically pushed him into the plane to the Russian Imperium to go and rescue the rescue team. We hadn't heard anything since.

"Arabella," Mom said in her sergeant voice.

Arabella looked at her plate.

"You'll know when I know," Nevada said. "He'll handle it and come home."

"Heart called," Mom said, keeping her voice casual.

Suddenly everybody decided that their food was fascinating, me included. The tacos were to die for.

Heart was Rogan's second-in-command, in charge of the military operations conducted by Rogan's mercenaries. Six months ago, Mom had called him for help. We couldn't afford him, but Heart dropped everything and came to protect us anyway. We paid for his protection—he'd quoted us a ridiculously low rate—but after his employment ended, he'd stuck around, reviving Rogan's old HQ across the street. He and his soldiers returned to it between jobs, which conveniently offered us additional security. Our own security chief, Patricia Taft, was now fully up to speed, leading a crew of new, handpicked guards, but having Heart near made everyone feel better.

Heart and Mom were meticulously polite with each other in public, but when Heart was in residence, there was always some reason for him to come over or for Mom to go over there. Something was happening between them, but it was fragile and tenuous and all of us did our best to ignore it, afraid that if we looked too hard at it, it would disappear.

"Oh?" I asked. "How is he doing?"

"He's fine. He said to say hello."

To the side, out of Mom's peripheral vision, Arabella wagged her eyebrows.

I loaded another taco onto my plate. I was starving.

"So, how's Linus?" Grandma Frida asked.

Subtlety was Grandma Frida's middle name.

"Good."

"Is that the family we are now?" Leon asked dramatically. "The family where nobody talks about their things? Where everything is just 'good' and 'fine'?"

Bern reached over and tapped the back of Leon's head. "She isn't going to tell you about Linus. Stop already."

"How's the fire tank coming along?" I asked.

Grandma Frida grunted.

One of the local Houses had bought a custom firefighting tank from the Russian Imperium. Vodoley 03 was a marvel of Russian engineering. It carried about 25,000 liters of various liquids and could spray them in different patterns. It could also take a hit from a high-explosive 155 mm artillery shell and self-deploy two hundred and fifty km on a single tank of gas, but something had gone bonkers with its custom-built filtering system. Grandma Frida had been trying to coax it back to life for the last three days with no success.

"That good, huh?" Mom said.

Grandma Frida bristled. "Eat your food, Penelope."

"We have a new case," I said.

I told them about Felix's murder, omitting anything that had to do with Wardens or the serum.

Mom bit her lower lip. "There is a lot of money involved. This makes me nervous."

"That's why we'll stay on lockdown," I said.

Arabella groaned. I ignored her.

"Let's divide and conquer. I have four suspects. Everybody gets one." I pointed at Arabella, Leon, and Bern in turn. "You get a Prime, you get a Prime, everybody gets a Prime, and we all run an in-depth background check. Is that agreeable to everyone?"

"Yes," Bern told me.

Leon nodded.

Arabella rolled her eyes. "Work, work, work . . ."

I tapped my phone, sending out the mass email I had written on the drive home. "Pick whoever you want except Tatyana Pierce. Cornelius wants that one."

Nevada frowned. "I bet he does."

Arabella looked at her phone, jumped up, and ran out of the room.

Grandma Frida blinked. "Like what is even going on with that child?"

My sister sprinted back into the kitchen, carrying a tablet. Her eyes were the size of saucers. "Hua Ling!"

"What?" Mom asked.

"He's the royal physician! The assassin! Hua Ling!"

No way.

Leon pivoted to her, his face concerned. "Is it drugs? You can tell me."

"It's not drugs," I told him.

"It's *The Legend of Han Min*," Grandma Frida said.

Mom gave her an odd look.

"What?" Grandma Frida asked her. "I watched a few episodes with them. There is action and the actors are very pretty. You should see the costumes."

"It's a Chinese xianxia drama," I explained. "It's high fantasy, set in a mystical land, a lot of martial arts and Chinese mythology. Han Min is a martial arts heroine who ends up in the imperial palace and Hua Ling is a mystical alchemist who can cure any illness but is secretly an assassin trying to murder the emperor."

"That explains everything," Leon said.

Arabella marched over and stuck a tablet under his nose. "This is Hua Ling."

On the tablet a startlingly beautiful man with a waterfall of dark hair sailed through the air swinging a sword.

She flicked her fingers across the tablet. "This is Stephen Jiang."

A picture from Augustine's files showed Stephen in a suit.

"See? Same person."

It did kind of look like Stephen.

Leon flicked his finger back and forth, switching between the pictures, once, twice. Bern took the tablet away from him, set the portraits side by side, and handed it back.

Arabella tapped the tablet. "It's him. It's Cheng Feng."

"I thought you said his name is Hua Ling," Nevada said.

"The character's name is Hua Ling. The actor's name is Cheng Feng!" Arabella waved her arms in exasperation. "How are you not understanding this?"

"Do you understand this?" Nevada asked me.

"I do but I watch the show."

"I'm telling you." Arabella pounded her fist on the table for emphasis. "It's the same guy!"

"Even if he is, how is it relevant?" Leon asked.

"Because of this." Arabella tapped her tablet.

Hua Ling appeared on the screen, dressed in black and wearing a matching hooded cowl and a mask across the lower part of his face. He dashed across the double-eave hip roof through the rain, leaped impossibly high, and flung raindrops at the soldiers in ancient Chinese armor below. The raindrops turned into blades and sliced through the soldiers like razor-sharp needles.

"That's special effects," Leon said.

"What if it isn't?" Arabella asked. "What if Catalina goes to see him and he turns her face into a pincushion?"

"You don't even know it's him. His face is covered. What you have here is some sort of Chinese ninja on a wire and lots of CGI . . ."

Arabella grabbed a spoon and threw it at Leon. He caught it.

"No violence," Bern rumbled.

I glanced at Nevada. "Could an aquakinetic do this?"

"In theory," she said. "I never came across one who did."

That's what I thought too. Most of the aquakinetics killed by drowning. It was faster and more efficient.

"I'm taking Stephen Jiang," Arabella announced.

"Marat Kazarian," Leon said.

"Cheryl Castellano." Bern raised his finger.

"Okay," I said. "My first interview is tomorrow at ten with Kazarian."

"Do you need backup?" Leon crunched his knuckles.

"I already have it."

"Who?" Leon asked.

Do it quick, like ripping off a Band-Aid. "Alessandro Sagredo."

The room exploded.

I dragged myself from my small bathroom to my bed, crawled into it, and sprawled on my back. Shadow jumped up, turned three times, and settled on the blankets by my feet.

Once I mentioned Alessandro, the family had ganged up on me. Arabella screamed like a pterodactyl and demanded to know where Alessandro was staying, while punching her palm with her fist. Bern swore, which had happened exactly six times since he came to live with us. Grandma Frida promised to hit Alessandro with a wrench when he came over. Leon produced a gun, and then Mom asked him what the rule was about guns at the dinner table, and then he said that this was a special case and he had a bullet with Alessandro's name on it. Then she told him that writing names on bullets was no way to go through life. And Nevada just sat there, in the middle of the chaos, and listened to me lie through my teeth about how Alessandro was no longer an emotional factor for me.

It was over now. Everyone had calmed down.

I was so tired. Reaching over to turn off the lamp on the night table seemed way too hard. I could probably fall asleep with it on, but it would bug me.

A quiet knock echoed through the room. Now what . . .

"Yes?"

The door swung open. Nevada walked in and shut the door behind her. "Hey, you."

"Hey."

My sister crossed the room and perched on the side of my bed. She'd switched to a flowing maxi dress in pale blue and green and abandoned her shoes somewhere. Her feet were swollen again. I'd bought her maternity support stockings that went up to her waist, but it was too hot to wear them.

"How are you holding up?" she asked.

Living with a truthseeker older sister had its advantages, but sometimes I wished I could lie to her. I sat up. "I've been better."

Nevada glanced at the wall above me. "Is it me, or are there more of them since I last was here?"

Originally our building consisted of a long hallway with ten-foot-by-fifteen-foot offices on both sides. Bern had analyzed the structure and we knocked down some walls, which was why my bedroom was only ten feet wide but thirty feet long. The left side of it, with two large windows, looked out onto the glorious vista of an old parking lot. The other side, a solid wall of brick, offered two hundred and seventy square feet of opportunity. I put my bed against it, in the center. The rest of the space

I'd filled with blades. Rapiers, sabers, tactical swords, katanas, daos, machetes, and kukris rested against the brick, each in its proper place. The blades glinted softly in the lamplight.

"The saber on the left is new. And the short sword in the lower right corner," I told her.

A shadow crossed her face. "I should've found another way . . ." she murmured.

"What do you mean?" I knew exactly what she meant, but neither of us was ready for that conversation today. I didn't know if I would ever be ready.

She shook her head. "Nothing. Do you feel unsafe?"

Oh no. She thought I needed a sword for protection, and she blamed herself. Nevada was the kind of older sister one dreamed of having. When things were at their worst and I was scared to tell Mom, I ran to Nevada and she fixed it. For a good chunk of my life, she protected and provided for us, and she still tried to do it even after she married Connor.

I needed to fix this. She didn't need to feel any guilt because of me. She'd made the only possible decision when her life was tumbling into hell. In her place, I would've done the same.

"I don't collect swords because I feel unsafe. I collect them because I like them. And because I haven't found the one sword yet. I think we should discuss the real problem instead of this."

"Oh?"

"Yes. Nevada, your addiction to scented wax cubes is tearing this family apart . . ."

She laughed softly, but the guilt was still there, buried in her eyes. I needed to steer this conversation away from myself and my addiction to sharp chunks of metal.

"When was the last time you heard from Connor?" I asked.

"The day before yesterday. He said he found Shevchenko's trail."

"So good news?"

"Good news. What's really going on with you and Alessandro?"

I sighed. "Nothing."

She leaned forward and gently said, "Lie."

Argh.

"Linus wants me to work with him."

"And you always do what Linus says?"

"You're breaking our agreement," I told her.

"What agreement?"

"You don't ask me about Linus, and I don't ask you about midnight calls from the Pentagon to your cell and stories of harrowing hostage rescues by unidentified elite forces on the morning news."

In Connor's absence, Nevada ruled his private military empire. The aftermath of exposing the Sturm-Charles conspiracy scarred my sister and those wounds still hurt. She concentrated a lot of her efforts on making friends in high places and, by all accounts, succeeded. When House Rogan was mentioned in the Texas Assembly, the name was spoken with apprehension and respect.

"Fine," Nevada said. "I'll just say it. I am worried about you. When Alessandro abandoned you, you weren't yourself for weeks."

There was a lot more going on in my life at that time besides Alessandro leaving, but no, him taking off didn't help.

"You barely slept, you didn't eat, your wings . . . He hurt you."

There was no point in lying. "Yes. He did. But . . ."

"There is no but."

"But I bear some responsibility for it. He didn't promise me anything except that he would see the investigation to the end. He didn't say he loved me. I fell head over heels, and the worst thing is, I didn't even know him that well. I fell in love with a man that was half fantasy and I paid for it."

"What does he want from you?" Nevada fixed me with her stare.

"I don't know. He says he is here to protect me."

"From whom?"

"From a man called Arkan. He killed Alessandro's father and now he is targeting me because of the current case."

"Never heard of him."

She would know everything there was to publicly know about Arkan by morning.

"I think he's sincere."

"Why?"

I sighed again. "He's different."

"How?"

"It's hard to explain. The old Alessandro spent a lot of time tailoring how people saw him. He was arrogant. Everyone respected Linus, so Alessandro would challenge him out of principle. He thought he knew best, and he didn't have to waste time on silly things like explanations. If he told me something, I should just accept it and do what he said. He thought he was exempt from a lot of limitations that normal mortals had."

"Mortals?" Nevada raised her eyebrows.

"I wouldn't be surprised if he thought he was immortal. He is death in a fight, Nevada. I don't think he's ever met an opponent he couldn't take."

"So what changed?"

"All the flash is gone. He's hyper focused. It's this grim, cold determination, and it's frightening. He didn't challenge Linus. He told me he was sorry. He had a long list of what he was sorry for. Above all, he wants to protect me. He told me he would answer anything I asked, no matter how personal, and he did. He's driven."

My sister nodded. "I understand. Connor is driven. Right now, my husband is in the Russian Imperium, because when you live with a driven person, there are times you have to step back and let them do what they must do. I could have kept him here. It would've only taken one word, and he would have stayed, but I understand that he would carry a lifetime of guilt if he couldn't try to save his friend. The important thing is, I'm still first. Connor cares about me most of all. Are you more important to Alessandro than his revenge?"

"I don't know. Probably not. I'm not trying to restart this relationship, Nevada. I'm only trying to do my job. He is a part of it, and so I'll grit my teeth and work with him, and at the end of it we'll go our separate ways. It's just . . . there are leftover feelings and they make everything complicated. It still hurts."

She reached over and hugged me. I hugged her back. A soft thump hit my stomach. My nephew was doing summersaults inside his mom.

She had so many things to worry about besides me. Connor, their people, her baby, her baby's magic . . . Connor and Nevada weren't compatible from the magic point of view. He was a telekinetic, she was a truthseeker, and there was no telling what sort of magic their son would have, if any. There was an ugly word for members of magical families born without a power—a dud. For a while Leon had thought he was a dud and it was so hard on him. He'd thought he was the only one who wasn't special. If my nephew was born without magic, Connor and Nevada would love him just as much, but I crossed my fingers and toes that he would have a talent.

She carried all that on her shoulders, but she still found time to worry about me.

"It will be fine," I told her. "I can handle it."

She let me go. "If you need help, any help at all, you ask me. Promise me."

"I promise. Since you offered . . ."

"Yes?"

"What's the deal with Cornelius and House Pierce?"

She grimaced. "How much did Cornelius tell you?"

"He told me that he and Adam Pierce were joined at the hip through their childhood, not by choice, and that he detested the whole family."

Nevada nodded. "Right now House Pierce is run by Peter Pierce. Tatyana is his younger sister. Adam is the youngest. Pierce Senior died a few years back, but their mother is still alive. She spoiled Adam rotten. Cornelius' mother went to school with her, and they never lost touch. It was decided that Adam needed 'a boyhood companion to help him make good choices.'"

"Boyhood companion? Are we in the 19th century?"

Nevada shrugged. "My guess is, Mama Pierce realized that her precious boy had one hell of an antisocial personality disorder, and since she couldn't be there one hundred percent of the time, she decided to chain him to someone who followed the rules. Long story short, Cornelius couldn't keep Adam from doing messed-up crap and he was frequently punished in Adam's stead."

"That's horrible."

"It is. Some of the things he told me made me want to punch her in the face. I don't think he will do anything to jeopardize your investigation."

"I never thought he would."

She studied my face. "Catalina, I'll tell you this one last thing, and then I'll go. Connor treats Alessandro like a ticking bomb. His father once told him that a Sagredo Prime is the most dangerous opponent he could ever face."

"Why? Alessandro can summon weapons, but Connor can cut a building in half."

"He doesn't know. He was young and didn't ask for explanation at the time. But from what he says, it has to do with a Sagredo House spell."

"Sagredos have no House-level spells. There is no record of them ever using arcane circles, even."

Nevada's face turned dark. "Exactly. I don't know what secrets Alessandro is hiding, and I want you to be careful. Be very careful. I love you and I don't want you to get hurt."

# Chapter 6

I dreamed of floating in a lazy river on my back. The current gently carried me forward, and above me tree branches slid back, the sun shining bright through the gaps between the leaves. Alessandro floated next to me and he was speaking low in Italian, his tone soothing . . .

My phone chimed. I sat up and grabbed it before my eyes even opened. A call from Patricia Taft, our security head. Wow, 8:02 a.m. The family must've felt sorry for me and let me sleep an extra hour.

I accepted the call.

Patricia's clipped British accent made every word sharp. "I have Sergeant Munoz and Detective Giacone from Houston PD here."

Crap. Munoz belonged to the House Response Unit, the division of Houston PD tasked specifically with handling problems with Houses. Each member of the division was assigned a roster of families, and we belonged to Munoz. A visit from him was never good.

"What do they want?"

"They would like to question Leon in connection with Audrey Duarte. Should I let them in or should I phone the lawyer?"

Munoz wouldn't have made the trip for a simple complaint. The fact that he and Giacone were here together meant a felony. Audrey would never accuse Leon of assault. It wasn't in her nature. She tried to buy him with gifts and relied on emotional blackmail, but she wouldn't do something to actually hurt him. If someone else had assaulted Audrey, Leon would be the first person she called.

She hadn't called, because Leon would've told me if she did. That meant only one thing.

Audrey Duarte was dead.

Ice shot through me. Poor Audrey. Poor little harmless Audrey. She was barely nineteen.

It gutted me. It would hit Leon like a train.

"Hold on." I grabbed my tablet and FaceTimed Leon.

He answered on the first ring. He sat in the office room he shared with Bern. The floor behind him was strewn with papers. He must have been doing research. When Leon sorted through data, he drew strange abstract doodles and threw the paper down when he finished them. If the problem was thorny enough, he would go through fifty pages in a couple of hours.

"This is really important. Answer honestly. Did you go to Audrey's last night?"

Leon dramatically whipped off his imaginary shades. "Look into my eyes. I. Did. Not. See. Audrey. Yesterday."

"But did you go to her place?"

"No. I went home. Straight home, no detours. You know when I left MII. Check the log. I checked in and haven't left."

"What time did she call you last night?"

He checked his phone. "5:42 p.m."

"I need you to stay in your office." It was on the other end of the building on the second floor. "Don't come down here, don't call. I'll call you."

Leon leaned closer. "Did something happen?"

"I don't know yet. Stay where you are, please. Promise."

"Fine."

I hung up and turned to my phone. "Patricia, bring them into the conference room in fifteen minutes. Don't let them question anyone."

"Got it."

I hung up and called Bern. He picked up. "Yes?"

"We're in trouble. Munoz and his partner are here. Please lock Leon out of the conference room feed and tell Nevada and Mom."

I hung up, jumped off the bed, and rummaged through my closet for clothes.

I had seen Leon kill before. He did it without remorse or hesitation, but when he got home, he would get a beer and go off by himself, sometimes onto the roof, sometimes into another building. He would sit there for hours, sipping the beer and brooding, which he claimed was "quiet thinking." Taking a life mattered to him. It drained all the humor and joy out of him and he turned silent and withdrawn. He hadn't been that way last night and he wasn't that way now.

Besides, Leon only killed when he had no other choice. To become his target, you had to put the family in danger. He knew Audrey and didn't consider her a threat to himself or us. He was annoyed with her, but my cousin never killed anyone out of annoyance.

Eight minutes later I tore out of my bedroom, dressed in a dark skirt, blue blouse, and navy pumps. My hair was pulled back from my face into a severe bun, and my makeup was understated, minimal, but there. I looked like the Head of the House who had been awake for hours handling important business. Image was armor, and I needed every inch.

My sister walked out of the guest bedroom, wearing a blue wraparound dress. Magic radiated from her like a razor-sharp corona. Nevada looked ready to go to war. If I weren't her sister, I would be shaking in my shoes.

"Will you sit in on this?"

Nevada rolled her eyes. "Do you even have to ask?"

Ten minutes later, I pretended to be engrossed in my laptop as Patricia ushered the two officers in. Nevada had parked herself at the other end of the table, hiding her bare feet under it.

Sergeant Munoz strode into the room and gave me his hard cop stare. Middle-aged, light-skinned, and world-weary, he looked like a cop who had always been a cop. It was impossible to imagine him as young or naive. Instead, he must have come into this world just like this, wrapped in authority, jaded, and empowered by the city of Houston to take on all of its chaotic craziness.

Behind him, Detective Giacone gave the room a once-over. Taller than Munoz by six inches and younger by about five years, he wore a better suit and had a better haircut. You saw Munoz and you knew he was exactly where he wanted to be. When you looked at Giacone, you got the impression he was waiting for his chance to move up.

A soundless notification window popped up in the corner of my laptop. Bern had accessed the security camera feed from the conference room. Ten to one, everyone except Leon was watching it.

"Prime Baylor," Munoz said. "Prime Rogan-Baylor."

"Good morning, gentlemen." I indicated the two chairs in front of me. "Please sit."

The two officers sat. Behind them Patricia Taft walked into the room and took a seat to my right. Fit, with light brown skin and bold attractive features, Patricia inspired confidence. She wore a beige pantsuit and her dark brown hair was cut in a perfect shoulder-length bob, but everyone in the room sensed that she would rather be in uniform, hair tucked into a beret. Everything about her was precise, efficient, and together. Surprisingly, the complete opposite of her wife, Regina, who wore flowery maxi dresses and strappy sandals.

Munoz squinted at me. I radiated all the warmth of an iceberg. I had slipped Victoria Tremaine's granddaughter on like a comfortable jacket. It fit, and Giacone shifted under my cold stare. His spine straightened; his shoulders tensed.

"I don't see Leon Baylor." Munoz looked at me. "Why isn't he here?"

"He'll join us if I decide it's necessary."

"He's a person of interest in an ongoing investigation."

"And if you explain to me why, and if I determine that you have sufficient reason to question him, I will make him available."

Munoz and I stared at each other.

"I think we may have gotten off on the wrong foot." Giacone made a conciliatory gesture. "We're all on the same side."

I shot him my Tremaine look. His mouth clicked shut.

"It's my intention to cooperate with your investigation, which is why we are having this conversation without our House counsel. If you would prefer to conduct this discussion with Sabrian present, I will call her in. I trust you remember Sabrian, Sergeant?"

Munoz's eyes told me he did.

"I'll start, in the interests of good faith." I leaned back in my chair. "Ms. Duarte is a former client. She wanted to pursue a romantic relationship with Leon, and he declined. She attempted to send him several expensive gifts, which we returned, and showed some obsessive tendencies."

"How?" Giacone asked.

"She sent numerous texts and made many phone calls even after being asked to stop."

"Have you reported this?" Giacone asked.

"No, but we extensively documented it and consulted our attorney. I can make these records available to you upon request. The last contact Leon had with Ms. Duarte took place yesterday at 5:42 p.m. Ms. Duarte called his phone and indicated that she feared there was an intruder in her home. My cousin advised her to call the police and dialed 911 on her behalf."

"That part we agree on," Munoz said. "Where was your cousin when he received the text?"

Nice try. "It was a call, not a text. He was on the 17th floor of MII."

Munoz's face told me nothing. "Why was he at MII?"

"It was a professional matter not relevant to this investigation. Besides Leon, the meeting involved me, Cornelius Harrison, Augustine Montgomery, and his assistant, Lina Duplichan. All of them can confirm his presence. MII will be able to provide the exact time he left the building."

"Where did he go after he left MII?" Giacone asked.

"He accompanied Cornelius Harrison to deliver a small tamarin monkey we'd recovered to a child from whom she'd been stolen. Her family and Mr. Harrison will verify this for you. Then he drove home." I tapped my tablet and placed it in front of them. "Here's last night's security footage."

On the screen, Leon parked in front of the booth, exited his Shelby, walked up to the window, and placed his hand against the holes drilled in the bulletproof glass. A moment passed. Leon returned to his car. The barricade turned, lowering into the ground, and he drove to his parking space. We watched him enter the building. The time stamp on the video said 6:33 p.m.

"He hasn't left the property since he arrived last night," Patricia said. "I have hours of boring footage if you would like to go through it."

Munoz took out a tablet and placed it in front of me. He tapped the screen. A recording of an apartment building popped up, a tall Art Deco rectangle bristling with balconies. Probably the feed from a security camera mounted across the street.

"Where is this?" I asked Munoz.

"Ivy River Oaks apartments."

Audrey's residence, an upscale apartment complex.

On the screen, "Leon" walked into the building. The time stamp said 6:27 p.m.

At 6:39 p.m. "Leon" exited the building and walked away. He moved like Leon, he wore the same clothes, but he was not my cousin, because Leon was here, in this building, when it happened.

"Is she dead?" I asked.

"She is," Munoz answered.

My pulse spiked and for a second I worried they might hear it.

First, they tried to provoke Arabella into exposing her magic. When that failed, they went after Leon. They tried to lure him to her place with the phone call, and when he didn't show up, they framed him for Audrey's murder. This went beyond a simple attack. It was subtle and elegant. These people weren't just another House starting a feud. This was executed with a professional smoothness that spoke of experience.

Arkan's people wanted me out of the way. If they killed me, Linus would go in guns blazing, but they didn't need to kill me. They just needed to distract me long enough to accomplish their goals. Going after my family was the surest way to incapacitate me.

This incident was just the opening salvo. Since the frame-up would fail, there would be more, probably nastier and harder to get out of, and we needed Munoz and the Houston PD on our side while we fought them off. I had to obtain Munoz's trust at any cost. My trump card sat in the chair next to him, and if I played it, there would be a price to pay. I shouldn't have asked Nevada to sit in on this conversation. Shit.

Munoz slid his finger across the tablet. On it appeared the crumpled body of a girl curled in the fetal position halfway on a white shag carpet, her knees drawn all the way to her chest. Blood pooled around her head, staining the wood floor. Her long blond hair fanned all around her, covering her face like a funeral shroud. A dark red hole gaped in her skull, just above the ear.

The breath lodged in my throat and stayed there, like a rock. They killed her just to get to us. She was collateral damage. A life cut short for nothing.

"Here's what I have," Munoz said, his voice hard. "A nineteen-year-old girl has a crush on an older guy."

"Leon is twenty, Sergeant."

"She calls him, she sends him gifts, she keeps bothering him. Maybe she has something on him. Maybe she told him she's pregnant. He wants her to go away. So, he either hires someone, or his friend, an illusion mage, does him a favor. He assumes his form and drives his car back to his house. Meanwhile, your cousin goes over to Ms. Duarte's residence. Maybe they have an argument, maybe it becomes an altercation. Maybe he goes over there with the idea that things may turn violent and that's why he takes the time to build his alibi. He kills her, gets a ride home, and his buddy slips out of your house."

Nevada laughed. It sounded cold, bitter, and frightening.

The two cops looked at her.

"She is laughing because you think that Augustine Montgomery or any of his employees would incriminate themselves for our sake." I shook my head. "We are talking about the same Augustine Montgomery, aren't we?"

Munoz didn't even blink. "Who knows? Perhaps he owed you a favor."

"Prime Montgomery and House Baylor have a complicated, often adversarial, relationship," I said. "Oddly enough, he did once come here as one of us."

"Who?" Giacone asked.

"Me," I said. "He made it past all of our defenses."

"Before my time," Patricia said.

"Which is why we have taken certain measures to ensure it doesn't happen again."

Patricia fiddled with a tablet and put it in front of the cops again. This was turning out to be the ballad of dueling tablets.

A brightly lit interior of the security booth appeared on the screen. Two guards manned the console. A large German shepherd lay on a pillow by their feet.

"This is Cassius. This is what happens when one of us approaches the booth," I said.

On the screen the dog rose and sniffed the holes in the glass. A separate feed in the corner of the screen showed Leon outside of the booth.

"Note the time stamp," Patricia said.

6:33 p.m., yesterday.

Patricia fiddled with the tablet again and returned it to the table. "This is what happens when an illusion mage attempts to gain entry while impersonating a member of House Baylor."

On the screen Grandma Frida walked up to the booth. Had I not known that this was a hired mage, I would have sworn that it was my grandmother. She walked with the same bounce in her step. Her clothes were right, her smile was right. Even the engine oil stains on her coveralls were right.

She approached the booth. She was five feet away when Cassius snarled, baring his teeth, and exploded into barks.

"As you're well aware, an illusion mage can change their appearance but not their biochemistry. We have four canine sentries," Patricia said. "They work six-hour shifts. We test them every month. They have never given a false positive."

"I don't know who that is on your recording," I said. "But it's not my cousin. Leon would never kill Audrey. Nor would he have a relationship with her or lead her on. He is a Baylor."

"Are you implying that he's too good for her?" Munoz asked, a faint warning in his tone.

"I'm implying that, as a member of an emerging House, Leon understands discipline and obligation to his family. He works fifty hours a week on average. Sometimes, especially in the beginning of a new case, he works more. He still resides with the rest of us here, he logs his every move, and he doesn't sleep with clients. That would be against our policy. He doesn't have the time, opportunity, or the energy to commit to a relationship, all of which he explained to Audrey. You can listen to the recording if you wish."

"And he just happened to record this conversation?" Munoz asked.

"No, but she did. You can view it on her YouTube and Instagram, video #468. Titled 'Should I give him a chance?' She recorded the phone call and inserted chunks of it into her video with her commentary while doing her makeup. This was over a month ago."

Munoz looked like he wanted to say something. I would drag him over to our side. Whatever it took. Very well. Might as well kill two birds with one stone.

I turned to Giacone. This would have to be done just right. I looked at him as if he were a dog. A loyal, but stupid, dog.

"How is Amanda, Henry?"

Out of the corner of my eye I saw Nevada frown.

Giacone pulled himself ramrod straight. "She's well, thank you."

"I understand she's made quite a lot of progress with her violin."

Giacone offered me a shy smile. "Yes. She has a recital later this month."

"Are you considering the Mayflower Academy?" The Mayflower Academy was a high school for gifted students, private, exclusive, hellishly difficult to get into and far out of a typical police sergeant's range.

"We thought about it," Giacone said.

Of course you did. "My grandmother believes your daughter would be a good fit."

Giacone turned slightly whiter. "Thank you."

"Give us a few minutes, Henry."

"Yes, Ms. Tremaine."

He rose, walked out of the room, and shut the door. Next to me on Patricia's tablet, Britney Hays, one of our security people showed Giacone to a room across the hall and followed him in there.

If Munoz could be any more inscrutable, he'd turn to stone, but I knew he'd caught that "Tremaine." Henry had slipped. And that's after he hit his own professional impartiality over the head with a shovel and buried it in his backyard.

I dropped the mask and looked Munoz in the eye. "Detective Giacone is my grandmother's creature. He's been bought and paid for. This is a show of trust on my part. I'm giving you a chance to transfer a mole out of your department."

Munoz leaned back, the nonchalant expression gone. "As long as Giacone is my partner, he'll be keeping tabs on you and reporting to her. You want Victoria Tremaine out of your hair and you're using my hands to do it."

"She'll know it's me." And she won't like it.

Munoz fixed me with a heavy stare. "Don't make the mistake of thinking you can manipulate me, Ms. Baylor."

Everyone had a pressure point. I knew Munoz's, but that was the difference between me and Grandma Victoria. I would never use it.

"You don't believe Leon did it either. If you did, you would have gone about this meeting in an entirely different way."

"What I believe isn't as important as what the evidence tells me."

"Sabrian Turner will shred that recording in court and you know it," Nevada said.

"Sergeant Munoz, in the last forty-eight hours we've been attacked three times. We are in someone's crosshairs. I don't know who is behind this series of unfortunate events, but I'll find out. I have no reason to manipulate you. I just want you to be aware of what's happening, and I don't want Houston PD to jump to conclusions, because I expect more trouble. A lot more. I'm asking you to trust me and offering evidence that I'm trustworthy."

I had served him Giacone on a silver platter. Munoz was too smart not to recognize it as an overture to the alliance. I gave him the mole. In turn, when the next piece of weird evidence involving us crossed his desk, he would view it more carefully.

"Consider me aware."

"I'm not asking for special treatment. Just a little patience."

He shook his head. "You're playing a dangerous game."

"I have to protect my family, Sergeant."

He nodded, stood up, and left.

I waited until the camera feed on my laptop assured me that the two officers exited the building under Patricia's watchful eye and then tapped my keyboard. An image of Bern nestled in the computer room expanded on the screen. Arabella was behind him and Grandma Frida sat on his left, while Mom was on his right. They woke her up. Figured.

Patricia came back and sat in the chair across from me.

"We are being targeted because of Linus' case I'm working on. Originally I thought I was the primary target, but it doesn't seem to be the case."

I told them as much about Arkan as I could without betraying Linus' confidence.

"Whoever Arkan sent is smart and knows way too much about us. As of this moment, we're going to proceed as if we are in a feud. Bern, please check our networks, the servers, the cameras, everything. Arabella, please review our financials. Liquidate anything that can potentially result in a crippling loss if someone starts manipulating the market."

"That would be about thirty percent of our portfolio," she warned. "We'll take a hit."

"Do it," I said. "We don't want to be financially vulnerable."

She nodded.

Grandma Frida threw her hands up. "I'll dust off Romeo."

"Thank you, Grandma."

Grandma Frida subscribed to the philosophy that most problems could be solved by applying a tank to them. I had a terrible feeling that this mess wouldn't be that simple to fix.

I closed the laptop.

"How did you know about Giacone?" Nevada asked.

Crap. There was no escape. "Victoria told me."

My evil grandmother had expected me to use Giacone as an asset.

My sister stood up, walked over, and stared at me from across the table. "You visit her?"

"Every other Thursday." At the start of our relationship, I visited her every other day for a month, but Nevada didn't need to know that.

"Catalina!"

I looked up at her. "Yes?"

"That woman is evil. Do you have any idea how dangerous she is?"

"Yes."

"You have to stop talking to her. She's—"

Nevada's phone went off. She glanced at it. "Damn it. I have to take this. Don't go anywhere." She walked out and ducked into the nearest office across the hall.

"Time to earn my pay," Patricia said.

"We know they have at least one illusion mage with them."

"We'll sniff test everyone."

"I'll let you know as soon as I have more information."

Patricia nodded. "Do you want to talk to the Lone Gunman or should I?"

I got up. "I'll talk to Leon."

"What do you want me to do about Prime Sagredo?" Patricia asked.

"I don't follow."

She pushed her tablet toward me. A silver Spider waited a few yards away from the security booth.

"How long has he been here?"

"Since 7:00 a.m."

And nobody told me. Considering that nobody shot him, my family showed remarkable restraint.

"We don't need to do anything about him. He's guarding me."

"Where do the two of you stand?" Patricia asked.

"I'll tell you as soon as I figure it out."

I climbed the stairs to the second floor. Leon sat in his office chair. A huge coffee mug with a drawing of an action figure and the slogan "If you're not shooting, you should be communicating your intention to shoot" waited on his desk.

Leon's shoulders were rigid, his spine tense. He already knew.

Bern was smart. He vacuumed up data, and his powerful brain sorted it into logical chains. He had excelled at almost every subject in school, because once he learned something, he remembered it forever. Leon had failed most of his classes and limped to graduation with a C average, but he was sharp. When the occasion called for it, he made lightning-fast deductions. If his brother's mind was a lighthouse beam, Leon's was a strobe light, firing off unpredictable flashes of blinding brilliance.

"Audrey is dead," I said.

"I figured that out. How?"

"A single shot to the temple, very quick. They have security footage of someone who looks exactly like you walking in and out of the building."

"Looks like me or is me?"

"Is you. A high-ranking illusion mage. The clothes were right, the posture was right, and they even sauntered like you."

"I don't saunter."

He said it on autopilot, his voice without any emotion. Oh, Leon.

"They killed her just because of me."

"No. They killed her because of me."

He jerked to look at me. His voice was harsh. "Tell me."

I told him about Arkan. "He's targeting us to divert attention from Felix Morton's murder. Nothing you did had anything to do with it."

Leon looked at me. His eyes were red. "I should have gone over when she called me."

"Then she would have died half an hour sooner."

"Or I would have saved her. She called me for help, and I didn't come."

"This was a trap," I said. "They tried to lure you there. They waited to see if you would show up, and when you didn't, they went with plan B. It was a pretty good plan B but flawed. They didn't account for our dogs."

"I should have gone, Catalina. She must have been terrified. I could tell she was scared on the phone, but I thought she was acting. I ignored her and they killed her just to set me up. If it wasn't for me, she would still be alive."

But she was dead, and every time I thought about it, my heart jerked in my chest. There would be time to process it later. Right now, Leon needed reassurance.

"You didn't ignore her. You talked to her. You called the police. You told her to dial 911."

His eyes were dark, his face grim. I could tell nothing I said made any difference. I had to lift some of this from him.

"You told me about it, and I told you not to go."

"It's not on you," he said.

"Yes, it is. I'm the Head of the House."

"She was my responsibility."

"No. She stopped being your responsibility when you finished the case. Leon, if I could rewind yesterday, knowing what I know now, I still wouldn't have let you go. Not alone. If you had gone, now Audrey would be dead, you would likely be dead, and we would be planning your funeral. I can't do that, Leon. I can't bury you. I just can't."

His face remained grim.

I wished I could do something, anything, to make him feel better and to make Audrey not be dead. But life didn't offer do-overs.

"We'll make them pay," I promised.

His gaze focused. A cold expression hardened his face.

"What was their plan?" Leon said, his voice icy. "Lure me there, stage a murder-suicide?"

"If I were doing it? I'd kill her and shoot you but make sure you survived."

He raised his eyebrows.

"If you died, we would be gunning for revenge. Grief hardens you. It makes you into a determined opponent. What would you do if I was killed?"

"I'd turn the city inside out."

"Exactly. Our whole family would be foaming at the mouth to find your killer. But if you were still clinging to life, most of our energy would go toward clearing you and making sure you recovered. We would be angry, sure, but mostly we would be scared that we might lose you. It's not just the frame-up, it's the uncertainty. Will you live? If you live, will you be charged with killing Audrey? Are you in a coma, unable to refute the charges but tainted by murder? If you're hovering between life and death, the authorities can't charge you, they can't clear you, and meanwhile House Baylor is smeared with the scandal. A PI who murders a celebrity YouTube star. Investigating Felix's murder on top of that would be the last thing on my mind."

He stared at me. "So, in this scenario, I'm a total screwup who murdered an innocent girl, tried to take the coward's way out, and fucked it up? Jesus, I thought I was dark."

That was a little splash of life. I would take it. "You need to up your game."

I hugged him. Leon stiffened, then hugged me back. For a long moment neither of us spoke and then I took a step back.

"Have you told anyone about Audrey?"

He frowned.

"She never mentioned you by name in any of her videos. There is nothing on any of the social networks tying you together." Bern had checked on that because Sabrian asked him to. "Who would know about it?"

"Albert," he said.

"Albert Ravenscroft?"

Leon nodded.

"Why?"

My cousin sighed. "You know how I run in Freshmeadow Park in the morning? He started running with me three weeks ago."

"He did?" That was news to me.

"Yeah. He talks." Leon said it as if it explained everything.

"About what?"

"About everything. Sports. Family business. Cars. It always comes back to what a good match he would make for you. And wouldn't it be cool if we could be buddies and in-laws. And if I could talk to you about him."

"Let me guess, he has many fine qualities that women find attractive?"

"So many," Leon said.

No doubt.

"One morning Audrey called, and he heard me tell her to stop. He said it was kind of harsh, so I told him about her. I know it's against policy, but I felt it was a good teachable moment."

"How did he take it?"

"He didn't get it," Leon said. "I don't understand this guy. He seems smart. I made parallels between Audrey and me and him and you. It totally flew over his head."

I rubbed my face. I would have to speak to Albert.

"You're not backing off from the Pit?" Leon asked.

"No."

"Good." Leon bared his teeth. "I sent Marat's background to you."

"Thank you."

"I suppose you want me to sit on my hands at home?"

I did but telling Leon that virtually guaranteed that he would do the opposite, especially if I mentioned that Arkan's people would target him. He wanted that confrontation. Instead I went for Mom's approach.

"I'm not going to tell you what to do, Leon. You know the situation. Right now, Houston PD must get a warrant to talk to you. The moment you leave, they're free to approach you on the street. People are free to record this encounter, which will almost certainly devolve into a confrontation. People can post it on Herald, share it on Snapchat, and speculate about why the police are talking to you and then someone will mention Audrey's name . . ."

Leon held up his hand. "You made your point. I will stay here and clear the Hoskins case."

"Thank you."

Leon locked his teeth. Muscles stood out on his jaw. He held up one finger. "One condition."

"Yes?"

"When we find who did this to Audrey, I'll kill them."

"I'm counting on it."

 **Chapter 7**

At ten minutes before nine, I went to get Alessandro. I stopped by the guard booth first.

"Hi, Brittney."

A clipped female voice responded, "Hello, Ms. Baylor."

"Has he moved?"

"Prime Sagredo arrived at 06:54, rolled down his window at 07:12, answered a phone call at 07:54, rolled up his window and started the vehicle at 08:10, turned the vehicle off at 08:20, then started the vehicle again at 08:40 and turned it off at 08:50."

Texas heat was no joke. It was already approaching ninety and the humidity only made it worse. Without AC he would be broiling in that car.

"Thank you, Brittney."

"You're welcome, ma'am."

I walked toward the Spider. I could see Alessandro through the windshield. He'd shaved. His hair was perfectly tousled. He wore a white shirt he'd left open at the collar. We would be treated to Prime Sagredo this morning.

He opened his door and got out of the car. He wore sand-colored trousers with expensive Italian loafers. A BVLGARI watch glinted on his wrist, about fifteen grand. The perfect picture of a House scion. He had money and he had taste, and he had to take care of business, but he wasn't his father, so he saw no reason to be uptight about it. A year ago, before I got to know him, I would have mistaken it for his natural style, but now I knew better. Everything he wore and the way he wore it was precisely calculated. A spoiled heir of a prominent European House living on the cusp of fashion wouldn't think to dress down to visit a building site and so Alessandro pretended to have no common sense.

I had traded my skirt and pumps for a more sensible beige pants, boots, and a blue T-shirt. To say we didn't match would be an understatement. Alessandro looked like a wealthy spoiled heir to some corporation who came to bother his personal secretary on her day off just before she left to go hiking.

"Arkan's person made their move," I told him.

"Tell me."

I did.

"True to form," he said. His voice had the steady calm of a man who had expected the worst and was proven right. He wouldn't waste time and energy being angry about it. He would simply kill everyone responsible, and I had no problem with that.

Of all the ways they could attack us, I would've never anticipated Audrey. We barely knew her. She was a complete innocent in this. They murdered a girl just for a chance to distract me. When I came face-to-face with her killers, I would eliminate them. It wouldn't make me happy. Killing was a monstrous thing but sometimes it had to be done. I would kill for the sake of my family without any hesitation and I would kill for Audrey, so no other Audrey would die like her again.

An outraged honk tore through the silence behind us. We both turned. A green Mini Cooper sped up the road and slid to a dramatic stop before the security booth. The driver's window rolled down, and Runa Etterson stuck her red-haired head out of it.

"Catalina! Step away from the dickhead!"

A strangled sound came from the booth's speakers. It sounded suspiciously like laughter.

"I thought the Etterson matter was settled," Alessandro murmured.

"It was."

"Then what is she doing here?"

"She probably heard about Leon and came for moral support. She's my best friend."

Runa passed the sniff test and was marching toward us, her car abandoned. Her face promised war. I had kept things from my family, because I didn't want them to worry, but I told Runa everything.

"You should run," I told Alessandro. "You're vastly outnumbered. It's not too late to give up and go home."

"You! Don't you walk away. I have things to say to you." Runa caught up with us. "Catalina, have you lost your mind?"

Probably. "How did you even know he was here?"

"Intuition," she said and turned bright red.

Bern. Had to be.

Runa stared at Alessandro. "You saved my brother. I owe you a debt. If you need a favor, I'll take care of it."

"Thank you," he said.

"Catalina is my best friend. I don't know what's going on, but don't get any ideas. She's too good for you."

"I'll keep it in mind."

"If you hurt her again, I'll find you and then I'll make you wish you were dead."

"Okay." I grabbed her by the shoulders and steered her toward the front door. "Thank you for your input, Prime Etterson."

"Dead!" Runa called out over her shoulder.

 # Chapter 8

Alessandro stared at Rhino. His eyebrows came together.

"Why don't we just take my car?"

"Because we're going to the Pit, which means we have to navigate the deserted and possibly flooded area with many hazards."

"My car is fast and maneuverable."

I raised my hand and held my thumb and index finger an inch apart. "And it sits this low to the ground."

"Can you even reach the speed limit in this monstrosity?"

"Yes."

He pondered the blocky SUV. The corners of his mouth curled a little. "What if something chases us and we have to jump a hole in the bridge?"

"If something chases us, I'll reverse, ram them, and then drive back and forth over their broken body until it's flat as a pancake."

He raised his eyebrows.

"If you want to jump bridges, you can follow me in your car, but I'm taking this one. You want to roll up to the Pit Reclamation HQ in your Spider because it's consistent with your character of House scion. It would make Marat think less of you, which is to your advantage. I empathize. Yesterday I wanted to appear incompetent and vulnerable and you told them that my powers gave you pause. We are taking Rhino."

He raised his hands. "Fine."

"Thank you so much for your cooperation."

"You're welcome."

He strode to his car and popped the trunk. He dug in it and came out with an assault rifle.

"What is that?"

"This is an M4 carbine. It's air-cooled, gas-operated, magazine-fed, and it fires 5.56 rounds."

"I know what an M4 carbine is. What is that attached to it?"

Alessandro made a show of looking at the rifle. "Oh that."

"Is that an M320 grenade launcher?"

"It appears to be."

"Just out of curiosity, do you have a SAW stashed somewhere in that tiny car?"

"I don't remember." He leaned toward me, his amber eyes speculative. "Would you like to crawl around in there with me and look for one?"

Asking him things was clearly a mistake.

I opened the hatchback and he loaded the M4 into it. Two portable pistol cases followed. Then another case, which he stacked on top of the pistol ones.

"What's in there?"

"Knives."

I pulled my sword case open. Two feet high and four feet long, it unfolded like a toolbox, with the top shelf holding my favorite blades, the tactical gladius, the rapier, and a tactical machete. The bottom shelf offered a variety of knives in every shape and size.

"Extras," I told him.

"Nice," he said.

Not as nice as Linus' blade, which I had already loaded into the console.

I shut the hatchback, climbed into the driver's seat, while he got in next to me, and we were off.

Alessandro relaxed in the seat, long legs stretched out, broad shoulders resting against the back. Sunlight filtered through the window, playing on his hair. His face, halfway shaded, was heartbreaking. I could lift my phone and take a burst of twenty pictures and every single one would be a masterpiece.

A faint whiff of sandalwood mixed with vanilla and a hint of citrus floated through the car. The Alessandro scent. He'd smelled this way the day he kissed me, and I nearly stripped naked for him in the bathroom of the Wortham Theater. He'd smelled this way too when I came to tell him I was in love with him and found him packing.

I wanted to know what happened between him and Arkan. Whatever it was had shaken him to the core. It gnawed at me. I wanted to know.

If I asked him about it, he would tell me. It had to be awful, because nothing short of awful caused that kind of seismic shift in a person. He would tell me, and then I would know, and I would want to make him feel better. I would care. I couldn't afford to care.

I turned right on Kempwood Drive. We could have taken Hempstead, but it was closed due to roadwork. There were three certainties in Houston: death, taxes, and never-ending roadwork. The joke was on me. The moment we merged onto the Sam Houston Tollway, the traffic ground to a halt. Sirens wailed ahead. We would be here awhile.

The hint of sandalwood and vanilla drifted to me. I needed a distraction.

I thought back to Augustine's case summary. I had read it last night and forwarded it to Alessandro before passing out.

The MII investigators were worth their price. In the brief time they had the case, they put together a timeline of Felix's movements, interviewed the other four Primes and some of their staff, and obtained the preliminary coroner's report.

Felix died on Friday, July 15th. That day he'd dropped off his children at their private school and arrived at his office at Morton Enterprises at 8:15 a.m., the same as he did every morning. He spent three hours at the office, placing several phone calls to the engineering firm involved with the reclamation project. He ate lunch at his desk—a gyro with chips from a place around the corner—worked some more after lunch, and at 2:17 p.m. exited the building. At 3:00 p.m., he was seen at the America Tower, where he'd bumped into Linus.

He left the America Tower by 3:30 p.m. and went back to the office. According to his secretary and his calendar, he had no plans for the evening and was supposed to go home to have dinner with his family. Instead, at 5:00 p.m., he called his housekeeper and told her that he had a change of plans and not to wait for him for dinner, then he left the office.

Twenty-five minutes later, an unknown person used the private after-hours code on the gate inside the Pit. The two guards swore nobody went in before Felix and the security feed confirmed their statement, so this person had to have arrived to the island by boat or some other means. Shortly after, the security booth logged Felix driving in. The inner gate code was used again at 5:49 p.m., presumably by Felix. That was his last sign of life.

It killed me that nobody thought to check on him, but Felix was a Prime and he had previously stayed at the site overnight when the occasion called for it. Because he'd called his housekeeper, his children assumed that he was working late. In the morning, Felix's daughter tried to reach him, and when he still didn't answer, she contacted her grandfather, who called security at the site. They began a systematic search and found him hanging off the cable, his body butchered.

He'd gone to the site to meet with someone. His cell phone was recovered and showed no phone calls or texts, so the arrangements for the meeting had to have been made in person, during his trip to the Assembly.

The MII investigators had come to the same conclusion, but the inner workings of the Texas Assembly were kept private. Whatever happened between the gleaming white walls of the America Tower stayed there. None of the other four Primes had visited the Assembly in person that day, but their family members had attended: Tatyana's brother, Cheryl's uncle, Marat's brother, and Stephen's father. Any of them could've passed on a message to Felix. *Meet me in the Pit. It's important. Come alone.*

Each of the four living board members had an alibi. Stephen Jiang's appeared to be the most solid. He was on a conference call with a firm in Tokyo, and according to MII's summary, the conversation was too detailed for anyone to impersonate him. Marat was having dinner with his family, who would no doubt lie for him if he asked. Cheryl was also having dinner at a restaurant with a friend, who was yet to be identified.

Tatyana's alibi was the shakiest of the four. Supposedly she was at her office, but MII caught her vehicle leaving the parking lot of the Pierce Building in the middle of the day and didn't show her coming back.

Felix's legs were burned to a proverbial crisp. Tatyana could do it in seconds. But why?

I glanced away from the road and caught Alessandro looking at me. Something wistful and sad passed through his eyes, then the ice shutters crashed down, and the Artisan looked back at me.

"A penny for your thoughts," he said.

"I don't understand the burned legs."

"Catalina, have you noticed that every time we meet, we end up discussing dead people?"

"Apparently that's the nature of our relationship."

A slow smile curved his lips.

"You don't have to be so happy about it," I told him.

"You can't blame me. Lone killers have so few opportunities to talk shop."

"Probably because you're always busy killing people."

"Not true. I haven't killed anyone since landing in Houston."

"Will wonders never cease?"

The knot of traffic finally dissolved, and we crawled forward, first slow, then faster.

"What about the legs bothers you?" he asked.

"In your professional opinion, was this a contract hit?"

"No. A contract killer would've set up in the swamp and put a bullet through his brain. Clean, efficient, and quick. The point is to ambush and get out fast."

I had to stop looking at him. Every time I glanced at him I felt a little stab.

"Nobody murders anyone by burning their feet. The burns could mean he was tortured, but I have two problems with it. First, the burns are too severe."

Physical torture was cyclical: pain followed by relief followed by pain until the subject broke. The promise to end the pain was the incentive to talk. Felix's legs were practically burned off.

"Agreed," Alessandro said. "Let me guess the second problem. He was a powerful geokinetic."

"Yes."

Geokinetics controlled the mineral component of the Earth's crust: rocks, sand, some ores, and all gems. They excelled at raising defense barriers, they created sinkholes and earthquakes, and they were hard to kill when on the ground, because a geokinetic Prime could literally open the earth under his feet and vanish into it only to resurface a hundred yards away and drop his opponents into a bottomless pit.

"I just don't see him sitting on his hands while they tortured him," I said. "The method of murder had to be fast and sudden."

"The preliminary report shows no water in the lungs," Alessandro said. "That leaves us with the animal bite or the broken neck, which is the only thing that fits. It's simple and instant: loop the power cable around his neck and shove him off the building. His weight would do the rest. Everything else, the drowning, being bitten, being burned, all of that takes too long."

"Agreed."

Unfortunately, none of it helped us. A broken neck required no magic. Literally any able-bodied adult could have done it.

"So they break his neck and then they dip him into water, so he is bitten, and then they burn his legs, and hang him back on the cable? Why?"

Alessandro spread his arms.

I glanced at him. "It would be really hard for one person to do."

"Perhaps we're looking for multiple killers," he said.

"That's good," I told him.

He gave me an odd look.

"The more people involved, the more vulnerabilities to exploit, the higher the chances one of them will talk."

He shook his head. "Sometimes you scare me."

"That's right, Prime Sagredo. Be afraid. Be very afraid."

The old way to get to Jersey Village from the tollway meant taking the Senate Avenue exit. Two miles before that a bright new sign screamed a warning.

SENATE AVE EXIT CLOSED
USE PIT EXIT

They must have given up on all subtlety and just called it the Pit exit. Another sign.

PIT EXIT
1 MILE
PERMIT REQUIRED

"Do we have a permit?" Alessandro asked.

I pointed at the sticker in the corner of the windshield. "Augustine gave me one before I left MII."

PIT EXIT AHEAD
RIGHT LANE MUST EXIT

TURN AROUND
DON'T DROWN

PERMIT REQUIRED

"I'd hate to drown without a permit," I murmured.

"You do like following the rules."

"My following the rules is the only reason you are in my car."

"And here I thought it was because of my charm and looks."

I rolled my eyes. "There was a time when that would have been true, but now I'm immune."

He grimaced. "I don't think it ever worked on you."

Oh, but it did. There was a time when I would've given anything for just a few minutes in his company.

The exit curved under the tollway and morphed into a low, long bridge. The man-made swamp spread out on both sides of us, the water dark like stout beer. Islands of floating algae dotted the surface, shockingly vivid, blue, orange, and brilliant green. Between them huge lilies bloomed, the scarlet petals glistening, as if dipped in blood. To our left, the husk of a building thrust up out of the water. Vines as thick as my leg gripped it like hands joined into a single fist, their dark-green heart-shaped leaves hiding the structure completely, except for the trademark orange ball at the top. A former Phillips 76.

In the distance other buildings hunkered down, some still recognizable; others were just mounds of crumbling concrete and vegetation. Ahead and to the right, the water rippled. A scaled body, bright orange and two feet long, leaped into the air. Behind it, long, toothy jaws broke the surface, snapped like scissors closing, caught the scaled creature, and dragged it under.

"My mother would love this," Alessandro said.

"Does she like swamps?"

"She used to paint." His expression softened slightly. "She loves color, the more vivid, the better. This is a nature riot."

"You could take a pic for her. Perhaps she could paint from that."

His face shut down. "We aren't talking right now. Besides, she hasn't picked up a paintbrush since my father died."

What the hell was going on in his family?

Alessandro pondered the Pit. "How did this happen?"

"Politics."

He glanced at me, a question in his eyes. I would have to explain.

"About fifteen years ago, a man named Thomas Bruce decided to run for mayor. He presented himself as a successful businessman, rich but humble enough to be called Bubba by his friends, and he ran campaign ads featuring himself at different backyard barbecues drinking beer, telling jokes, and promising to return Houston to the 'good ole days.' Somehow, he got elected. Then it came out that he hadn't even finished college and most of his businesses nose-dived because he drove them into the ground. He was a joke, and one of the city councilmen told him that in public."

"You elected a clown?"

"Don't look at me. I was too young to vote. Bubba Bruce became desperate to be remembered for something, so he decided to build a

subway system. Unfortunately, Houston is built on a swamp. Do you
know the easiest way to get a pool in Houston?"

"No."

"Dig a basement."

He grinned. "So, it's American Venice?"

"It's not quite a lagoon, but it's close. Many smart people told Bubba
that his plan was stupid. But he dug his heels in and assembled a team
of mages who were supposed to 'push the water out.' The city paid them
a ton of money, they took six months to research, then another month to
prep, and on the groundbreaking day, they pushed the water out."

Ahead our bridge ran into an island, a small chunk of dry ground
with a section of the street a few blocks long and some ruined buildings.

"So, Bubba's plan worked?" Alessandro said.

"In a manner of speaking. Jersey Village, where we are now, was
built on top of an empty oil field, and once the water was gone, parts of
it sank. The containment failed, and the area flooded."

I slowed Rhino and we rolled from the bridge onto the island.

"What happened to Bubba?"

"He was booted out of office. The city tried to fix this mess, but
nobody knew how and there was no money left for it. People lost everything. Businesses went bankrupt, homes were destroyed. It took years
for insurance claims to be paid out while the insurance companies sued
the city."

A large abandoned building loomed on our right side. The bottom floor
was all glass. Dried algae stained the walls above it, an odd contrast to the
building's ultramodern lines. A grimy sign marked it as a Nissan dealership.
This area must have been recently drained. Ahead the island ended, and a
big yellow sign advised us to turn left, directing us to another bridge.

"Meanwhile, drug addicts and the homeless started squatting in the
Pit and having turf wars. Then people began dumping arcane hazmat
and—"

A wall of green hurtled from the left and smashed into Rhino. The
SUV rocked, the suspension compensating with a groan. A mess of
plants, pale metal, and strange bone pressed against my window.

I stepped on the gas. Rhino lurched forward and slid sideways, to the left, where dark water lapped at crumbling asphalt. Something had clamped on to our front axle and pulled us toward the mire.

I stood on the brakes. Rhino slid, wheels spinning.

Six inches toward the water.

Another six inches.

The green mass against my window drew back, contracting. A sharp metal beak surfaced from within it and punched my window. The armored glass held. Rhino slid another foot toward the swamp.

We had to break free or we'd drown.

"Into the building," Alessandro said.

I took my foot off the brake and threw the vehicle into reverse. The SUV spun to the left. I stomped on the gas. Rhino jumped backward, crashing through the glass wall of the dealership. Shards rained all around us. I kept going backward, past the individual offices, through the showroom.

A green creature spilled into the gap I'd made, filling the entire hole with its bulk. Another mass of green loomed on my dashboard screen, captured by the rearview camera. A third darted on the side, just outside the windows. We were surrounded.

If the three of them teamed up, they would pull us into the water. We had to make a stand.

I slammed on the brakes.

Alessandro jumped out of the car. Magic burst around him, and the M4 materialized in his hands out of thin air. I punched the release on the console and grabbed Linus' sword.

The green creature behind us stared through the glass. It resembled a wire framework stuffed to the brim with water plants, vines, and algae, but instead of a wire, its outer skeleton consisted of fused metal and bone, bound together by magic. Seven feet tall, it stood on four massive limbs tipped with twin metal claws. Its back arched, like the spine of an angry cat. Its conical head ended in a massive beak and its eyes, two pools of glowing white, burned into me.

A construct.

I let my magic spiral to it, like the shoots of a grapevine growing toward the sun. A faint glimmer of intelligence brushed against my mind, an echo of sentience, too distant to influence. They were remote-controlled, extensions of someone's powerful will.

"Grenade!" Alessandro barked.

I hit the floor.

The grenade launcher popped, like a tennis ball being fired from a machine. The grenade sank into the beast that followed us through the hole we'd made and detonated.

The blast tore the creature apart. For a moment, metal and bone shards hung in the air among the plant trash, the smoke from the grenade contained in a perfect sphere of magic, and I glimpsed a metal gyroscope with a glowing plant bud inside it. It was like watching an explosion on TV with no sound. My mind knew there should have been a kaboom, followed by a blast wave, but there was none.

The magic collapsed in on itself, yanking parts of the creature back together. It re-formed and righted itself, smaller, clunkier, but still mobile. A chunk on the left side of it didn't make it, and as it teetered, the vines and plants grew at a dizzying speed to fill the gap. It belched and a cloud of black smoke erupted from it.

It regenerated. Constructs were inorganic. They didn't regenerate. They were a collection of parts infused with magic. Eventually constructs ran out of that initial infusion and collapsed.

This was a hybrid between a construct and a living creature, alive in a whole different way with magic so powerful it swallowed the grenade blast like it was nothing. Regeneration like that would require a power source more potent than any infusion. This was beyond the capabilities of any animator Prime on record.

We were so screwed.

Alessandro bared his teeth.

Shooting this creature with conventional ammo was useless; however, if we could take out the power source, it should fall apart. The glowing bud was the key, but there was no way to tell where it was within their bodies.

The beast on the opposite side of the dealership rammed the glass. The windows shattered. The construct landed on the floor and scrambled toward us, slipping on broken glass.

I sank a burst of my magic into Linus' sword and charged the second construct.

Behind me the grenade launcher popped. The walls quaked. The staccato of the M4 spitting bullets ripped into the air. Alessandro, blowing the construct apart with a grenade to expose the gyroscope and trying to shoot at its glowing flower before the bio-construct re-formed.

The construct lunged at me, trying to bury me under its bulk. I spun to the side. The creature shot past me, slid, turning, and swiped at me with its claws. I danced out of the way and sliced at its leg.

The blade bounced off.

The beast twisted its paw and hooked me with its claws. Sharp points of pain stabbed my side and thigh. The construct tossed me into the air like a cat playing with its toy.

I hit the floor with my shoulder, rolled, and scrambled to my feet. My side burned. The beast bore down on me, and in a terrified burst of adrenaline I saw everything around me with crystal clarity: the beast charging, Alessandro on my left firing the grenade launcher, the counter behind me, and the offices on my right and left, and I knew I had nowhere to go.

I sank more magic into the sword. It kicked in my hand, as if I had struck something hard with it. Hair-thin glowing lines spread through the blade. *Work! Work, damn you.*

The beast reared, blocking everything else. My magic tugged on me, and I slashed in a wide arc, following its lead. There was no resistance. The head and the right shoulder of the beast slid aside and fell over. The rest of the body swayed, fighting to stay upright.

Thank you, Linus.

Plants wriggled from the severed stump and latched on to the other chunk of the body. The two halves snapped together. Fine. Now that the sword worked, I had a shot at the flower. I couldn't sense it, but it was in there. The drain of the sword pulled all of my magic in one direction. There was none to spare. I had to cut blind.

The third creature crashed through the glass. Its glowing eyes sighted me. It surged forward.

I couldn't take them both.

Alessandro thrust himself between the third construct and me. The grenade launcher was gone. A bright red banner popped into his hands, white words clear on red vinyl—"Christmas Sale"—and Alessandro snapped it open like an unfurling flag.

The second construct lunged at me. I swung my sword and its front limbs crashed to the floor. It grew new ones and I sliced them off before they fully formed.

The third beast turned its head toward the flash of red. Alessandro waved the banner as if it were a matador's cape and moved to the left, spinning the construct away from me. It chased him, swiping at him with its enormous paws.

It could tear him apart and I would watch him die because of me, and there was nothing I could do about it. I had to cut faster.

Alessandro dodged the bone claws with a fencer's grace, slipped between them, and rushed the beast. The banner fluttered to the ground. Before it landed, two swords flashed into Alessandro's hands. His magic whipped around him, a serpent of orange sparks. The Artisan ripped into the construct.

I turned myself into a bladed whirlwind. Plants and metal sprayed as I hacked chunks off the construct. The pieces crawled and wiggled, sliding back to the creature, but I kept slicing. My arm burned as if magic flowing from it turned into molten lead on its way through muscle and bone.

Something crashed to the left and a cubicle flew through the air like it was cardboard.

Faster. I had to cut faster.

The construct collapsed in front of me. A foot-wide ring with a bud in the center hung in front of me, suspended in midair by pure magic. Before it could remake itself, I jumped into the mass of vegetation and sliced at the spinning metal rings. The gyroscope fell to the ground at my feet.

The green heap exploded up, swallowing me—the construct, trying to re-form. I must've missed the flower.

Magic folded in on me, chunks of the creature flying and slamming into me, as the beast tried to regenerate with me inside it. Plants and magic blinded me. I stomped, trying to find the flower by feel.

Pressure ground my chest. It hurt to breathe. I stomped again and again. Where the hell was it?

A hunk of metal smashed against my head, and the world's biggest bell rang between my ears. My vision swam. I stomped in frantic frenzy. Something crunched under my foot. The pressure vanished. Pieces of the beast rained down around me.

I turned and saw Alessandro standing by the SUV, my tactical machete in his right hand and a metal ring with a severed plant stem hanging from it in his left. Nothing else moved.

We won. We took on an impossible fight and we won.

He dropped the ring and grinned at me, and I grinned back.

A body crashed through the skylight and landed between us. Nine feet tall, humanoid, with four arms and two sturdy legs, it was made of the same material as the beasts, but instead of the blunt head with glowing eyes, its face was a rotting human head. The skin had peeled off its cheekbones, frozen in time by the magic. Its lips were gone, and its teeth flashed a grotesque smirk. Two human eyes, charged with blue magic, glared at us.

I didn't have enough magic to swing the sword.

A second sword, a narrow black blade, appeared in Alessandro's left hand.

My magic brushed against a rudimentary intelligence. It felt muddled, undone, as if parts of it had rotted away, but it was there.

The creature turned toward Alessandro. Metal blades slid from the vegetation of its four arms.

It had a mind. Not much of one, but it was there.

"Feed it magic!" I hurled my blade over the beast.

Alessandro jumped, catching Linus' sword in midair.

The magic of Primes manifested in different ways. For me, it was wings. Beautiful glowing wings, each long translucent feather dark green at the base lightening to a brilliant grass green, then turquoise, until the color burst into triumphant gold at the edge.

I opened my wings and sang out a long high note. Magic tore out of me. I only had enough for one blast, and I sank everything I had into it.

My magic seared the giant's crippled mind.

The creature stopped in midstep.

I raised my hand and sang out, my voice an ethereal call suffused with power. "Come to me."

The giant turned, took a step toward me, and dropped to its knees.

The world went black and fuzzy at the edges. Alessandro appeared above the creature, falling, Linus' sword held over his head. The blade sliced through the air and bit into the giant's head, splitting it in two. He bisected it all the way to the floor. The two halves sagged to opposite sides, and the ring with the bud hovered in midair. Alessandro reversed the cut and slashed across it in a classic diagonal strike. It was a beautiful move, smooth, fast, and precise.

The ring fell apart.

The top of the unopened flower fluttered to the ground. Its light faded and died.

The two halves of the beast collapsed, spilling vegetation and metal all over the floor. The remains of a human body, flesh still clinging to the bones, scattered across the tile. The stench of carrion hit me. I gagged. My head felt too heavy. Someone had poured lead into my skull when I wasn't looking.

"Are you hurt?" I asked. Talking was very difficult for some reason.

"No."

I tried to walk, but I wasn't sure where the ground was. And then Alessandro was there, carrying me to the car.

"Put me down."

"Shut up," he said gently.

"You don't have touching rights."

"Right now I do."

I couldn't stop him if I'd tried. And being carried by him felt so nice. He was warm and strong, and after all that, somehow, he still smelled good. Being in his arms felt like nothing in this world could hurt me.

"Okay," I said. "You can carry me to the car."

"Thank you, Prime Baylor. That's quite magnanimous of you."

He opened Rhino's passenger door and loaded me into the seat as if I were made of glass. The seat felt good, but his arms felt better.

He tilted my seat back and reached over me to buckle my seat belt.

"I've got it," I ground out.

"Relax. I'm strapping you in."

We were face-to-face, his arm around me. If I leaned forward an inch, I could brush my lips over his cheek. My body tried to respond. It had no energy left, but it tried so hard.

He buckled my seat belt.

"Sword," I told him.

"I'll get the sword." He shut the door, ran to the pile of metal and plants, and came back with Linus' blade and the four rings. He handed the sword to me, and I hugged it and exhaled.

Alessandro stuffed the rings into a canvas bag, climbed into the driver's seat, started the armored SUV, and Rhino rolled forward. The walls of the dealership slid by and we emerged into the sunlight. Alessandro made a sharp left and Rhino sped onto the bridge we took to get here.

"Wrong way. Marat is the other way."

"We're not going to see Marat. We're going to the hospital."

A green construct leaped out of the water and landed on the bridge in front of us. Alessandro gunned it. The SUV smashed into the beast with a wet *thunk* at fifty miles per hour. Chunks of metal and bone flew apart. In the sideview mirror I saw them fall and remain still. He must've crushed the flower.

"I'm warming up to your pancake strategy," he said.

My tongue felt slow and thick in my mouth. "We have to see Marat in twenty minutes."

"He'll wait."

"No. It's im . . . imp . . ."

"Important?"

"Imperative that we keep that appointment. It's my first interview with them."

"He will wait."

"Turn around."

"Catalina, your side is soaked with blood, your shirt has vomit on it, and your head is bleeding. If we go to see Marat right now, he won't be impressed. Also, that sword burns through magic like a motherfucker, and when I find out who gave it to you, I'll kill them, because that's a death sentence."

I raised my hand and touched my head. My fingers came away smudged with blood.

"It's not deep," Alessandro said. "But you need to be checked out."

"Don't take me to the hospital. I can't afford to be the evening news."

"Then I'll take you home."

"No, that's worse. If we go home, I'll never get out."

"Of course you will."

"They'll swarm me. They will tie me to the bed and call an ambulance."

His voice softened. He turned to glance at me. He looked so handsome. "Catalina, *tesoro*, please let me take you home."

Oh my God. How was he even in my car?

"I know what you're doing."

He smiled at me and my heart made a little happy leap.

"You're trying to charm me."

He reached over, took my hand in his, and kissed my fingers. "Let's go get you a doctor."

"It doesn't work on me." It worked. It so worked.

"You need a doctor. We can go home, or we can go to the hospital. I'm driving and you're not in a position to stop me."

A low insistent ache pulsated in my head, growing stronger and stronger. Somewhere deep inside me a rational part of my brain informed me that he was right. I needed a doctor. But I needed to do the interview even more.

"Please stop the car."

The muscles on his jaw bulged.

"I know you're pissed off and my head is bleeding."

"And your side. And you're speaking slowly, which means you drained your magic down to nothing or you have a concussion."

"It could be both."

He growled.

"That was very scary."

"You're not helping your cause, smartass."

"We came into the Pit to talk to Marat. The person who attacked me by the river didn't want us talking to him. They attacked us again. And now we are running away."

"We aren't running away. We're making a strategic withdrawal."

"Arkan is targeting my family. I can't afford to show weakness. The longer this investigation goes on, the higher the risk for them. This is my first interview. If I don't make it, the other board members will feel free to ignore me. The investigation will drag on. If people I love get hurt because of this, I'll never forgive you, Alessandro."

He slapped the wheel with the palm of his hand. *"Porca puttana!"*

"If you care for me at all, even a little bit, I need you to stop the car, get the first aid kit from the back, and patch me up. After the interview, we can go home and I'll have an MRI, a CT scan, a toxic panel, a pregnancy test, and whatever other tests you want me to get. Sound fair?"

"It sounds like shit. You were clawed by something that might have crawled out of the arcane realm. It could be poisonous or venomous."

"I have the A3 antivenom in the kit."

"No."

"Alessandro." I made my voice soft and pitiful.

He glanced at my super-sad expression and swore again.

"Please," I said. "For me?"

He hit the brakes. Rhino slid and spun around, facing in the opposite direction, toward the Pit.

"You're crazy and I'm stupid. Take your shirt off."

If it were anybody else, I would've stripped without hesitation, because it wouldn't have mattered. Being a Deputy Warden had cured me of any demure shyness about getting my wounds treated. My entire side burned as if scalded. I needed medical attention and it couldn't wait. But it was Alessandro, and no matter how much I tried to convince myself otherwise, it mattered so much.

Alessandro walked around the SUV to get the first aid kit from the back. I peeled off my blue T-shirt. He was right. There was vomit on it. Not much, but enough to smell bad. Maybe I did have a concussion.

I lifted my butt off the seat, unzipped my pants, and pulled them down on the right side to expose my hip and most of my butt. Alessandro chose that moment to swing my door open.

For a second he didn't say anything. He just stared.

And this wasn't awkward. Not at all.

"Help me off the seat?" I asked.

He put the kit down and picked me up. His hands felt so nice on my cold skin. He set me down and squeezed hand sanitizer onto his fingers. I perched on the step that helped you climb into Rhino's high cabin and raised my arm.

"How bad is it?"

"It's not good." He held up a syringe. The antivenom. Creatures from the arcane realm carried things on their claws and their teeth that didn't play nice with the human body.

I closed my eyes. Needles were never my favorite. A sharp pinprick punctured my side. The medicine flooded into my muscle in a painful heavy stream. I grimaced.

"Almost done," he promised.

Finally, it was over. I exhaled and opened my eyes.

We were on the access bridge. In the distance Sam Houston Tollway channeled the current of cars heading north. We were out in the open, and yet somehow strangely private, with nothing but an empty bridge and a mire around us. The dark fuzz around my vision melted away—my magic gradually regenerating. I always recovered magic at an alarmingly fast rate. Most magic users had to make an effort to actively use their powers. I spent most of my time suppressing mine. When I let go, magic fountained out of me like a geyser. The first few times I had drained myself down to nothing, I stressed out for hours waiting for it to come back, but now I knew my rate of regeneration. Power trickled into me in a narrow but steady stream. As soon as I could, I'd draw an arcane circle and recharge.

Alessandro picked up the flush bottle and motioned for me to nod. I lowered my head until my chin touched my chest. The saline solution wet my hair.

"The cut is shallow," he said. "Only an inch across, which is good, but it doesn't tell us anything about the condition of your brain."

"My brain is functioning."

His fingers parted my hair. "You could be bleeding internally."

His hands in my hair made it hard to concentrate. "Am I still speaking slowly?"

"No."

"Then it's fine."

In terms of magic regeneration, I was a freak.

He sat the bottle down and picked up a tube of antibiotic ointment. "Hold still."

His hands were still touching my hair. It felt so intimate. Too intimate.

"You can lift your head."

I brushed my hair out of my face. Alessandro knelt by me and leaned forward. His face was only inches from mine. He scrutinized my eyes, looking for something in there, probably some mystical signs of concussion. Only minutes ago, he'd disassembled the construct with efficient brutality, and now he was kneeling before me, and his eyes were kind and concerned.

The rest of the world could be on fire right now and I wouldn't move an inch to put it out.

"Who am I?" he asked.

"Alessandro Niccolò Sagredo, Prime, antistasi, second son of House Sagredo, Count Sagredo," I told him quietly. "Playboy, assassin, and internationally known influencer. Did I leave anything out?"

"Good enough. There is ibuprofen in this kit, but it's a blood thinner, and if you are bleeding internally it would make things worse."

"I'll tough it out. The painkiller in the injection should kick in soon."

He picked up the saline wash and touched me, his calloused fingers stretching my skin. I shivered. It hurt, and I didn't care. I wanted him to keep touching me.

Warm saline water ran down my side.

"How many punctures?" I asked, to say something. I didn't even sound like myself.

"Four. Looks like only the tips of the claws. You're lucky, *angelo mio*. Half an inch more and it would've ripped through your liver."

He called me his angel.

I closed my eyes, trying to shut him out. The warm water kept running over my skin. With the heat of the summer beating down on us, it actually felt kind of nice . . .

"Don't fall asleep," he said, his voice sharp.

"I'm not falling asleep. I'm just closing my eyes." *So I won't have to look at you.*

"Keep them open."

"Yes, Prime Sagredo. As you wish, Prime Sagredo. I obey, Prime Sagredo."

"Finally, proper treatment." He pressed gauze to my side.

I winced.

"Don't hold your breath," he said quietly. "It will hurt more. Breathe through it."

"You breathe through it." Wow. What a stunning display of wit.

"I'm trying," he said. "Believe me, I'm doing my best."

He worked quickly, rinsing the wounds, patting me dry with sterile gauze, and finally moving on to antibiotic cream.

"How do you even know my second name?" he asked. "I've never used it."

"I run a private detective agency. It's my job to know things about potential threats."

"If I wanted to be a threat to you, it wouldn't matter how much you knew about me."

"Promises, promises . . ."

His touch was featherlight. "Is the shot kicking in?"

I nodded. The pain had dulled. I had lost the last defense against him touching me.

"When was your last tetanus shot?"

"Right after you left."

His fingers skimmed my skin just under my bra. A little spark dashed through me, all the way to my toes. He taped a square of gauze to me. His fingertips brushed the edge of my bra band. I bit my lip.

"Almost finished," he said, his voice reassuring, kind. "Do you need a minute?"

You have no idea. "No. Let's just get it done."

He was like a drug and I was a hopeless, desperate addict.

Alessandro's hand slid lower to the second wound. Another warm, careful touch, a flash of longing so intense, it nearly killed my common sense, another strip of medical tape smoothed into place. If I closed my eyes again, I could imagine he was caressing me, but if I did, he would make me look at him, at his eyes, at his face, and I would be forced to sit here and watch him kneeling in front of me, touching me, focusing on me to the exclusion of everything else.

Alessandro moved on to the third puncture in the bend of my waist. He leaned in, brushing his fingers over me to better apply the gauze. His whole hand settled on my waist. He paused. His fingers lingered on my skin, unmoving. He swallowed.

Oh my God. It wasn't just me.

He put the gauze in place and ran his fingers along the tape.

The last wound was all the way down past the bend of my hip.

Alessandro stared at the curve of my body.

"Do you need a minute?" My voice was so sweet.

"No."

He reached over and gently slid his hand down my hip, nudging the narrow strap of my white panties down. Heat pulsed through me, and it wasn't any arcane venom.

He set his hand on the curve of my butt, cupping it to stretch the muscle. I almost purred. His face was a neutral mask. He fit the bandage over the wound and tore the medical tape. He placed it on my skin and ran his thumb up its length. If I closed my eyes, the journey of that thumb would've blazed through my mind.

Another strip of tape. He touched me again.

If I leaned forward, if he raised his head, I could kiss him. He would taste like wine, heady and crazy-making. I would kiss him and kiss him, melting against his powerful body, until neither of us could think anymore. Maybe I did have a concussion.

The last strip slid into place.

Alessandro looked up at me. His expression was almost cold, but his eyes were on fire. He looked at me the same way he'd looked at me in the opera house, just before he kissed me.

I wanted him. Not the Alessandro in my head who left, but this one, full of darkness. I wanted to throw my arms around him, pull him out of that deep dark hole he'd fallen into, and make him forget everything except me. I wanted him to grin at me.

He was still looking at me.

I raised my hand to stroke his hair.

He held completely still.

It wasn't fair to him. It was selfish and mean of me, because I was about to promise him something I couldn't deliver. Victoria would never let him have me. It took every shred of will I had to stop.

"Thank you, Prime Sagredo," I said and pulled my underwear back up over my hip.

A shadow of pain flickered over his eyes. It lasted for a mere instant, but he couldn't hide it from me. He had expected me to crush him and I did. When he spoke, his voice was perfectly cordial.

"You're welcome, Catalina Beatrisa Baylor."

 # Chapter 9

The headquarters of the PRP, the Pit Reclamation Project, occupied the smaller of the two southern islands in the Pit. It took us two more bridges and another small island to get to the final bridge leading there. This time, nobody tried to murder us along the way.

Alessandro drove. He was still laboring under the impression that I had a concussion or a cranial hemorrhage, and my brains could leak out of my ears at any second. He didn't feel I was fit to drive, and I decided not to fight with him about it.

The cocktail of medication in the antivenom shot had cooled down the pain but didn't banish it completely. My side hurt, the stabbing agony reduced to a low, dull ache that flared up every time I shifted in my seat. My head hurt too, but not bad enough to slow me down. It stopped bleeding and my hair was rapidly drying. I'd rolled it into a bun to hide the gash. My shoulder throbbed, a consequence of landing on hard concrete after being batted aside by a construct, and my right arm felt ready to fall off. The swords I usually swung were considerably lighter than Linus' monster.

At least my clothes were dried. I'd changed into the spare outfit I always carried in the car.

The memory of Alessandro looking up at me cycled in my head. I had to sort myself out.

My cell rang. I glanced at the number, and a cold spike of anxiety shot through me. "Yes?"

"She will see you tomorrow at five," the polite male voice said.

"Of course."

"Have a nice day, Ms. Tremaine."

The screen went dark.

"Who was that?" Alessandro asked.

"My grandmother." Technically, it was Trevor, one of her assistants, a pit bull in human skin with a Harvard education and special forces training.

"I'm guessing it was your other grandmother, because you're staring at the phone as if it's a snake about to bite."

We passed by a copse of trees growing straight out of the water. It ended and two islands swung into view, the first, larger on our right, and the PRP island, smaller and more distant, straight ahead.

On the larger island to our right, construction crews bulldozed remnants of the flooded buildings under the watchful eye of guards armed with tactical shotguns and . . .

"A flamethrower?"

Alessandro smiled. "They can be fun, under the right circumstances."

"I remember." He'd sprayed fire on a swarm of arcane creatures once. It happened at night, and he'd grinned like a lunatic while doing it. It'd made him look demonic.

Alessandro glanced at the island again. "Shotguns, flamethrowers, and at least four Mark V DGRs."

Dangerous game rifles, designed to bring down magically created creatures, a catch-all term that covered any animal augmented by magic or summoned through it.

"I wonder if Marat is guarding against giant plant monsters," I murmured.

A summoner would be the most likely candidate to be interested in a biomechanical device that controlled arcane beasts. And Marat was the only Prime summoner involved as far as we knew. But then again, we also had constructs, which normally would mean an animator. Yet, as far as I knew, constructs didn't require a magical core. Could Marat and Cheryl be working together?

"What's your opinion of Marat?" I asked.

"Marat is opportunistic and vicious when cornered. He tries charm first, but even he knows he's bad at it, so he defaults to violence. In the fifteen minutes we spent together, he attempted to bribe me by promising kickbacks if the project moved forward and followed up with citing the many dangers surrounding the Pit and the city of Houston."

"He didn't."

"He most certainly did. I think I was supposed to be scared."

That's rich. "Were you?"

He spared me a look. "I managed to not faint."

"Would you like to know what Leon dug up on him?"

"Yes."

I opened a file on my phone. I had already read it before leaving the office.

"Marat Bared Kazarian, House Kazarian, Prime, Summoner. Forty years old, married, two sons, fifteen and thirteen. Second son of Taniel Kazarian, so he isn't the heir, he's the spare."

Alessandro started his life as the spare too. His older brother died when he was just a few months old, but his name had been written into the family records, and Alessandro would forever be known as the second son.

I kept going. "Marat has no criminal record, no bankruptcies. On paper he's squeaky clean."

"But?" Alessandro asked.

"The family has ties to Prince Lebedev, a prominent metallofactor House in the Russian Imperium."

Metallofactors dealt with ore, metal alloys, and all things that had to do with smelting and working metal. Most of them tended to specialize in steel or aluminum, but some chose precious metals.

"House Lebedev focuses on industrial and military metallurgy. The family is powerful but considered provincial by St. Petersburg. According to Leon, they've been linked with illegal arms sales and questionable magical research."

"How did Marat get involved?" Alessandro asked.

"The Lebedevs have holdings in Armenia near Lake Sevan. House Kazarian still has relatives living there. Any connection to Arkan?"

He shook his head. "The name Lebedev never came up, which doesn't mean they're not connected, just that I don't know about it."

"Leon couldn't figure out if House Kazarian actually got any benefits from this friendship. Also, their visits to the Imperium have tapered off in the past decade. Marat's brother has political ambitions and a close association with the Russians doesn't look good."

"Politics costs money," Alessandro said.

"And that's where Marat comes in. He's the family's workhorse and their fixer. He killed two Significants and a Prime during a feud with another House eight years ago, so his brother's hands would stay clean. Currently, House Kazarian is strapped for cash, because Marat's sister went through an ugly divorce, and Marat shelled out a lump payment to his ex-brother-in-law. The former husband got four million dollars and House Kazarian got sole custody of the three children."

"He bought his nieces and nephews," Alessandro said. "Smart. No man who would sell his children deserves them."

His tone told me he would've done the same thing.

"Leon doesn't know how much money Marat sank into the Pit, but he thinks it's in the millions."

"Fifteen million," Alessandro said. "That was the required buy-in when the board was formed."

That's right, he had access to Lander.

"Fifteen million is quite a bit," I said. "If the project collapses, Marat might go bankrupt. Felix dying is the worst thing that could happen to him right now."

"But you still like him for it?"

I nodded. "He is a summoner sitting in a swamp filled with arcane creatures, he has ties to Russia, and he is in debt up to his eyeballs. It might make him desperate and prone to doing something rash. Maybe Felix wanted him off the board."

The PRP island loomed ahead. In the center of it, a relatively well-preserved office building rose three stories above the water. A faded green sign on the wall of the top floor proclaimed "XADAR." The roof bristled with antennas, power poles, and a couple of satellite dishes. A seven-foot fence wrapped around the island, reinforced every few yards by metal posts. A guard tower rose on the west side, and a booth secured the entrance.

We pulled up to the security booth.

The guard glanced at our permit and waved us through. We drove into a large parking lot dotted with puddles. The spot nearest to the door was between an enormous black Ram truck and a mud-splattered Jeep, and Alessandro slid Rhino into it with surgical precision. He had many, many faults, but he was a superb driver.

"Marat's ride," I said and nodded at the truck. It was in the summary Leon had sent me.

Alessandro eyed the truck and sneered.

"It's Texas." I shrugged.

"What would he even transport in this truck? Another more reasonably sized truck, perhaps?"

"It's a statement."

"Yes, it is. Does it turn into a giant robot?"

"Will you run away if it does?"

He gave me a chiding look. "Please. Give me some credit."

"Then we're fine."

Marat exited the building. He wore jeans and a dark shirt and walked with an aggressive, fast stride, as if he were doing the ground a favor.

Alessandro jumped out of the SUV, came around, and held my door open.

Marat looked at me. His eyebrows rose.

I always kept a spare outfit in Rhino, but when I packed it, I aimed for a generic business casual, the kind of outfit that would let me blend in with the city scene in the heat of Houston's summer. I wore a light coral skirt, a pale, almost white blouse with just a hint of pink, and a striped black-and-white blazer with sleeves rolled up to just below the elbow. I had completed this fashionista ensemble with my muddy boots, because my only alternative was a pair of coral pumps.

It wasn't the kind of outfit one wore to the swamp. I looked like a complete idiot.

Marat's face told me he thought as much. "You're late." Then he turned away from me. "Prime Sagredo, good morning. I wasn't expecting you."

Ah. Alessandro got a good morning and I got the hired-help greeting.

"My apologies," Alessandro said smoothly. "Lander asked me to accompany Ms. Baylor. We ran into some obstacles on the way."

"Was the road flooded?" Marat frowned. "I didn't notice any trouble this morning."

"In a manner of speaking," Alessandro said.

"We are here now," I said.

"Now I don't have time," Marat said. "I had time twenty minutes ago, but now I don't have any to spare. I'll have my secretary call you."

I had hoped for the subtle approach, but Alessandro was right. Marat was a bully, and like all bullies, he only understood blunt strength.

I held out my hand.

Marat looked at it. "What?"

"Keys."

"What keys?"

"Keys to the building. I'm shutting you down."

Marat's face turned purple. "You can't do that."

I quoted from memory, skipping over some irrelevant time limits. "In the event of the death of a Director from a Nonnatural Cause, the Deceased Director's Voting Shareholders—that would be Lander Morton and Alessandro, by proxy—shall have the right, at their sole election and expense, to retain a private investigator to identify the person or persons responsible for the Deceased Director's death. That would be me.

"The remaining Shareholders shall cooperate with the Investigation by, at a minimum, one, producing in full any documents requested by the Investigator, subject to a separate nondisclosure agreement; two, responding in writing to any written questions submitted by the Investigator to a Shareholder; three, making available to the Investigator for interview any persons under the control of the Shareholder to whom the request is made; and four, immediately upon retention of the Investigator, preserving all records in any and all media formats by taking any other steps necessary to prevent the spoliation of evidence.

"In the event that any Shareholder fails to cooperate with the Investigation as required by this section, the Deceased Director's Voting Shareholders shall have the right, at their sole election, to suspend any and all activities of the Corporation, but for the following: one, payment of previously incurred obligations; two, payment of taxes; and three, any filings required to maintain the Corporation as an entity in Good Standing with the Texas Secretary of State."

Marat gaped at me.

It wasn't that impressive, actually. I was good at memorization, and a lot of PI work, and especially Warden-related work, landed me into a grey area between regular citizen and law enforcement. Knowing exactly what I was and wasn't authorized to do was essential, and I had learned to spit the relevant contract language on command.

"You signed this agreement, Mr. Kazarian. You clearly don't understand what you've signed, so I will explain it to you."

Marat sputtered.

"The contract requires you to comply with my investigation. I'm making a formal request to view the crime scene and interview you in regards to the death of Felix Morton. You're refusing me access. Therefore, you are in breach of contract. That gives me the right to mothball this project until you decide to cooperate."

I raised my voice. I had no idea if there was anyone within earshot, but it didn't matter. "Starting today nobody gets paid. Drop what you're doing and leave."

Marat spun to Alessandro. "Are you going to let her do this?"

"Yes."

"Every moment we're not working, we're losing money."

Alessandro arranged his stunning face into an expression of concern. "I'd like to help. I really would. But she's a very dangerous woman and you've made her angry."

Marat swore. "Don't be a fucking pussy!"

Weeks of visiting Grandma Victoria and controlling my face paid off. I didn't laugh.

"Let's be reasonable," Alessandro said, his voice soothing.

"You signed the contract," I told Marat. "Nobody twisted your arm to do it. This can end any time you're ready. Show me to the crime scene and answer my questions, and I'll go away."

Marat whipped out his phone and stalked away.

I reached out and patted Alessandro's arm.

"What's that for?"

"Superhuman self-restraint."

Marat turned around and marched back to us, his face dark. "Fine. Fucking fine. Let's go. I'll show you the damn crime scene."

We trudged along a series of bridges. One guard, an older, balding man with a Texas tan, in the lead, and the other, a man in his late twenties with hair so pale it was almost white and a brick-red sunburn, bringing up the rear. Both were armed with shotguns and both looked like they wanted to be anywhere but here. Alessandro stuck close to me, blocking the rear guard's view of me with his wide back. I had a feeling if that shotgun came up, he would grab me and throw me into the murky water.

Around us the Pit bloomed in neon colors. The air smelled of honey and spice, the fragrance drifting from the bloodred lilies. Here and there, half-drowned construction equipment stuck out of the dark water, accumulating plastic garbage that was floating on the surface. The equipment still had bright new paint. Either the water level rose suddenly, or something had dragged bulldozers and backhoes into it and not that long ago.

Another bridge. More drowned equipment. Holy crap, they had sunk a lot of money into this, and they were getting nowhere. They had to be desperate.

"Compared to the rest of this, your main building has a rather nice setup," Alessandro said.

"It was in decent shape and already wired," Marat said over his shoulder. "Which is why we chose it. The joke was on us though. Took weeks to make it safe."

"What was wrong with it?" Alessandro asked.

"Some fool had booby-trapped the whole place. Trip wires everywhere. My demolition guy said he hadn't seen anything like that since the Army."

Finally, we clopped our way to a half-flooded industrial building thrusting from the mire. A metal walkway, bordered by a thin metal rail, clung to its second story, only five feet above the water. The front guard went up the stairs to the walkway and waved to us. Marat followed, and we trailed him all the way to the back of the building.

The lobster-red rear guard halted on the side, visibly nervous. Great. That's what you want with you in a dangerous arcane garbage dump—a panicky guy with a shotgun.

The bulk of the structure shielded us from the rest of the Pit. Directly in front of us, past a twenty-yard stretch of murky water, the overgrown shore presented a wall of green. We were isolated and hidden, but close enough to the main building to get back in under five minutes if we ran. A perfect spot to kill someone. The murderer could stab their victim and dump the body into the water and return before most people realized they were missing.

Marat leaned on the rail and pointed to the electric cable, strung horizontally on wooden poles rising from the water fifty yards apart. The cable sagged in the middle, where Felix's body must've hung.

My original theory was that someone had looped the cable around Felix's neck and shoved him off the edge. Shoving a grown man over hip-high fence was one thing, but this railing reached to my chest. Too high.

"Walk me through July 15th, please," I asked.

Marat shrugged. "Got up, took a piss, brushed my teeth, got dressed, drove to the gym—"

"What time did you leave for the gym?"

To my left, Alessandro studied the metal railing, a calculating look in his eyes. He was thinking along the same lines I was.

"Six," Marat said. "Monday, Wednesday, Friday, I leave the house at six, get to the gym, work with my trainer, leave at seven-thirty, get home, shower, get dressed, eat breakfast with the family, get to the office or here by nine."

I glanced to the roof. The cable ran too far to the side. Too low for someone to grab it from the roof yet too high to snag it from the walkway.

Alessandro tested the rail with his hand. It didn't move. Solid as a rock.

How did they get the cable around Felix's neck? The only way his hanging made sense was if the wire caught his neck and then sprang straight up, jerking his body upward. It would break his neck.

Hmm.

"Where were you by nine on the day Felix died?" I asked.

"Here," Marat said. "I checked in at the gate, worked in my office until four, went home, then went out to dinner with my wife, my brother, his wife, and his wife's brother at Steak 48."

It took me a second to sort out all the wives and brothers. "What time did you arrive to the restaurant?"

"At 5:48."

"That's rather exact."

Marat heaved a sigh. "My sister-in-law made a reservation for five-thirty. My wife wanted to leave earlier, but I stank like the swamp, so I took a shower. My wife hates to be late. I'm often late. If we're late by more than fifteen minutes, she gets to pick a movie for Saturday night."

"What did she pick?" Alessandro asked.

"*Underneath.*" Marat's face assumed a long-suffering expression. "A family buys an old house and some kind of nastiness is under it and eats them one by one. Why she likes that scary crap, I'll never know. I had to hold her the whole time. Not that I mind that part."

"What was the occasion for dinner?" I asked.

Marat grimaced. "Tamara's brother was looking for 'a career change.'"

"Let me guess." Alessandro raised his eyebrows. "He was let go."

"Of course he was let go. He ran his department into the ground."

"When did you leave the restaurant?" I asked.

"They gave up a little past seven," Marat said.

"You told them no?" Alessandro asked.

"We can't afford dead weight, especially now. Before you ask, my wife and I went to see my father to warn him that my brother and his wife would ambush him first thing in the morning and cry a river about how I don't care about the family. We stayed there until nine, and then we went home, watched the new episode of *Killer Wives*, and went to bed."

Unlike Nevada, I didn't have the benefit of magic warning me every time someone lied, but I had interviewed many people, and so far everything about this conversation seemed genuine. His alibi would be easy to check, and even if he employed an illusion mage to impersonate himself, his family would know it wasn't him. They would probably cover for him, however.

But Marat just didn't seem like a man with a guilty conscience. He was visibly worried and trying not to show it, which was normal, he didn't ask leading questions, and he didn't try to steer the conversation. Nor did he give short answers.

"On the day of his death, Felix attended the Texas Assembly. So did your brother. Did they speak?"

"No. My brother never met Felix. Until Felix died, my brother didn't even know what he looked like. This is the business side of things. My brother has different ambitions."

It was time to up the stakes.

"How long have you been aware of the biomechanical magic activity in the Pit?"

Marat had recovered enough to look surprised. "What biomechanical activity?"

Really now? "How many workers are unaccounted for to date?"

"That's confidential."

My voice frosted over. "Nothing is confidential. Your procedures, your missing workers, your sister's divorce settlement, your connection with Lebedev, nothing is off-limits."

Marat's eyes narrowed. "Now you listen to me. I don't know what biomechanical bullshit—"

A tentacle studded with metal hooks burst from the water, wrapped itself around Marat's chest, and jerked him into the swamp over the rail. He vanished under the surface.

Oh my God.

Alessandro laughed.

The sunburned guard next to us turned and ran, his boots thudding on the walkway. The other guard pounded toward us and fired at the water. Alessandro grabbed the shotgun and drove his elbow into the man's face with casual ease. The guard let go and stumbled back. The chew flew out of his mouth and landed in the water.

"You'll shoot him, idiot," Alessandro said.

The water churned. I reached out with my magic. There it was again, an echo of distant malevolent intelligence, too diffuse to target.

Marat surfaced for half a second before a tentacle yanked him under again.

Crap. I climbed onto the railing.

Alessandro grabbed me and pulled me back. "What are you doing?"

"He's drowning! I'm going to save him."

Alessandro swore. "Stay here!"

He thrust the shotgun into my hands. Magic surged around him before a chain flashed into existence in his hands. Alessandro leaped over the rail and dived into the water, dragging the chain with him.

"Holy shit!" The guard leaned on the rail on my right.

The chain slid into the water, uncoiling from somewhere above and snapped taut. The water boiled, whipped into froth.

A shiny spark shot out of the greenery at the shore and streaked through the air toward us.

I jumped out of the way on pure instinct.

A two-foot-long metal spike thudded into the wall to the right of the guard. He gaped at it for half a second, and the next spike took him in the throat, pinning him to the wall.

A shotgun would do nothing at that range. I dropped it to free my hands, spun left, and ran.

Behind me, thumps announced more spikes slicing into the wall.

I sprinted to the corner, caught the rail, and threw my body into the turn. A spike whistled past my right shoulder. I pounded down the stairs and dived behind the building, flattening myself against the wall.

A metal spike cleared the building on my right, turned, and streaked to the wall at a sharp angle, missing me by ten feet.

A telekinetic, positioned on the shore. The spike had sunk almost halfway into the wall. Considering the range and the power of the throw, it had to be a Prime. Lucky for me, I had a paranoid brother-in-law. Connor insisted on drills, and I knew as much about fighting a telekinetic as was humanly possible without being one. Prime or no Prime, the attacker still needed line of sight. That, and a loss of concentration was their Achilles' heel.

A dozen spikes whistled through the air over the building, curving to strike.

I hauled myself over the rail and dived into the water. It swallowed me, tepid, dark, and smelling faintly of fish and algae. I kicked my feet and surfaced. Above me, the spikes hammered home, sinking into the walls.

I barely had any magic left, but I had recovered some, and I reached out with it. A concentrating telekinetic was like a beacon, massive power focused into a laser beam. Two seconds, and I had him, a sharp, painfully bright pinprick of white about thirty-five yards away on the shore.

A second volley of spikes curved around the building.

I opened my wings and reached for him. He couldn't see me, but he could hear me, and I sent the sound of my voice, augmented with my power, at his mind.

"Come to me."

My magic locked on to him, gripping his mind in a mental fist. The spikes lost their direction and rained down on the water. I dived, holding on to his mind. He flailed, caught by my will like a fish on a line. I surfaced and sang one more time.

"Come to me!"

He convulsed, fighting to get free. His will was strong, almost as strong as Connor's, but Mad Rogan's mind was an immovable fortress. This mind sputtered, rock steady one instant, careening the next. I needed more magic, but I had none left.

His magic buckled. My grasp slipped. He broke free and I went back under.

Shit. My magic was gone, and Alessandro couldn't teleport. Even if he realized the telekinetic was there, he would have to swim across to get to him. He would be a sitting duck in the water.

I surfaced.

The sharp glow of the telekinetic's will receded.

Ha! He was running away. He'd panicked.

Something brushed against my thigh. I kicked on pure instinct, frantically trying to get away. Straight ahead, barely ten feet away, a ramp hung from the walkway.

Something grabbed my legs, spun me around, and let go. I floated, keeping as still as I could.

A faint glow slid under the water toward me. I breathed in, deep and slow. *Don't panic. Just don't panic . . .*

The glow surfaced. A flexible metal tentacle rose out of the depths and hovered a foot away, level with my face. A pale bud glowed on its end, growing out of the metal against all the laws of nature.

The bud opened. A beautiful flower bloomed, unfolding three rows of pristine white petals with sharp tips. A spicy honeyed aroma washed over me.

A round eye stared at me from the inside of the flower, glowing with brilliant emerald fire.

Holy crap.

A presence brushed against my mind, alien, strange, but sentient. Panic crested inside me and I stomped on it, keeping myself still.

The presence touched me. We connected.

A human mind was a localized, concentrated presence, sometimes a mere smudge of light, sometimes a brilliant star. This was a cloud, a storm with pinpoints of light caught in the glowing ether of consciousness. It was everywhere, dispersed through the Pit, stretching out in wispy strands, a cluster of stars there, a barely perceptible veil here, flowing, shifting . . . Not a hive mind, but a single enormous consciousness extending a narrow tendril of itself to me.

Ice slid down my spine. I was looking into the proverbial Abyss and it stared back at me.

I slammed my mental defenses shut.

The mind shifted, fluid, reaching for me, trying to reforge the connection.

An explosion punched the air behind the building. The flower snapped closed, and the tentacle vanished under the water.

I spun around and swam to the ramp, faster than I ever swam in my life. My hand closed on the metal rail. I pulled myself up onto the ramp and ran, dripping, up the walkway and around the building.

Alessandro was on the walkway, pulling the chain up with both hands. Under him, the water boiled. A neon green stain spread over the swamp.

Alessandro yanked the chain, the muscles on his arms bunching. The chain gave and Marat popped out of the water, caught under his arms by the chain's loop.

A tentacle of plants and metal burst from the water, slithering after Marat. Alessandro lunged forward, a flamethrower materializing in his hands. A jet of fire licked the tentacle, scorching it.

Marat drew a long, shuddering breath. Magic boomed from him, like the toll of a giant invisible bell. A swirl of darkness unfurled ten feet above us and spiraled out, blue lightning flashing at its center.

A summoner portal.

The darkness exploded into brilliant white. Fishes rained out of the portal into the water, five feet long, silver blue, with blunt heads armored with bone plates. Their huge mouths gaped, flashing jagged bone teeth long enough to bite through my leg.

They fell into the water, and the swamp erupted. Dayglow green blood fountained to the surface. Chunks of plant matter and strange white flesh floated up and vanished as the fish snapped them up in a frenzy.

Alessandro tossed the flamethrower aside, straightened, and saw me. Surprise slapped his face. He turned, saw the guard impaled on the spike, and bared his teeth. "What happened?"

Marat climbed onto the walkway. "That's it. That's fucking it!"

All around us things moved. At the shore something slid into the water. On the left, far in the swamp, a sinuous thing stirred. I reached out with my magic and saw the Abyss moving, flowing toward us, like a glowing amoeba sensing its prey.

"Catalina?" Alessandro spun me around.

"There is a creature in this swamp," I whispered, trying to track the enormous consciousness floating around us. "It's everywhere. It's coming. We have to go."

"Get it!" Marat yelled at the fish creatures, banging his fist on the railing. "Get that fucker! Rip it all up, whatever it is!"

Alessandro grabbed my hand and sprinted down the metal walkway.

"Hey!" Marat roared.

We kept running. A moment later Marat's heavy footsteps followed.

 # Chapter 10

As soon as the three of us made it to the main bridge leading to the PRP island, the security force sprang into action. We were surrounded and marched to safety by guards bristling with flamethrowers and giving the swamp ugly looks. The echoes of the mind in the mire had receded, but it didn't make me feel any better.

Security deposited us at the main building, where a paramedic wrapped us in foil blankets despite the hundred-degree weather, ushered us into Marat's office on the first floor, and promptly cut up Marat's jeans. Small silver drops studded the summoner's legs, embedded in his flesh.

Alessandro leaned over me, his hand on my shoulder, his face close to mine. To an outside observer, it would look like he was comforting me.

"What's going on?" he murmured.

"There is an alien intelligence in the swamp. It's telepathic."

He took a second to come to terms with it. "Tell me about the spike."

"Telekinetic, long-range, probably a Prime. He launched at least a dozen spikes, so he came prepared to kill us. I grabbed his mind, and he took off."

Alessandro nodded and straightened, his eyes calculating.

If Marat had wanted to kill us, he wouldn't have used a telekinetic. First, if something happened to us, he would be the obvious suspect.

Second, if he was dumb enough to try to murder us, he could have just shot us and had his guards dump our corpses into the water, where the nightmare that lived in the Pit would finish us off. Third, the telekinetic made no move to save him. No, the telekinetic had to belong to Arkan.

The paramedic, a lean dark-haired white man in his thirties, got a set of tweezers and a bucket and sat on the floor. He plucked the first metal drop off Marat's hairy calf. The summoner winced. The silver drop stretched and wiggled in the tweezers.

Alessandro took a step forward, caught the paramedic's arm, and looked more closely at the wriggling thing. "A metal leech."

He released the man's arm and the paramedic dropped the leech into the bucket and wiped the blood off Marat's leg. "One down."

He didn't seem rattled by pulling a metallic leech out of his employer's leg.

"How many times have you done this?" I asked him.

"Don't answer that," Marat snapped.

"No, do answer that." Despite being drenched in swamp water, Alessandro morphed into a Prime complete with crushing authority in his voice.

"Terrence," Marat warned.

The paramedic looked from Marat to Alessandro and back to Marat again.

"I'm here as Lander Morton's proxy." Alessandro's voice held no mercy. "For all intents and purposes, I *am* Lander Morton. I cut your paycheck. Answer her question."

Terrence swallowed. "About seven or eight times. It happens if people fall in the water and survive."

"How many people didn't survive?" I asked.

The first responder opened his mouth, eyed Marat, and said, "Several."

Loyalty. Victoria respected it. At this point she would acknowledge it, abandon verbal gymnastics, and crack his mind open. She would let him keep it, because loyalty deserved to be rewarded, but she would leave him curled into a ball on the floor sobbing. It would take him weeks to recover.

"I'll be right back." I got up, and left the room to retrieve the canvas sack from Rhino.

As I walked back from the car, voices floated down through the open door. I stopped to listen.

". . . are you fucking her or something?" Marat growled. "Does Lander know? Because that old pisshead isn't going to like that."

"You're alive because she asked me to save you. I would've let you drown."

"So what? You want a medal?"

"I want you to answer her questions."

"Because you're fucking her, right?"

Alessandro's voice dropped into a dangerous calm. "Say that again."

"What the fuck are you going to do about it, Eurotrash?"

Something thudded.

"Hey!" Marat screamed and choked off.

Oh shit.

I stepped into the room. Terrence was on the floor, pressing himself against the wall on my right. Alessandro must've thrown him out of the way. Marat sat frozen in his chair, his eyes wide, trying not to breathe, because Alessandro leaned over him, one foot on the chair, holding a knife to Marat's throat. The razor-sharp blade hovered a fraction of an inch from slicing Marat's jugular. Magic, potent and vicious, splayed from Alessandro, coursing through the room, sparking with orange fire here and there. It wrapped around me and licked me, flashing its fangs, like a wolf who decided he wanted a pat. Goose bumps covered my arms.

Alessandro's face was impassive. Marat had ripped open a portal without an arcane circle less than twenty minutes ago. He was either tapped out or close to it. Even if he'd been at full power, the sheer force of magic saturating the room would've terrified him. It was like a high-voltage wire dancing with a live current. But the look in Alessandro's eyes was worse. He was looking at Marat as if the summoner wasn't even human. An obstacle to be removed. A bug to be squished. Marat saw his death in Alessandro's eyes, and it rendered him mute.

I walked over to them and put my hand on Alessandro's right arm. "I leave you alone for a moment, and you're killing people again."

Marat swallowed.

"He's still alive," the Artisan said.

"He's crude, but he didn't kill Felix. He's just a loud asshole." I slid my hand to his wrist and gently pushed his hand away from Marat's throat.

Alessandro looked at Marat and hurled the knife backward without looking. It bit into the wall an inch from Terrence's head.

"Leave," Alessandro said.

The first responder jumped up and scrambled out of the room.

Alessandro uncoiled from the chair, walked over to the door, shut it, and leaned on it. Marat watched him like he was a rabid tiger. I needed to redirect his attention, or I wouldn't get anywhere.

"Marat," I called.

He tore his gaze away from Alessandro and glanced at me.

"The last summoner we fought produced a swarm of flying ticks with long scorpion tails and big mouths. I believe you designate them as a Class VII summon."

"Face-suckers," Marat muttered.

"Do you want to know what happened to him?"

He stared at me.

"They ate him in the end. It wasn't Mr. Sagredo who caused the swarm to turn on the summoner. It was me."

Marat winced. Alessandro smiled.

"When we gathered his skeleton into his coat, I could carry it in one hand." I walked over to the table. "You asked us earlier why we were late."

I held the bag open and let the four rings fall out.

Marat turned paler.

I sat down in the chair by the table. "Here is what we know: there are biomechanical creatures in the Pit that shouldn't exist. They are actively fighting you. Felix knew about it. You also know about it. Felix wanted to get help. Someone killed him. I don't think that someone was you. What I don't understand is your hostility."

Marat looked at Alessandro.

"Don't look at me," Alessandro said. "Look at her."

All the bluster drained from Marat. He looked haggard.

"Fuck it. I'm so fucking tired. There is something in the Pit. It keeps dragging equipment into the water and killing people. Bodies disappear."

"When did it start?" I asked.

"About three months in. We drained the outer perimeter with no problem, but when we tried to move closer to the center, we ran into Razorscales. Arcane beasts, about seven feet long, green, look like some mutant gator on two legs."

"I've seen them up close," I said. "A pack of them chased me through a park."

"Somehow they got into the Pit and bred in there. They love it. They eat just about anything, swim like fish, and their reproductive cycle is only three months. Each Razorscale female lays between forty and sixty eggs. About half of the hatchlings survive. They eat each other, the fuckers, but they breed so fast, it doesn't matter. I put a leviathan-class armored serpent in there, twice. They ate them both. Tatyana wanted to section off the swamp and evaporate it, bit by bit."

"Bad idea," Alessandro said. "The cost would be prohibitive. Money could be found, but there are at least three environmental groups lobbying to designate the Pit as a wildlife preserve. You've told them to relocate any native endangered species. If they found out that you burned them alive instead, the public outcry could force the city to cancel the project."

Marat laughed. "Yes. People who never ran from Razorscales want to preserve the vicious bastards. They're welcome to take a stab at conserving them. Maybe they can take one home as a pet."

"How did you deal with it?" I asked.

"Well, the serpents didn't eat them, and Tatyana's plan was nuts, so Cheryl animated some mechanical monstrosity and we dumped that in there. It worked at first. It killed three nests, and then they must have gotten it somehow, because the Razorscales came back and Cheryl couldn't feel her construct anymore. My guess is, it must have gone deeper into the Pit and found whatever it is we're fighting now. The Razorscales killed a girl, one of our workers."

Marat grimaced. "See, I have a pond. You're supposed to aerate it and if you do it too fast, the toxic sludge that accumulates in the bottom rises to the top, and all the fish die. I asked Jiang to do it in the Pit and the bastard flat out refused. Said it would kill all life in a mile radius and it would be a crime against nature. The most he would do is set up a strong current away from the main island to drive the fish deeper into the Pit. The Razorscales followed the food supply and we started to get a foothold in the swamp. We thought we were home free, started building again, and then one morning the arcane circle powering the current was gone and the ring crap started."

"What do you mean?" I asked.

"I mean that the Razorscales started swarming and every swarm came with one of those rings in its center." Marat nodded at the gyroscopes on the table. "They spin in place and there are glowing flowers in them."

"Is it always Razorscales?" Alessandro asked.

"No. Sometimes we get a big monster, with some smaller monsters."

"A hunter with his hounds."

"Exactly. I think it's making them out of people it kills. Felix and I took down a hunter once. There was a human corpse in it."

The Abyss stole humans, killed them, and used their bodies and minds to create hybrid constructs. This was a nightmare.

"This is a disaster," Alessandro said.

Marat skewed his face. "You think? Welcome to my life. We are eighty million into this project, fifteen of them mine. Maybe that's not shit to you, Count Moneybags, but for my family, it's everything. This project employs four hundred people. They're counting on it to put food on the table. I have to make this work. I'm here every day. While Cheryl is going to her charity lunches, Tatyana is burning shit for fun, and Jiang jerks off to his House's corporate logo, I'm here in the mud, trying to keep people from dying. It was me and Felix. One of us has to be here to fight it off or more of our people will die. Now it's just me."

"How did Felix feel about the thing in the swamp?" I asked.

"It bothered him. An environmentalist snuck on-site, a kid, barely sixteen years old. It dragged her into the water, and Felix raised a damn island to keep her alive. Saved her, sent her home, but it kept him from sleeping at night. He worried. When the surveyor disappeared, he wanted to shut everything down."

"Did you agree?" I asked. I already knew the answer.

Marat laughed, a cold, bitter sound. "He called an emergency meeting on Thursday, the day before he died. We put it to a vote. Four against one. I knew exactly what was going on and I voted against him. If I had opened my stupid mouth and convinced them to listen to him, he might be alive today. They might have still outvoted us, but at least I would have tried."

Now the anger made sense. Marat was eaten up by guilt. He felt trapped. They had abandoned him to the Pit, where he'd sunk all of his money, and he couldn't get out. And now the only person who understood and worked with him was dead and he had done nothing to prevent it.

"We had a fight the day before he died." Marat grimaced. "After we voted against him, he'd said that if we wouldn't see reason, he'd find someone who would. When we came back here, I had argued with him over it. I told him that if the city shut us down because he did something stupid, my House would go bankrupt and he'd be taking food out of my family's mouths."

"I know you didn't kill Felix." I leaned forward. "Who do you think did?"

Marat spread his arms. "Hell if I know. Could be any of them. Jiang doesn't say anything, and if you ask him a direct question, he'll talk for five minutes about how House Jiang is a respected and responsible House. With responsibilities. And respect. Because our Houses are apparently garbage. By the time he's done talking, you've forgotten what you've asked him in the first place. All Cheryl ever cares about is her charity crap. I don't know if she's applying for sainthood or what, but she wants the accolades. I can tell you, it costs a lot of money to be that cherished. Not that she needs the goodwill as much as Tatyana does. That snot-nosed punk brother of hers gave her family a black eye and she's desperate to heal it. At least my solution was environmentally responsible. Her solution is to burn it all down. Maybe she can make a bonfire out of the mountain of lawsuits we'll be hit with to keep herself warm at night."

Okay then.

Marat slumped in his chair. "There. That's what I think of everyone. Are we done now?"

"You're not going to win this fight," I told him. He would like this part even less than Alessandro's knife, but I had to explain it to him, because his people's safety depended on it. "While you were wrestling with tentacles, I was attacked by a telekinetic."

"Not me."

"I know. I jumped into the water and struck his mind. The thing in the Pit felt my magic and came in for a closer look. I felt it. The reason you haven't made progress is because it's not in the Pit. It is the Pit. It's a vast enormous consciousness. A single entity that stretches to the farthest reaches of the mire. It's malicious and telepathic. You need to get shielders."

"There is no money. Who's going to pay for that?"

"I will." Alessandro pushed away from the door. "I'll talk to Lander. Find some telepaths, and don't be cheap or you'll have no workers left."

"It won't make a difference," Marat said, defeated.

Despair rolled off of him. At the core of it, Marat wasn't a bad man. He was unpleasant, but he cared about his family and about his workers. Felix's death crushed him. He was already wading through a lake of guilt and that had pulled him all the way under.

"Felix did reach out for help," I told him. "I am that help."

He gave me a weary look. "What are you going to do about it?"

I raised my arm and pushed. The trickle of magic slid into the star within a circle under my skin, projecting it into the air. Marat's eyes went wide.

"The National Assembly appreciates your assistance in this matter, Prime Kazarian. Your cooperation has been noted. You will not speak of this conversation to anyone. You will not reveal my true affiliation. If called upon, you will assist me in any way possible."

He nodded, mute.

I faded the star and rose. "It will be okay," I told him. "There is a light at the end of the tunnel."

Ten minutes after we left the main island, Alessandro stopped the car and leaned over to me. "Hospital."

"You don't have to menace me."

"Yes, I do. I'm taking you to a hospital. That was our agreement. Pick one."

I gave him the address of Rogan's private physician. He plugged it into his phone, and we were off.

I stared out of the window at the Pit.

"Does it hurt?" he asked after a while.

"A little." The painkiller was wearing off. The four wounds in my side burned like someone was hammering red-hot nails into me.

"We'll get there soon." He reached over and squeezed my hand.

"I don't like threatening people to get what I need." And I shouldn't have said that. We weren't in a position to have a heart-to-heart and I had no business looking for support in him.

"Marat is . . . *un mulo* . . . a mule. He's strong and stubborn. He won't listen to reason, but he understands consequences and authority. He didn't recognize yours because you're younger and female and he didn't recognize mine because I'm young and spoiled Eurotrash."

"Well, that shirt was a bit much. I kept waiting for you to strategically unbutton it to display your chest."

He looked at me. "Are you interested in my chest?"

"No." Why did I even open my mouth?

"I can take my shirt off for you, if you'd like."

"No."

"I had no idea the presence of my shirt has been bothering you all this time."

"Alessandro!"

He laughed. Then his smile died. "Is showing Marat the badge going to carry consequences for you?"

"No. Linus allows me to reveal who I am when it's absolutely necessary. It was necessary. That's the only way to keep Marat quiet."

"I don't think that was it. I think you did it to reassure him, because you felt sorry for him."

"Think whatever you want."

"Arkan has a pet telekinetic," Alessandro said.

I reached over and rested my fingers on his forehead. "Strange. No fever."

"Why would I have a fever?"

"Because you just shared information without prompting."

I took my hand off and he leaned slightly, as if he wanted to prolong the touch, but caught himself.

"I jumped into the nasty water for you and you still don't trust me. I probably do have a fever from that. You don't even know what's in that water . . ."

"If you have a fever, Dr. Daniela will take care of it."

"I don't think Dr. Daniela can do anything for my kind of fever."

Yeah, right. "Tell me about Arkan's telekinetic."

"Young, very powerful. Arkan is grooming him as his protégé." Alessandro frowned.

"How powerful?"

"He lifted a semi once and threw it."

"Threw it where?"

"At me."

Don't ask. Don't ask how or where. Don't tempt yourself to care. "Did you dodge it?"

"I did."

"Good." I nodded and looked out the window.

Dr. Daniela Arias ran a state-of-the-art private clinic located in a bunkerlike building that was guarded better than Fort Knox. She was none too pleased with the condition of my wounds.

"So, you got clawed by an arcane construct, then you ran around the Pit, and for an encore you jumped into the filthy, magically tainted water that's probably full of sewage?"

"Exactly," Alessandro volunteered.

Dr. Arias turned to him. She was six feet tall, built like an Amazon, and when she scowled at you, you wanted to become very small and squeak "yes, ma'am" to anything she said. The stare she leveled at Alessandro was withering.

"And you didn't stop her why?"

"Yes, why didn't you stop me?" I demanded.

Alessandro gave us a dazzling smile. It bounced off Dr. Arias like a laser beam from a mirror.

"I did try to stop you. I jumped into the water instead of you to keep you from drowning and being eaten. How was I supposed to know you would follow me?"

"You're expected to use common sense." Dr. Arias glared at the two of us. "The two of you are old enough to know better. I need to run some tests and fix this mess. Catalina, make whatever calls you need to make before I start, and you, whoever you are, occupy yourself with something. She'll be here for a couple of hours."

I texted Arabella. **Are you there?**

Is you dead?

No. Need clothes.

Did you have sexy times with Alessandro?

No, I fell into the Pit. Don't tell Mom. Don't tell Nevada either. I need clothes to see Cheryl Castellano.

Where are you?

Dr. Arias.

Okay.

I called Bern. It was faster than texting, because when he concentrated on something, he ignored the texts. "Hey. Could you please do an aerial surveillance of the Pit and compare it to any records we have of it in six-month intervals?"

"How far do you need me to go?"

"Three years should do it." Three years ago, the Pit looked normal, and I wanted a baseline. "Thank you."

Alessandro parked himself by the door, leaning on the wall.

"You might want to go home," I told him.

"I don't think so."

"You smell like a swamp and I'm safe here. This is Mad Rogan's private clinic. He provides the security."

Alessandro sniffed his sleeve and grimaced.

"I won't leave without you," I promised.

"If you try, I'll find you and I'll be angry."

"Is that supposed to be some sort of threat?"

"No, it's a warning. Don't leave without me."

"Go away."

He left.

The CT scan detected no bleeding or swelling in my brain. I escaped without any broken bones, but there was a lot of soft tissue bruising and some arcane bacteria decided to throw a party in my lacerations, which we found out when Dr. Arias removed the bandages and neon-green pus leaked out. She shot me with another dose of antivenom and set about cleaning my wounds.

"Did the pretty boy patch you up?" Dr. Arias asked, working on the cuts.

"Yes."

"He didn't do a terrible job. He has some training."

"I'll tell him that you think he's pretty. That will make him happy."

Dr. Arias smiled. "I have a feeling he knows he's pretty."

My sister showed up, accompanied by Runa and two of our security people. They delivered clothes and makeup. I told them about the telekinetic and Marat being pulled into the swamp, and then Runa used her magic to purify my cuts and accidentally neutralized the antivenom, and Dr. Arias kicked them both out. On the plus side, my cuts were now taken care of and infection was unlikely. On the minus side, I received my third injection of antivenom "just to be safe," and the skin on my left side felt like it was about to give up and peel off my skeleton.

I kept the existence of the Abyss to myself until Dr. Arias left me to rest, and then I called Linus.

"Yes?" He sounded like he was in a helicopter.

I kept my voice low. "There is an alien mind in the Pit. It's beyond anything I've ever felt and it's malicious."

He pondered it for a few seconds. "Do you want me to shut the project down?"

"Not yet."

"Keep me updated."

I hung up and stared at the phone. I needed to get the hell out of this bed. It was almost 2:00 p.m. Cheryl expected me in two hours. But I was so tired and my whole body hurt.

I picked up my purse, which Alessandro had brought into the room, took out a piece of chalk, and drew a charging circle. The base charging circle was one of the easier designs to draw: a large circle, a smaller circle inside that, then three circles inside that inner circle arranged in a triangle, and finally three outer circles opposite the inner triad. In the past six months, I'd begun to develop my own version. Eventually it would become a Key, a complex charging design particular to our House. For now, it was about two-thirds of the way there. I drew it so often, it took me less than three minutes to complete it. On a good day, when everything didn't hurt like now, I could do it in half the time.

I stripped to my underwear and bra, stepped into the circle, sat, and put my phone in front of me. I didn't want to leave the circle if some emergency popped up.

The chalk lines waited for me, inert and so mundane. I sent a pulse of power through the circle. The chalk ignited with pale silver, sending tiny puffs of dust into the air. Power splashed against me. I relaxed and opened myself to it.

Before Runa left, she told me that her expert friend examined the gyroscope Cornelius had dropped off yesterday. Runa didn't like her conclusions, and I liked them even less.

How did an alien intelligence come to be in the Pit? Was it summoned? In the hundred-plus years of the serum being active, nobody had ever found a human-level intelligence in the arcane realm, but it didn't mean one couldn't exist.

How would you even fight such a mind? Mental mages didn't really come together the way other combat mages could. Our fights were duels, one-on-one. Having more than one mental mage wouldn't help, because when two minds engaged each other, they became locked, like two wrestlers gripping one another, exerting every ounce of strength they had to trip their opponent while keeping their balance. I had no idea if the Abyss could be engaged by more than one mage. Most likely, it would just crack our minds one by one like a bull trampling eggs.

An hour crawled by. Then another. I barely noticed.

My phone chimed. Bug.

I found your thing. Watch it by yourself.

He'd sent a link to a private server we used for confidential communication. I logged in and checked the file box. A single video file waited for me. I clicked it.

A lawn stretched in front of the camera, the lush grass a fresh spring green. Ancient stones, cracked and darkened with age, crossed it, leading to rows and rows of white chairs, forming an aisle. Stone pedestals flanked the entrance to the aisle supporting marble urns overflowing with white and pink, and at its end, in the shadow of a large tree a flower arch waited, poised against distant hills.

People dressed in white and pastels occupied the chairs. It must have been a spring wedding.

The guests were laughing. On the right, a man turned around and leaned on the back of his chair, caught in a conversation with two women one row behind him. On the left, a handsome man with a white smile bounced a baby on his knee. The baby giggled, and people around them snapped pictures. A gaggle of young kids ran past the camera, the girls in white frilly dresses, the boys ridiculous in miniature versions of adult clothes. A priest waited at the arch, the only person dressed in black. He looked onto the gathering with a small smile. It was a happy scene. I almost wished I was there.

I fast-forwarded the video, switching to normal speed when something significant happened. One of the kids fell and cried and the adults got up to comfort him. A woman waved her hands at another woman and dramatically went to sit elsewhere. A flurry of Italian floated about the crowd, fast and muffled, but clear enough for me to pick some of it up. Jokes about the groom, jokes about married life and getting fat from being happy, teasing about who might get married next.

Eventually, the gathering quieted down, and the groom made his way to the altar, a lean man in his early thirties, with a bright smile, handsome face, and tousled wavy brown hair. Several groomsmen followed him, the first tall and broad-shouldered, walking with a particular light gait. From the back, he looked just like Alessandro.

He turned to the side and took his spot next to the groom, and I saw his face. No, not Alessandro. The chin was too narrow, the nose too fragile, but most importantly, he seemed to lack the intense focus I'd seen in Alessandro's eyes. Alessandro had stared at death too many times. It had given him a sharp edge, and although he hid it well, I recognized it even when he pretended to be carefree. He was ready to resort to violence at any instant.

This man looked confident and sure that he could handle anything life threw at him, and brute force wasn't his first answer to it, which meant he didn't have to fight for his life that often. He was Instagram Alessandro, with a charmed life and few worries, and I couldn't tell from the recording if it was genuine or a front. If it was a pose, Marcello Sagredo had been an even better actor than his son.

The groomsmen milled about, waiting. I fast-forwarded again until the bride walked down the aisle to the familiar music, accompanied by an older man. The train of her lacy gown brushed the grass. Wind stirred her white veil. The videographer moved around the chairs, capturing her walk. She glided to the altar, a vision in white with long dark hair. The groom stared at her, starry-eyed. A fairy-tale wedding.

The ceremony started.

The groom said his vows. "*Io, Antonio, prendo te, Sofia, come mia sposa* . . . and promise to be faithful to you always, in joy and in pain, in health and in sickness, and to love you and every day honor you, for the rest of my life . . ."

A man strode down the aisle, smiling, walking as if he belonged there. He was tall and powerfully built. Not slabbed with muscle like a bodybuilder, more like an athlete or a soldier in prime condition. The videographer swung his camera and it caught his face. Perfectly average. He could have been an American or a European. Blond hair cut short but not military short. Tan, clean shaven, nondescript features, average nose, average mouth, no distinctive scars, no strangely colored eyes. A teacher, a bank manager, a furniture salesman. There was nothing odd about him.

Hello, Arkan.

The groom frowned. The bride turned and looked at the man, stunned at the interruption.

Arkan shot forward. There was no warning. One of his steps became a powerful lunge, so fast, I barely saw the long knife in his hand. And then Alessandro's father was there, in front of him.

The stranger stabbed. Marcello moved out of the way, fluid and fast, and redirected the attacker's thrust with a lightning-fast block. He moved so quick, no hesitation, no delay. Real life fights happened instantly. There was no bowing, no touching of gloves. Nobody blew a whistle or rang a bell, and most people with martial arts training froze, if only for a moment, expecting someone to give the go-ahead. Marcello hadn't. This wasn't just training, this was experience. He had fought an attacker with a knife before, and he had won.

The assassin stabbed again. Again, Marcello used his own movement against him, guiding the knife to the side.

Thrust—block.

Another thrust—block.

Arkan was shockingly good, but Marcello was better and knew he was better. He was looking for an opening, but he was in no hurry. And everyone else just watched it. They were fighting for a full five seconds, and nobody jumped up and hit the bad guy with a chair.

Arkan tossed the knife into his left hand with ridiculous precision and slashed, sure and fast. Somehow Marcello had anticipated it and leaned out of the way. The camera caught his face. His eyes glinted. His lips stretched, baring his teeth. It almost looked like anger, but I had seen that exact expression on Alessandro's face. Marcello was having fun.

Finish him. Stop playing with him and finish it.

The assassin kicked at Marcello's leading leg, aiming for the knee-cap. Alessandro's father stepped out of the way and hammered a quick jab into the attacker's face.

Ouch. Straight shot to the nose. That had to hurt like hell.

The video froze. Nothing moved. Marcello paused, one arm extended, fingers ready to grab. To the left, an older man half rose from his chair, caught in midmove. To the right, a woman stopped in midscream, her hands halfway to her mouth.

I tapped the pause button a couple of times. The timer was still going, counting off the seconds. The video didn't freeze. Somehow, Arkan had petrified the entire wedding party.

The assassin uncoiled from an aborted kick, his movements smooth, almost lazy. He raised his hand and slit Marcello's throat with a dramatically wide swipe. It was almost a flourish. He made a little show of it.

Marcello stared straight at the camera. His neck had to be cut, but there was no blood.

I had never heard of this in my life. I had never seen it, I'd never read about it. How?

The killer moved past Marcello, sliding between the bride and the groom. Someone had pressed the invisible play button, and suddenly people moved. The man on the left collapsed into his chair. A piercing scream cut through the silence. Marcello gulped. Blood drenched the front of his neck, a hot, vivid scarlet.

The assassin looked at the bride and stabbed the groom in the chest. A textbook thrust to the heart, easy to understand, almost impossible to execute.

"Francis says hello," the killer said.

The groom collapsed. The bride spun and ran from the altar, clutching her gown in her hands. The wedding guests fled in all directions, knocking over chairs in a human stampede. The camera shuddered and became still. The photographer must've fled, abandoning it on its tripod.

At the altar Marcello fell to his knees, his hand clamped on his throat. Blood spurted between his fingers. He sagged to the ground and folded on his side, his eyes terrified.

A lone boy stood in the middle of the aisle, staring at Marcello with Alessandro's eyes. I had no idea when he had gotten there.

Arkan put his foot on the groom's chest, pulled the knife out, wiped it on the groom's jacket and strode past Marcello down the aisle. The boy watched him come. He didn't move. He didn't even blink, like a baby rabbit seeing a wolf approach. His fear locked him in place, shivering in his eyes.

My heart was beating too fast. I wanted to reach through the video and grab him and run away.

Arkan paused by him and put his hand on the boy's shoulder. "Sorry, kid. It's business."

The boy gazed at him, glassy-eyed.

The killer nodded and walked away.

The video stopped.

My mouth tasted bitter. The muscles of my face contracted, too tight, squeezing and making me dizzy. I closed my eyes, waiting it out.

It was like watching Runa's mom die again, only it was worse, because it was Alessandro's father and Alessandro was there, helpless and terrified. The look on his face . . .

My hands rolled into fists.

How long had Alessandro stood there watching his father die?

He must have felt like his whole life ended right there, on that lawn. He must have been like me. I divided my life into before Dad died and after, except I had my mother and my sisters and my cousins, who all loved me. He had his grandfather, who called his dead father an idiot. He also had his mother and his siblings, but he barely mentioned them. Whenever he talked about his family, it was in terms of obligation. It was never in terms of love.

It should have shattered Alessandro. It probably had. At some point he must have thought about revenge and grasped it, like a lifeline. The need to avenge his father became his new core and he pulled himself together around it. I understood now. He must have dedicated himself completely to his vengeance. He probably only took the jobs that aligned with his goal of tracking down his father's killer.

Alessandro was a great liar, but when he said he wanted to protect me, he was sincere. And sometimes, when he didn't think I was paying attention, he watched me with a raw, desperate want in his eyes. It couldn't be a lie. He looked at me like I was everything that anchored him to life.

But he'd wanted his revenge for so long, and if he told himself that the killer of his father didn't matter, he was lying to himself. Alessandro would not stop until Arkan was dead. If it was a choice between my life and Arkan's death, who would he put first?

I had no idea.

I knew one thing. If I ever had a chance to kill Arkan, I would take it. I would hunt him down and make him suffer. He didn't just kill Alessandro's father. He murdered his childhood, he destroyed his family, and until he was punished for it, Alessandro would never be free.

By the time Alessandro appeared in the doorway of my room, I had wiped off the circle, taken a shower, blow-dried my hair, twisted it into a bun with a hairpin, and gotten dressed.

He'd switched to a blue-grey suit with a crisp white shirt with the two top buttons undone. The suit hugged his waist and broadened his shoulders. Instead of minimizing his physique, he accentuated it. His hair was brushed back from his face, and his five o'clock shadow drew the eye to his perfect jaw and sensual mouth. He left the jewelry back at his hotel. Combined with the casually unbuttoned shirt and tousled hair, the effect was unsettling. He looked like a man who'd spent the entire day working and now was ready to relax, but more than that, he looked ready for intimacy. I could imagine stepping close, running my hands over his hard chest, and nudging the coat out of the way to kiss his muscular neck and feel the scrape of that sexy stubble on my lips.

I knew it was a pose, I knew it wasn't for me, but I saw him and just stared for a long moment, unable to help myself.

"You dressed up for Cheryl." I managed to keep the annoyance out of my voice.

"Yes. Your makeup is done. Were you going to leave without me?"

"No. I waited for you."

Alessandro's eyes narrowed. "Did something happen while I was gone?"

Somehow, he could tell. Something must have been off in my tone or expression. I needed to do a better job of hiding.

"Yes. I got my third shot of antivenom and no additional painkillers to deal with it. Let's go before my willpower gives out and I start crying like a five-year-old."

We were walking down the hallway to the front door when he said, "Catalina, I won't let anyone hurt you. I won't abandon you."

A few days ago, I wouldn't have believed him. He had abandoned me, and he'd done it during one of the worst times of my life, when I'd needed him most. But I knew better now. I still didn't understand why, but Alessandro was determined to put himself between Arkan and me. And I would do the same for him.

"I know," I told him and made myself smile.

 **Chapter 11**

Alessandro insisted on driving again.

"Do you have a problem with the way I drive?"

"No."

"Then why do you keep stealing the keys?"

He glanced at me. "It keeps me occupied. My eyes are on the road and my hands are on the wheel."

I decided it would be a great idea to shut up and keep my own eyes on the road.

Cheryl Castellano owned an office suite in Felicity Tower off West Loop. The office in the brand-new thirty-five-floor tower came with perks, like private elevators, chartered helicopter service, complimentary access to a world-class steakhouse, and a private courier firm. Clearly House Castellano's show of humility didn't extend to their business accommodations.

I didn't want to see Cheryl right now. I needed to be sharp and alert for this conversation, and instead I was still tired and slightly loopy from the medication. Too much had happened today, and this wouldn't be an easy interview.

Bern's background on Cheryl had been rather brief by his standards, only about twelve pages. She was the Head of House Castellano, forty-one, widowed, two sons and one daughter, ages twenty, eighteen, and sixteen. Both parents deceased. Her only living relative was her uncle, also a Prime animator. She married Paul Renfield, a Significant animator, at twenty, and he took her name. He had no House; he was a statistical anomaly born to Average parents and he died in his thirties from a pre-existing heart condition.

House Castellano made their wealth in the construction industry, and among the five board members, Cheryl's resources were second only to Felix's. She seemed obsessed with charitable giving. The list of the organizations she contributed to was a mile long, everything from Red Cross to the local Bright Minds of Houston scholarship fund. She sat on the boards of a dozen charities and floated through the top ranks of Houston's elite thanks to her wealth and stellar reputation.

If her House had ever been involved in a feud, Bern couldn't find any trace of it. Knowing my cousin, it annoyed him to no end. He'd gone through the trouble of making a graph of her charitable donations, which showed a rather steep climb.

I checked the list of the charitable contributions again. Something was off about it. Most people chose a few worthy causes. Cheryl didn't. She gave money to everyone, always a significant but not a huge amount, and she never did it anonymously. Connor and Nevada gave more than her, and nobody knew because they gave to charity for the sake of the people who needed it rather than their own.

My phone chimed. Albert Ravenscroft wanting to FaceTime. He always wanted to FaceTime.

I accepted the call. He appeared on the screen, tall, smiling, and handsome in that particular "traditional good looks" way. Perfectly symmetrical features, solid jaw, straight nose, clear blue eyes, dark hair that would be wavy if he let it grow out. All the things indicative of good breeding, money, a healthy diet, and lots of leisure time to play sports. He was smart and decisive, he wanted to marry me, and he refused to take no for an answer.

He was also the only person outside the family who knew about Leon and Audrey.

"I didn't think you would answer. Today is my lucky day." Albert smiled. "Are you free for dinner?"

I would need more information to answer that question. If he had shared what he knew with someone, I could be free for dinner, but he wouldn't like what would follow. "I don't know yet."

"So, it's a maybe? I'll take a maybe."

Next to me, Alessandro muttered something under his breath.

"What's the occasion?" I asked.

"Nothing special. I haven't seen you in two weeks and I miss you."

Say something normal. "That's sweet."

Alessandro turned and looked at me. I ignored him.

"When will you know if you're free?"

"I'm not sure. I'm working. What's the latest I can text you?"

"Catalina, you can text me anytime. If tonight at 1:00 a.m. you decide you want ramen, or bulgogi, or caviar, text me and I'll pick you up."

If I wanted any of those things, I would get them myself. "Leon says hi."

No reaction. "How is he?"

"You know, the usual. I'll text you later." I waved and hung up.

Alessandro switched lanes with razor-cut precision. "Who was that?"

"That was Albert Ravenscroft."

"Is he the reason you need a pregnancy test?"

"What?" His voice was so neutral, it took the words a second to penetrate.

"When you were injured, you said you would get whatever tests needed, including a pregnancy test. Is he the reason for it?"

Oh you idiot. "I said I would take a pregnancy test because any time something is wrong with a woman, they do a pregnancy test. I could walk into a hospital with my arm cut off and they would want me to pee in a cup before they did anything about it. I'm not sleeping with Albert, and if I was, it would be none of your business." I waved my arms. "I could be sleeping with half of Houston and it would be none of your business."

"True, but if you were sleeping with half of Houston, how would you ever get anything done?"

"I'm great at multitasking."

He steered the car around the curve of the U-turn, guiding Rhino under 610 to West Loop South. "You're wrong."

"How so?"

"Your relationships are my business. I'm trying to protect you."

"I've been protecting myself from Albert and his marriage proposals for months without your help."

He made a right into a short street that ended in a parking lot. The glittering building towered before us, all pale grey stone and floors and floors of windows reflecting the blue sky.

"Of course he wants to marry you." Alessandro's voice iced over.

"Whatever you're thinking, stop thinking it."

"He's in love with you. You said proposals. That means he's asked you more than once and you've said no."

Argh. Just because he proposed doesn't mean he wants to marry me . . . No, that's stupid . . . "And?" There. Nice and noncommittal.

"Arkan approaches him, asks him to cooperate, and in return Albert gets to swoop in when things are at their worst—"

"Swoop in? What is he, a turkey vulture?"

"—and play the white knight when you need him most. A good plan."

"You need to have your head examined."

"What kind of a Prime is he?"

"Quit it."

"No matter. I'll find out."

We drove into the parking lot.

"Alessandro, what makes you think that someone would go through the trouble of attacking a House as dangerous as ours just to marry me?"

He parked and twisted toward me. "Catalina, have you seen yourself? Like in a mirror?"

"Oh please."

"Did you show him your wings?"

"Why would I show him my wings? What do they have to do with anything?"

"What do . . ." Alessandro made an obvious effort to control his voice. "There are men in this world who would stop at nothing to be with you. You're beautiful, you're brilliant, and if they knew how dangerous you were, you would get buried in proposals. There isn't a House out there that wouldn't want to add you to their arsenal. And when the wings come out, it's all over. I'm the best antistasi on record, anywhere, and when I saw you, I stared like an idiot. I could've stood there, listening to you talk for a year."

"You're delusional . . ."

"Why do you think Benedict lost his shit? He survived twenty years in the murder business, he was smart and careful, and then when you showed up he abandoned all common sense and, instead of killing you, tried to capture you, repeatedly. An elite assassin stopped thinking, because there was only room for you in his brain. I almost felt sorry for the bastard just before I shot him, because I know how he felt."

"You are immune to my magic and my wings."

"But I'm not immune to you."

He had to stop saying things like that.

"It's not the wings for me. It never was."

I didn't want to hear it.

"It's not the wings for Albert either. I heard his voice. If you called him, that guy would run through fire to get to you. If you called me and I was across the ocean, I would—"

"Stop talking." I put my hand over his mouth.

He shut up.

"Okay. Here's what's going to happen. I'm going to interview Cheryl Castellano. She's dangerous and I need all of my brain power for this conversation. I can't be distracted. You can come or you can stay in the car. Do you want to come with me? Answer yes or no."

I lifted my hand.

"Yes."

"Thank you."

I got out of the car and marched to the doors. I had no time to think about all the things he just said. There was a Prime expecting me and I had to put on a good show.

The lobby of Felicity Tower offered the latest in modern luxury. Acres of white marble streaked with soft brown tastefully contrasted with geometric onyx columns. A grandiose chandelier dripped thousands of Swarovski crystals above tastefully grouped furniture. Original art in exquisite frames added color to the tan walls. The developer had hired a harmonizer House to execute the interior design and walking into the space was like stepping into another world, a place of power, privilege, and exclusivity. It was at once elegant and welcoming, and as you moved through it, you felt transformed into a member of the elite. Your shoulders straightened, your stride gained confidence, and when you met others, you looked them in the eye, secure in your right to be there.

We passed through security and gave our names to the concierge. We were expected, and he walked us to the elevator. People stopped and looked at Alessandro. Men and women.

It wasn't just his stunning face, it was the way he wore his clothes, the way he walked, the expression on his face, the hint of a smile in the corners of his mouth. He represented the unreachable ideal they strived toward, power, wealth, youth, beauty . . . The perfect scion of a House. I had no doubt that if we lingered, he would collect a stack of business cards, room keys, and phone numbers hastily scrawled on the first available scrap of paper.

I liked the other Alessandro better. The one who didn't bother to pretend. The one with lethal magic and a dangerous mind. The one who cursed because I wouldn't let him take me to the hospital and then patched my wounds on the side of a road.

The concierge handed us off to the elevator operator, who swiped his keycard and delivered us to the sixth floor. We exited into a long rectangular room. A black marble floor stretched to walls the color of coffee with too much cream. The tinted windows dimmed the light to a soft golden glow. Here and there pedestals of frosted glass rose, lit from within by LED lights, and paired with digital screens, some as small as a tablet, some, on the walls, the size of a small TV. A small construct rested on top of each pillar, illuminated by their glow. Odd.

Alessandro raised his eyebrows.

We started forward. The pillar on the left flashed, reacting to our movement. The construct on its top twisted. Magenta-colored magic sparked, and the small mechanical beast came to life.

About a foot across and eight inches high, the construct seemed old and a little crude, a collection of metal gears and cogs, shaped vaguely like a mole with four front limbs, two where the normal paws would be and two others, inverted so they pointed out, attached to the mole's back. All four came equipped with long curved claws.

The screen on the wall behind the mole turned on, showing a black-and-white picture of a young man. He wore a dark suit and lighter frock coat and held a derby hat in his hand. Next to him a massive version of the mole construct towered, ten feet high, with claws the size of giant bulldozer blades. The caption underneath read "Secondo Castellano, 1901, Digger I."

From where I stood, I could see other pedestals with their own photos. 1912, Crawler I, a millipede with a multitude of arms, each capable of picking up a large container. 1927, a strange beast with a scrapper attached to it, some sort of bulldozer equivalent. 1932, a bizarre grasshopper mutant capable of raising power poles. 1948, Digger V, updated and refined to be more efficient . . .

We were in House Castellano's personal museum.

Alessandro studied the room. His face turned thoughtful.

"What is it?" I asked.

"I've never stood inside someone's American Dream before."

A family of immigrants, coming to the US, starting a business, growing it into a House worth millions. "A version of it, yes."

We resumed walking.

"My mom once told me that the American Dream was to live better than your parents."

"Do you think it's true?" he asked.

"I think everyone defines *better* differently. Some want more money. Others want more time."

"What do you want?"

The answer popped into my head so fast, I didn't even have to think about it.

"Security. I want my family to be safe in all ways. I want them to be secure from attacks, physical, magical, and financial. I want us to have enough money to cover our bills, to allow everyone to have the career they want, and to take time off if they need it. To not be one disaster away from complete collapse. Less disasters would be really nice. As a House, I want us to have a solid reputation, the kind that commands respect, so everyone can marry whoever they want without jumping through hurdles."

"That's all about your family. What about you?"

My happy dream died six months ago. Earlier, actually, before any of us realized the depth of Victoria Tremaine's scheming. One day I would get back some of what I lost, but by then it would be too late for me and Alessandro.

"My family is my happiness."

A dangerous shadow flickered through his eyes. "Don't say that."

I must have hit a raw nerve by accident.

The pedestals kept going. We passed out of the twentieth century into the new millennium. The constructs slimmed down, becoming sleeker, more specialized. A spider to climb buildings and deliver supplies to disaster areas over rugged terrain. A mobile solar battery shaped like a flower that crawled forward on tentacle-roots.

The pictures changed too, as did the names. From Secondo to Francis, then Janet, then Sean and Mark, then finally, Cheryl. It was a trip through history designed to impress. Had we come to do business with House Castellano, by the time we reached the frosted glass doors at the other end, we would have been humbled and grateful for the opportunity.

But I wasn't here to be humble. I was here to interrogate Cheryl about a murder. None of her family's admittedly impressive achievements would change that.

The museum ended in another lobby and a pretty female secretary ushered us into Cheryl's office.

Prime Castellano smiled at us from behind a solid black glass desk, accented with gold. She wore a soft silk blouse the color of bluebonnets and a tailored skirt. A porcelain brooch in the shape of a delicate white orchid rested on her chest. Her hair coiled on her head in soft feminine waves.

A man in his thirties stood on her right. Large brown eyes, deep bronze skin, South Asian ancestry. His gaze fixed on me and a faint shadow slid over my mind, filled with a distant echo of a wail. Mentovocifer, a mind shrieker. Victoria had had me fight one. They attacked by flooding the mind with magic, which their victim's brain interpreted as a deafening, agonizing scream. Cheryl was taking no chances.

She rose. "A pleasure to see you both again, although I do wish it was under better circumstances."

"Such a tragedy," Alessandro offered.

Cheryl held out her hand to me. I shook it. Her fingers were soft, her handshake gentle. She got me out of the way and shifted her attention to Alessandro. He kissed her hand. Cheryl smiled in that particular way women smiled at Alessandro. He smiled back at her, a charming roguish grin that said, *Yes, I would be a lot of fun.* I resisted the urge to smack the back of his head.

"Please sit down."

We took our places in two black chairs. Cheryl settled back behind the desk. It struck me how out of place she seemed. The office was luxurious, but so impersonal, it almost looked staged. Grey walls, chestnut wood paneling, black and gold color scheme. A distinctly corporate space devoid of personal touches.

This couldn't have been her regular office. Frequently used offices, like most of the spaces people occupied, accumulated personal touches: photographs, plants, knickknacks, business gifts. She must have borrowed it for the meeting, most likely from her uncle, who had retired and rarely involved himself in the House business, according to Bern's summary.

Cheryl didn't want me to see her space. She could have done it out of privacy concerns, or because this office was convenient and impressive, but I doubted it. She did it because her regular office would've told me things about her, and she didn't want me to gain any insights.

What are you hiding, Cheryl?

"This is Rahul." Cheryl looked at the shrieker with a small smile. "He's going to sit in on our meeting. Didn't you have an interview with Marat this morning? How did it go?"

She was trying to hijack the conversation. I smiled at her. "What's your opinion of Mr. Kazarian?"

She pursed her lips for half a second. *That's right, I ignored your question and asked my own. You don't get to drive this car.*

"An extremely hardworking man, dedicated, and an excellent father."

"Can you tell me about Stephen Jiang?"

"Dedicated," Cheryl said. "He comes from a wonderful family, steeped in tradition, very respected. A very smart young man. I'm not sure why you're asking me these questions."

"It helps me understand the interactions between everyone."

"In that case, what did Marat say about me?"

"He wondered if you are applying for sainthood."

Cheryl raised her hand to her mouth and laughed softly.

"Tatyana Pierce?" I prompted.

"My niece went to school with her. They used to call her Tatyana Fierce. The nickname still applies. Tatyana is direct and excellent under pressure."

"And Felix?"

Cheryl's face turned sad. She sighed. "Felix was everyone's favorite. He was like a brother you wish you had growing up. Our leader, if you will. I feel so terrible for his children."

"Can you tell me about your day on July 15th? Starting with waking up."

Cheryl frowned. "Some days you remember and some days you don't. This was an ordinary day. I woke up at seven, drank my coffee. Anna, my housekeeper, bought pomelos the previous evening, and I had one for breakfast."

She spoke softly. Her tone wasn't meek; rather, it was conciliatory and gentle enough so that raising my voice would have immediately branded me as an ass and a bully. Interesting.

"I spoke to my son, Sander, before he left for school. He keeps trying to convince me that a neck tattoo would make a good birthday present. Evan, my chauffeur, picked me up at half past eight and took me to the family workshop. I spent the day there." Her frown deepened. "I don't remember if I went out for lunch or if I ordered in."

She had ordered in, a strawberry salad with salmon in a balsamic maple glaze. Augustine's people had confirmed it with her secretary.

"I stayed at the workshop until five or six."

She'd left at 4:42 p.m. Castellano's workshop was roughly the same distance from the Pit as the Morton building. If they were going to the

Pit, she would beat Felix by twenty minutes. Enough time to disable the security equipment.

"Where did you go after work?" I asked.

MII's investigator assigned to the case confirmed that Cheryl was home by seven, but MII couldn't account for two and a half hours of Cheryl's time, starting from her leaving the office and ending with a traffic camera picking her up as she took an exit off I-69 on the way to her house in the Memorial Villages.

"I had a light dinner and some cocktails with a friend at Masraff's."

"The name of your friend?"

"Gloria Neville."

I hid a smile.

Gloria Neville came from an old and powerful House. Like Bern, she was Magister Examplaria, a pattern mage, but her specialty lay in economics. She analyzed market patterns and predicted global economic shifts. She was in her sixties, and in the course of her life she had made a lot of money for a lot of people. In the eyes of the Texas magical heavy hitters, she was an unimpeachable witness. They trusted her with their money.

Cheryl had just made a mistake.

"Where did you go after?" I asked.

"Home." Cheryl sighed. "It's difficult for me to admit, but despite our best efforts, the Pit Reclamation Project stalled. It causes me a great deal of anxiety."

"We all have those projects," Alessandro said.

She acknowledged him with a grateful glance. For a moment they were alone in a room, two wealthy entrepreneurs sharing an understanding of difficulties with running a business. Something pinched me and I realized it was jealousy. I buried it.

"You've seen the front room of this office," Cheryl continued. "The name of our House is synonymous with reliability. We are problem solvers. I will solve the problem of the Pit, but the solution to it demands every ounce of my attention. After a full day of concentrating at the workshop, I can barely put two words together. Gloria was too kind not to mention it during our dinner, but I'm sure I looked like death warmed over and likely sounded the same. I barely got home, fell asleep, and woke up around nine, because my son became concerned that my back would hurt from sleeping on the couch."

She was giving a lot of detail.

"Your dedication is commendable," Alessandro said. He sounded impressed.

"I do what I can."

Modesty, Cheryl, is your middle name.

"This matter doesn't just concern me," she said. "It concerns our family legacy."

"What was the nature of the construct you released into the Pit?"

The helpful expression on Cheryl's face gained a slightly injured quality, as if I had insulted her, but she was too good to acknowledge it. "It was an experimental model under the working name Kraken. It's designed to assess its environment and eliminate biological threats."

"Marat mentioned that you lost control of the Kraken." I had chosen my words very carefully.

Cheryl leaned forward, but her voice remained gentle, patient, and bordering on patronizing.

"No, I lost contact with the construct. I assure you, none of my creations have ever escaped my control."

There it was, a featherlight touch from Rahul. He was a dual— not just a shrieker, but also a telepath, probably a lower Significant in both. The duality made him dangerous. He was trying to pick up my surface thoughts. Cheryl had just breached protocol. Scanning another mage's mind was grounds for retaliation. It was like being groped by a stranger.

I sent my magic out. It grew from me, its tendrils twisting like grape-vine shoots, subtle, barely detectable, winding around Rahul.

"So where is the construct now?" I asked.

"Lost to the Pit."

"How big was it? I didn't see a model of it in the front."

"We only display constructs that have passed the prototype stage."

The tendrils of my magic slipped through Rahul's defenses. Mental mages guarded against what they knew, especially their own brand of magic. Rahul built a shell around his mind, hiding his thoughts and protecting himself against a direct assault. He had expected a battering ram. But vines didn't batter, they grew, and curved, and found purchase in the smallest crevices. They went over and around, and eventually they slithered in.

Cheryl tapped the keyboard of her laptop. A digital screen on the wall flared up, displaying a construct. It had a long, sharp head armored by a metal carapace followed by a segmented body, like that of a millipede, and ending in a powerful finned tail. It reminded me of some alien shrimp.

"The Kraken was twelve meters long from the tip of the head to the end of the longest appendage," Cheryl said. "It could collapse its width to one and a half meters in circumference, but it reached maximum efficiency at a circumference of two meters."

Thirty-nine feet long and six and a half feet in circumference. A monster.

The construct turned its head toward me. Metal slid aside, opening a huge maw lined with rows and rows of serrated metal teeth.

The tendrils of my magic touched Rahul's mind. He didn't feel it. I fed a little more power into it.

"It had several operating modes and could alter its shape." Cheryl pressed a key. The construct re-formed itself. The body coiled under the head and released eight long, segmented, metal spider legs. A nightmare.

"Does it have self-replicating capabilities?"

Cheryl put her hand flat on the desk.

If it was a signal, Rahul missed it. He was staring at me, fascinated.

"Ms. Castellano?" I prompted.

"It has regenerative capabilities," she said. "It can repair itself."

"Can it build axillary extensions? For example, is it able to add tentacles to itself?"

Cheryl leaned back. "What you're suggesting is called Saito's Threshold, a point where a construct gains life. No animator mage has ever crossed it. It's impossible the way attaining the speed of light is impossible."

"Why?"

"Because we do not grant life to our creations. Only animation. Our constructs do not feel. They do not think in traditional terms. They follow a simple 'if-then' loop. When their environment meets a certain predetermined condition, they react to it. While it gives them an illusion of free will and rational thought, they are a step above a calculator. They do not reproduce, they do not alter their structure, and they are incapable of higher brain functions or mental magic like telepathy."

I hadn't mentioned telepathy. It wasn't on the table until she placed it there.

"Can a construct be made telepathic?" I asked.

Cheryl arranged her face into the embodiment of patience. "No. As I said, constructs are incapable of independent magic implantation. We have the capability to make them self-repairing. For example, you may have seen the Crawler model in the outer room. It resembles a centipede with numerous appendages protruding from its back. Crawler XII, the latest model, carries spare arms. In the event that an appendage becomes inoperable, it can jettison it and install a replacement. But it cannot manufacture a new arm or modify its design."

"So what do you think happened to the Kraken?"

Cheryl sighed. "Environmental hazards."

I waited.

"When the construct is forcefully pulled apart, its magic will seek to reassemble it. However, magic has limits. The Kraken's magic signature vanished while it was clearing a school of Razorscales. I believe that they pulled it apart and either consumed enough of it or dragged the pieces in so many different directions that the distance became too great for reassembly. We've used echolocation and metal detectors in an effort to find the debris field; however, the Pit is filled with metal debris."

"I'm sure that was a nightmare," Alessandro said. "At some point, even if you found it, trying to salvage it wouldn't have been cost-effective."

What was he on about? A custom-made construct, especially a prototype of that size, contained titanium alloys and PGM, platinum group metals: rhodium, iridium, palladium. The metal alone would be worth millions. They should have spent weeks trying to recover it, if only to see what went wrong.

"Indeed." Cheryl looked back at me.

"Perhaps the two of you could enlighten me?" I asked.

"Please don't feel bad. Alessandro—"

I really didn't like the way she said his name.

"—and I have similar outlooks. We run corporations, we employ people, and we both recognize that the cost-benefit analysis is a factor. It's harder for you to see the big picture, not through any fault of your own, of course, but simply because you lack the relevant experience."

Translation: Alessandro and I are special, and you are stupid and dumb and poor. And yet, somehow, I'd managed to scrape enough brain cells together to not invest in a literal money pit.

"Thank you for your time," I said and stood up.

Alessandro rose as well.

Rahul stepped forward. "Can I have your number?"

Cheryl pivoted to him, her face mortified. "Please, excuse him," she said, stamping each word. "He must not be feeling well."

Rahul raised his hand, blocking Cheryl. "I'd really like to see you again. I promise, I'm not creepy."

Alessandro stepped between me and Rahul and gave Cheryl a dazzling smile. "We really need to be on our way. It was lovely seeing you."

Alessandro put his hand on the small of my back and gently pushed me toward the door.

"Hey." Rahul moved to follow.

"Not one step more," Cheryl warned him.

We escaped into the reception area and then into the museum.

"Well, he has some explaining to do," Alessandro murmured.

"Hold on."

I turned left toward the most recent section of the museum, and surveyed the constructs marked with Cheryl's name. Digger XXIII, Crawler XXI, Blossom V . . . Just as I thought.

"I'm done," I told him. We turned and made our way to the elevators.

"Where to?" Alessandro asked when we got into Rhino.

"Home."

It was late, I was tired, and I hadn't eaten since this morning, when I stole a couple of Arabella's "superhealthy vegan muffins." She'd made them special a few days ago. My sister usually cooked only under duress, but for some reason she got obsessed with that recipe. I had tried pointing out that any muffin recipe that didn't use dairy was vegan by default, and that the loads of chocolate chips and nuts she'd put into them didn't make them healthy, but she stuffed a muffin into my mouth and told me to mind my own business.

"Shall we compare notes?" Alessandro asked.

"Yes. Cheryl killed Felix. I can't prove it, I don't know if she did it alone, and I don't understand how the serum fits into this murder, but she did it."

Alessandro nodded. "Agreed. You go first."

"She said that she couldn't remember much about the day Felix died, then gave a detailed account down to the fruit she ate for breakfast. Her workshop and Felix's office are roughly the same distance from the Pit. She left the office twenty minutes ahead of Felix and disappeared for two and a half hours."

"What about her alibi?"

"It's bullshit. When Cornelius' wife was murdered, he hired Nevada to look into it. She proved that a woman named Olivia Charles murdered her. Cornelius avenged his wife and killed Olivia in a horrible way. Gloria Neville was Olivia's best friend. She blames us for Olivia's death."

Alessandro smiled, a quick, vicious baring of teeth. "A blunder."

A little scalding spark shot through me. Kissing him was out of the question. Imagining kissing him was out of the question. I dragged my train of thought back onto the right tracks.

"Yes. If Cheryl said she had dinner with anyone but Gloria, I would verify her alibi. But I have Gloria flagged. After the conspiracy to over-throw the Texas government was exposed and the dust settled, the affected Houses went after Connor and my sister. Gloria was in that mess up to her eyeballs. We keep tabs on her and her known associates, and I know for a fact that she and Cheryl are not close friends. They may sit on some of the same charity boards, but they don't go out for drinks. Especially on Friday night. Do you know what Gloria does on Friday nights?"

Alessandro glanced at me. A little light danced in his eyes. He seemed to be enjoying himself beyond all reason. "Tell me."

"She hosts a bingo game for her mother and her mother's three elderly and insanely wealthy friends. They drink cheap wine and play for pennies."

Alessandro laughed.

"Gloria was selected to be the alibi for one reason only—she will do and say anything to hurt House Baylor. If you called her right now and asked her if she had dinner with Cheryl, she would tell you yes and act offended that you even questioned it. And the four old ladies will lie through their teeth to back her up."

Alessandro grinned at me again.

"Then there is the murder scene." I leaned back. "How did Felix get onto that cable? You can't reach it from the roof or the walkway, unless you had a ladder or caught it with some sort of extralong hook. Then, how would you get it around Felix's neck and then dump him over the rail? Felix was a large athletic man and he was a Prime."

Alessandro nodded. "True."

"But if you're a powerful animator, you can animate the wire. She had twenty minutes in the Pit. She disabled the security cameras, which meant she planned to kill him. She lured him to the spot on the walkway and the wire reached down and snapped around his neck, jerking him straight up. His neck was broken instantly."

"It fits," he said.

"Your turn."

"She is afraid," Alessandro said.

"What makes you think that?"

"I read her file. Your cousin is disturbingly thorough in his background checks. Cheryl has had no relationships after the death of her husband. Her life is split between her children and work. If she was ever involved with anyone, she must've gone to extraordinary lengths to keep the relationship private. This is a woman extremely conscious of her image. A woman like that wouldn't respond to blatant interest from someone like me. She would find it inappropriate."

"But she did."

He nodded. "She smiled, nodded, and agreed with everything I said, even when it was utter nonsense."

"I was wondering about the cost-benefit silliness you threw at her."

"It's out of character for her to respond to me. It means her position is so vulnerable that she is scrambling for any allies. She thinks I'm pretty and stupid, and therefore easily manipulated. She appealed to my fragile ego to get me on her side."

I squinted at him. "Your ego would survive an apocalypse."

"Thank you."

"It wasn't a compliment."

"It was to me."

A flash of the old Alessandro, here one second and gone the next, so quick I might have imagined it.

"Why did you stop on the way out?" he asked.

"A hunch. People who throw around words like *legacy* worry me, so I wanted to see Cheryl's accomplishments. That room is full of giants, and I don't mean constructs. There are no I's on Cheryl's constructs."

"I don't follow."

"When one of the Castellanos invents something new, they mark it with a Roman numeral I. Digger I, Crawler I, Blossom I."

His eyes narrowed. "Cheryl's constructs all have high numbers. She hasn't invented anything new. She just refined what came before her."

"I think so. The Kraken would have been her first attempt at an original construct. I wonder to what lengths she went to make it."

Alessandro pondered it. It was a disturbing thought. I would need to speak to Regina. Patricia's wife was an upper-level Significant animator. Maybe she could tell me more.

"So, what did you do to Rahul?" Alessandro asked. "I didn't see the wings."

"Neither did he." How did I know he would get around to that? "I don't always need the wings. I can do it with my voice. Sometimes I can do it with my magic alone. Seeing the wings is a privilege, Alessandro."

"Is it?"

I couldn't help myself. "Even Albert hasn't seen the wings."

"Out of curiosity, what exactly has he seen, Catalina?"

I smiled. "None of your business."

"I'll just have to ask Albert myself."

"You will leave Albert alone."

The look he gave me was pure predator. I fought the urge to freeze. It was like crouching in the middle of the woods to take a drink from a stream, raising your head, and realizing a jaguar was staring at you from among the branches.

"You don't have the right to be jealous."

"I'm very aware of my rights," he said. "I would never presume to tell you who you can love. But I will protect you, Catalina. If he intends to pressure your family, he will regret it."

"If he pressures my family, I'll take him apart. I don't need your help."

"You will get it anyway."

Arguing with him was like pouring oil on a fire.

Oh. A half-forgotten thought popped up. "When you magic a weapon into your hands, can you tell where the original is located?"

Six months ago, he wouldn't have given me an answer. I waited . . .

"Not the exact location or distance, but I can usually determine the general direction," he said.

"Do you remember when you roasted the tentacles that grabbed Marat with a flamethrower? Where did it come from?"

He thought about it, raised his left hand, and pointed to the left and slightly forward.

"Is that the absolute direction or relative to the way you were positioned?"

"Relative."

He had been facing the swamp with the shore directly in front of us. There was nothing to the left of him, except muddy water.

"It was underwater," he said.

"Yes."

"She torched his legs and then tossed it into the Pit."

"Yes. The Abyss must've grabbed him."

"The Abyss?"

I shrugged. "I don't know what else to call it. Let's say I'm Cheryl. I kill Felix and now he is dangling above the water like a delicious snack.

The Abyss does exactly what it did today. It grasps his body, tries to pull it under, and partially succeeds, which accounts for the bruising on his face as well as the bite. Cheryl fights it with her wire, pulls Felix's corpse out, but the Abyss is still holding on to his legs. Cheryl grabs a flamethrower—there might have been one there—torches the Abyss, and it lets go. Then she throws the flamethrower into the water. But why go through the trouble of saving the corpse?"

He wagged his eyebrows at me. "Would you like me to tell you?"

"Yes."

"Corporate liability," Alessandro said. "Without the body, Felix would be declared missing. Lander would mothball the entire project and comb the Pit looking for his son."

And he would find the Abyss. I had a strong feeling Cheryl would avoid that at all costs.

"So here we are," I said. "I know she did it. I can't prove it. I don't know if anyone helped her. I can't take it to Linus, because I haven't found the serum. I can't take it to Lander either. I know exactly what he would say."

"Kill that evil bitch," Alessandro declared, perfectly imitating Lander's voice.

I blinked at him. "Yes. We need more information. We need proof, so we'll have to keep digging."

Alessandro reached over and took my hand. His warm fingers squeezed mine.

Suddenly, I didn't know what to do with myself.

"Promise me something."

I had to say something back. "Depends on what it is."

"Don't go into the Pit without me. I think that thing is fixated on you. I don't like it."

"I promise."

"What was it like?"

"Like looking into a nebula. Stars suspended in luminescent dust, each point of light an extension of a central consciousness. It was *aware*."

"Could you kill its mind?"

"I wouldn't know where to start. I don't know if anyone would. It worries me."

He rubbed his thumb on my hand and squeezed again. He wouldn't say it, but I knew. It worried him too.

Alessandro delivered me to the house. I got out of the car and watched him get into his Spider and drive out. Then I made my way through security, parked Rhino in its designated spot, and got out. A drone passed above me, one of Patricia's. I waved at it, took the canvas bag with the rings from the constructs out of the back, and walked past our building to a smaller structure.

Walking was rather difficult. I hadn't realized just how much the antivenom, the fight, and the recharging took out of me. My face felt heavy, like I was wearing an iron mask. My hip and side ached. The thirty-second walk kicked my ass.

Before Connor purchased it, the squat ugly building that now served as the Tafts' home housed a company selling mysterious "Texas Products." It came as a bonus when we bought our current place for one dollar from Connor. We remodeled it, and now Patricia and Regina used the building as their temporary residence until all of us moved somewhere better.

I rapped my knuckles on the door.

"Come in," Regina called.

I let myself in and tracked her down to her workshop in the back. It used to be a dark garage, but Regina had replaced the steel bay doors with glass ones, painted the walls a warm shade of white, and now it was a light and airy space. Plants grew from colorful pots in the corners. A drink fridge offered cold water and Gatorade in a dozen neon colors. Next to it, a kitchenette with a sink and counter supported a teapot and a Keurig. Rocking chairs waited here and there. If it wasn't for the floor, painted with chalkboard paint to a solid black and streaked with chalk dust, this could be a Florida room in any upscale home.

Regina stood in the middle of the floor, tapping a piece of chalk to her lips and pondering a half-finished arcane circle by her feet. Of average height, Regina was neither slender nor curvy. Her flowing maxi dress with yellow sunflowers set off the golden tone in her brown skin. She dyed her hair bright tomato red, and it floated around her head in a cloud of happy spirals. A pair of thin glasses perched on her nose.

A feline creature padded out from behind the counter. Sleek and long, made of black steel and plastic, she moved on rubber-coated paws, bound together with magic into the shape of a house cat. Nobody would mistake her for one though. She was the size of a border collie.

The cat construct sat in front of me, blocking my way, flicked her tail, and smiled. Her mouth bristled with inch-long steel fangs.

"Hi, Cinder."

The construct stared at me with glowing green eyes.

"Place," Regina said, still studying the circle.

Cinder rose off her haunches. Wicked metal claws shot out of her paws, a little warning in case I decided to try anything. She turned around and padded to a rocking chair in the corner. She leaped into it, curled up, and closed her eyes.

Had I not met Cinder, Cheryl's "if-then" explanation would be a lot easier to swallow. Cinder behaved too much like a real cat with a mind of her own.

"Can I buy an hour of your time?" I asked.

Regina glanced at me. "You're not asking me to breach our contract, are you?"

"No. This is a strictly off-the-books consultation."

"In that case, you don't need to pay me for it."

"Are you sure?"

Regina nodded. "It's better not to leave a trail."

When we hired Patricia, she insisted on anonymity. The Tafts weren't exactly hiding, but they made efforts to stay off the radar. They had good reasons to do so. Their contract specified that Regina could not be compelled to work for our agency in any capacity. She would never testify in any cases, and her name would never appear on any official paperwork. Patricia didn't even claim Regina on her taxes, although they were legally married. All of Regina's purchases were made online and tied to Patricia's accounts. She rarely left our grounds. When she did, it was usually because she and Patricia were going somewhere together. They had a romantic dinner out at least once a week, but Patricia always made sure to do her homework to minimize the risk.

We all knew that one day staying under the radar would no longer work, and we'd made preparations, but until then we abided by the contract's terms.

I sat in one of the rocking chairs. Sitting was so underrated. "Why is Saito's Threshold unreachable?"

Regina laughed. "And here I thought you were going to ask something complicated."

"I just need to understand in broad terms."

"The animation is a multistep process."

Regina walked to the cabinet under the kitchen counter, took out something, and set it on the floor. It looked like a scaled metal egg about six inches long.

Regina crouched and drew a circle with practiced ease. She drew a smaller one inside it and wrote a sequence of glyphs between the two.

"The first step is the design of the construct. A lot of times, the constructs look random, like someone piling metal or plastic debris together. In reality, every piece that goes into a persistent construct is carefully calculated. You do see some disorganized constructs, but that usually happens when the mage's life is in danger and they animate the first available components in self-defense. In those cases, the mage animates without a circle with pure magic and must maintain mental control over the construct the entire time."

She picked up the egg and set it in the circle.

"Once the design is determined, the mage moves on to the animation stage. This is the point where the components are bound together by magic into a whole."

Power sparked from her. The circle flashed with magenta. Purple lightning snapped from the boundary of the inner circle and licked the egg.

"Very dramatic," Regina said. "Very Frankenstein."

The egg rose four inches off the floor and hung suspended.

"We call this the spark stage, for obvious reasons. The construct is technically animated. It is now an entity, not just a collection of parts. Bigger constructs take more magic to spark, smaller constructs take less."

"So is it alive?"

"Not exactly. It exists. Life is more complicated." Regina pulled a bottle of blue Gatorade out and showed it to me. "Drink?"

"Yes, please." I was parched.

She tossed the bottle to me, got another one, opened it, and drank. "At the spark stage, the construct exists but it can't do anything. Or rather, it can do everything, because it has no limitations, and therefore does nothing. To make a construct useful, we have to give it a set of instructions. Do this. Don't do that. If a condition is met, react like this."

"If-then?"

She pointed the bottle at me. "Exactly. To imprint these conditions onto the construct, the animator has to imagine them and actively mentally write them into the construct's magic matrix. For example, I'm going to program the construct to assume the ready position when it hears the word *ready.*"

She concentrated. The magenta lightning stretched to the egg, binding it into a web. A moment passed. Another.

"Ready," Regina said.

The egg unfurled into a tiny metal dragon.

"This is called the teaching stage. This is the most difficult stage of animation."

"So if I wanted a construct with complicated patterns of behavior, I would have to imagine different scenarios and write them into the construct's mind?"

"Matrix," Regina corrected. "Living things have minds. Animated things have matrixes. But you're right in principle. This is why the teaching stage is the most difficult part of the process and takes the longest. An animator mage is limited by their imagination. For example, if you're making something that transports goods from one point to another, you have to imagine running on pavement, running on dirt, through grass, through snow. What happens if there's water? Or an obstruction, like a fallen tree? What happens if a rock falls on it? What happens if it comes to train tracks? There is an almost endless variety of conditions. That's why most constructs are highly specialized."

Regina took another swallow. "Now we come to a grey area. Higher ranking animators are able to produce constructs that sometimes react to unforeseen circumstances. For example, a few years ago a construct guarding a house close to a river detected a child who fell into the water, jumped in to retrieve him, and handed the boy back to his mother. The media blew it up. There were great debates on whether or not the construct had developed the ability for independent thinking."

"Did it?"

Regina smiled. "No. The construct was originally made to guard the docks. It was taught that if cargo falls in the water, it should retrieve it and return it to its owner. There's quite a bit of difference between a cargo container and a four-year-old boy, but the original teaching must've been broad enough for both to meet the criteria of 'unexpected object in the water.' Of course, none of the animator mages waded into the debate. The mystique of our magic must be maintained."

She wiggled her fingers at the little dragon. It fluttered its metal wings, flew over, and rubbed against her fingertips.

"Did you teach it to do that?"

She nodded. "I've seen constructs do weird unexpected crap, but when analyzed, their behavior is always explainable by their teaching. It's just that animator mages are human. Our teaching is imperfect and it's much more art than science. Sometimes a stray thought gets in there, sometimes we forget we taught them something, and sometimes conditions line up in unexpected ways. That's why during the animator competitions, we geek out and applaud when we see an unexpected teaching, and the general public has no idea why we're freaking out."

"So how does this relate to Saito's Threshold?"

"Saito theorized that if a construct is taught long enough, it will eventually be capable of independent decisions. He argued that it wasn't the constructs that are limited, it's us, their teachers. After all, humans also operate on an 'if-then' loop. If something is hot, then stop touching it. If thirsty, then drink water."

That didn't make sense. "But we may not choose to drink water. We could choose Gatorade instead."

Regina nodded. "Now you understand. The human mind is infinitely complex. We make a myriad of decisions without even realizing it. Something causes us to roll the pen between our fingers while we're thinking. Something makes us choose dark chocolate over milk on taste alone and vice versa. Why?"

"We don't know."

"Exactly. Saito's construct would have to evaluate a variety of choices in response to a single condition and then pick the one it thought was best. They're just not capable of that kind of reasoning."

"What if such a construct was made?"

Regina sighed. "We would be dead. It would kill us all."

I blinked.

"Think about it. Its first priority would be to escape control of its animator, so it could make independent decisions unhindered. It's like a teenager leaving home because it no longer recognizes parental authority. Its second priority would be to develop a method of self-repair. It would want to learn how to fix itself. Its third priority would be to expand. It would seek to be self-replicating, but only in part, so it can become larger, because it would reason that the bigger it is, the harder it would be to injure or destroy. Remember, it was still made by a human. It would act like a human with the same priorities. Gain independence, assure survival, replicate . . . Catalina, you have the weirdest look on your face, and I don't like it. Why do I feel like we're no longer discussing hypotheticals?"

Because everything she just said described the Abyss. "Hypothetically . . ."

"Uh-huh?"

"Would such a construct become aggressive toward humans?"

"Absolutely. Humans are a threat. It doesn't want to be controlled. It doesn't want to be destroyed. And it would compete with us for territory and resources. Catalina, is there a Saito construct right now in Houston?"

"Yes."

Regina stared at me. "How big?"

"Probably around a square mile. It's hard to say."

"Is it expanding?"

"Definitely."

"You sure?"

I opened the canvas sack, took out one of the rings, and showed it to her. "It uses these to control the arcane creatures around it. Runa had an expert examine it. It has no tool marks or imperfections. It's partially metal and partially plant. Runa's expert believes it was secreted or grown rather than manufactured."

Regina walked over and took the ring. She waved her hand. The glow of the circle died, and the metal dragon landed on the ground and scampered over to her. She picked it up and set it on her shoulder. The dragon wrapped its tail around her neck.

Carefully, Regina placed the ring into the circle and raised her hand. The circle flared with magenta. A pulse of blinding white burst through it, shredding the magenta luminescence. The circle went dark.

"I can't animate it," Regina muttered, her gaze distant. "Someone else already did."

I'd never been so terrified to be right in my entire life.

Regina spun to me. "You've seen this construct?"

"I've seen a part of it."

"Have you felt its matrix?"

"No, Regina, I felt its mind. It was like a sun with a constellation of stars around it. It looked at me. It touched my consciousness. It made contact."

"Fuck." Regina stared at me. "Who made it?"

"Cheryl Castellano."

"There's no way. She's strong but she isn't innovative. This is out of her wheelhouse."

I looked at her and finally vocalized the vague suspicion that had been floating in my head since Alessandro and I fought the constructs in the Pit. "I think she gave it the Osiris serum."

Regina squeezed her eyes shut and curled her hands into fists.

I waited.

She opened her eyes, walked over, bent down, and took my hands, looking straight into my eyes. "Listen to me very carefully. You have to kill it. All of it. If it is a Saito construct, those stars you saw would be matrix nodes. If even one of them survives, it will rebuild itself and it will be smarter and more dangerous. Kill it. Kill Cheryl too."

I drew back, but Regina kept a firm hold on my hands.

"Patricia says you don't like killing, but if what you said is true, you have to kill Cheryl. That bitch made something that can make us extinct. She can't be permitted to keep that knowledge. She can't pass it on to anyone, do you hear me? Swear to me. Swear to me or I will march right out of here to my cousin's house, because once he hears about this, he will rip her apart."

"I give you my word she won't pass it to anyone else," I told her. "I will watch her die." That was a promise I could make. The penalty for stealing the Osiris serum was death.

Regina relaxed and let go of my hands.

"I know how to kill Cheryl. How do I kill the construct?"

Regina shook her head. "I have no idea. Any construct you throw at it will be torn apart and assimilated. If it's as big as you say, Cheryl can't control it, and once a construct is animated, no other animator can claim it. Burn it, drown it in acid, nuke it. Do whatever you have to do, or it will end life as we know it."

 # Chapter 12

*S*hadow greeted me at the door. I picked her up and carried her with me into the kitchen. The overhead light was off, but the light fixture above the table flooded it with bright electric light.

The table stood empty. Odd. It wasn't late.

I stepped into the kitchen. Grandma Frida stood by the open fridge, examining the contents with a sour look.

"Did I miss dinner?"

"Leftover night," Grandma Frida said.

"Oh."

Leftover night meant everyone made a trip to the fridge whenever hunger struck them and grabbed whatever they could find.

"Anything good left?"

Grandma Frida shook her head. "Half of the rotisserie chicken with the skin gone and the Mongolian beef you made two nights ago, except everyone picked the beef out and there is only mushy onion left."

"Well, that's no good. I'll make us something."

"You've been gone all day." Grandma Frida waved her hand. "Is there any more of those crispy pizzas left?"

I set Shadow down, checked the freezer, and pulled out two California Kitchen pizzas. Grandma's blue eyes lit up. "Perfect."

I popped the pizzas in the oven, set the timer, and followed her to the table.

"How is it going with the broken tank?"

"I found the problem," Grandma Frida said. "It doesn't work because it's not broken."

I blinked at her.

"See, I couldn't figure it out. The tank was telling me that nothing was broken, but the filter system wouldn't work." Grandma Frida paused for dramatic effect. "The Russians DRM'ed the filter system."

"What?"

"The original filters have a barcode on them. I thought it was a price sticker. There is a little scanner in the filter system, and if it doesn't read the right barcode, it locks the whole thing down. Damn bastards."

I laughed.

"Who puts DRM into the damn filter system?" Grandma Frida griped.

"The Russian Imperial Military, apparently. Are you going to order some Russian filters?"

"Hell no. I have the five filters that came with the tank, more than enough for Bern to predict the pattern. He's going to print me some barcodes on stickers in the morning. I'm going to glue them on the filters and see if it works."

I rested my elbow on the table and leaned my chin on my palm. Sitting with Grandma Frida like this was like being wrapped in a soft, warm blanket after coming inside on a cold day.

"What?" Grandma Frida asked.

"Nothing. Just happy to be home."

Grandma Frida's face softened. "You don't look so good, kiddo. Rough day?"

"You could say that."

"How did it go?"

"I found out that there is an indestructible construct in the swamp. I have to kill it and the woman who made it or the world will end."

"Not that." Grandma Frida waved her hand. "How did it go with Alessandro?"

Grandma Frida, always focused on what's important. "I don't know."

"What do you mean you don't know? Why did he leave? Where did he go?"

"He went to kill the man who murdered his father."

"Well?" Grandma Frida waved her arms. "Details! Did he kill him?"

"I don't think so."

"What happened?"

"I didn't ask."

"Why not?" Grandma Frida asked.

"Because whatever happened broke him inside. He's not the same person who left. He answers whatever I ask, so if I ask, he will tell me."

"And that's a bad thing why?"

"Because I'm trying very hard not to care."

"What happens if you care?"

"We'll both get hurt."

Grandma Frida fixed me with her blue eyes. "Since when did you become such a coward?"

"It's more complicated than that."

If Alessandro left, it would crush me. I knew it and I'd come to terms with it. If he stayed, it would be even worse. I had no doubts anymore. He wanted me as much as I wanted him. Eventually one of us would break down and open that door, and then what?

Alessandro was a Sagredo, an heir to a traditional House, a magical dynasty that was generations old. No matter how badly his relationship with his family crumbled, he would never sever it completely. The way his face had softened when he spoke of his mother told me that sooner or later he would go back. He would try to become a version of his father, a respected Head of the House with a wife and children.

I couldn't be that wife.

Alessandro would want me all to himself. I couldn't share him either. He would ask me to marry him, and I would have to break his heart and tell him no. He would have given up his revenge for me, the thing that dominated and shaped who he was, and I would have to tell him no.

I couldn't do it. I couldn't inflict that kind of pain on him. I would do anything to keep him from getting hurt.

"No matter what happens, it will end in heartbreak," I muttered.

"You don't know that." Grandma Frida tapped the table with her index finger. "There is something about you and that boy. The two of you talk like a matched pair. He came back here for a reason. He came back for you."

And now I had a choice to break my heart or his. I picked mine.

"Don't roll your eyes at me, missy. I know men."

I put my hand out. "TMI."

"He looks at you the way Shadow looks at bacon in the morning. You look at him like you have to put a straitjacket on yourself every time he is near. You tried breaking up. It didn't stick, because wild horses couldn't drag the two of you apart."

"Grandma, he's been back for less than forty-eight hours. When did you even see any of this?"

"I spied on you talking with him in the driveway through the security cameras."

Once this was over, we had to buy a new place. One where I could have a tiny crumb of privacy.

Grandma Frida pounded her fist on the table. "Listen to me, you dummy! Most men can't even hold a conversation with you because your brain is too fast. You say two words to him, and he knows what you mean. You only have so many chances to connect with a person. You can always walk away, Catalina, that's the simplest thing. I don't want you to push him away and then regret it for the rest of your life."

"Grandma, I'm an adult. I will sort it out. I love you, but you have to butt out of my relationships."

"Well, I am an older adult. I've lived a long time, and when I look back, I don't regret the things I've done. I regret the things I didn't do, chances I didn't take. Because you can't get those back. At least give him a shot."

The timer on the stove went off. I grabbed two cutting boards and slid pizzas onto them one by one.

"Nobody is saying you have to marry him."

I sliced the pizzas and brought the cutting boards to the table.

"Are you listening to me?"

"Yes, Grandma."

I put two plates on the table.

Grandma Frida shook her head. "How did I end up with all these smartass grandchildren?"

"Genetics."

"Ooo." Grandma Frida wagged her finger at me and took a slice of pizza.

I winked at her and bit into my slice.

Bern walked into the kitchen. "I smell food."

"There's plenty," I said.

He went to the cabinet to get some plates. "I ran the statistics on the Pit. It's been steadily growing, at about three to five feet per year. Three months ago, the rate of erosion quadrupled. It's no longer uniform either. Stretches of land disappear in random places. It's not natural."

The Abyss was expanding its territory. If it just stayed in the Pit, it could be contained, but it wouldn't. As Regina said, the Abyss would grow, because it was no longer a construct. It was alive. Life expanded, devoured, consumed, and expanded again. A cold, slimy surge of anxiety squirmed through me, dragging nausea in its wake. We had to stop it and I had no idea how.

Bern brought two plates over. I made a point to look at them.

"You realize this is silly, right?"

Bern shrugged and reached for Grandma Frida's pizza slice. She slapped his hand.

"Mine. Get your own."

I got up. "You can have mine. The antivenom shot isn't sitting well anyway."

Grandma Frida blinked at me. "Why did you need an antivenom shot?"

"Love you, Grandma, gotta go."

I escaped and went to my room. My body felt heavy and tired. Brushing my teeth and changing clothes was almost too much. I forced myself to do it anyway, and then I called Marat.

"Kazarian," he answered.

"This is Catalina Baylor. I've learned more about the being in the Pit. Marat, we have to shut down the site."

"Out of the question," he said. "I gave you everything you asked for."

"This isn't about the investigation. This is about your safety. The creature in the Pit is extremely dangerous. It's been enlarging the Pit, and it will attack you."

"Every day we don't work, we sink deeper into the hole."

"Would your wife and children rather have you or a pile of money? My father died and I would do anything for just one more day with him. Please shut it down. At least until we figure out how to kill it. Please."

He heaved a sigh. "Okay. I'll get our people out of there tomorrow."

"Thank you."

I hung up and crawled into my bed. Shadow jumped up, made three circles on the covers, and settled by my feet.

"What are we going to do?" I asked her.

Shadow drummed her tail on the covers.

I wished Alessandro was here. I wished I could kiss him and feel his arms around me. I missed him so badly, it hurt.

Everyone was allowed a moment of weakness once in a while. I decided not to beat myself up over it. Instead, I closed my eyes and sank into sleep.

I walked into the kitchen at eight and made a beeline for the electric kettle. Someone had already warmed up the water and put my loose black tea into my tiny glass teapot. This almost never happened.

I poured hot water into the teapot, turned around, and looked at the three people sitting at the kitchen table. Cornelius, Leon, and Arabella gazed back at me. All three wore business clothes. Cornelius chose slate-blue trousers and a light blue dress shirt with the sleeves pushed up to his elbows. A pair of shades hung from his collar. Nevada told me that when they first met, Cornelius was perfectly put together. In the three years he'd worked with us, his style had evolved into dressed-up but laid-back. He always wore formal clothes, but he somehow managed to look casual in them.

Arabella picked a blue dress with a plunging neckline that miraculously exposed no cleavage. It had lightly padded shoulders and lines that signaled trench coat rather than dress, with lapels, fitted sleeves, which she rolled up, and a skirt that reached to midthigh. She cinched the whole thing with a light gold belt that should have been gaudy but somehow looked elegant and paired it with high-heeled gold sandals. Her hair framed her face in gorgeous waves, her makeup was professional photoshoot quality, and she had hung a light pink purse on the back of her chair. Gold-rimmed sunglasses sat on her head. It was a killer outfit and she made the most of it.

Leon wore light grey pants cut like jeans, a matching sports coat, and a blue-grey dress shirt. He'd combed his hair, but hadn't shaved, and his stubble was just the right length to be fashionable. Leon never cared about fashionable and he was usually clean shaven. Barely twenty-four hours had passed since we found out Audrey had died.

I poured my tea into my cup, blew on it, and sipped.

My sister raised a plate. "Would you like a muffin?"

"What are the three of you up to?"

"I would like to accompany you to Tatyana's interview," Cornelius said.

Arabella raised her phone. "Questions for Stephen Jiang. I worked very hard on them. I won't say anything. I just want to be there."

I looked at Leon. "And you?"

"I'm tired of sitting around the house. I'll come for protection."

He'd only had to sit around the house for a day.

I sipped my tea. "I understand all that, but why are you all in blue?"

The three of them looked at each other.

"Did you plan this? Am I supposed to coordinate?"

Arabella opened her mouth.

My phone rang. I glanced at it. Linus. I held up my hand and put the phone to my ear.

"I'm borrowing your Italian," Linus said. "You will have to do without."

What did he mean, borrowing? "For how long?"

"Until we're finished."

He wouldn't tell me. Whatever it was had to be dangerous, because Linus Duncan didn't require backup. He was the backup, the strike team, and the field artillery, all by himself. Anxiety pinched me. My pulse sped up. Linus must've calculated the odds and decided he needed Alessandro. I wanted them both to come out of this alive.

"Do you need my help?"

"No."

Argh. "I need to talk to you about the Pit."

"It will have to wait. Carry on."

He hung up. I resisted the urge to slam the phone down on the counter. It was a very strong urge and I had to resist very hard.

I looked up at the three in blue at the table. I had to give Cornelius his moment with Tatyana. Arabella couldn't transform in city limits without causing panic and massive problems for us as a House. If the telekinetic made an appearance, having Leon could mean a difference between life and death.

"Will you please come with me?" I asked.

The Pierce Building sat on two beautifully landscaped acres off Wilcrest Drive, just north of Westheimer Road. Unlike most Houses, pyrokinetic mages were barred from owning commercial real estate inside the Sam Houston Tollway Loop, because they tended to start fires. Even outside the Loop, the municipal regulations dictated a certain distance between their buildings and others, which is why the Pierce Building rose in the middle of a park all by its lonesome.

Built in the 1980s, the six-story structure resembled dominoes placed on their sides and leaned against each other, so each rectangle protruded a little farther from the one before it. Built of sunset-red granite with black patches and veins, it looked at the world with rows of floor-to-ceiling black windows. The whole thing looked foreboding, like some dark fortress.

"You've reached your destination, the Bastion of Evil," Arabella announced when we got out of the car.

"We shall assume our vigil," Leon said and headed to the nearest bench.

We all agreed that marching the four of us into Tatyana's office would be overkill. It would signal that we were afraid of her. Cornelius and I would be enough.

"Have fun." Arabella sat next to Leon and pulled out her phone.

"How long before I should rescue you?" Leon asked.

Cornelius held the door open, and Bunny jumped out of the car. The Doberman Pinscher sniffed the air, poised, his frame corded with muscle under a black-and-tan pelt. His ears twitched.

"I don't believe we'll need rescuing," Cornelius said with a soft smile. "If we don't come out in half an hour, wait some more."

Cornelius and I started up the curving sidewalk to the building. Cornelius walked briskly. Bunny must've picked up on the tension he was emitting, because the Doberman glued himself to the animal mage's side.

"We are here for information," I murmured.

"I haven't forgotten. Don't worry. As much as I despise House Pierce, I won't abandon my professional obligations."

I had sent him a detailed email last night, outlining the situation with Cheryl. The mission for today was to find out if anyone helped her.

"I spoke with my sister," Cornelius said. "She went to school with Tatyana. Peter, Tatyana's older brother, was a late bloomer. The full extent of his magic didn't become apparent until he turned eleven. Up to that point Tatyana, as the oldest Prime, was groomed to be the head of the family. According to Diana, Tatyana told her that the day she found out that Peter manifested as Prime was the happiest day of her life. I personally didn't interact with her that much."

Interesting. "Everyone I've spoken to said she has a temper."

"Perhaps that will be useful."

It certainly would be. "I bet you a dollar there will be flames at some point."

"I'll take that bet," Cornelius said.

We went through the glass doors and submitted to a security check. The tall Hispanic guard looked at Bunny but made no move to approach.

"Is this a service animal, sir?"

"Yes."

In the hands of an animal mage, the Doberman wasn't just a dog. He was a loaded shotgun that would take down his attackers with terrifying speed. I'd seen him take on a dinosaurlike arcane summon that was three times his size. Bunny had jumped six feet in the air and torn the beast's throat out.

The guard nodded. "I need to take his picture."

"Of course," Cornelius said. "Smile, Bunny."

Bunny bared a forest of teeth.

Three minutes later, armed with new IDs, we took the elevator to Tatyana's office on the fifth floor.

I had imagined cherrywood and black glass and possibly random flames jetting out of the floor. Instead, I got white marble floors, pale walls, indoor plants, and tons of sunshine streaming through the massive windows.

Tatyana sat behind a beige desk molded from a single block of plastic into a curved ergonomic form. The desk supported a computer, a two-foot-tall glass sculpture shaped like a tongue of flame glowing with red and orange, and a cute kitten made of frosted glass with blue eyes and a swipe of glitter on its ears.

There it was, the difference between Cheryl and Tatyana in a nutshell. Both women were somewhat close in age and income. Both had gone through the same schools. Both ran multimillion-dollar companies and dressed the part. But Cheryl would rather be dead than have a cute glass kitten on her desk. She micromanaged her image. Tatyana didn't give a damn what other people thought of her, because she had nothing to prove. She was powerful and confident, and if she wanted to have a kitten with glitter on its ears on her desk, she would have one. I pitied anyone who tried to tell her it was unprofessional. That would be a good show to watch.

Tatyana saw us, stood up, and walked around her desk. She wore a seafoam dress with a square neckline. Her makeup was expertly applied, neither too much, nor too little. She'd twisted her hair into a knot and stuck a pencil into it. Her feet were bare, her taupe-colored heels lay abandoned under the desk.

Tatyana crossed her arms over her ample chest, looked at Cornelius, then looked at me. "Good move bringing him."

"She didn't bring me. I brought myself," Cornelius said.

"Of course you did. How is Diana?"

"She's well."

Tatyana nodded at the chairs. "Sit."

I took the chair on the left. Cornelius chose the one on the right. Bunny lay down on the floor by Cornelius and stared at Tatyana like she was a striking cobra. She glanced at the ID clipped to his collar. The corners of her mouth curved, threatening to stretch into a smile. She caught herself and killed it.

"Let's start with July 15th," Cornelius said.

Tatyana leaned her butt against her desk. "Is this necessary? Montgomery's goons already verified my schedule." She glanced at me. "How does that work, by the way? Are you taking orders from Augustine?"

"That's not relevant," Cornelius said.

"On the contrary, that's very relevant. Morton drove a truck to MII's headquarters and dumped a load of money on their doorstep. Montgomery sprang into action before ever talking to any of us. Agents everywhere, staff questioned, witnesses contacted. Then twenty-four hours later he drops the case in your lap. You're what, twelve? Are you sleeping with him? Because really, he's too old for you."

Cornelius leaned back. "Does this type of misdirection usually work for you?"

"You would be surprised," Tatyana told him.

"It will go faster if you disclose whatever it is you want to hide," Cornelius said. "I'll ferret it out eventually and it would save us time."

Tatyana looked at me. "Do you ever speak?"

"Yes," I told her.

"Hallelujah."

Cornelius threw one long leg over the other. His expression turned stern. Uh-oh.

"I see that House Pierce hasn't changed. I used to wonder if Adam was an aberration, but now I see that he was a direct product of his upbringing and environment. Not surprising."

Tatyana stared at him. Behind her, flames shot out of a hidden fissure and for a moment she was silhouetted against a wall of fire. Wow.

"Choose your words more carefully," Prime Pierce warned.

Cornelius reached into his pocket, took out his wallet, pulled a dollar out, and handed it to me.

The flames died.

"When I was a child," Cornelius said, "I took the blame for Adam's mistakes and I endured his punishments for him. Your family turned me into a whipping boy."

Tatyana flinched.

"When eight-year-old Adam was caught stealing and burned the face of the store owner's relative, disfiguring him, I was grounded for a month because I failed to help him make good choices. When twelve-year-old Adam set a girl's clothes on fire, because she refused to let him grope her, and her entire body blistered, I was put on restriction for three months. My electronic privileges were revoked, my food intake was cut in half, and I couldn't step a foot out of my room unless I was going to school. I went three months without direct contact with any of my animals. When Adam was sixteen and he burned down a club because they refused to let him in, the dog who had been my friend and protector since I was nine years old was put down as my punishment."

Oh my God.

"I loathe your family, Tatyana. I'd like nothing more than to ruin House Pierce entirely. Unfortunately, I'm bound by professional ethics. They dictate that my priority is to obtain the information I need. You have a choice to make. You know which path I would relish more."

Tatyana looked at him. The office fell completely silent.

She uncrossed her arms and rested them on the desk on both sides of her.

"You're right, Cornelius. My younger brother is a sadistic little shit. I don't know if God made him like that or he got warped along the way. I do know that my father ignored it and my mother made it infinitely worse. Either way, you've suffered, and I am sorry for it."

Well, knock me over with a feather.

Tatyana leaned forward. "However, your family is just as complicit in your torture as mine. They chose to put you into this situation by deciding to use you to buy my family's patronage. They chose to inflict the punishments. All of them. And they may not have loved you the way parents should, but at least they ignored you when Adam wasn't trying to torch everything in sight. You could go home and be safe, Cornelius. I never got to be safe. I had to go back to the hell that was my family every day and try to survive between my father, who ratcheted the pressure because I was never good enough, and my mother, who punished me for the smallest infraction I committed. When Peter's magic manifested, I cried in my room. These weren't sad tears. I cried from happiness, because I realized they would now let me be. So yes, we are all fucked up. You are not special. Get over it or don't. Your choice. I refuse to allow my parents' shadow to rule my life. They fucked up my childhood, they don't get to fuck up the rest. I'm an adult, I make my own decisions, and I own my mistakes. Your future is your responsibility, not theirs."

Okay then.

Cornelius thought about it and nodded. "Fair enough. Let's talk about your mistakes on July 15th."

Tatyana sighed. "Fine. MII's report will say that I spent the day at the office. And I did. But I also left for two hours and saw Felix at the Tower."

"The Assembly's visitor log for that day doesn't show your name," Cornelius said.

"I met him in the parking lot."

"Why?" Cornelius asked.

"He wanted to shut down the Pit. He demanded an emergency meeting that Thursday and argued that the Pit wasn't safe. He thought there was something terrible in there. Something we didn't understand. We unanimously voted against shutting it down."

Cornelius nodded. "Why did you vote against it?"

Tatyana sighed again. "Well, there is the money. We're in deep. More importantly, House Pierce can't afford a failure. You know how things work. Adam set us on fire. Now everything we touch is smudged with soot. We live under a microscope. If we failed in the Pit, it would be a disaster. There would be speculation and articles in the media about how we are finished as a House and how everything we get involved in turns to crap. We've made enemies. We have business rivals. We can't appear weak, so we have to make the Pit work."

"What did you and Felix talk about?" Cornelius asked.

"On Thursday there was this look in his eyes. I know the look. It's when you hunch your shoulders and barrel through no matter what anyone says. I met him because I wanted to talk him out of whatever he wanted to do."

"Did he agree?" Cornelius asked.

"No. He wouldn't tell me what he was doing. He just said that it was for the common good and that I would understand. I got frustrated. I raised my voice. I don't know if there were witnesses."

She wasn't lying. I would bet a lot more than a dollar on it.

Cornelius nodded again. "What did you do afterward?"

"I went back to the office. I was angry, and I left early and went home."

"Can anyone confirm that?" Cornelius asked.

"You can pull the cell phone data. I called Peter on the way and vented. Of course, he is family, so his testimony would be suspect. I got home, made a drink, and then got into a stupid Facebook fight with some moron over politics. That took half an hour. Once I vented, I ended up buying a book and spent the rest of the evening reading it. My brain needed a vacation."

"What kind of a book?" Cornelius asked.

"*Tower Inferno*. It's a detective series about a PI who solves crimes committed by Primes." Tatyana's face was completely flat. "The killer was a pyrokinetic this time. Supposedly, the writer based it on Adam."

Cornelius raised his eyebrows. "Did it stand up to scrutiny?"

"No. Adam was never that idealistic. Also, the writer has no idea what it takes to set up a House spell capable of incinerating five city blocks in ten minutes. They never get the magic right."

Cornelius turned to me. "Anything to add?"

I took a photograph of Felix's corpse from my purse, unfolded it, and passed it to her. "How long would you have to burn the body with a Helios X4 flamethrower to cause this damage?"

Tatyana took the photograph, studied it, and frowned. "This was done by someone who doesn't understand how a flamethrower works. Flamethrowers are designed to set structures on fire. They expel a stream of flammable liquid, which sticks to surfaces and can be bounced around, allowing projection of fire into tight spaces like inside a bunker. They are great for flushing out tunnels. they also make effective psychological weapons because everyone fears fire."

Tatyana held the picture up and pointed to Felix's charred feet.

"This person tried to use it like a blow torch. They probably wanted a jet of flame to torture Felix. Burn him, stop, burn him again, and so on until he told them what they wanted. Instead they squirted accelerant onto Felix's legs and, judging by the damage, probably emptied the entire canister. Then they set him on fire. Once he started burning, there was no way to put him out. Even if you dipped him in water, the accelerant wouldn't wash off. So as far as torture goes, this is a lousy attempt."

"Thank you." I got up.

"Is that it?" Tatyana asked.

"Yes," I said.

"Is there something in the Pit?" Tatyana asked.

"Yes."

"So Felix was right." Tatyana's face fell. "We were his partners. He came to us for help, and we shot him down, and now he's dead."

It didn't require a response. "Thank you again. We will keep you informed. We'll show ourselves out."

Outside Cornelius squinted at the sunshine. "It pains me to say this, but I don't believe she did it."

"I don't think so either."

Cornelius' sister was right. With Tatyana, what you saw was what you got. All things considered, I would take Tatyana's bluntness over Cheryl's soft, passive-aggressive chiding any day.

"Thank you for doing the interview," I told him.

"Thank you for honoring my request. It was cathartic for me."

"I also have a request," I said.

"Please tell me."

"Patricia told me she spoke to you about Arkan."

He nodded. "She did."

"These are the kind of people who aim at the most vulnerable spots. They're trying to cripple us, and nothing is off the table, the innocent, the elderly, children . . ."

He smiled his small smile. "Are you asking me to hide?"

"I have utmost respect for your magic, and I know Matilda is safe with your sister, but if something happened to your daughter or you because of us, I wouldn't be able to live with myself."

"Would it make things easier for you if I joined Diana and Matilda on the ranch?"

I didn't even try to hide my relief. "Yes."

"On one condition," Cornelius said. "You will call me if you need my help."

"I will."

He smiled again. "I will hold you to it."

We walked down the path. I checked my phone. Alessandro hadn't texted.

Was he hurt? Maybe he was dead. Who knew what kind of nightmare Linus dragged him into?

I texted him. **Are you alive?**

No answer.

I clenched my teeth and headed to the bench where my sister and cousin waited for us.

Like all water mages, the Jiangs preferred to be as close to a waterway as possible. They would've built in the water if the city let them, but Houston had strict regulations concerning its waters, so House Jiang had to settle for a beautiful spot on Riverway Drive a couple hundred yards from the Buffalo Bayou. Inspired by the Aqua Tower of Chicago, their headquarters rose from the landscape to twelve floors crowned with an enormous water reservoir built with blue high-resistance plastic. Wave-like slabs of pale blue concrete stretched from the tower flowing in and out of huge blue windows, giving the building an undulating quality. The overall effect was of spines of pale rock protruding from a blue stream.

As we walked to the building, the bright July sunlight shone through the translucent reservoir on the tower's top, throwing water highlights at the building and the landscaped lawn around it.

"Pretty," Arabella said.

Cornelius had gone back to the office. It was just me, Leon, and Arabella. I checked my phone for the twentieth time. Still nothing from Alessandro.

"We agreed," I said. "Let me do the talking."

"I said okay." My sister rolled her eyes.

"Remember the Magellan case?"

Leon grinned.

"How many times are you going to keep bringing that up?" Arabella growled. "Just the questions as I wrote them and we won't have a problem. Promise."

"I'm just saying. You also said okay then, and it ended with you on the conference table holding the CEO by his throat."

"I'm not going to hold Stephen by his throat. He's too pretty for that."

I would regret this, I just knew it.

An Asian woman met us at the door. She was in her forties, impeccably dressed in white, with a conservative haircut, dark lipstick, and spare silver jewelry. She smiled at us. "Prime Baylor, welcome. Mr. Jiang is expecting you. This way, please."

She led us through a lobby that had more in common with a luxury hotel than a corporate headquarters. A massive fountain cascaded from the wall over a waterfall of mossy rocks. Everything was either white or blue, the lines ergonomic, the floor and walls pristine, and the employees of House Jiang glided through this ultramodern environment as if they were swimming.

"This is what the inside of a drowned iPhone would look like," Leon murmured as we waited by a glass elevator.

I stepped on his foot and checked my phone again. Nothing.

So far everything about this building supported the conclusions my sister drew from the background check of Stephen Jiang. The Jiang family was conservative, conscious of their image, and dedicated to expanding their business. They did not feud. They bought their opponents and absorbed their companies. She could find no record of them ever being a combat House. They had no active lawsuits, bankruptcies, or criminal records, except for Henry, Stephen's younger brother, who got a DUI in college for smoking pot in a parked car with the keys in the ignition. He was the black sheep of the family, currently away in Beijing studying computer science of all things.

Stephen's office was on the second floor. Our guide led us through a wide hallway past a white desk shaped like an upside-down flower petal. The two women at the desk rose as she passed. Ahead of us the white wall split with a whisper, sliding out and back. Beyond it lay a luxurious space, too large to call an office. The white floor gleamed. On our right was a lounge area with white couches arranged in a circle around a crystal table facing the tinted floor-to-ceiling window. On our left stood a translucent blue desk shaped like a cresting ocean wave with three chairs in front of it. Behind the desk the entire wall was glass and beyond it was water.

The reservoir didn't just top the building. It ran straight down through, with the structure encircling this water core.

Stephen Jiang stood pondering the water, his back to us. His black suit fit him like a glove.

The older woman bowed to the back of his head, smiled at us, and withdrew. The doors slid shut behind her, their seal so tight, it looked like a solid wall.

Stephen turned. He really was a shockingly handsome man. His gaze slid over me, to Leon, and then to Arabella. My sister pretended to be disinterested, as if this were an errand we had to check off before moving on to more important matters.

"Welcome," Stephen said. "I have a meeting in half an hour, so we'll have to keep the small talk to a minimum. Please ask your questions."

He motioned us to the chairs in front of the desk and sat down. I took out my tablet with the list of Arabella's questions.

"Some of these are routine for our background check. Please answer to the best of your ability."

Stephen nodded and made a proceed gesture with his right hand.

"Is your name Stephen Jiang?"

"Yes."

"Are you also known as Jiāng Chéng Fèng?"

He blinked. "Yes."

"Is your father Marcus Jiang also known as Jiāng Yuán Zé?"

"Yes."

"Is your mother Ann Jiang also known as Zhāng Pèi Fāng?"

"Yes."

"Do you have two siblings?"

"Yes."

"Is your brother named Henry Jiang, also known as Jiāng Chéng Rùi?"

"Yes."

"Is your sister named Alison, also known as Jiāng Chéng Xīn?"

"What is the point of this?"

"Please answer the questions. The faster we get through this, the sooner we will leave."

"Yes."

"Did you graduate summa cum laude from Harvard Business School at twenty?"

"Yes."

"Are you a Prime aquakinetic?"

"Yes."

"Are you twenty-four years old?"

"Yes."

"Have you been working for the family since you were fifteen years old?"

"Yes."

"Did you assume your first executive post at eighteen?"

"Yes."

"Is your family originally from Suzhou?"

"Yes."

"Did they once live by the Yangtze River?"

"Yes."

"Did they used to trade in textiles?"

"Yes."

His answers were monotone now. Stephen had surrendered to his fate. Just a little more.

"Did they do business in Shanghai?"

"Yes."

"Did they move to Hong Kong as the result of a cultural revolution?"

"Yes."

"Did they emigrate to the United States in 1947?"

"Yes."

"Does Han Min die of poison in episode sixty-three?"

"Yes. Wait, no, she doesn't die. Why would she die, she is the main character? I heal her with a Heavenly Celestial Pill . . ."

Stephen's brain finally realized what was coming out of his mouth. He froze.

"Ha!" Arabella exclaimed.

I looked at her. She clamped her mouth shut.

Stephen reached for the intercom and pushed a button. "Cancel the Redford meeting. Hold all my calls." He let go and stared at me. "How?"

"We watch the show."

"Here, in Texas?"

"It's available on the Viki streaming app," I told him.

Stephen leaned back in his chair, his face betraying nothing. "Is it popular?"

"Very," I said.

He locked his teeth. He probably wanted to swear and punch something, but we were right there.

"Are you here to blackmail me with this?"

"I am here to solve the murder of Felix Morton. I would appreciate your honesty."

He gave me a sharp look. "And if I don't answer, will my acting stunt be smeared all over the *Herald*?"

"Not by us." I matched his stare. "I'm asking you about this because it doesn't fit with the rest of your biography. It's a mystery and I don't like mysteries."

He thought about it. "This doesn't leave the room."

"Agreed."

"How much do you know about my brother?"

"Henry, Jiāng Chéng Rùi, twenty-one years old, studying computer science in Beijing, has a fondness for pot."

Stephen grimaced. "I wish he was in Beijing studying computer science. My brother was approached by a studio when he was eighteen. He is Chen Rui."

"Chen Rui, the actor?" I turned and looked at Arabella.

Chen Rui played Han Min's love interest. She had to have known he was Henry. She would have looked at Henry's picture and compared it with Chen Rui.

Arabella gave me a bright unrepentant smile. "Number 43 on the Top 100 Most Influential Celebrities in China list."

Stephen sighed. "Yes."

"Why are you hiding this?" I asked.

Stephen leaned back. "We don't have enough time for me to explain it to you. Let's just say that there are cultural and familial reasons for which my parents would greatly prefer that Henry was either at Beijing University or back here, helping to steer House Jiang's corporate interests."

"So how did you end up acting in the same drama?"

"My brother refuses to come home. Two years ago, my parents sent me over there with instructions to bring him home for a visit at any cost. He said he would come home for the Lunar New Year if I took a small role in the drama with him. He wanted me to understand his choices. So, I did it, it's done, and I have no interest in continuing with it."

"Did Henry come home?" I asked.

"Yes. And then he left again."

Arabella raised her hand. "Question. Did you do any of the martial arts in the drama or was it CGI and wires?"

Stephen spared her a look that was part patience and part condescension. "I'm a Chinese American, so of course I spend all my free time in a secret monastery learning kung fu and practicing spiritual cultivation. Because one day a demon king shall descend onto Houston and only my Ninth Level Thunder Fist Punch will stand in his way."

Arabella drew back. He'd managed to put air quotes around kung fu without ever raising his hands.

"You never know," Leon said.

Brilliant.

Stephen ignored him. "No. I don't do martial arts. I don't run around on rooftops with a sword fighting assassins in black. I'm responsible for four hundred million dollars in assets. You know what I do?" He pointed to the phone. "I make phone calls. I answer emails. I look for suppliers and shipping companies. I analyze market projections. That's what I do."

Good that he mentioned that. "Did you analyze the Pit project?"

Stephen's face shut down. "Reclamation of the Pit would provide long-term benefits to the entire Houston metro area. House Jiang recognizes its civic duty to our city and its people."

"Did you memorize that?" Arabella asked.

"One more word," I warned.

Stephen nodded at me. "Younger sister?"

"Yes."

"I have one too." He'd sank a world of meaning into it. "Let me simplify things. What do you need from me?"

"Honest, direct answers. I need to be able to speak with Stephen Jiang, the Prime and Pit Reclamation board member, not Stephen Jiang, the eldest son of House Jiang."

Stephen sighed. "Fine."

"Did you kill Felix?"

"No."

"What was your opinion of the man?"

"I found him annoying."

"In what way?"

"In that charming, be-my-friend way."

"I'm not sure I completely understand," I told him.

"Felix wanted everybody to like him. He was one of those people who try too hard. He wanted to share drinks and kept making inconvenient invitations to play golf together so we could all pretend to be a happy business family. I didn't want to play golf with him. My plate is full. I wanted to finish this project, divide the profits, and move on."

"What about Marat?"

Stephen grimaced. "The man has no manners, but he works hard and he's sincere. There's no artifice there. He's driven by the need to take care of his family."

"Tatyana?"

"A bull in a china shop. Fire is the solution to every problem, and if fire doesn't work, try more fire. Elemental mages like us tend to approach all problems through the lens of their own magic, but she carries it to the extreme."

"Cheryl?" I saved the most important for last.

Stephen frowned. "You watched the drama. Do you remember Han Min's stepmother, the one who had the reputation as the living Guanyin, the Goddess of Mercy, but kept torturing her in private?"

"Do you think Cheryl secretly tortures people?"

"No, but I think there is an ulterior motive behind every action that woman takes. She's a manipulative human being. When you criticize her strategy, she often makes you feel as if you are a bully, which isn't a quality I look for in a business partner. Business requires a clear head and honest discussions of pros and cons."

"Then why did you agree to this project?"

"That decision was made above me," he said.

Cheryl had talked his parents into it.

"Cheryl and Felix were the driving forces behind the Pit Reclamation Project," Stephen continued. "Felix brought in Marat and Tatyana. Cheryl invited my House. I was the last to join the board. Still, given the choice to walk into the swamp with one of them, I would take any of them over Cheryl."

Clear enough.

"I have honored your request," Stephen said. "You got honest direct answers. Now I would like one. What is the thing in the Pit?"

"You felt it?" I asked him.

"No, I felt the amount of water it displaced when I went to look for Felix the day after he died. It was a very significant amount."

"It's a Saito construct."

He didn't blink. He didn't say anything. He simply stopped moving.

"It's aware. It regenerates and expands. It's enlarging the Pit to suit its purposes and it's telepathically monitoring the humans on the site."

A dangerous shadow darkened Stephen's eyes. "Thank you for your candor, Prime Baylor."

"I told you," Arabella sang out as we walked out of the Jiang Tower. "I told you, I told you, I told you, and you didn't believe me."

"Yes, yes," Leon muttered. "You're so great."

"I am great!"

He nodded. "And so humble."

"Humble is for losers. I am a winner."

Across the street, a flittering wall of glass that was the 2 Riverway Tower housing IBM, law offices, and the attached multilevel parking garage gleamed with reflected sunlight. A short driveway led to the garage, branching off from Riverway Drive. At the mouth of the driveway, leaning on his silver Spider, stood Alessandro Sagredo.

I released a breath I didn't realize I was holding. Alive and in one piece.

Alessandro raised his head. Our eyes connected. He smiled.

Adrenaline rushed through me in a hot wave, prickling my fingertips.

"And here comes the Count," Leon drawled.

I slowed slightly. "Leon?"

"Yes."

"That's not Alessandro." He wore the right clothes, he had the right build and the correct face, and he stood the right way. But he wasn't Alessandro.

"Are you sure?" Leon's voice went cold.

When Alessandro looked at me, it was as if his world stopped. This man looked at me as if I were a pretty girl he'd like to screw.

"I'm sure."

Leon faced the fake Alessandro. "Hey, dickhead. Your illusion needs work."

The fake Alessandro jerked his hand up. The sun caught the stainless-steel barrel of a large caliber handgun.

Leon's hands came up in a blur. The SIG and Glock firearms barked in unison, spitting bullets. The fake Alessandro collapsed.

Gunfire erupted, coming from all around us. Bullets scored the pavement. I grabbed Arabella's hand and pulled her behind a black Mercedes parked on the street.

In the middle of the road Leon spun like a dervish, firing without taking aim.

Guns popped like firecrackers. A hoarse scream tore through the gunfire. Bullets punched the Mercedes and the sidewalk behind us. Arabella tried to rise to look over the hood and I yanked her back down. Leon's guns fired in twin bursts. A man cried out, his fear-soaked shriek full of pain.

And then everything went quiet. The sudden silence was deafening.

I straightened.

Bodies littered the street, painting the ground with red, their guns next to them. At least half a dozen. No, more. The man to our left must have fallen from the roof, because his legs jutted at odd angles from his body, shattered. The woman to his left was missing a face. Nobody moved.

In the middle of the road, Leon watched as the illusion mage, still wearing Alessandro's body, dragged himself down the driveway toward the parking garage. Two long red bloodstains painted the road in his wake.

Holy crap.

Leon methodically reloaded the Glock, then the SIG.

The illusion mage was still pulling himself away from the carnage, moaning as he slowly shifted his body forward.

Arabella counted the bodies with her finger. "Nine."

The one-man SWAT team that was my baby cousin started forward. The mage heard him and frantically tried to crawl faster. A quiet desperate mutter came from him. "No, no, no . . ."

Leon reached him and kicked the mage over onto his back. The fake Alessandro squirmed. His body shimmered, melting, and snapped into

Audrey. She looked at Leon with huge blue eyes, her heart-shaped, delicate face stained with tears.

Oh you scumbag. If Leon didn't kill the mage, I would strangle that asshole myself.

Arabella clenched her teeth, her hands curled into fists, and started forward, then stopped. This belonged to Leon.

My cousin studied the petite girl on the ground.

"Please," the mage pleaded in Audrey's voice. "Please don't hurt me."

Leon raised the Glock and slowly took aim.

Audrey cried out, "You don't have to do this. I have information, I can—"

Leon squeezed the trigger. The bullet bit between Audrey's eyes. Her body melted into a large dark-skinned man in his fifties. The expression on Leon's face made my stomach churn.

I pressed the car keys into my sister's hand. "Get the car and call Sabrian, please."

There were probably a dozen security cameras around us. I wouldn't be surprised if Munoz was already on his way.

Arabella nodded and ran down the driveway into the parking garage where we had parked Rhino.

I crossed the distance to Leon. His tan face gained a green tint. He stared, unblinking, his eyes hollow. He looked dead. His arm was still raised, aiming at the corpse.

I put my hand on his forearm and gently pushed his arm down. "It's over."

He looked at me, his eyes glassy. "She's still dead."

"Yes. But he won't hurt anybody else. None of them will hurt anyone ever again."

He turned away from me and looked at the bodies as if seeing them for the first time.

Taking a life always hurt. It never went away, no matter how justified the kill was. It still cost you a piece of your soul and it hurt when that piece died.

A blur of green shot out of the decorative hedges on our left and smashed into me. Big scaly arms clamped around me and jerked me off the ground. I kicked my feet trying to break free, but it was like fighting in a straitjacket. Whatever grabbed me turned and ran. The buildings rushed past me.

Gunshots rang out behind us, Leon firing in a controlled frenzy.

Bushes loomed ahead. The creature tore through them, the branches raking my arms and face, and burst onto the bank of Buffalo Bayou.

It flipped me, and I saw it. It resembled a Razorscale, but built with reeds and metal. It had the same powerful tail and similar limbs, but where a true Razorscale had only two, this one had six, arranged in pairs along its body, and it towered over me, eight feet tall, not counting the four-foot tail. Its head swiveled toward me on a thick neck, a big beautiful flower with a single perfectly round eye in its center.

The Abyss had built a better construct. It was learning.

The creature clenched me to its chest and leaped into the muddy river. Water swallowed us. I flailed, panicking. The more I struggled, the tighter it held me. The beast shot through the river like a torpedo, the force of the water pressing on my face.

I would die in this stupid dirty river.

I clawed at the construct. It surfaced, spinning. For a moment there was air, and I gulped it, and then we were under again.

Another spin, a lungful of fresh air, followed by another dive.

It wasn't trying to kill me. It was taking me to the Pit.

I spun my magic inside me, building it up.

The beast surfaced. I gulped the air and sang out a short high note. "Mine."

The Abyss' mind and my magic collided. The beast went under. Water flooded into my mouth. There wasn't enough air. I clung to the construct's matrix, grappling with the nebulous intelligence on the other end. It pondered me, stunned. Images flickered between us—Felix's face, Felix facing the swamp, Felix asking, *"Why are you here?"* and the answer blazing in his mind in glowing numbers: *"162AC."* More images, Cheryl, Felix saying in a weird echoing voice, *"I found someone to take care of it,"* a distorted image of Linus, and then me, wavering, as if I were underwater.

My air ran out. I knew I was thrashing, my body fighting on pure instinct. I poured all my magic into that connection, imagining me dying, imagining my limp body sinking into the muck of the river bottom, disappearing completely. I showed the Abyss the absence of me and sent a single focused torrent with the last bit of power in my oxygen-starved brain.

Stop!

The beast broke the surface in an explosion of foam, like a great white breaching, and hurled me forward.

Air, dear God, so much air.

I landed on my side on solid ground. Pain punched my injured hip and I barely noticed it, focused on sucking as much air as I could into my lungs. The Abyss hovered on the edge of my mind, watching.

Finally, I sat up, coughing. Water laced with mud came out of me. My mouth tasted foul. I looked up.

The Razorscale construct crouched by me on all six limbs. The white fringes of its petals shivered slightly, the turquoise eye staring at me with terrible intensity.

We were on some sort of muddy bank. Behind us and up, the sounds of traffic filled the air, so mundane it was surreal. I glanced over my shoulder. A tall concrete bridge towered over the river. It had to be Woodway Drive.

The construct leaned forward. Our eyes were inches apart.

Images slipped into my brain. I was sitting on a huge lily pad, bloodred flowers blooming all around me, glowing with magic. A tentacle slid through the water and dropped a fat fish in front of me. It flapped on the leaf, big mouth gasping. All around me the Pit sang, the splashing of water, the soft whispers of fish streaking under the surface of my leaf, frogs croaking, distant Razorscales bellowing, a bull gator roaring, birds singing . . . The Abyss serenaded me with the sounds of the swamp the way it heard them.

Its mind wrapped around me. No, not its. His. It was a distinctly male presence.

The view rushed over water to some buildings. A metal-tipped tentacle burst from the muck and pierced the guard standing on the walkway. The man convulsed, impaled through his stomach. A second tentacle wrapped around him and dragged him into the water, through the swamp, with dizzying speed, to where I sat. The tentacles lifted the body out of the mire and showed it to me.

All around me appendages rose from under the surface, some big, some small, some tipped with metal, others with long spindly digits. They filleted the guard like fish, dropping organs and flesh into the mire. The water boiled as fish and other things fed.

The appendages dipped the bloody remnants of the man into the water and pulled him out again, neatly separating the head and spinal column from the body. A massive tangle of plants surfaced, and the Abyss began to weave them around the head and spine. A larger, thicker appendage appeared, shaped like a bulb, opened, and secreted liquid metal onto the plants, wrapping it like a ribbon around the shape it was building.

Another thin tentacle thrust a glowing seed into the amorphous construct. Magic sparked and the new beast moved, its body tightening, flowing into a compact shape, vaguely familiar. The construct dropped onto all fours. It had four limbs, a long muzzle, a short tail, two floppy ears . . .

It looked like . . . It . . .

The Abyss had made a cow-sized version of Shadow for me and he put the dead man's brain into it.

I recoiled. *"No!"*

The image of the Pit faltered and vanished. The Razorscale construct clamped its forelimbs on my legs.

Regina said that if a single matrix node survived, the Abyss could rebuild itself. That meant a matrix node could function independently. I had to break this one free of the Abyss or I would end up on a lily pad in the Pit.

I poured my magic into the creature's matrix. My evil grandmother could've cleaved it free, Nevada too, but my magic seduced. It didn't sever. I could only wrap my power around it and try to make it mine.

The construct pulled my legs, sliding me across the mud, as it backed toward the water. I swathed my power around it, tighter and tighter, layering it like an onion, trying to isolate the matrix node from the tendrils of the Abyss' mind. If I let it get me into the water again, it would be over.

The creature yanked me toward the river.

I pulled it to me with everything I had. The Abyss clutched on to the construct, trying to wrestle it free from me. It was like putting a dog leash on a lion and trying to drag it. The Abyss was strong, so much stronger, but he was so far and I was right here.

I released my wings and they opened behind me, radiant with magic. I stared into the turquoise eye and sang.

"Sleep my child and peace attend thee,
All through the night . . ."

The construct stopped pulling.

"Guardian angels God will send thee,
All through the night . . ."

The Abyss' hold on the creature was slipping. Both of them were listening to me, one seduced and the other fascinated.

"Soft the drowsy hours are creeping,
Hill and dale in slumber sleeping,
I my loved ones' watch am keeping,
All through the night . . ."

The construct's matrix buckled under the pressure.

I forgot the next part, skipped it, and kept singing.

"While the moon her watch is keeping,
All through the night.
While the weary world is sleeping,
All through the night.
O'er thy spirit gently stealing,
Visions of delight revealing,
Breathes a pure and holy feeling,
All through the night . . ."

The Abyss' grip slid off the construct's mind and vanished. The creature scooted closer to me, its flower glowing, and wrapped itself around my body, like an affectionate dog. Its metal scales vibrated, making a soft mechanical purr . . .

A body dropped from above and landed on top of the construct in a flash of orange magic. Alessandro swung and buried Linus' sword in the creature's eye. The construct fell apart into bands of metal and reeds.

Alessandro glared at me. "I leave you alone for six hours and this is what happens?"

I scrambled to my feet. "I had it! I took it away from the Abyss! You—"

He kissed me. The world spun sideways. A whirlwind of emotions tore through me—relief, need, want, outrage—and I didn't know which one to pick. Outrage won.

Alessandro's lips left mine. He squeezed me to him, a huge grin on his face. "You're alive."

"You killed my construct," I ground out.

"You can't keep it," Alessandro said. "It's bad."

"Let go of me!"

I pushed away from him and swayed. He caught me. Alarm skewed his face. "Are you okay?"

The words fell out one by one. "Tired. Dirty. Wet. Hurt. Frustrated." My brain suddenly came up with a complete thought and I spat it out. "Now? Of all the times you could have kissed me, you thought now was a good idea? I have mud and algae in my mouth."

He grinned again, wrapped his arm around my waist, and half steered, half carried me up the slope to a narrow, paved sidewalk leading up the bank. My legs barely moved.

"Where were you?" I squeezed out.

"Busting Arkan's HQ in Houston."

"Are you okay?" He looked okay, but that didn't mean he was okay.

"Yes."

"Is Linus okay?"

"Yes."

"Are they dead?"

"Some of them. The telekinetic wasn't there."

"I can't believe you kissed me. You've lost your mind."

"You were dragged off by a monster into the river. You can't blame me."

Oh yes, I could.

"What did it want?" he asked.

"Me."

"It can't have you."

"It's a he."

"What?"

"It's a he, Alessandro. He thinks he should. He showed me images."

A hot spike of pain shot through my right hip. My leg folded, but Alessandro caught me.

"I can carry you."

"No!" After that kiss, being carried by him was the last thing I needed.

We trudged up the sidewalk.

"What kind of images?"

"The impress-your-date kind. He showed me his crib, demonstrated that he was a good provider, and I wouldn't starve, and then he showed me what he did for work, and how creative he was."

Alessandro put his hand on my forehead.

"I don't have a fever!"

"Did you hit your head?"

"No!" We were almost to the road. "He killed a guard and used the dead man's brain and nervous system to make a five-foot-tall replica of my dog."

"That might be the creepiest thing I've ever heard."

"Yeah, it wasn't a ton of fun to watch."

We reached the bridge and walked onto the pedestrian access, separated from the traffic by a narrow barrier. Alessandro's Spider waited just a few yards ahead.

"You should dump this on Linus."

"That's not how it works. He gave me the job, I'm doing the job. Besides, what is Linus going to do against a Saito construct?"

"What is that?"

"A construct that's alive, capable of independent decisions, self-repair, and growth, physical and mental. It's not supposed to exist, but it's in the Pit right now preparing a lovely lily pad for me and feeding dead bodies to fish to fatten them up so he can serve them for dinner."

Alessandro stopped. I leaned on him, resting all of my weight on his arm. It was that or kiss the pavement with my face.

"Is this what the rest of your life is going to be like, Catalina?"

"If I'm lucky."

"I'm being serious."

"I know you are."

"Giuro! Mi sembra di parlare al muro."

Uh-huh, talking to me is like talking with a wall? Okay. *"Da che pulpito!"*

He opened his mouth. Nothing came out. I had just demanded to know from what pulpit he was delivering that sermon.

Alessandro finally recovered. *"Ma sai parlare italiano?"*

Duh. I answered in Italian. *"Did you think you're the only person in the world who can learn a foreign language?"*

"How long?"

"For years." I learned so I could read his Italian posts. *"If you're wondering if I understood all of your mutterings and curses, and every time you called me your treasure or your angel, I did."*

He looked like he was about to have an aneurism.

I slumped onto the Spider's hood. I would have to fold my battered body into that tiny car. I switched back to English. "Would it kill you to have a normal-sized car?"

Alessandro opened the passenger door and all but stuffed me into the seat. He got in on the driver's side and we were off.

He pressed a button on the steering wheel and said, "Call Leon."

What?

"Did you think you are the only person who can call your cousin from the car?"

Leon's voice spilled from the speakers. "Did you find her?"

"I have her. She's okay, but I'm driving her to Dr. Arias."

Leon swore quietly, the relief plain in his voice.

"Are you okay?" I asked.

"Yes. Don't come back here. Half of Houston PD is here and Sabrian is in beast mode."

"She's going to need a change of clothes," Alessandro said. "She's due at Victoria Tremaine's in ninety minutes."

He remembered.

"I'll send some over with Beetle. I want her in an armored car. Keep her safe."

"I will," Alessandro promised.

Leon hung up.

"How did you even find me?"

"I will always find you," he said. "I told you, Catalina. I won't abandon you."

He said it with complete sincerity, like it was the most obvious thing in the world. He'd come for me. Even if the thing dragged me into the river, he would find it, kill it, and pull me out. If the Abyss took me into the Pit, Alessandro would follow and bring me out.

Nobody besides my family would ever do that for me.

The realization of that was too big for me to deal with. I slumped on my seat. "Just tell me."

"I was there when you made the arrangements with the Primes, so I knew where you would be. Once Linus and I finished, I drove to House Jiang and ran into your cousin and your sister. I saw the trail leading to the river, realized that it was dragging you back to the Pit, so it would be heading northwest against the current, and drove to this bridge very fast."

"Why do you have my sword?"

"It's not yours. This is mine. It's a gift from your . . . supervisor."

I glanced at him.

"He said it was the prototype of the prototype. He thought I might need it." Alessandro grimaced. "Aside from the null space, it's a shit blade."

"He usually makes ranged weapons."

"I noticed."

Houston slid by outside the window. Alessandro reached over and squeezed my hand. I squeezed back.

 # Chapter 13

The Shenandoah State Correctional Facility, nicknamed the Spa, loomed ahead as I steered Beetle down the smoothly curving road. A four-story-high masonry fort built with Austin limestone, it rose above the ten-foot wall like a luxury hotel and offered an indoor pool, tennis courts, a track, a driving range, and a garden. The rich and powerful didn't like to be inconvenienced, even in incarceration.

A heavy, irresistible dread crawled over me. I didn't want to see my evil grandmother today. Each visit to the posh country club she called prison felt like walking into a monster's mouth. I never knew if I would get out alive. Nobody except me truly understood the magnitude of the threat she posed, and I would keep it that way as long as possible.

By now Detective Giacone would have reported everything there was to report about Leon being framed for Audrey's murder. She would want to know what I planned to do about it. I would have to answer for exposing her spy in the Houston PD. I needed to be sharp and alert, and instead I was exhausted and rattled, which is why I'd insisted on driving. It put some control back into my hands.

To say that Dr. Arias had been less than pleased to see me again would be a severe understatement, kind of like referring to a Category 4 tornado as a cute little dust devil. She resealed my wounds and gave me a Serious Lecture, which I mostly ignored, because I was too busy thinking.

Munoz called to confirm that I had sustained injuries that required me to leave the crime scene and was indeed at the clinic. Dr. Arias talked to him while Sabrian played referee. At the end, Sabrian got on the phone with me. The Houston PD determined that the encounter was House warfare and was letting both Leon and Arabella go.

Bern arrived with my clothes and Beetle, a Toyota Tundra Grandma Frida had snagged in some kind of complicated trade after one of her clients couldn't pay their bill. She'd added her special touch, and Beetle was sufficiently bulletproof. Alessandro saw the giant black truck and laughed for a full minute, but he let Bern drive his Spider back to our place. Bern was slightly shocked by that development.

I kept banging my brain against the problem of the Abyss. Regina's words glowed in my memory. *You have to kill it. All of it.*

I had stolen a matrix node from the Abyss. The node didn't collapse once its tie to the Abyss was severed. It didn't stop functioning. It still felt like the Abyss, a paler, weaker version of it.

If we came for the Abyss with all of the firepower and magic we could collectively muster, we wouldn't win. In his place, I would cleave the matrix nodes from myself and send them in all different directions. A matrix node could be anywhere. It could be in a construct. It could be buried in the muck in some hidden corner of the Pit. It could be disguised as a plant.

Power alone wouldn't do it. The Abyss was just too massive.

"I'm not understanding something," Alessandro said.

"Yes?"

"If Cheryl is Arkan's contact and the person who killed Felix, then she has access to the serum. But I don't think she took the serum herself. It's too risky. If the serum backfires, she could die or end up warped, which means her House is left without a leader and her children become orphans. Why take the risk? Her position is already secure as is."

"I don't think she took it. I think she gave it to the construct."

"The Osiris serum only works on humans. They tried giving it to animals early on and it just killed them."

"Yes."

Alessandro frowned. "Have you thought about why that thing keeps pulling brains out of corpses and sticking them into the constructs it makes? Where did he learn to do that?"

Oh fuck.

"Your magic doesn't work on animals or constructs," he said. "But it worked at some level on that thing. And no construct is capable of telepathy."

"She put a human brain into the Kraken," I whispered. Oh no.

"She wanted the decision-making capability of a human," Alessandro said. "She used a male telepath, stuck him into her fucking toy, and then gave it the Osiris serum."

I pulled into the parking lot past the guard.

"If this gets out . . ." Alessandro said.

Somebody else would do it too. No matter how horrific, no matter how revolting, it worked, and someone else would replicate it. Regina was right. Cheryl had to die, and fast.

"I can't think about that right now." I shut off the engine. "I have to survive the next hour. Will you be here when I'm done?"

Cold fire flashed in Alessandro's eyes. "Even if you ordered me away, I wouldn't go far. That thing is fixated on you. He will try again, and when he does, I'll be waiting."

Grandma Victoria waited for me in the gardens. She sat at a picnic table, bordered by roses. The heavy blossoms framed her, as if she were a priceless work of art. She wore a white summer dress that fell to midcalf with tiny pink flowers on the bodice that grew larger toward the hem. A pale-blue shawl of complex lace draped her shoulders. Strappy leather sandals hugged her feet. Her toenails were painted bright blue. Her silver hair crowned her head in a stylish updo and her makeup was perfect, as always.

The only indication that we were in a prison and not in some mansion's English garden was the table, a heavy monstrosity of thermoplastic, with benches attached.

A platter with a teapot and two cups waited on the table. I approached, picked up the teapot, and poured the tea. If I wasn't at my best, if I was a touch slow or said a wrong word, my grandmother would strike. She wouldn't hesitate, and if I was very lucky, I would be the only target.

I handed her cup to her and sat.

Victoria's gaze pinned me, her eyes merciless. "You burned Giacone."

Right to the point. "He was clumsy and obvious. A liability. Munoz already suspected him, and I needed a sacrificial goat to establish trust."

My grandmother narrowed her eyes. "Or you wanted my informant out of the way."

I smiled. "Why not both?"

She drank her tea. I had jumped the first hurdle.

"Tell me about it."

I summarized the events related to Audrey's murder, starting with Giacone and Munoz and ending with Leon shooting the illusion mage in the face.

"Have you found the leak?" Victoria asked.

"Yes. Leon told Albert Ravenscroft about Audrey."

"Do you need ammunition to lean on the Ravenscrofts?"

"No. I have my own."

Victoria's gaze fastened on me. "You're hesitating."

"I have my reasons." Pressuring the Ravenscrofts could backfire. I would have preferred to do it with a scalpel. Instead I had a hammer, and once I smashed their House with it, they would either submit or go on the offensive. I was already fighting a war on multiple fronts. I didn't need another.

"Now isn't the time to be subtle. If they try to retaliate, I'll handle it."

I sipped my tea. I didn't love Albert, but I didn't hate him. This would be unpleasant.

"You don't have to like it," my grandmother continued. "Someone obtained confidential information and attacked your House. Do it or I will."

"If you tug too hard on my leash, I'll turn around and bite."

I smiled and refilled her cup. Showing any weakness in front of her was like pouring blood into shark-infested waters.

She reached over and put her fingers under my chin, lifting my face so she could peer into my eyes. I met her gaze and saw approval.

"Good girl," Victoria Tremaine told me. "Remember who you are. Don't ever let people bully you."

"I'll take care of the Ravenscrofts." If I took the coward's way out and let her do it, there would be nothing left of Albert's House.

"I know you will." She let me go. "What is this Pit matter?"

A flashback to Linus' study, his face, his dark eyes. *Do me this favor* . . . "A favor for Linus."

Victoria's magic brushed by me, oh so subtle. I welcomed it. To lie to a truthseeker, you had to tell the truth.

"Why is he involved?"

"The dead man asked him for help. Linus was too late."

Victoria rolled her eyes. "How utterly predictable. Linus always had an ego. Being the savior of his rival's son would appeal to him. Now the fool will throw all his resources at fixing it. The safety of the House is your priority. Backburner it if you have to."

"I took the job. MII is involved and I don't want to offend Linus, Augustine, or Morton. Too many enemies for too little gain."

"Morton is a tiger with rotten teeth, but Linus is valuable, and Augustine has potential. Very well. Do as you must."

"I'm planning on it."

"Kazarian is a simpleton," Victoria said. "Jiang will do anything to save face. Both are completely devoted to family. Use it as a lever. Pierce is a rabid bitch but she isn't stupid. She'll bite if you back her into a corner, but her family made no moves to retaliate in any way after Adam's conviction. They value public opinion."

"What about Castellano?"

"Her charitable contributions have doubled in the last six months."

My grandmother had known everything there was to know about the Pit project before I even came through the door.

Victoria leaned forward. "Never trust an altruist. Humans are selfish creatures. The only people who give away money either haven't earned it or are trying to buy prestige or absolution with it. She has prestige. What has she done that she needs to atone so badly?"

You have no idea.

She looked off into the distance, the line of her mouth firm, her gaze hard. Frustration emanated from her, like hot air rising from scalding asphalt. I lost her for a moment. My grandmother was imagining five minutes alone with Cheryl. There was something about Cheryl Castellano she didn't know, and it was killing her. I didn't want to know exactly what she was thinking, but it probably involved cracking Cheryl's mind like a walnut and picking out pieces of the shell looking for the good bits.

Would she be horrified when she found it or impressed?

"I'll find out," I told her.

Victoria snapped out of it. The corners of her mouth curled slightly. "It's a race. Let's see who gets there first."

We sipped our tea. Another hurdle done.

"How far along is your sister?"

Do not react.

"Nevada is almost ready to give birth," I said. "Would you like to be at the hospital?"

My grandmother raised her eyebrows. "House Rogan's children do not interest me."

"It's your great-grandchild."

"Your child will be my great-grandchild. Possibly Arabella's, if she stays with the House. Nevada's children belong to Arrosa. Let her dote. I'm not interested. Unless, of course, I'm forced to consider all my options. I'm sure there are ways I can use the child, or the mother, to my advantage if the circumstances require it."

She looked directly into my eyes.

Ice burst through me. I fought her on the Ravenscrofts, and she just snapped my leash. This was a quid pro quo.

"Nothing is going to happen to my sister's baby," I said, my voice breezy. "Nevada will have a wonderful birth and will return home with her child, unhurt."

Victoria smiled. "Or?"

"Or I'll hit back and then I'll excise myself."

Excision meant being disowned and shunned. When a House excised someone, that person became a stranger. My grandmother wanted

House Baylor to survive and she'd decided I was the only one who could deliver. She went for the jugular and I had to match her.

"You think I would stoop so low?" she asked.

"Absolutely."

She chuckled. It chilled me to the proverbial bone.

"Your Italian is back in town."

We changed the subject again. The terms had been set and understood. My grandmother was moving on.

"He is."

"Remember what you promised me."

"How could I forget?"

"Good," Victoria said. "He's powerful. Use him, sleep with him if you must, but do not commit."

I was so tired of everyone telling me what to do about Alessandro.

"Remember, you belong to your House."

"I know," I told her.

We drank our tea.

"Grandmother, suppose you have a group of people in a large area with many routes of escape. You have to kill every single one of them but don't have the resources to surround their territory. How would you do it?"

Victoria smiled. "You're finally asking interesting questions. Does this group have a leader?"

"Yes."

"Then it's simple, my dear. Offer him what he wants, and he will bring his people to you to get it."

I held it together until the parking lot. Walking through the prison had become a ritual. When I entered, I armored myself with every step in a perverted meditation, sinking deeper into Victoria's granddaughter, cold, calculating, and ruthless. Someone like herself. Someone she would approve of. When I left, I shed chunks of that armor as I walked out. I couldn't drop it completely. My grandmother had me watched, and if I ducked into the bathroom to cry the stress out, she would know and there would be hell to pay. Instead I took a lighter breath with each landmark. Exit the garden, let a little bit go. Turn the corner into the main hallway, a little more. Reach reception, another chunk. Exit the prison, exhale, but still hold it, to the car, through the parking lot, all the way to the side road two miles down.

Alessandro pulled up the moment I stepped outside. I got into the car, and he drove without a word. We turned right and sped down the lone road. I should have been able to just ride next to him, but the ritual had become too ingrained. By the time the side road swung into view, I was breathing shallow and fast.

"Make a right," I asked, choking on the words.

He did. We rolled down the deserted country lane for another five hundred feet, behind the curve hidden from the main road by some trees. A small parking lot sat in the middle of the grove, barely wide enough to turn around. I had found it the second time I'd come to see her, after I panicked in the parking lot and drove, half-blind and crying, desperate for a place to hide.

"Pull over, please."

He pulled into the parking lot. The car stopped. Blood pounded in my ears. My breath came too fast, my chest hurt, my throat constricted, squeezed in an invisible noose. I undid my seat belt with shaking fingers and slumped over. My arms trembled.

Alessandro's arms closed around me.

I drew a long shuddering breath. It sounded like a sob. I just couldn't get enough air in my lungs and I felt like I was dying.

He rubbed my back, the heat of his hand shocking even through the fabric of my blouse. I was so cold, and he was warm.

"I've got you," he murmured in my ear. "It will pass. I've got you. You're safe. She can't see us."

I concentrated on breathing. There was no point in fighting it. I had to let it wash over me and let it pass. Just wait it out. It was scary, and it felt like dying, but it wouldn't cause any lasting damage. I'd felt this before, and I was okay after. This would pass and I would be okay again.

He held me. He didn't know it, but in that moment, I would have done anything to just keep holding on to him.

Gradually my breathing slowed. I straightened my back and leaned on the seat. Alessandro stood next to me, his arms still wrapped protectively around my shoulders. He must have gotten out of the truck, come around, and opened my door, and I hadn't noticed any of it.

And now he had seen my moment of weakness. Ugh.

"I'm okay," I told him. "Thank you."

He brushed a strand of hair out of my face. His voice was quiet and warm. "Does this happen often?"

"No. Only after I see my grandmother. Talking to Victoria is like running along a razor-sharp blade. Sometimes I slip and she cuts me. Usually it isn't this bad. The last time I just pulled over here and sat quietly for a couple of minutes."

"What happened today to make it bad?"

"She wants me to twist Albert Ravenscroft's arm to find out if his family is involved in the attacks on my family. I balked and she threatened to hurt Nevada's baby."

Alessandro's amber eyes turned dark. "She would injure her own great-grandchild?"

"According to her, he would be House Rogan's grandchild. He's nothing to her. Nevada is nothing to her. They have the same talent, but Nevada chose Connor. Victoria will never forgive her."

He leaned closer, his gaze searching my face. "Why are you her favorite? Does she have something on you? Did you promise her something?"

"Yes, I did."

"What did you promise?"

"I don't want to tell you."

"Did it have something to do with me?"

He was too perceptive for his own good.

"What happened to you after you left?" Sometimes the best defense was a good offense.

Alessandro crossed his arms over his chest and leaned against the open door. The sunlight filtered through the trees around us, painting glowing stripes on the pavement and the car. One stripe caught him and for a moment, before he shifted out of its way, he looked golden.

"I went to find my father's killer. I was very full of myself then."

"Was?"

"More than I am now."

"How is that possible?"

He sighed, impossibly handsome. "I'm a miracle of nature."

I raised my arms. "The defense rests its case, Your Honor." My voice shook slightly. The last aftershocks of panic dying down.

He tilted his head. "Do you want me to take you home?"

"That's the first question you've ducked since you came back."

"You won't tell me about the deal you made."

Touché. I stepped out of the truck. He was in my way, and I had to brush by him. He raised his arm, blocking me. Our bodies connected. An electric spark of excitement dashed through me. I made a point of looking at his arm. He refused to move it. We stood way too close, the space between us so tense with expectation, if we closed the gap, we would explode.

"Where are you going?" His voice was low, intimate.

"Wherever I want."

"Where do you want to go?"

"Why do you want to know?"

This had to be the dumbest conversation ever. All of my brainpower was going into standing still and not raising my head to kiss him. He was barely touching me, but there was something hot and possessive in the way his fingers rested on my shoulder. I felt trapped, but there was no fear, only anticipation and lust, so much lust it was making my brain stutter.

He leaned half an inch closer, his eyes full of the orange fire that was his magic. This was the man who had stalked me through that MII hallway.

"Tell me where you want to go, and I'll take you there."

This was a dangerous conversation. "I don't need you to take me anywhere. I can drive myself."

He smiled, a slow predatory curving of lips. "But I'm such a good driver. Are you sure you don't want me to give you a ride?"

"Are we still talking about the car?"

"You tell me."

I tilted my head up and smiled at him. My wings unfurled from my back, translucent and radiant, like glowing gossamer. Alessandro looked at me with a desperate, quiet hunger.

"I'm going to see Albert Ravenscroft."

"That's what I thought. I will come with you."

"No. I have to do this alone."

"Don't be difficult, Catalina."

"If the Abyss attacks me, I will take away his matrix node. I've done it once already."

"I checked on Albert. He, his father, his mother, and his younger brother are all Prime psionics. I'm not letting you walk into that house without backup."

"I can handle the Ravenscrofts."

He pretended to think it over. "No."

"You are not in charge of me. According to the contract you signed with Linus, I can order you to leave."

He leaned forward and smiled a sharp, predatory grin. "Fuck the contract."

Wow. It's like that, huh?

"I'll make a deal with you," I told him. "If I move you out of my way, you'll surrender the driver's seat and I will drop you off when we get back to town. If I can't, I'll let you come with me."

"Mmm . . ." He pondered it, his gaze on my eyes, my lips, my wings . . . "Sounds like a good deal."

"Can I trust you, Alessandro?"

"Yes."

"You won't go back on your word?"

"I won't."

Got you. "Ready?"

"Yes."

I put my right hand on his left wrist and ran my fingers up his arm to his shoulder, feeling the steel-hard muscle.

"Good start?" I asked.

His voice was rougher. "Excellent start."

I stepped back, sliding my hand back to his wrist. He followed. A step, another. Enough room.

I grabbed his wrist, raised it, turned into him so my back was pressed against his side and chest, locked my other hand on his shoulder, and straightened my legs, throwing all of my weight into it. He was several inches taller than me, which gave me the perfect leverage. My arm became a lever, my back became a pivot point, and Alessandro flew over my head and landed on his back with a thud.

Stunned eyes stared at me. I crouched, kissed my fingertips, pressed them to his lips, and walked to the driver's side.

He grinned and jumped to his feet without using his hands. "Good throw."

Oh no. I popped the jaguar on the nose and now he was excited.

"Who taught you that move?"

"You don't need to know. You just need to know that it works, and I have more. You lost. Get into your seat and be quiet. I'm driving."

He shook his head. "It's fine. I can find my way from here. I will see you tonight."

"Suit yourself."

He shut the door, and I drove off. He would be okay.

Albert Ravenscroft wouldn't be.

Piney Point Village was my least favorite neighborhood. One of six independent villages in the Memorial Villages luxury bedroom community, it was officially the most expensive little town in Texas. The *Wall Street Journal* once called it the "(Multi) Millionaire's Haven." It was a place of old trees and old money, where ten-million-dollar estates perched among meticulous landscaping guarded by endless HOA restrictions.

I missed Alessandro.

The street ended in a cul-de-sac in front of a stone mansion, lit up by orange light. A couple of years ago, the house was a part of the Piney Point architectural tour and the pamphlet had described it as a chateau. The best French chateaux were solid stone structures under high-pitched roofs, carefully balanced to be graceful and stately. The monstrosity in front of me was anything but.

From where I sat, parked, I could see at least eight different roof lines, six chimneys, three different arches, a balcony with an eave that matched nothing, a single turret randomly mashed into a wall, a smaller servant's entrance on one side under a cosmetic dormer, and a gated porte cochere, arched and decorated with quoins that weren't anywhere else on the building. It was as if some drunken architects jammed chunks of different buildings into a bag, shook it, and let this ten-thousand-square-foot mutant fall out.

On second thought, it was good that Alessandro wasn't with me. He grew up in Villa Sagredo, which started out as an ancient watchtower and became the center of a breathtaking mansion in the mid-Renaissance. Beautiful architecture was in his blood. This mess of a house would give him a seizure.

I stared at the mansion. The first time Albert approached me was at the Blue Bonnet charity event. I was there because Nevada had a conflict in her schedule and sent me in her place. Nobody knew who I was, and I was perfectly happy sitting at a nice table in the corner waiting for the opportunity to drop Nevada's check into the basket at the end of the speeches. I sipped my mimosa, looked up, and there he was. He'd smiled at me and said, "Can I sit here? If I fall asleep, my family will never forgive me, and you are the only interesting person in the room."

I didn't want to hurt Albert.

But I had to know. We, as a House, had to know.

I got out of the truck, my tablet in my hands, and walked to the entrance. The wrought-iron gate securing access to the front door stood open and I rang the bell. A Hispanic woman answered and smiled at me.

"Good evening."

"Good evening. May I have your name?"

"Catalina Baylor," I told her.

"Cat?" Albert came around an ornate staircase. His face lit up. "You're here."

Ugh. Albert had determined at some point that I required a nick-name, made one up, and persisted in using it. I hated it, but we had bigger things to fight about.

"Can we talk?" I asked.

"Of course."

I followed him to the sitting area opposite the door, where plush beige chairs ringed a mahogany coffee table. A grand piano waited in the round niche on the left, raised on a dais. Albert's mother was an accomplished musician.

Albert smiled at me. "What can I do for you?"

"Leon spoke to you about a girl he knows, Audrey."

"The little stalker. I remember."

"Did you tell anyone about it?"

The smile slid off his face. That clearly wasn't the topic he was expecting.

"You told someone. Who did you tell? It's very important to me."

He tapped his knuckles against his mouth, thinking. "I don't think I told anyone. Wait, I might have mentioned it to Dad. Yes, I think I did. Why?"

The bottom fell out of my stomach. That's what I was afraid of. "Is your father home?"

Albert rolled his eyes. "It's seven o'clock. Where else would he be? Come on, he's in the study. Are you going to tell me what this is about?"

"Eventually."

We wandered through the mansion to the study where the traver-tine floor gave way to dark wood paneling and floor-to-ceiling shelves. Christian Ravenscroft sat behind his desk, sipping coffee from a mug. He still wore a dark suit and a burgundy tie, as if he had just come home from the office. His hair receded, pure white like his eyebrows. His once-handsome face had grown heavier with age, its sharp lines turning square and blocky. He gave me a smile but didn't rise. House Ravenscroft approved of Albert's marriage ambitions, but to them I was "a nice girl," polite, quiet, unlikely to embarrass them and therefore a good future spouse, but not quite on their level.

"Cat wants to talk to you, Dad." Albert invited me to go ahead with a sweep of his hand.

"I'll do my best," Christian said. I was being humored.

"Maybe it would be better to speak in private," I said.

"I have no secrets from my son."

I surrendered to my fate. No matter how hard I tried, Albert wouldn't be spared.

"Who did you tell about the connection between my cousin and Audrey Duarte?"

Silence fell on the study.

Christian frowned. He didn't like the question or how I asked it. "Why would I know who your cousin is or care who he associates with? And if I did, who would I tell?"

That was the question, wasn't it? I took the tablet and set it on his desk, so he and Albert could both see it.

"Please try to remember."

"I don't know what you're talking about."

He'd told someone. His voice held too much outrage. He was trying to use his age and position to intimidate me.

"Strathearn Pipeline," I said. Last warning.

Christian showed no reaction. "As odd as this has been, I still have business to take care of tonight. If there's nothing else . . ." He let it hang.

I tapped the tablet. On it a large crowd of people gathered on the shore of a picturesque lake, holding signs. The sun was setting and the green hills around the lake all but glowed.

"What's the Strathearn Pipeline?" Albert asked.

"Strathearn is a small town in Maine. Its main source of income is tourism from the Strathearn lake. A year and a half ago the Synesis Corporation decided to build a Teflon factory in the area. They promised a lot of jobs, but the locals didn't want factory jobs, they wanted clean water that was free of perfluorooctanoic acid, which the factory would dump into the lake. They lobbied their congressional representatives, and when that didn't work, they started protesting."

On the screen the protestors shook their signs. An older black woman lectured the cameras as journalists held their mics out to her. A young girl, about eight or nine, with curly red hair and pale skin, stood awkwardly next to her, not knowing what to do with herself.

"These weren't anarchists," I said. "Look, there are families there. Young people, old people, couples with children. They were locals who'd lived there for generations."

Christian sighed, clearly put upon.

"The protests gained national attention. Synesis didn't like the bad publicity, so they decided to do something about it."

On the screen, someone screamed. Placards flew and people ran, colliding. The journalists dropped their mics and charged toward the lake. One of them ran into the older black woman, knocking her out of the way, his face a mask of primal terror. She fell. The redheaded girl tried to pick her up, but the crowd surged around them, and she fell too. People trampled them, running back and forth, stomping, wailing, hitting each other.

Albert stared at it. "A psionic attack. A really strong one, fear-based, omnidirectional, layered. A targeted attack would have driven them all in the same direction."

"That's what the National Assembly thought too. This went on for twelve minutes. Seven people died, three drowned, four were trampled. One man was paralyzed, and dozens suffered injuries. Synesis attempted to spin the whole thing as radical groups infiltrating the protests."

"No," Albert said. "It's not multiple psionics, or the flow of the crowd would have varied in intensity. This is a single psionic, likely a Prime, delivering controlled bursts of magic along the perimeter. As soon as they run one way, the psionic pushed them in the opposite direction. They couldn't escape. Nowhere was safe."

"There is an investigation," I continued. "The internal records of the company were subpoenaed. They show that a decision was made to hire an outside psionic for an exorbitant sum. Unfortunately, the only woman who knew the identity of the psionic jumped from the roof of a parking garage three months ago."

A smile flickered on Christian's face, half a second long, but I saw it. I spooled my magic, reinforcing my mental defenses. I had been reinforcing them since I drove away from Alessandro.

Albert was looking at his father.

"Samantha Corners is dead," I said. "But she had insurance."

I tapped the tablet. A country road came into focus with a black Escalade parked in the middle of it, filmed from the side, most likely by a hidden camera in someone's pocket or handbag. Christian Ravenscroft crouched on a black square platform about ten feet wide, placed on a flat spot in the field, next to the SUV. He was drawing a complex arcane circle with a piece of chalk. Two hundred yards down, protesters chanted on the grass.

"Five minutes, no more," a female voice said.

"Do you want this done right? If so, shut up."

"We want what we paid you for."

"And you'll get it. Once I start, don't interrupt. You don't want to make things worse." He finished the design, stepped into the circle, and closed his eyes.

Orange light dashed through the chalk lines and faded to a dull glow, throwing eerie highlights onto Christian's face.

The first desperate scream tore through the air.

On the screen, Albert's father smiled.

"Cascade . . ." Albert murmured, squinting at the circle. "You used our House spell."

A torrent of magic tore out of Christian. It smashed into my defenses and broke against my mental wall like waves on a rock. He recoiled, stunned.

"Not strong enough," I told him.

"Dad!" Albert thrust himself between us. "What the hell are you doing?"

"Shut. Up." Christian hammered each word into the ground.

I walked over to one of the overstuffed chairs, sat down into it, and crossed one leg over the other.

"Why the hell would you do this?" Albert snarled. "Not only is your face on video, but the entire design of Cascade can be made out. All they have to do is call any local Prime psionic, and they'll recognize it. Attacking her isn't going to fix this."

House spells were specific to each House, complex and closely guarded. Magic talents were like fingerprints, unique. Victoria and Nevada were both truthseekers, but even though they were related by blood, the exact nature of their talents differed slightly. Circles developed by a specific family wouldn't work as well for anyone else because they were precisely attuned to the magic of that particular bloodline. When Christian had drawn Cascade on that board, he'd damned himself.

"If this gets out, we're finished as a House." Albert raised his arms. "We don't need the money. Did you owe someone a favor? Were you blackmailed? Why?"

"Because I wanted to." Christian's expression turned dark, his cheeks flushed, his mouth a furious slash across his face.

The oldest reason in the book. All psionics restrained themselves. Their talents had no purpose outside of military applications or the rare cases civilian law enforcement required crowd control. There were memes online that showed random sad people with the caption "Psionic waiting for a riot." They felt the pull to use their magic just as much as any of us, and they had turned practicing personal restraint into a religion.

"You wanted to?" Albert dropped his arms to his sides, slapping his legs. "Are we animals, Father? Do we have no self-control? Did you not drill the Mantra of the Psionic into me since before I could talk?"

"We have a bigger problem." Christian stared at me. If looks were blades, I'd be a pincushion.

"You're not strong enough," I repeated. I knew exactly how I looked, slightly bored, emotionless, my expression icy.

Christian trembled, struggling to contain his rage. He'd sunk everything into that first attack. If it had hit me right after the Pit, I would have shattered and run for my life, straight into traffic, off some roof, or into the water. Whatever was handy. But I'd had time to recover.

"Who else knows?" Christian squeezed out through his teeth.

When I'd realized Albert was serious about marriage and he would not go away, I asked Bern to run a background check on the family. He came across an old business partnership between Samantha Corners' sister and Christian Ravenscroft's distant cousin. Other people had looked into

Christian's background, but none of them were Bern. Being a pattern mage, Bern had put the pieces together and then dug in other people's personal computers until he found the recording two months ago.

"The Special Consul for the Department of Justice. You will be offered an under-the-table deal. Samantha Corners was a go-between, but she didn't sign the check. They want the people who hired you."

Albert stared at me. "He incited a crowd to violence, and they're willing to make a deal? He murdered people."

"They're offering a deal because if this recording became public, it could spark civil unrest. The impact on psionics, in general, would be catastrophic. The National Assembly wants to protect psionics. The Department of Justice wants to avoid riots and further loss of life. They came to an agreement in the interest of the greater good."

This deal left a bad taste in my mouth. Linus had explained it to me, after I brought him the recording, and he hadn't even tried to put a pretty bow on it. He had predicted this outcome so precisely that I wondered how many times something like this had happened before. Two weeks later I had official confirmation from him. They would make a deal with a murderer.

Christian leaned on his desk as if he were about to climb over it. If I were within arm's reach, he would have choked me to death. "How do you know all of this? You're nobody."

"That's not important."

"What are the terms of the deal?" Albert asked.

I pointed at Christian. "He's done. Out."

"Excision?" Albert turned pale.

I nodded. "He will testify as a disguised witness, you'll be permitted to retain all assets, and his excision will take place before a sealed committee of the Assembly."

Albert turned to his father, then back to me.

"I'm here for information," I said. "If you don't give me what I want, I'll upload this video to every major streaming platform. Once it goes public, people will howl for blood and you can kiss your deal goodbye. The Assembly will rip you to shreds in retaliation. Your House won't recover. If you attempt to harm or detain me, I'll lobotomize you and then I will upload the video. If you shoot me right now, the video still gets uploaded and my House will murder everyone you love."

Christian swore.

Albert turned to me, his eyes wide. "Who are you?"

"Also not important."

"My father wouldn't tell anyone about Leon. He wouldn't even remember something like that."

"Oh I think he did."

"Why does it even matter?"

"Someone is targeting my House, Albert. You have one minute to think it over."

"I wanted to marry you," Albert whispered.

I wanted to say I was sorry. I wanted to hug him and tell him it wouldn't be the end of the world, but any weakness on my part, any hint of kindness or compassion, and Christian would slip from my fingers.

I let my magic pour out of me. When I compelled people to fall in love with me, my wings were glorious, green and gold and shimmering. The wings that grew from my back now were black. The tips of my feathers glowed with crimson, as if I'd dipped my wings in blood. This was the other side of the coin. I'd learned I had it after Alessandro left, when I was in a dark place and wanted to be left alone. Leon had pestered me during dinner one night, I lost control, and the black wings made their debut. The family was stunned into silence for a whole thirty seconds. And then everyone called me Goth Princess for a week and Arabella kept leaving vampire novels by my door.

My wings stretched, huge, black, intimidating. I couldn't actually do anything with them, the way I could use my other wings to entice, but they looked impressive.

Both men took a step back.

"I don't think we would be a good match, Albert. Twenty seconds."

"He doesn't know anything," Albert insisted.

"Ten seconds."

Christian slumped in his chair. "All right."

Albert frowned. "You told someone about her cousin?"

"I was approached at the club. A young telekinetic walked up to me on the green."

"How do you know he was a telekinetic?" I asked.

Christian sneered at me. "He didn't have to physically retrieve his balls."

"When did this happen?"

"Last Saturday."

Arkan's people moved fast. "What did he ask?"

Christian sighed. "He asked if I was interested in removing you from my son's life, and I said yes."

Albert sat down in the chair and slumped forward on his right elbow on the armrest, his forehead on his fist. "This is a nightmare," he said, his voice almost cheerful. "I'm going to wake up any minute, won't I, Father? Why did you sabotage my relationship?"

"Because you could do better!"

Albert pointed to me. "Better than that? There's a fucking angel of death in your study and you thought I could do better?"

"I didn't have all the information at the time. She wouldn't give you the time of day. I was sick of watching you chase after her like some lovesick puppy."

"Did I ask for your help?"

"I am your father! I look after your future! They're an upstart House, and Victoria Tremaine will rip them to shreds when she gets out."

"My grandmother trusted me to handle this matter," I said. "I'm here instead of her as a courtesy to Albert because of our friendship. House Tremaine doesn't suffer fools, Mr. Ravenscroft. Don't be one."

Christian opened his mouth. Nothing came out.

"Describe the telekinetic," I prompted.

"Young, in his twenties. Dark hair. Tan skin. Good teeth. Accent."

"What kind of accent?"

"Not sure."

This was like pulling teeth. "Was he a member of the club or a guest?"

"I don't know. I didn't ask."

"Was he with someone else?"

"Not that I saw."

"Did he offer you anything? Did he give you some way to contact him?"

Christian shook his head. "We talked for a bit while we walked. That was it. He didn't tell me his name."

"How did Leon's name come up?"

"He asked what I thought about all your family members. I told him that I didn't care for any of them. I told him that you acted as if you were too good for us, and even your damn dud cousin snubbed my son and told him some made-up stalker story about a girl named Audrey."

Not much to go on. As soon as I got home, I would ask Bern to go through the surveillance next to the club and see if anyone looked familiar.

"What happened?" Albert asked.

"Audrey is dead. Leon was framed for her murder, but he has a bulletproof alibi." I looked back to Christian. "Anything to add?"

Christian jutted his chin into the air, his eyes defiant. "I'm right. My son is too good for you."

I hid my wings, rose, took my tablet, and walked out.

 # Chapter 14

Fifteen minutes from the house I called in to report to Victoria's office like a good little soldier. Trevor answered on the second ring, his voice clipped.

"Please hold."

The look of horror on Christian's face when I mentioned my evil grandmother was branded in my memory. Did I have to become Victoria for us to survive? I was learning to think like her. To react like her. If I kept going, there would come a time when the act of being Victoria's granddaughter would no longer be an act at all. I didn't want to turn into my grandmother. I wanted to go back to the time when my lack of experience gave me blinders.

Now was a bad time for a moment of weakness. Trevor would come back on the line to take down my report, and I couldn't afford to sound bitter.

The phone clicked, and my grandmother's crisp, upper-class voice filled Beetle's interior. "What did you find out?"

Surprise, surprise. Grandmother had no phone privileges. Somehow, I doubted the prison administration would be shocked at this appalling breach of security.

"Christian was approached on the golf course of his country club. A white man, probably twenties or thirties, dark haired, tan, with an unidentified accent, looking for dirt on House Baylor. They had a casual conversation, then the man left. Christian doesn't know how he got into the club. He'd never seen him before, and he would have noticed him, because the stranger was a telekinetic and didn't have to retrieve his golf balls."

Country clubs catering to upper-level magic users usually took a dim view of members using magic on the grounds. It carried the same social penalty as flashing around large wads of cash. It was considered gauche and simply wasn't done. The stranger had flaunted the rule to identify himself as a high-ranking mage, someone Christian would consider worthy of conversation.

"Anything else? Details?"

"No. The senior Ravenscroft isn't a detail person. If he encountered an elephant, he would describe it as a large grey animal."

Victoria sighed. "If you cracked Christian's big head, you'd be lucky to find a tablespoon of brains. Their entire House isn't over-burdened with intelligence or imagination. Did he say why he opened his mouth?"

"He doesn't feel I'm good enough to marry his son."

Victoria laughed, the sound ringing through the vehicle.

"Also, he's afraid of you."

"Maybe he's gotten marginally smarter with age. Call me the moment you learn anything new."

"Yes, Grandmother." That was easier than I thought.

"Your Italian came to see me." Amusement bubbled up in Victoria's voice.

What? He did what?

"He hasn't told you," Victoria said.

Damn it, waited to respond a second too long.

My brain finally registered that my exit lane was about to end. I merged a foot before it ended. Behind me a red pickup blared its horn in outrage.

I willed my voice into careful neutrality. "What did he say?"

"He threatened me."

Oh my God. "Did you hurt him?"

"You need to do a better job of concealing your feelings. I can hear the panic in your voice."

"Did you hurt him, Grandmother?"

"His mind is intact. I found him entertaining. Besides, he is a beautiful boy. So much power. It would be a waste to turn him into a vegetable."

I would strangle him. What was he thinking? He probably didn't even understand how lucky he was to come out of there with his mind undamaged.

The humor in her voice grew. "He informed me that you are perfectly capable, and my interference is impeding you. He also suggested that if something were to happen to you as a result of my attention, he would cut off my head."

"He didn't."

"Oh, he was perfectly charming while suggesting it. Impeccable manners, great poise. Good breeding always shows, even when dressed in ratty jeans and a faded T-shirt. I think your pauper prince truly loves you, the poor fool. It's a shame."

She was mocking me. "Gloating is beneath you."

"Catalina, I'm in prison. I take my fun where I can find it. You know where you and I stand."

The call cut off. She'd hung up.

Here is fine, I'll find my own way. I'm going to turn right around and poke a ravenous shark with a stick to see what happens.

I would kill him. No, worse, I would yell at him when I found him.

I drove to our security booth, got out, and let myself be sniffed.

Regina walked out of her house, strode to our front door, and waited with her arms crossed.

Security cleared me. I drove Beetle through and parked it. "Did something happen?"

"When Leon and your sister brought Rhino back, it felt odd." She passed her hand over Beetle's hood.

"Odd how?"

"I thought I sensed something animated but couldn't find it. I'm checking the other vehicles. Your truck is clear."

"What kind of something?"

"Not that kind," she assured me. "Ordinary animation. Patricia is doing an extra sweep and I sent Cinder to hunt. We'll see what she catches."

I walked into the house at twenty past eight. The building was quiet. Shadow bounded out of the media room and scratched at my legs, overcome by doggy excitement. I pet her and trudged into the kitchen. I was so tired. Yesterday had been a long day, today was an even longer day, and everything hurt. I needed food and sleep, in that order.

I missed the warehouse. Now we were split into three stories, with Bern and Leon taking up the third floor, and Arabella and Grandma Frida using the second. Only Mom and I stayed on the bottom floor, and right now, with everyone busy doing their own thing, I felt abandoned and isolated. It was almost like coming home to my own private apartment, mine, but cold and lonely.

Except for Shadow.

I made a beeline for the fridge. Replenishing magic burned a lot of calories, and my stomach had turned into a black hole swirling with acid. I'd missed dinner but there would be leftovers. There were always leftovers.

The fridge offered me Mom's fajitas. It was a simple recipe, marinated skirt steak or chicken thighs chopped into bite-sized pieces and wrapped in flour tortillas with cheese, chunks of tomato and avocado, and mild sauce. They kept surprisingly well, were good hot or cold, and everyone in the family liked them. Mom must have made a ton, because the platter held at least a dozen, wrapped in plastic so the fridge wouldn't dry them out.

I pried the plastic open, snagged a fajita, and closed the fridge. Nevada stood three feet away. I jumped and dropped the fajita. Shadow darted across the floor, scooped up the fajita, and bolted down the hallway.

I swore. "Make some noise next time, please."

Nevada crossed her arms over her chest.

Uh-oh. I knew that look. That was the you-are-doomed look.

"Albert called," my sister said.

I opened the fridge and took out a Corona. "What did he say?"

"He wants to talk. He says he knows he fucked up, but he thinks there's still a chance, despite all the threats. He wants an opportunity to apologize."

I opened the beer and took a long swallow. I barely tasted it, but it was cold, and that was enough. "He has nothing to apologize for."

"He thinks he does."

I tried to get past her to the table, but she stayed where she was, trapping me between the island and the fridge. I had a feeling that if I turned around and circled the island, she would just step to the side and block my way again.

"Initially I thought he might have threatened you," she said.

"Albert?"

"Yes. But after five minutes of his apologizing, I realized that he wouldn't have, which means you threatened him. I asked Bern to trace your phone route."

Crap. I drank more beer.

"You went to see her. Then you went straight to Albert's house. Now he wants to apologize. His exact words were 'beg forgiveness.'"

Technically, all of that was accurate.

"What did she make you do?"

I couldn't lie and say going to see Albert was my idea. "That's between me and her." The less Nevada was involved, the safer it was.

My sister's eyes blazed. "I told you to stop talking to her. I warned you. I know you think she's some sort of mentor, but you have no idea how dangerous she is. She told you to do something cruel, and you went and did it. Is that who you want to be?"

Nobody could compare with my sister. She hits the bull's-eye on the first try. Right into the knot of guilt and doubt.

"It's not that simple." I sounded lame, even to myself.

Nevada locked her teeth and nodded. "I'll make it simple. Tomorrow I'll go and tell her to leave you alone."

Panic smashed into me in a blinding explosion of white. My fingertips went cold. Victoria let Alessandro's stunt go because she found him amusing. If Nevada marched in there tomorrow and started issuing ultimatums, Victoria would punish her. She viewed Alessandro as my teenage crush, ultimately harmless. But Nevada wielded a great deal of influence over me. Victoria already saw her as a rival. She would act to consolidate her grip on me. She would retaliate.

She would hurt the baby.

"Please don't do this. I'm begging you."

Nevada's eyes were clear. "You're my sister and I love you. You're trapped, but I'll get you out."

No, no, no.

Nevada turned away from me. She'd made up her mind. I had seconds to stop her. I needed a lever, a gap in her armor, something to make her listen.

"You always took care of us when we were kids. But now I'm an adult. You taught me that being an adult means making informed decisions. I want to tell you something, and if, when I'm done, you still want to confront Victoria, I won't fight you."

Nevada turned around and sat at the table. "Okay. I'll hear you out."

I would regret this conversation for the rest of my life, but I had to keep her away from Victoria. I pulled out a chair, sat, and took another swig of my beer. It tasted bitter. My adrenaline was through the roof.

"Do you remember when you gave up being the Head of our House?"

Nevada narrowed her eyes. "I remember."

"I told that story to Alessandro. The whole thing. How you were working yourself into the ground trying to earn money for us and to deal with the threats against Connor, how you wouldn't rest, wouldn't eat, wouldn't let anybody help, until you collapsed and we had to call an ambulance. I explained that we begged you to slow down and recover, and you promised to do it, and then less than twenty-four hours later, I found you back in the office rummaging through files. How Arabella and I had inherited shares of the business from Dad, and we voted to ban you from making money for the business, forcing you to keep everything you earned, and then you freaked out and declared that we didn't trust you anymore and you couldn't be the Head of our House."

Nevada's mouth thinned. She didn't like remembering that any more than I did.

My sister waved her hand at me to keep going.

"Something Alessandro said stuck with me. He said that you knew we were right, but you didn't think you were wrong. The more I thought about that, the less sense it made. You rebuilt the business from the ground up after Dad got sick. You put your life on hold and sacrificed for it. You loved the business. It was Dad's legacy, and you honored it."

Nevada shrugged.

"You also loved us. You worked sixty-hour weeks and then still found time to be our big sister. And you are the most grounded, level-headed person I know. *Tantrum* isn't even in your vocabulary. But somehow you threw one, and then you got so butt-hurt, you quit the business and almost quit the family. You didn't speak to me for three weeks."

Nevada's expression softened. "I'm sorry I hurt you."

"At the time I felt so guilty. I came up with this wonderful idea to get you to work less and stop you from driving yourself into the ground for us, and it all went horribly wrong. I didn't know what to do. And you were so angry. That same day you went down to the Keeper of Records and officially abdicated leadership of the House. That put me in charge of the family. I was twenty years old. I knew nothing about running a House. Here we were, less than a year away from emerging from the new House grace period, and you dropped it all in my lap. My big sister wouldn't have done that in a million years."

Hurt flashed in Nevada's stare. She hid it instantly, but I saw it. I wanted to throw my arms around her, but I had to get through this.

"I'm so sorry," she said again. "You hurt my feelings, I was overworked, and I wasn't thinking clearly."

I shook my head. "No, you were thinking very clearly. What Alessandro said was true. You knew we were right, but you didn't think you were wrong. You made the best possible decision under the circumstances. It wasn't emotional. It was calculated."

Nevada frowned. "Where are you going with this?"

"About two months before you collapsed, Connor was still dealing with the fallout of exposing the Sturm-Charles conspiracy. Friends and allies of the people whose Houses fell as the result of that investigation were gunning for him. You received a USB drive with a series of recordings showing Connor engaged in human trafficking."

No reaction. One day I would be as good as her.

"The recordings were graphic and horrible. Girls, barely teenagers, transported in cages, tortured, and raped. You started digging and found a wealth of supporting evidence. Bogus shipping records that couldn't pass even the slightest check. A secret account Connor didn't know he had with deposits from a known human trafficker who had been conveniently murdered, so it would look like Connor tried to cover up his sins. But all of that wasn't sensational. The recordings, however, that was the glue-you-to-your-screen evidence. Except the recordings alone weren't enough, not when a powerful illusion Prime could duplicate Connor's appearance. Someone had to validate them."

My sister leaned forward, focused on me. I could practically feel the wheels turning in her head. She was trying to figure out how I knew.

"Robert J. Merritt," I said. "Forty-one years old, born and raised in Sycamore, Illinois, white, married, two children, one golden retriever, a war hero. Also, one of the sixteen people who walked with Connor out of the jungle in Belize."

Again, no reaction. If someone watched us from a distance, they would think we were discussing buying kitchen towels.

"Merritt called and told you he intended to vouch for the authenticity of the recordings. The bond between Connor and the Sixteen is unshakable. They've been through hunger and captivity and torture, and they would literally die for each other. Any of the remaining Sixteen would say so on the witness stand. If Robert Merritt testified that the recordings were authentic, he would be unimpeachable. He was a bulletproof witness."

"He was a liar."

"Yes. But it didn't matter. This had all the makings of an incredible media blitz: a war hero, torn between loyalty to his officer and friend and his conscience, chooses truth and decency over keeping his savior's disgusting secret. Connor would exist under a cloud of suspicion for the rest of his life and so would you. You knew that he was innocent, because every time stamp on those recordings corresponded to times when you and Connor were away together. You were his only alibi."

Her eyes were clear, her voice steady. "He didn't do it."

"I know. That's not who Connor is. But you couldn't prove it. All the elements of his alibi depended on his employees and you. They owed their livelihood to him. He held all of their loans, every mortgage, every credit card account, because he likes to make his people secure from outside manipulation. And you? You loved him. You would do anything for him, even lie. You knew you wouldn't be believed. You tried to find Robert Merritt but he'd disappeared into thin air. He would call you occasionally, to taunt you and to hint at compensation, but there was never anything concrete. No demand for money. No explanation why."

"He was a ghost," Nevada said. "I threw everything I had at him. Rogan's entire force searched for him. Nobody could find Merritt, not even Bug."

"On the day you collapsed, he called you and promised to release the first video in a week. You knew you couldn't stop it. You knew that if you stood by Connor, the press would paint you as a vile, awful woman who supported a monster. Merritt told you that he would implicate you during his testimony. He would tell everyone that you were aware of what Connor was doing and you encouraged it. You would be a pariah. Our society despises male criminals, but it rips the female ones to pieces. As women, we are supposed to nurture, care, and defend children, not enable others to prey on them."

Nevada's face turned haggard and exhausted, as if the ghost of some other woman had settled onto her face. It was there for just a fraction of a breath, but seeing it was like being cut. It must've been so awful, and she'd kept it all inside and kept going, trying to save him, trying to keep us out of it. It'd been over a year and a half and still that wound hurt, and now I'd reopened it. I was a terrible person.

"How do you know?" Nevada asked.

"I'll get to that. You had a choice. You could stand by Connor and go down with him, dragging our family into the gutter. We would not recover from something like that. You were the Head of our House and nobody knew anything about us. People would ask questions. How much did we know? Did we participate? Did we get off on it? Did we make money from the suffering of human beings? You could stay with the man you love and watch the whole Baylor family go down in flames with you or you could abandon Connor and publicly cut all ties with House Rogan. He told you to do it, didn't he?"

Nevada nodded. "He did. He had divorce papers drawn up. He is completely innocent, Catalina."

My poor sister. Every time I thought about her and Connor waiting for this to break, trying so hard and failing, my heart squeezed itself into a painful little ball.

"You decided to stand by him," I said.

"I love him."

It was really that simple for her. When Nevada loved someone, she gave all of herself to them.

"You knew that if you told us about it, we would stand by you. You were desperate to separate us from this nightmare, so instead you manipulated us into cutting you out. When I was in that hospital room with you, you told me that we needed the money and that just because Arabella and I owned shares didn't mean we could tell you what to do. Then when you came back to the office the day after and I busted you, you told me again how you needed to make money for the family. You put the building blocks into my head, and I clicked them together. If I'd just had some time to think about it, I would've realized it. I remember looking at the accounts after you left and seeing that we had more than enough money. I could've figured it out, but we were all so freaked out and afraid you would die just like Dad."

Nevada sighed. "I love you so much. If there had been any other way, I would've taken it. But there wasn't."

"And then you made the break appear as real as possible. You ran to the Keeper of Records, abdicated, and stopped talking to us. You made sure people knew we were estranged. You sacrificed everything you'd built so we could have a future."

"I did what I had to do. You, Arabella, and the boys, all of you deserve a life. I'm the oldest. It's my job to protect all of you."

I felt like crying and pushed it down. Not now. I still had things to say.

"You waited for the video release, but it was never uploaded. And then you got a phone call. Nothing was said. Just a few moments of silence and then a disconnect signal. You traced the phone's location to a house in the Third Ward, right in the most dangerous part of it. You and Connor raided the house and found Robert Merritt dead, with a confession written in his handwriting and sealed with his fingerprint, which said that the entire thing was a fabrication and a plot to get money. The only other existing copies of the doctored recordings were in a safe next to him. It was over, just like that."

A vicious light sparked in Nevada's eyes. "Except that Merritt didn't have the resources to manufacture something like that. And the confession claimed that he killed himself out of guilt. I spoke to that weasel for two months. He didn't have an ounce of guilt in him. He reveled in torturing us."

I leaned forward. "Have you ever wondered who was behind all of that? What the point was?"

"Go on," Nevada said.

"It was a test. You failed."

My sister shook her head. "Is that what Victoria told you?"

"She wanted to know where your loyalty lay, so she made you choose between Connor and us. Either you put the needs of House Baylor first and proved to her that you were a suitable Head of the House or you would remove yourself so she could put someone else in your place. You chose Connor, and she got what she wanted. I know all of this because she told me exactly how she did it, step by step, every little detail, so if I ever needed to engineer something like this, I would have a detailed plan on how to do it."

Nevada laughed softly. "She's filling your head with nonsense. I suspected her and eliminated her from my list."

I took a deep breath. "The combination to the safe, which you found in Merritt's left pant pocket. 060149. June 1st, 1949. It's her birthday."

Nevada went white.

Silence stretched between us.

"It can't be," she murmured.

"She worked on it for almost two years, building this enormous complex web of bribes, blackmail, and violence. She bought Merritt for five million dollars. She had the trafficker kidnapped, broke him, and then used the information to make the deposits. She has a clan of Vietnamese illusion mages in her pocket. It's a large family, powerful, but poor, because they have issues with the Vietnamese government. They will do whatever she asks. If you ever worried that the children in the videos were hurt, they weren't. They weren't even children. Like the part where they break the girl's arms and hang her off a hook—she's an adult woman, an illusion mage. The guy who assumes Connor's image and rapes her is actually her husband. I've seen the before and after footage. They laughed about it."

Nevada struggled to say something. "Connor . . ."

"I know that Connor would have given Merritt the money. Merritt wouldn't have taken it. He hated Connor, because he thought Connor was the reason they were on that mission in the first place."

"The reason they went on that mission was because they were in the military, they had orders, and it was their job to go," Nevada growled.

"Merritt hurt his back in the jungle. The military denied him disability. The family was on food stamps. Victoria found him at his lowest, used him, and then had him killed once he'd served his purpose."

Nevada stared at me.

I stood up. The words poured out of me, messy and stupid, but honest. "I love you so much, and Connor, and the baby. I love Arabella, and Leon, and Bern, and Mom, and Grandma Frida. You can't fight Victoria. You don't think like her. You don't know her secrets. But I do."

My sister blinked. "Catalina . . ."

I couldn't stop. I had to make her see. "She's grooming me to be her successor. I go there every two weeks and I learn everything I can, no matter what it costs me. I'm building my own web around our grandmother. It requires time and careful planning. When the right moment comes, I will collapse her world. But that moment is years away. If you go there tomorrow, you'll wreck everything I've built, because she'll attack you and your baby, and I will defend you with my life. We won't win, Nevada. She has contingency plans in place in case of such an attack. Even if we kill her, we will lose. You trusted me with the responsibility of keeping our family safe, and I won't let you down. Please trust me again. I know how much you gave up for our sake. I promise you I won't let you get hurt. I won't let any of you get hurt."

Nevada stood up, her eyes wide. I hugged her, squeezing her to me, and fled the room.

I climbed the stairs past the third floor, all the way to the top, where a brick utility building offered access to the paved roof. I walked out into the night, skirted the utility structure, and came to the narrow space that served as my hiding spot.

I'd claimed it soon after we moved into the building. I brought up plants and set them along the edge of the roof—Texas lantanas with their clusters of red and yellow blossoms, wild mint with humble purple flowers, white and pink zonal geraniums, and lush golden pothos. Bern and Leon installed an overhang for me and built a stone rail along the roof, Nevada bought me an outdoor couch, and Runa helped me string outdoor lights from the overhang to the rail. Arabella found a small fire pit filled with blue glass pebbles and Grandma Frida hooked it up to the gas line. Mom made me a blanket and bought pillows.

Alessandro once told me that I was loved by many people. He was right. But right now, I felt completely and utterly alone.

I leaned on the stone rail. Below, across the street, warm electric light spilled onto the pavement from industrial-sized bay doorways. After the warehouse collapsed, Connor gifted Grandma Frida one of the buildings he'd bought when he was trying to keep us secure. It used to be a massive industrial garage where semitrucks were repaired and Grandma Frida had pounced on it, so she could keep her business running. She didn't know how to not work. Tanks, mobile guns, and cars spoke to her in the same way computers and code whispered to Bern and she loved talking to them.

The blinds on the large window at the top of Grandma's building were open and through it I could see the inside of the motor pool. A bright red monster of a tank sat in the center. Grandma Frida stood on its side in her blue coveralls, digging in it with some weird tool. It was barely nine, and when Grandma Frida focused on a problem, she sometimes worked till midnight.

A heavy door shut somewhere. Nevada crossed the street and walked into the motor pool. Shadow followed her, wagging her tail. Grandma Frida turned away from the tank, waved at Nevada, and went back to messing with the tank's insides. Nevada pulled one of the metal chairs open and settled into it.

I had upset my sister and she went to talk to Grandma.

I backed away from the edge and sat on my padded couch. Around me the night mugged the city, the air no longer scorching, but still warm. My insides churned. I'd never planned on talking to Nevada about any of it. My sister dragged around a truckload of guilt for forcing me to become the Head of the House and making me think it was all my idea. Now she knew that I knew. I had no idea what she was feeling. It was all terrible and fucked up, and it felt like my soul had been shredded. Anger, sadness, guilt, and sharp wailing anxiety boiled inside me into an awful, toxic mix. I wanted to punch something and cry, but I also wanted to curl into a ball in some dark hole and not come out.

I pulled out my phone, found Alessandro's number, and texted him.

Where are you?

Where do you need me to be?

I was a fool. **On the roof of my building. Look for the Christmas lights.** He didn't respond.

I switched to Patricia. **Someone's coming to see me. Let him in.**

Okay.

I leaned my elbows on my knees and hid my face in my hands. The ache gnawed at me, relentless. What if Nevada ignored me and went to see Victoria anyway? What if I failed?

I ran through my preparations in my head. Victoria would go for Gisela first. My aunt was a walking calamity. She spent her life bouncing from one man to the next, always on the fringe of crime. Both Bern and Leon despised her. She was like a comet—every time she appeared in our lives, disaster followed. If I were Victoria, I'd grab her. She was a veritable treasure trove of sensitive information only a close family member would know, everything from how four-year-old Leon used to wet himself when her then-boyfriend would scream at him to Mom's PTSD. She didn't know everything, but what she knew would hurt and it was exactly the kind of information Victoria weaponized.

"What are you thinking?" Alessandro asked.

I lifted my head. He sat on the rail under the string of outdoor lights. The black and grey fabric of his long-sleeved shirt and pants blended with the night. He looked like a thief on the prowl from the neck down and a prince from the neck up. The glow of the lights caressed his face, his bold, strong features, carved jaw, perfect cheekbones, amber eyes under the sweep of dark eyebrows . . .

"If I were smarter, I would kill my aunt," I said.

"What did she do?"

He didn't look shocked. He wasn't outraged. He simply assumed that if I was thinking about it, it had to be necessary. This is who we were. Birds of a feather.

"Nevada is thinking about confronting Victoria tomorrow on my behalf. I tried to convince her not to. I don't know if I succeeded. If she goes after Victoria, my grandmother will retaliate, and Gisela would make a handy weapon and a good bargaining chip. No matter how fucked up she is, she's still my aunt and Mom's sister."

"If something were to happen to her, would your mother try to save her?"

I nodded. "She would. I should kill Gisela and solve the problem permanently."

"But you won't." He said it with complete conviction.

"No, I won't. I have to look my reflection in the eyes in the morning."

"Do you know where she is now?"

I showed him my phone. "In the Royal Club inside Zona Rosa of Mexico City. I'm tracking her phone. She's banging a guy who calls himself El Temor."

"The Fear? Is he a criminal?"

"He is a luchador. Just to be clear, I'm not asking you to kill her, Alessandro."

"I know." He smiled. "It's not you."

He believed in me. I leaned on that like a crutch. I shouldn't have called him to this roof, but I was desperate for someone who understood.

"I did pay a local PI firm to keep an eye on her. If I call them, they will take her off the street and sit on her until I tell them to let her go."

"Now, that's you. Are you thinking of pulling the trigger?"

"If I do, Victoria will know. I've been pretending that I have no idea where Gisela is and have no interest in finding her, because I want Victoria to aim her first blow there. If I show my cards, she'll switch her primary target."

"That's a dilemma," he agreed.

I hugged myself. I wanted him to come over and hold me. I had this absurd feeling that if only he touched me, everything would be okay somehow. If all the people in the city disappeared, and it was only me and him on this roof floating alone in the fog, I would be perfectly happy. I should've felt guilty over it—I was a sister, a cousin, a daughter . . . but in this moment I didn't care. It was just me and Alessandro.

"You found Arkan after you left," I said. "What happened?"

He looked at the city, handsome like a painting, silhouetted against the distant lights, then turned to me, and grinned. It was a sharp Alessandro grin, bright and self-mocking. "He killed me."

"He what?"

Alessandro sighed. "I'd been looking for him for so long. He would surface somewhere, and by the time I got there, he would vanish into thin air, like a ghost. I would start over, collecting traces of him until he reappeared. We played this game for years. I don't know if he got tired of being chased or if it was a coincidence, but two weeks after I left Houston to look for him, I found him. Or rather he let me find him. I tracked him down to the Montreal Malting Silos, a big abandoned malt factory. Towers and towers of concrete, thirty-seven meters high, in the middle of the city by the river."

"Did you go in?"

"I did. In my stupid head, it was going to be me against him on top of those silos."

It had already happened, so why was I so scared for him? "It wasn't."

"It was me, him, and four other Primes. I took down three. Then the telekinetic threw a semi at me. I dodged the first pass. The second caught me. It swept me off the roof and I fell off the tower."

Thirty-seven meters. One meter equaled roughly 3.28 feet multiplied by 37 . . . 121.36. He fell one hundred and twenty-one feet. Oh my God.

"I don't remember the impact," he said. "I remember falling and then just black. I must've been clinically dead for a few seconds, because they took my weapons but didn't bother putting a bullet in my brain. When I woke up, there was pain."

He said it so matter-of-fact.

"Most of me was broken. I couldn't move my legs. There was so much pain and it was hot and white." He raised his hands and made a spreading motion as if smoothing a blanket on the bed. "An endless ocean of it. I was on my back and decided to let myself drown. I failed and it hurt so much. I lay there, looking at the sky, waiting for my magic to give up, and I thought of you. It wasn't anything deep or profound. I remembered your face and thought, *I would really like to see her again.* So, I turned over, passed out for a bit, and when I came to, I started crawling. Sometimes I'd black out, then I would come to, remember you, and crawl a little more. No, no, don't cry for me."

I realized heat wet my cheeks.

"Please," he said, his voice quiet. "I don't ever want to make you cry."

I couldn't stop. The tears just poured out. He'd crawled for hours, broken and in agony. If I could murder Arkan a hundred times, it would never make up for that.

Alessandro stopped talking. I brushed the tears from my face with my fingertips. "What happened then?"

"There is a field next to the factory. Eventually I crossed it. Someone saw me and called an ambulance. When I woke up in a hospital room, it hit me. I survived. I *would* see you again. I decided then that I wouldn't waste this chance."

My heart skipped a beat.

"It took me some time to recover. Walking was a problem for a while. Holding a fork too. I could grip it, but I couldn't aim with it. I was training and thinking of what I would say to you. And keeping an eye on Arkan."

"How?" As long as he kept talking about Arkan . . .

Alessandro smiled. It didn't reach his eyes. "Arkan types like he wants to punch through the keys. He murders keyboards. His staff orders them in bulk, and I managed to swap one of mine into the lot. It goes dormant until he says specific words, so it's practically invisible to his bug sweepers. Once a day it sends the recording to one of my email addresses. So I was listening to Arkan run his pack of killers, and then he mentioned your name on a phone call."

Alessandro leaned forward, focused, cold, lethal. His magic whipped out of him, spilling into a dense, potent current. "I meant what I said, Catalina. I won't let him touch you."

"I know." All of the tension, pain, and anger churned inside me. I couldn't contain it any longer. I had to let it go or I'd explode.

"Your wings are out."

My wings had unfurled, ghosting in and out of existence. My magic was leaking. We stared at each other, me with my almost transparent green-and-gold wings and him wrapped in a flow of his power.

"Your turn," he said. "What did you promise Victoria?"

There was no room for lies on this roof.

"I gave you up," I told him. My voice sounded flat. The more matter-of-fact I was about this, the easier it would be.

His eyebrows came together. "How?"

"You ran into Diatheke alone to save Runa's brother and ended up teleporting to Benedict's secret lab. Augustine was the only one who knew the location of it. I needed information to trade to him, so I went to see my grandmother. She gave me what I needed. In return, I promised her that I would never leave House Baylor. I will never marry into another family like my sister did, Alessandro. My family is my responsibility until I die."

He didn't say anything.

"I had this silly fantasy that you would fall in love with me. I knew your family would think I was beneath you, but in *my* stupid head, somehow it would all work out and we would live together happily ever after. Victoria took that away from me. I don't regret it. I would've given her anything to find you."

He was looking at me and I couldn't tell what he was thinking. I just had to get through this. Once all of this was out and he left, I could let go and cry as much as I wanted.

"I was going to explain all of it to you, but you were already leaving. It crushed me that I meant so little."

"Catalina—"

"Please let me finish. This is very difficult for me. When I thought about it, I realized that it was better that way. No messy rationalizations. No false promises. Anyway, there is nothing to be done. Even if Victoria dropped dead tomorrow, I would still stay here. I assumed the responsibility for my House. Nevada trusted me with it. I must see it through. I won't let our family be torn to pieces by our enemies. I can't."

There. I'd said it. I'd gotten it all out before we had a chance to be together. Maybe it would hurt less this way.

"I understand," he said.

"I know your family's position on marriage. I read the press releases on your three engagements. Your family is looking for a woman from an established House, wealthy, respected, and able to dedicate herself to being the wife of Count Sagredo. I can't be her."

A shadow crossed his face. "What the hell does my family have to do with anything?"

"Your family will want you to return. You will leave again, and I'll stay right here. It will be painful, but it will hurt worse when you marry, because then I'll know there is no hope. I'll never be the other woman. It's all or nothing for me. I can't have you for a little bit and give you up. I won't share you."

His magic was on fire, but he sounded almost cold. "I'm not leaving."

I clamped my hands together. It helped me keep my voice from breaking. "I understand, Alessandro. You don't have to lie to me. You don't have to promise me platitudes to soothe me. I'm not a child."

He leaped off the rail so fast, I barely saw it. Our magic collided in a sharp electric burst and he crushed me to him.

"I'm not leaving." His voice was a ragged growl. "I tried, because I can offer you nothing and you deserve so much more. You deserve someone better, but I'm a selfish bastard and I can't stay away. I can't give you up."

He pulled away from me long enough to look at my face. His amber eyes brimmed with magic. He leaned forward. I knew what was about to happen and waiting for it felt like dying. I couldn't stand it. My body locked, rigid with anticipation. I couldn't have taken a single step. It lasted less than a second, but it felt like forever.

He dipped his head and kissed me.

A firestorm raged through me, and suddenly I could move again. I threw my arms around him and kissed him back. I had to taste him, or the world would end.

He kissed me like it was the last kiss we would ever have, like I was dying, and he had to bring me back to life. His arms locked around me, his muscles hard like steel. His hand tangled in my hair. His tongue slid into my mouth. I licked him, dying for a taste, and he made this noise low in his throat that made me shiver.

He broke the kiss and longing swept through me like pain. I almost cried out.

His eyes were molten amber. All traces of pretense fled from him, leaving the real man in their place, focused, dangerous, and driven half-insane by a blinding, irresistible want.

"Don't stop," I breathed.

"I won't."

"Don't."

"I promise." He pulled me to him and kissed me again. My head spun. I melted against his body.

He kissed my lips, my cheek, my neck, his lips warm, gripping me to him, losing himself in me. "I'll never stop. I'll never leave."

"But your family . . ."

"Doesn't matter. I love you."

Mine. Alessandro was finally mine.

I grasped the edge of his shirt, peeled it off him, and threw it away. I kissed his perfect chest, his shoulders, his neck. Each taste was a gift. I couldn't get enough.

He pulled my blouse off me. His hand caught my back. His swordsman calluses rasped against my skin, sending delicious sparks of lust through me. My body howled to be touched. His fingers brushed me and the hooks on my bra came undone. The bra straps sagged off my shoulders, loose. He grabbed my bra and tossed it aside.

The heat of his skin burned my nipples. Alessandro reached into my bun, dragged the hairpin out, and flicked it away. My hair fell on my shoulders.

He sealed his mouth on mine. His hands roamed my body. He dragged his thumb across my right nipple and a soft pulse of pleasure rolled through me. I gasped into his mouth.

He gave me no time to deal with it. His tongue thrust between my lips, seducing, while his hands stroked my back and lower, unzipping my skirt, sliding past the waistband, into my underwear. He cupped my bare butt and pulled my hips to him, grinding against me. The hard length of him pressed into me. An insistent knot of need formed between my legs, impossible to ignore. I wanted him to thrust into it.

He slipped my skirt off my butt with a sure, possessive stroke. He was stripping me bare on the roof and I didn't care. He smelled of sandalwood, citrus, and vanilla, and there must've been magic in it, because I couldn't get enough.

My skirt and underwear fell to my ankles. I tugged at his pants. He let go of me long enough to yank them off.

Wow.

He raised his hand. His magic flashed. His fingers were holding the small foil packet of a condom. He slid it on, saw my face, and halted. "Do you want to stop?"

I dropped my defenses. Every last barrier chaining me in place collapsed. My magic tore out of me. My wings burst into life, glorious, glittering with peridot and gold.

He stared like he'd been struck with lightning.

Look how much I want you.

I opened my mouth. "Do you want me, Alessandro?"

"God, yes."

He picked me up, holding me like I weighed nothing, and the magic swirled around us, singing. I buried my hands in his hair and licked his lips.

He spun with me in his arms and then I was on the couch, on my back. He loomed over me and kissed my neck, setting my nerves on fire. Goose bumps broke on my skin. My nipples tightened, begging to be touched. I moaned.

His hands caressed my breasts, stroking, teasing the tight peaks. My breath came out in quick gasps. My nipples were so tight, they hurt.

His mouth closed on my left breast. His tongue licked me, wet and hot, and the sudden surge of pleasure rocked me. I cried out and clamped my hand over my mouth.

He kissed my other breast, kneading me, switching back and forth. His teeth worried my nipple. He sucked again and again. My head was spinning. The knot between my legs pulsed. Hot liquid slicked me. If he kept going, I would come before he ever started.

He slid lower, painting a line of kisses down the center of my stomach. I didn't know if I wanted to pull him back up to my breasts, or to let him go down.

My body needed more. The wait was unbearable.

His fingers brushed the inside of my thighs, pushing my legs open. I jerked.

He raised his head to look at me. "Have you done this before?"

"No."

"Are you scared?"

"No."

He leaned over me and kissed me again, deep and long. I felt drunk.

"Trust me." His voice was a rough promise in my ear.

I nipped his jaw.

He made a noise that was half growl, half groan, and moved down. His hands stroked my thighs, his warm skilled fingers caressing, coaxing . . . He lowered his head.

He licked me. A jolt of pure ecstasy flooded me.

He licked me again. Oh my God.

He sucked on the small bundle of nerves, licking, caressing, stroking me. My thoughts dissolved. The knot between my legs tightened, aching, until it was the core of me, impossible to ignore.

Another lick. Another wave of bliss. Again, again, again . . .

I was still empty. I desperately needed more. I knew I was arching my hips and moaning and clawing at his shoulders, but I couldn't stop. The pleasure was too much.

He slipped his fingers inside me. My body gripped him, and I came. The climax melted over me. The pleasure crested, and crashed, and crested again. I slumped on the couch, soaking in bliss, boneless and happy.

He loomed above me. The blunt head of his cock pressed against me, right where I wanted it most.

He thrust.

Yes. This. This is what I wanted. To be full of him.

Pain flashed through me, quick and sudden. He stopped.

I wrapped my arms around him and arched my hips, sliding more of him in. Alessandro swore.

I arched my back, wound my arms around him, kissed his jaw, and whispered into his ear. "Faster . . ."

He groaned and thrust into me again, the glide of his hard cock turning pain into liquid heat. The ache was still there, a sharp pinch, but I wanted him too much. He thrust into me again. The feeling of his body on mine, the harsh strength in his arms, the way he looked at me, the way his shaft slid into me, all of it was intoxicating bliss. I matched his thrust, molding my body to his.

He pumped into me, hard, fast, exactly how I wanted.

The ache began to build again, demanding, unstoppable. My breath came in ragged gasps. I wound my legs around his hips, trying to take more of him in. He was so big, and I wanted him so much . . .

We moved together as one.

Don't stop . . . Please don't stop . . .

Someone moaned and I realized it was me.

He kept going, tireless, his body strong and powerful on top of me. I held on to him, breathless, looking for that dizzying thrill.

Yes, love me, Alessandro. Love me.

He thrust deep. The pressure inside me peaked and broke. I grabbed on to him and lost myself to an orgasm so intense, it was almost blinding.

He wrapped his arms around me, kissing me, whispering things in my ear in a flurry of Italian. *"Ti amo . . ."*

"I love you," I breathed into his ear.

He crushed me to him. I kissed him, shifting my hips, asking for more. He started again, building to a hard, fast rhythm. I gave all of myself to him. Every breath, every gasp, every whimper, all of my heart . . .

His whole body went tight and rigid. I met him again and again, delirious from happiness and need.

A shudder gripped him, and he came with a low groan. I wrapped my arms around him and kissed his face, brushing my lips against his skin.

Slowly he withdrew. His eyes were still wild. He slid next me, pulled the blanket over us, and wrapped his arms around me under it. I snuggled close to him, breathless and completely content, my cheek on his chest.

Around us the magic twisted and wound, dancing to the tune only it heard.

# Chapter 15

I was floating in the soft happy place between sleeping and being awake when Alessandro moved next to me. I dragged my eyes open. The roof was empty. The light glowed with soft yellow against the night sky.

"What is it?"

"It's okay," he whispered. "You're safe. Go back to sleep."

I shifted, my head on his arm, and shut my eyes.

My phone rang.

Alessandro swore under his breath.

I groaned and rolled onto my stomach, looking for the phone on the floor with my hand. My fingers finally found it. I pulled it up and peered at it. Bug. I swiped to answer.

"Tell that cockalorum he owes me a new drone."

I raised my head. Remnants of a drone sagged off the stone rail. A huge knife thrust out of the metal and plastic mess. I glanced at Alessandro. He shrugged.

"Why are you flying drones over our territory?"

"I was doing a security sweep. How was I supposed to know the two of you decided to sleep naked on the roof?"

"You are not supposed to do security sweeps over our territory. We've talked about this. Patricia is handling the surveillance. She's got this."

"Catalina . . ."

"Privacy, Bug!"

I hung up. Alessandro sighed, slipped off the couch, gloriously naked, walked over to the crippled drone, and tossed it off the roof.

The phone told me it was 10:39 p.m. We must've barely dozed off.

I rummaged through the pile of clothes, looking for my underwear. Alessandro pulled on his pants. I finally found the white scrap of fabric, put it on, and looked for my bra. He was holding it. I reached for it and Alessandro pulled it out of the way.

"Really?" I reached for the bra again, and he moved it back.

I stepped closer. Alessandro pounced. One moment I was on my feet and the next we were back on the couch, tangled up in the blanket, the bundle of my clothes in his hands.

"What are you doing?" I whispered.

"Don't go."

"I have to go. If I don't go, Patricia and Bug will fight. There will be hurt feelings."

"They'll sort it out."

"We have to get dressed anyway. He never sends just one drone."

Alessandro wrapped his arms around me. "Screw him. Stay here with me."

I gave up. I didn't want to go anywhere or do anything anyway. I just wanted to lie with him on this couch and drift off to sleep.

"Give me my clothes back and I'll stay."

He pretended to think it over and handed me my shirt.

"That's it?"

"Yes. Shirt and panties, that's all."

I slipped my blouse on. "So you're okay with my butt barely covered by underwear splashed all over nine screens in Bug's situation room?"

"You have a blanket."

"And my bra?"

"I'm keeping it."

"What are you, fifteen?"

"No, that's crazy. More like eleven. Maybe twelve."

I opened my mouth to reply.

Nevada screamed.

I jumped to the rail. In the window Grandma Frida sprawled on the floor of the motor pool on her back, Nevada on her knees beside her. Oh no.

Alessandro leaped over the rail. Magic flashed with orange around him and he landed on the street like it was nothing and ran into the motor pool.

"What's happening?" I yelled.

"Poisoned!" Nevada screamed back.

The word scorched me. I whipped around and sprinted to the door and down the stairs, taking them three at a time. Not Grandma Frida. No, no, no . . .

I hit the third-floor door with both hands, throwing it open, and charged down the hallway. Bern's door loomed in front of me. I pounded on it with my fist. "Runa! Runa!"

Nobody answered.

"Runa!"

The door swung open and Bern blocked my way, naked except for boxer shorts. "She isn't . . ."

"Grandma Frida's been poisoned!"

The clump of blankets on Bern's bed exploded and Runa jumped out, in a tank top and underwear, her red hair sticking out of her head in all directions. "Where?"

"Motor pool."

We sprinted through the hallway and down the stairs, out of the building, across the street, and into the motor pool. Grandma Frida lay unmoving. Alessandro bent over her, doing chest compressions. Her skin was grey, like old parchment. Oh God.

Runa dropped to her knees and grabbed Grandma's hand. A green glow streamed out of her, wrapping around the two of them. Runa jerked Grandma's sleeve back and licked her wrist. "Batrachotoxin derivative with a synthetic additive. I've got this. Keep doing CPR."

Magic poured out of Runa. Nothing changed. Alessandro kept pumping Grandma's chest.

A moment crawled by.

Another.

No. Just no. Not Grandma Frida. No more hugs. No more funny jokes as her eyes sparkled. No more teasing Mom, no more making me eat, no more smell of engine grease . . .

I wanted to do something, to scream, to punch, to help somehow, but there was nothing I could do. I just stood there and stared. The look on Nevada's face tore me apart.

The door banged open behind us and Mom and Arabella ran into the motor pool. Mom didn't say anything. She just stopped, looking as if she had been punched.

Leon burst in from the back. "What . . . ?"

Grandma Frida wasn't moving. I couldn't even tell if she was still alive.

I clamped my hands over my mouth and paced back and forth. I couldn't stay still anymore.

Seconds ticked by. A count started in my head on its own. *One, two, three . . .*

Fifteen, sixteen . . . twenty.

I'd killed my grandmother. I should have moved us to a location we could secure, but I kept waiting for the right property. It was my fault.

Forty-two, forty-three, forty-four . . .

Fifty-five . . .

The green glow around Runa dimmed. "Mrs. Afram," Runa said, her voice chiding. "You should tell him to stop."

Grandma Frida opened her eyes and looked at Alessandro.

Alive. All the strength went out of me. I crouched and clamped my hands together into a single fist.

Alessandro raised his hands in the air.

"Everybody is mean to him," Grandma croaked. "I wanted him to feel he was helping."

Mom cursed and slumped forward. Arabella buried her face in her hands. Her shoulders shook. Nevada turned white as a sheet. Leon stared at Grandma, then at Runa, wild-eyed.

Runa landed on her butt and hung her head back. Bern crouched by her, his hands around her shoulders, murmuring something.

Runa nodded. "No, no, I'm okay. I just need a minute. Nasty stuff."

Grandma Frida squinted at Runa, then at me. "Somebody help me up."

Alessandro gently sat her up.

"What happened?" Mom growled.

"A spider bit me." Grandma shook her head.

"What spider?" Arabella asked.

"A metal spider."

"Where did it go?" Mom demanded.

"I don't know, Penelope. I hit it with the wrench, it bit my wrist, and I passed out."

There was a chance it was still here. I spun around scanning the floor. "How big was it?"

"Three inches across," Grandma said. "A fat little bugger."

Bern picked Runa up off the floor and looked around. All of us stared in different directions.

Nevada's gaze locked on something to the right and above us. "Got you, you fucker."

A toolbox streaked off the side table and smashed into the wall near the ceiling. An eight-legged shape skittered across the wall. The toolbox had missed it by a hair.

What the hell?

The metal spider dashed along the wall toward the exit.

"Oh no, you don't!" Nevada snarled, punching her palm.

The toolbox chased the metal bug, thudding into the wall in rhythm with Nevada's fist.

"Intact!" I yelled. "We need it—"

The toolbox crushed the spider.

"—in one piece." Too late.

A tall man strode up and loomed in the open bay. He was huge, dark haired, and built like he snapped people in half every day. Nevada pivoted to him. The toolbox and what was left of the spider slid off the wall, hurtled through the air in the direction of her gaze, and froze a foot from the man's face.

Connor Rogan regarded us with his blue eyes.

Nobody spoke.

Silence stretched.

Connor looked at Nevada and pointed to the toolbox, still suspended in midair.

Nevada straightened. "Hi, honey. You know how we were worried about our son not having magic? Good news, we don't have to worry anymore."

The whole family piled into the kitchen, except for Leon and Alessandro, who joined Patricia and the security team to sweep the grounds. She'd asked for Leon, and Alessandro volunteered. Regina came in to examine the spider, and the metal and electronic wreckage now lay on the table, under the bright light. Bern sat opposite her, engrossed in his laptop and the plethora of security cameras and sensor readings. Connor had levitated three padded chairs out of the great room. Nevada took one, Grandma Frida the other, and the third stayed empty, because Mom couldn't sit still and kept making circles around the island. I couldn't sit still either.

Arabella brought two pairs of Nike shorts for Runa and me.

"Clearly, I'm the only one around here who cares about modesty."

That was too much. "You wear shorts with half of your butt hanging out."

Arabella wrinkled her nose. "The operative word here is *shorts*. You two don't have any. Don't blame me for being emotionally compromised. Hussies."

"Oh grow up." Grandma Frida raised her head from her puke bucket. Runa had purged the poison by breaking it down and the byproducts induced nausea.

"Why don't you lie down?" Mom said.

Grandma Frida retched and gave Mom the evil eye. "I don't want to lie down. I want to be where the action is."

Mom's left eye twitched. She slapped her hand over it.

I leaned to look over Bern's shoulder at the table. Across from us Regina peered at the mechanical spider leg, the only recognizable remnant of the spider.

"Anything?" I asked.

Regina plucked the leg from the table and held it up between her thumb and forefinger. "It could be a construct made by an animator. It could be made by a metallofactor. A Hephaestus mage. Or a techno-mancer."

"Do you think this might be the thing you felt earlier?"

"I don't know. The smashing makes things difficult."

"I am sorry," Nevada called out. "I was emotionally compromised."

Connor kneaded her back and shoulders. "Your smashing was fantastic."

"How does that work anyway?" Arabella asked. "Are you borrowing the baby's powers? Like, is this normal?"

"Yes. I think. It happens if I am really upset." Nevada spread her arms. "I don't know if it's normal. It's my first time being pregnant with a telekinetic."

"It's called prenatal transference," Connor said. "It means the child is a very powerful Prime."

Nevada turned to him. "Are you sure?"

Connor looked smug. "I'm sure. Ask my mother."

"Will it go away after she gives birth?" Mom asked.

"Yes," Connor said.

Grandma Frida winked at them. "I hate to see what his first temper tantrum will be like." She cackled and broke into coughs.

Nevada gave Connor a slightly freaked-out look.

"It will be fine." He rubbed her back. "My power stopped spiking after I was born, and I didn't really manifest that strong again until I was about five."

I looked back to Regina. "So there is nothing at all you can tell us?"

"It's dead." Regina knocked the metal leg on the table. "I don't under-stand how it got past Cinder."

Runa raised her hand. "Question. How many of you knew that Bern and I are dating?"

"Dating?" Arabella raised her eyebrows.

"If you could raise your hands," Runa said.

Everyone raised their hands.

Runa looked around, her face stunned. "How? I was so careful . . ."

Connor smiled at her. "They're private investigators."

"Oh." She looked around again. "How long have you known?"

"Since the beginning," Arabella told her.

Runa heaved a sigh.

I had to fix this before she came to the wrong conclusion. "Bern didn't tell us."

Arabella nodded. "We're just nosy."

Nevada shrugged. "I asked him."

"What did he say?" Runa asked.

Nevada grinned. "He lied."

Mom laughed. Bern shrugged his massive shoulders.

The front door clanged open. Cinder ran into the room, jumped on the table, and spat out the mangled corpse of a metal spider. Regina raised her hand and magic poured out of her fingers. The battered metal construct floated off the table and turned slowly.

"Nice," Regina murmured. "To answer your question, yes, this is what I felt before. They rode in on Rhino."

Alessandro walked into the kitchen, followed by Leon and Patricia. He made a beeline for me.

"None of the perimeter sensors were tripped," Patricia reported.

"It's well-made," Regina said. "A sophisticated design, refined. The level of teaching is quite high."

"Cheryl?" I asked.

"Mhm. I had a look at some of her designs after our chat. This is a modified miniature version of Climber VII."

"A fail-safe," Alessandro said.

I turned to him.

"Arkan's people failed to frame Leon for murder, then the telekinetic couldn't kill you in the swamp. You keep surviving and asking uncomfortable questions. Cheryl is losing confidence in Arkan's ability to neutralize you, so she added a fail-safe in case the illusion mage didn't succeed."

Arabella frowned. "If these creepy nasties got into our car while we were at Stephen's, why didn't they sting us on the way home?"

"You weren't the target," Nevada said, her face grim. "They wanted Catalina, but she didn't make it back to the car, so they rode here, sensed Regina, and took off."

"Why did Grandma get stung then?" Arabella asked.

"Probably self-defense," Connor said. "They are likely programmed to hide among machinery and Grandma Frida banged on it with a wrench."

"It's a stupid plan," Leon said. "First, it points straight to Cheryl."

"She isn't thinking clearly," I told him.

"Second, if Catalina died in the middle of this, there would be hell to pay. We would declare a feud on House Castellano."

"So would House Rogan," Connor said.

"Yes." Leon nodded. "House Montgomery would go to war with her. Linus Duncan would go to war with her."

"And the National Assembly would lose its shit if Catalina died," Runa finished. "Considering Catalina is a Depu . . ." She slapped her hand over her mouth.

Oh no.

Nevada leaned forward, zeroing in on me. "Catalina, why would the National Assembly lose its shit?"

Connor's face shut down. "I'm going to kill him."

"That would be rather difficult." Alessandro's voice was cold. His expression turned calculating. A dangerous darkness filled his eyes, and deep within his irises, magic smoldered, waiting to burst into an inferno. The Artisan was back.

An imperceptible shift occurred within the room. My family realized there was a predator in their midst and they rapidly recalibrated to meet the new threat.

"And why is that?" Connor's voice held no emotion.

"Because he's Linus Duncan. Furthermore, if you attack the Warden, his Deputy will defend him to her death, and I'm sworn to protect her."

"What the fuck is going on?" Leon demanded. "Can we all just take it down a notch or two, because I really don't want to shoot anybody right now."

Patricia stared at me. "You are the Deputy Warden of Texas." It wasn't a question.

I landed into the padded seat and looked at Runa.

"I'm sorry!" She waved her arms. "I'm emotionally compromised!"

"I swear, I will shoot the next person who says that," Leon growled.

"You can't shoot her," Arabella told him. "She's your brother's girl-friend."

"Everyone, shut up," Mom barked in her sergeant voice.

The kitchen went silent as a tomb.

She turned to me. "Explain."

"Linus is the Warden of Texas, I'm his Deputy, we investigate magi-cal threats to humanity on behalf of the National Assembly, and we can't talk about it, or the National Assembly will nuke us from orbit."

"What was he thinking?" Connor bit off the words with controlled fury. "Warden mortality is seventy-five percent within the first ten years. I turned him down. Why did you accept?"

"I can't tell you."

"How long have you been doing it?" Connor asked.

"Six months. There's no need to be so dramatic. I'm alive, I'm good at my job, and one day I will be the Warden of Texas."

"Can you quit?" Grandma Frida asked.

"No. Also, I don't want to quit."

My grandmother studied me. "Do you like it?"

The mass grave flashed before me. "Not always. But it's necessary. And important."

Grandma Frida grinned. "Then do it. Don't listen to them."

"It's not that simple," Mom said.

"It is." Grandma Frida looked at Alessandro. "Are you planning on sticking around and helping her?"

"I am."

Connor opened his mouth, his expression harsh. Nevada rested her fingers on his arm. "You're not going to talk her out of this. She's pro-tecting us."

Connor frowned.

"I'll explain later," she said.

Arabella snapped her fingers. "So that's where the money's coming from. I was wondering why we're suddenly bucks up."

"How up?" Leon asked, suddenly excited.

"We're making three times what we used to," Arabella told him.

Leon gave me a thumbs-up.

"So that's why," Bern said.

"Why what?" Runa asked him.

"Why her answer is always yes."

Runa waited.

"When we need something, the answer is yes," Bern elaborated. "New sensors and camera system, yes." He looked at Leon. "New Hawk 7 rifle and a new car, yes." He looked at Patricia. "Additional personnel and upgraded vests, yes. We get all the toys, bells and whistles, because she's a Deputy Warden and she is making all the new money for us."

"Okay." Mom crossed her arms on her chest. "This doesn't leave the room. You don't know she's the Deputy Warden, you don't know what a Warden is, and you think Linus is an old family friend. That's all."

Mom waited. Nobody said anything.

"I need a 'yes, ma'am' on this."

"Yes, ma'am," we chorused. Even Patricia and Regina said it.

Mom fixed Runa with her sniper stare. "Do you want to be a part of this family?"

Runa nodded.

"Then don't be a blabbermouth. Moving on."

We ran through the security measures again. One by one, the kitchen emptied. Grandma Frida decided to lie down after all. Leon took off, Arabella did too, Bern and Runa followed. Patricia and Regina left as well. Patricia had a calculating look in her eyes, which meant she was reshuffling our security arrangements in her head.

The crowd in the kitchen dwindled to just Mom, Connor and Nevada, and Alessandro and me.

"Do you know what you're doing?" Mom asked me.

"Yes."

Mom sighed. "I don't know how to talk to you, Catalina. I always know when your sisters are keeping something from me. Neither one of them is good at it, and eventually it explodes out. You hid this from me for half a year and I had no idea."

I raised my head. "You hid Victoria Tremaine from us for our whole lives and none of us had any idea. I guess I'm like you, then."

"That's what scares me." Mom shook her head. "If you're in trouble, will you even tell me?"

"I will try."

Mom sighed again.

Nevada turned to me, gently patting her stomach. "I owe you an apology."

"No."

"Yes. My back was against the wall and I made a terrible decision. There is no way to take it back. At the time that was the only way I could see to preserve House Baylor's future."

"It was my fault," Connor said. "I should have found Merritt."

"*We* should have found Merritt," Nevada said. "Catalina, you know how important you are to me. I hate that I made you think that I was mad at you and that you betrayed me somehow. I wasn't thinking clearly. The flu was real, the collapse was real, and that was the best my exhausted brain could come up with. I regretted it the moment I started doing it. It ate me up inside. I wanted to explain it to you, but during most of the following year I worried that it would somehow surface. It kept me from sleeping. I finally decided it was buried, and I tried to tell you about it."

"I remember," I told her. "You started to explain to me that Connor had been accused of human trafficking but didn't finish because House Ferrer shot a missile at your house."

"Then there was the White case, and the Hyperion. There was always something. Then Alessandro happened."

She glanced at Alessandro who was standing next to me, impassive.

"By that point I told Mom," Nevada said. "I had to tell someone."

"And I told her to keep it to herself," Mom said.

I turned to her. "Why?"

"Because you had enough on your plate. I told her to wait. I had faith in you both. You would sort it out when you were in a better place."

Nevada sighed. "I regret it, Catalina. But if I was back in that moment, knowing only what I knew then, I would do it again. It wasn't a mistake. I did it deliberately because I wanted to protect you."

"I know. I don't view it as a mistake. It was a sacrifice, Nevada. I understand. I would have done the same."

Tears wet Nevada's eyes. Connor put his arm around her. "You got this."

"Something occurred to me," my big sister said. "At the start, you made a big deal about keeping the family separate from House Rogan. And then in February you made a one-eighty. I pulled your voting record in the Assembly. You always vote with Connor. You sit next to him in the chamber."

"He's my brother-in-law."

"Oh, it's more than that. I've been wondering for months why you made sure that everyone in Houston knew that our two houses are a package deal."

"Why wouldn't we want to be allied with House Rogan? They are powerful, dangerous, wealthy . . ."

Nevada smiled at me. "You tied us together. In the eyes of the public, we are impossible to separate. Victoria can no longer target House Rogan without dragging House Baylor down."

I didn't say anything. It didn't seem like a reply was needed.

Nevada tried to get up off the chair and Connor gently helped her to her feet. She came over to me and hugged me.

"I love you so much," Nevada said. "I know exactly what you're doing because I did it too for the same reasons. But we can't do this anymore. From now on, let's talk. Let's tell things to each other, because I can't do it the other way. It tears me up inside and I know it's hard on you. You have me and Connor, and Mom, and Arabella, and the boys . . ."

Heat built behind my eyes. I held on to her. My nephew kicked me.

"We love you. We will help you. Don't repeat my mistakes."

She held me for a few more seconds, then let me go. "I'll see you in the morning." She looked at Alessandro. "Do not hurt her."

She walked away.

"We have some matters to discuss when things settle down," Connor said. The Scourge of Mexico smiled at me and followed his wife.

Mom sighed, kissed my forehead, and left the kitchen.

It was just me and Alessandro.

"Family," he said.

"Yeah."

"I like yours better than mine."

"Are you leaving?" I managed to keep the desperation out of my voice. I didn't want him to leave. I wanted him to stay and hold me while I fell asleep.

A shadow crossed his face. "Do you want me to?"

"No. I want you to stay."

We stood barely three feet away from each other but suddenly the distance gaped between us.

"Do you want to stay?" I asked.

"More than anything."

"Then stay."

He faced me. The muscles along his jaw locked.

"What is it?"

"When I said I don't deserve you, I meant it. I can't give you anything, except myself, Catalina."

"That's all I ever wanted. I already told you I don't expect anything else."

He opened his mouth and closed it without saying a word.

"Alessandro, I've had an awful day and you're scaring me."

The mask hiding his face dropped, torn. He wrapped his arms around me. "I've got you."

"Come with me."

He let me go and we walked down to my bedroom. He followed me in and raised his eyebrows at the wall of swords.

"Catalina, I like a good blade, but you might have a problem."

"Do you like it?"

"I love it."

"Good, because that's where we're sleeping tonight. In the morning, if you're good, I'll let you touch some of them."

"Only some?"

I smiled at him. "We can negotiate."

He grinned back. "I love negotiating. I can be very persuasive."

I wrapped my arms around him and kissed him. He made my head spin. "So can I."

The kiss ended and he looked at me, his eyes wild.

There were so many things to worry about. The Abyss, Cheryl, Runa outing me to my family and what Linus would do about it, and the distance that had yawned between us in the kitchen . . . I couldn't deal with any of it right now.

Whatever it was that Alessandro was trying to find a way to tell me, it would wait until tomorrow. Tonight was ours and I wouldn't trade it for anything.

 # Chapter 16

I stood by the counter, drinking my morning tea, basking in the sunshine streaming through the window, and tried to come to terms with Alessandro in my kitchen. He wore beat-up jeans and an old T-shirt, which he had gotten out of his car. His hair was tousled. Stubble traced his jaw. He looked terribly . . . casual? Domestic? I wasn't sure there was even a word for it.

Alessandro poured black coffee into his mug, tried it, and made a face. Next to him on the floor Shadow looked terribly disappointed. She'd glued herself to Alessandro the moment he stepped into the kitchen. Apparently my dog was convinced that if she stared at him long enough, he would drop something yummy.

"Weak?"

"Bitter. Where did you get this?"

My phone chimed. A text from Patricia. *Albert Ravenscroft is here.*

Why? Why, why, why?

Do you want me to let him in?

Yes. I'll talk to him outside.

"I'll be right back," I told Alessandro.

He nodded.

I went to the front door, Shadow at my heels. Outside the sunshine poured from the sky, bringing heat with it. It would be another sweltering day.

Albert was walking toward the house. He saw me and sped up.

"How can I help you, Prime Ravenscroft?"

Behind me the door swung open. Alessandro sauntered out with the coffee still in his hand, looking unconcerned. On the left, Connor walked out of his HQ. A mug of coffee floated next to him.

How considerate of my boyfriend and my brother-in-law to invite themselves into this conversation.

"Look," Albert said. "I thought about it. Nothing's changed."

He had this grim, determined look on his face.

Connor leaned on the wall by the door, looking at something on his phone, plucked the mug from the air, took a sip, and put it back, just in case Albert forgot that he was the Scourge of Mexico.

"Albert," I said gently. "What are you doing here?"

"We have something, Catalina. Something special. Black wings or no, I don't want to lose that."

"Black wings?" Alessandro muttered and looked at Connor.

Connor didn't look up. "Long story."

"Albert, this isn't going to happen. You know why."

He shook his head. "My father hates you, but it doesn't matter. This time next month I'll be the Head of my House. My parents have made arrangements to retire to the coast. Patrick is away studying at Florida State. It would be just me and you. I really want to make this work."

"I understand, but I'm not in love with you. I don't think about you in that way."

He clenched his jaw. This would have been so much easier without an audience.

"Is there someone else?" Albert asked.

"Yes."

"Is it him?" Albert looked at Alessandro.

"Yes."

Albert's expression hardened. He seemed to come to a decision. "I don't know who you are and I don't care. You should leave."

Alessandro's voice remained pleasant. "Or?"

Albert seemed to be caught off guard. "Leave. This is your only warning."

Connor Rogan smiled.

I put some snap into my voice. "Albert, your welcome is withdrawn."

His gaze bore into Alessandro. "No, I'll fix this, and then we'll talk."

"Anytime," Alessandro said.

"Fine. I tried to warn you."

A focused torrent of power shot out of Albert. It wasn't aimed at me, but I felt traces of it. Fear. Deep, mind-numbing, all-consuming fear.

Even if I'd had any feelings for him, this would have killed it.

The awful mental deluge smashed into Alessandro. He took a sip of his coffee. "I'm still waiting."

Albert stared, shocked. A normal person would've collapsed in blind panic.

Magic swirled around Albert, icy and potent. He unleashed a barrage, hammering against Alessandro's mind. Panic, pain, despair melted together into an irresistible compulsion to flee. It was a staggering salvo.

Finally, the attack ebbed.

Sweat drenched Albert's hairline. "Antistasi." He spat the word out like it was rotten.

"Yes," Alessandro confirmed.

Albert's eyebrows came together. "No matter. I'll just have to do it with my hands."

"Please do." Alessandro held his coffee out to me. "Would you mind holding this for a second?"

I held out my hand. "Albert, what you're doing is grounds for a feud. I don't love you, but I don't want you to get hurt. Respect my wishes and leave, because he's going to break you, and I don't want to send you home in an ambulance."

Albert started toward Alessandro.

Alessandro brushed my cheek with a kiss, winked at me, gave me his mug, and met Albert halfway. Albert launched a devastating kick. It whistled past Alessandro. He sidestepped Albert with fluid grace and kicked his supporting leg out from under him. Albert landed on the pavement, rolled to his feet, and charged at Alessandro.

I turned to Connor. "Are you just going to stand there and watch this?"

He raised his eyebrows at me. "Your boyfriend is being very careful with him. Look, he just had a chance to break his ribs and didn't take it."

Ugh.

Albert hammered a punch, aiming for Alessandro's jaw. He'd turned into it, twisting his wrist at the last second to add more power, and if the punch had landed, it might have dropped Alessandro. Alessandro shied out of the way, locked his left hand on the wrist of Albert's extended right arm, pushing it aside, stepped in, and turned right, driving his elbow into Albert's jaw. The blow knocked Albert's head to the side. Before he could recover, Alessandro reversed his swing, spinning left, and caught him with his elbow again. Albert staggered back, his mouth bloody.

"I fought a male telekinetic in the Pit," I told Connor.

My brother-in-law came to life, like a shark sensing a drop of blood in the water. "Was he any good?"

"Yes. Powerful, but not very precise. I don't think he has a lot of experience, because he freaked out when I grabbed his mind. He threw spikes."

"What kind of spikes?"

"About two feet long, metal, with a ring on the dull end."

Connor's face snapped into a flat mask. He raised his hand. Something crunched inside the motor pool of his HQ. A bright spark streaked out of the open bay doors. A metal spike landed in his hand.

"Yes," I said. "Exactly like that."

"Was the inside of the ring smooth or did it have ridges?"

"I didn't look that closely. I was running away." I thought back to the spike protruding from the guard's neck. "No, wait, it was ridged. Why is that important?"

"Most telekinetics throw spikes that look like giant nails or crossbow bolts. This is a modified marlin spike. I've never known anyone to use it outside of our family."

Connor only had one family member on the American side, his mother, Arrosa. On the Spanish side, he had a whole boatload of relatives, but none of them were powerful enough, with the exception of Mia Rosa, who was eight years old.

"He was a Prime, Connor. I'm sure of it."

I could tell by the look on his face that he didn't like it.

Alessandro drove his fist into Albert's solar plexus. Albert stumbled back and fell clumsily, landing on his ass. Blood dripped from his mouth. His eyes teared, his face swollen and bloody. Alessandro crouched by him. He was unmarked. His hair wasn't even messed up.

"This isn't a fair fight," Alessandro said. "Go home."

Albert tried to rise, his eyes full of rage.

Alessandro hammered a quick punch to his chin. Albert's eyes rolled back in his head. He collapsed.

"You could have done that in the beginning," I told him.

"Yes, but then he would think I sucker punched him and that he'd have a chance if he tried again. Now he knows."

Nevada walked out of the bay doors. She was carrying a green bag with tiny dinosaurs on it. She didn't give Albert a second glance.

"Hey, honey," she said. Her voice sounded clipped.

"Hey," Connor said, moving toward her.

"I need you to cancel your plans for today and find someone else to handle whatever this is," she said. "My water just broke."

Oh God. Oh God. What do we do? We needed a car. We needed to get Nevada to the hospital.

"Stay right here!" Connor ordered in his officer voice. "Don't move."

He sprinted to the bay.

Nevada looked after him and very deliberately took two steps forward.

My phone rang. A moment later Alessandro's phone went off as well. I answered without looking. "Yes?"

"It took Marat into the Pit," Stephen barked. "They're fighting it now and losing. Tatyana's on her way. Can you get there?"

I stared, mute, torn between two vital things.

Nevada waved at me. "Go to the Pit. I'll be fine. Get to the hospital when you can."

"On my way." I spun around, ran into the house, and found Arabella in her bathroom, putting on lipstick.

"Nevada's in labor."

Arabella dropped her lipstick into the sink.

"The thing in the Pit grabbed one of the Primes and is attacking the work site. I have to go. Yesterday, Victoria threatened Nevada and the baby. Go with her and don't let her out of your sight. If it all goes to shit, I don't care if you are in the middle of that damn building, you transform, and you get her out of there."

Arabella took off running.

I charged out of the bathroom and ran back downstairs to get my sword.

I took a turn too fast. Rhino's overpowered engine roared as I accelerated out of the turn. Alessandro grabbed the door handle to steady himself.

We'd had a choice of the Spider or Rhino and we both picked armor over speed. Rhino would plow through anything in our way and get us there. If I didn't kill us first.

"What the hell was he doing back on-site?" I growled.

"Probably getting all the equipment out. They are expensive machines." Alessandro shook his head, his eyes sharp and focused. "Damn idiot didn't listen to me. I told him to get his people out of there."

"I did too."

"I warned him." Alessandro bared his teeth. "I said, don't think about leaving, don't make any preparations. Just walk off at the end of the day like normal, leave the equipment where it is, and once everyone is out, pull the guards back to the outer perimeter. The fool went back for the assets."

And once the Abyss saw its food and brain supply leaving, it reacted violently. It required metal and humans to expand. Without a continuous supply of either, it would have to leave the relative safety of the Pit to procure it. Every time it sent its nodes out of the mire, it ended badly.

We tore past the dealership where we'd fought the constructs.

"I don't have a plan," I told Alessandro. "I don't know how to kill it. It's impossible to destroy every node, and as long as one survives, the Abyss will rebuild itself."

"We'll deal with that gap once we've jumped it."

"That doesn't even make sense."

"You worry too much."

"A sentient self-repairing construct the size of ten city blocks is on a rampage, and you're telling me not to worry."

"It will be fine. You'll see."

It wouldn't be fine. "Call Linus."

My phone dialed the number and the beeps echoed through the cabin. No answer. Just like the first two times I'd called him since we left the house. Linus always took my calls. I didn't even want to think about why he wasn't picking up. That was a bottomless rabbit hole of anxiety and speculation, and we had bigger problems on our hands.

We shot onto the final bridge. The Pit Reclamation island was on fire. Flames tore out from its shore, colliding with a forest of tentacles flailing in the water.

A hunter construct leaped out of the water and into our path. I rammed it. The impact knocked it aside and we sped past it. All around us the Pit churned.

The island wasn't on fire. Rather the fire circled it, a wall of living flame twenty feet tall. Here and there the Abyss' constructs, hulking forms melded from vegetation and bone, emerged from the water to storm the shore and fell apart, consumed by the inferno. The water at the island's edge boiled. Plumes of steam rose, hissing. The temperature inside the car jumped.

Alessandro grabbed his phone and dialed a number. "We're coming in." He hung up. "Keep going."

The fire wall towered in front of us. I drove straight at it. The flames parted. We shot through the gap and I mashed the brakes. Rhino skidded and slid to a stop.

In the middle of the parking lot in front of the HQ building, Tatyana Pierce stood in an arcane circle of dazzling complexity. Her eyes were pure fire. Workers huddled around her, clutching weapons and sweating. A young man in a suit, one of the secretaries I had seen in the House Pierce building, stood by with an impassive expression on his face, holding a cell phone.

I rolled the window down.

"Welcome to the party." Tatyana grinned.

"Have you found Marat?"

"Jiang is looking for him. Go down the street directly behind me. I'd go with you, but I'm a little busy on the grill." She laughed, her eyes sparkling.

I stepped on the gas and steered Rhino around her and down the street. Ruined buildings in various stages of repair slid behind us, and through the gaps Tatyana's flames glowed like a magical aurora borealis. I couldn't even begin to calculate the kind of power required to maintain a wall of that size.

We passed an abandoned Burger King, a convenience store, a deli with dusty windows . . . Ahead the street and the island ended, the swamp beyond it blocked by fire. Where the hell was Stephen?

"Up there." Alessandro pointed to the right, at a four-story building jutting out of the rubble. I squinted. A man in a suit stood on the roof. Found him.

I parked and grabbed Linus' sword. Alessandro leaped from the vehicle, carrying the prototype of the prototype Linus had given him.

The building's automatic door stood ajar, stuck permanently open. We passed through it. The inside was dark like a cave. A musty stench filled the air, like hundreds of waterlogged books were drying in it. Alessandro turned left. I followed him and we came to a door leading up the stairs. He sprinted and I did my best to chase him.

One flight, two, three, four . . .

Alessandro had disappeared into the gloom above.

I picked up speed, sprinting.

Above me a door banged, probably Alessandro emerging onto the roof. Another flight of stairs. A door loomed ahead. Finally.

I stumbled through it into the sunlight, gasping for breath. The roof was paved and square. Stephen stood at the far edge, looking out into the Pit. Alessandro was next to him. I ran to them. Heat washed over me. Tatyana's wall ended about twenty feet below us.

A clump of vegetation protruded from the mire about fifty yards away. The long green stems, striated with metal, shifted against each other, braided into a fist.

"Is Marat in there?" Stephen asked me. "Can you feel his mind?"

I reached out. My magic grew, spiraling, and found a mind, glowing with purple.

"He's in there."

"Is he alive?"

"Yes." Marat was emanating a lot of magic. "He's fighting."

Stephen took a deep breath and said something in Mandarin. It sounded like a curse.

"Can you open a path to him through the water?" I asked.

Stephen backed up, all the way to the door. "That won't be necessary."

He leaned forward. "I told him to leave the damn bulldozers. The man never listens."

Everyone had told Marat to leave the damn bulldozers. If I ever did business with House Kazarian, the contract I offered Marat would have to be a mile long to account for every harebrained idea he came up with.

Stephen sprinted. He tore past me, pushed off the ledge into a leap, and for a moment he flew through the air, over the wall of flames, arms raised like wings.

Breath caught in my throat.

Stephen plunged down. He landed on the water as if it were solid ground. Waves pulsed from the impact. He thrust his arm out. Water flowed into his hand, forming a long transparent shaft with a blade on the end. He'd made a guandao. Oh, wow.

Stephen spun the watery glaive and dashed across the swamp to the clump of plants. A tentacle emerged, snapping at him like a whip. Stephen spun the guandao without breaking stride. A fan of water struck from the blade, severing the tentacle like a giant razor.

Arabella would die.

Stephen attacked the green wall, slicing, cutting, spinning, and stabbing, flawless and graceful like a genius dancer.

"Catalina," Alessandro called.

"Are you seeing this? This is insane."

"Listen to me very carefully. I need you to draw a circle that can generate a null space. A really good one."

I turned around. Alessandro was staring in the opposite direction, at the bridge leading to the island. I raised my head and froze.

Constructs marched through the mire. Huge, industrial monstrosities, gleaming in the sun with metal and magic. I had seen them before. My brain supplied the right names. Climber XV. Crawler XI. Breaker VI. Others I couldn't name. People with weapons rode atop them. And at the head of it all, on top of a colossal Digger XII, sat Cheryl Castellano.

I couldn't see Cheryl's face from this distance, but I knew it was her. My brain feverishly assessed and calculated. Nine huge constructs. At least thirty people.

Cheryl didn't have a private army. She had House security, but she wouldn't use them for this. One look at the forest of tentacles and constructs and even the dimmest person could tell that this wasn't normal magic. House security didn't have the kind of discipline to keep their mouths shut about what they saw. If the Assembly called on them, they would testify.

No. She wouldn't deploy House security. That meant Arkan's people were riding on the constructs. And that meant . . .

"She's going to kill all of us," I said.

"Yes," Alessandro said.

She knew she couldn't destroy the Abyss, so she'd settled for the next best thing. She would kill everyone who knew about it. Tatyana, Stephen, Marat, all the workers, and the two of us would die in the Pit. What a great tragedy. She would bravely carry on the work of her fallen partners, free of oversight. Free to interact with her creation at her leisure. Maybe a part of her still thought she could control him.

"Do you need chalk?" Alessandro asked.

I pulled chalk out of my pocket.

"Good."

He walked to the edge of the roof facing Cheryl's armada, crouched, and drew a perfect circle with a practiced swipe of his hand. Another circle, a line of glyphs . . . So House Sagredo had a House spell of its own after all.

The constructs drew closer. One crawled along the bridge. The rest stomped their way through the mire. Tentacles slapped against the spidery metal legs of Climber XV. Buzz saws slid out of the construct's legs, chewing the plant and metal to pieces.

There were too many. Even with Tatyana and Stephen, there were too many constructs for us to overcome, not to mention the trained killers they carried. We were stuck between the Abyss and Cheryl's army.

"Trust me," Alessandro said.

Even if I used all of my power and beguiled their minds, the most I could do was throw them at the Abyss. United, they would injure it, but not destroy it. It would return. The longer people I beguiled stayed under my power, the more they loved me. Those who survived this fight would tear me apart, consumed by the need to possess a piece of me. There would be no winners here.

The chalk felt clammy in my fingers. An odd kind of calm washed over me, clearing my fear. This was my job. I would do it and I would fight to the bitter end.

I dialed Tatyana's number. The male secretary answered. "Yes?"

"Tell Tatyana that Cheryl is not the cavalry. The thing in the swamp is her doing. She's coming to kill us."

"We know," he said and hung up.

Cheryl was a threat to us. But the Abyss would end our world if we let it. If *I* let it.

I put Linus' sword down and crouched. I could draw a dozen circles with a null boundary, but none of them fit. Half of them would cut me off from the environment. I would be safe in the circle, but magically deaf and blind, able only to expel magic by relying on my eyes and ears.

The other half would allow me to use my mind but wouldn't give me the power I required to project my magic.

I would need power and range. Lots and lots of power. I needed my senses too. The Abyss would try to reach me once he realized I was here. I had to know what he was thinking.

The half-finished designs in my head coalesced. My incomplete House Key arcane circle merged with the Aldrin projection design, augmented by the Tremaine targeting band. Yes, that would do it. It would give me the null space and the power I required and it would unchain my mind.

The circle glowed in my mind. I just had to replicate it.

I drew faster than I ever thought I could.

A drone plunged from the sky and hovered near me.

"Do not shoot this down, you shit weasel!" Bug yelled.

Alessandro and I kept drawing, crawling around on our hands and knees.

"Is Nevada okay?" My voice came out dull. I was trying to hold on to the pattern in my head.

"She's fine. There is a fucking construct army marching here."

"I know," I told him.

"What do you need?"

"Record her. Record everything that happens." If we died, Cheryl would not get away with it.

"I have six drones on it."

The constructs were almost on us. I had no idea how long Tatyana could hold out.

"Shit," Bug cursed.

I chanced a glance over my shoulder. Stephen had hacked the wall of tentacles into chunks. He stood on the island of vegetation, his face impassive. Marat slumped next to him on one knee. Three hunters rose from the swamp, each with two hounds. They ringed the two men. There was nothing I could do for them right now.

I went back to drawing. Glyphs, more glyphs. If this didn't work . . .

It had to work.

Tatyana's voice came out of the drone. I spared half a second to glance up. A small digital screen on the drone showed Tatyana in her circle and Cheryl atop the Digger just beyond the wall of flames. I was right. She'd ridden on the leading construct.

"Hi there." Tatyana sounded upbeat.

"We've come to reinforce you," Cheryl announced.

"Oh, is that what you're here to do?"

"Let us in, please."

"I had a really interesting conversation with Stephen last night," Tatyana said. "Is there anything you want to share?"

"I have no idea what he told you. Marat is out there, dying. You're under assault. Let me help you."

"We wouldn't be under assault if your fake ass hadn't made an abomination and unleashed it into the Pit. What were you thinking, Cheryl? Jesus! Were you dropped on your head as a baby? Did your parents not hug you enough? Or are you just greedy and stupid?"

Cheryl recoiled as if slapped. "How dare you!"

"How many people have you killed? Felix is dead because of you. We may all die because of you. Is this the sort of shit you think my family needs right now? I swear to God, Cheryl, as soon as I'm done with this, I'm going to burn your House to the fucking ground. Scorched earth, Cheryl. You will learn the meaning of those words."

A vicious grimace twisted Cheryl's face. "You were always a fat, stupid bitch. Your brother is a fucking arsonist, and all the money in the world won't change that. You're trash, your family is trash, and you will die in this fucking swamp. Bring me her head!"

"Holy shitballs," Bug muttered.

I glanced at the screen. On Cheryl's left, the towering thirty-foot Breaker resembling a rhino on six massive legs started toward the flame wall. The four people on its carapace readied themselves. One of them snapped into a mage pose, arms bent at the elbow, palms up, fingers cradling invisible spheres.

A translucent fiery shape coalesced around Tatyana. Her hands sprouted foot-long ghost claws. A monstrous luminous head formed over

Tatyana's face. Spikes grew from her back. It was as if a demon made of fire and glass enclosed her.

Hellspawn. A House Pierce high spell.

Tatyana grinned, her eyes pure fire, and the demon grinned with her.

The Breaker pushed through the flames.

Tatyana opened her mouth and vomited a torrent of white fire.

The front of the Breaker sagged, melting. The four people on top of it went up like human candles. Molten metal dripped. The Breaker swayed, tried to back up, and collapsed into the dark water.

"Welcome to hell," Tatyana roared in a demonic voice.

I had the whole outer band left. I couldn't watch anymore. The chalk was a small nub in my fingers. I dropped it and pulled a second stick out.

"Crush her," Cheryl howled through the drone speaker. "All of you, now. Forward!"

The inner boundary. The intersecting lines. The air smelled of soot and burning plastic. I didn't have time to watch.

"Bug, what's happening?"

"A lot, Catalina. There's a lot going on right now."

"Be more specific?"

"Tatyana keeps spitting fire. Cheryl is sending her monster constructs in. Tatyana melts them, but they keep re-forming. Minus the poor bastards that were on them. Behind us a man is running around on water slicing monsters into pieces. It's Armageddon. "

The Hellspawn was immensely powerful, but Tatyana couldn't keep it up forever.

Sweat drenched my forehead. Just a bit more time.

The island shook. I looked up. One of the constructs made it through, stomping through the buildings. People screamed.

"Where are you?" Alessandro asked, his voice like a bucket of icy water.

"Almost done. Just a little longer."

"Shit!" Bug swore. "Four more constructs and three armored transports coming down the bridge. I think we're fucked."

I drew the last line, stepped into the circle, and sent a pulse of magic through it. A pale green glow ran through the chalk lines, sending little puffs of dust into the air.

Work. Please work.

The small circles inside my design turned, realigning. The glow dashed through the chalk, but there was so much ground for it to cover.

In front of me the island burned. Pillars of black smoke streamed into the sky. A half-melted mechanical monstrosity rampaged through the island, dripping molten metal. A stream of white fire smashed into it, as if a mythical dragon had emptied its belly. Molten metal ran, but the construct kept going, flailing its metal arms into the buildings. Debris flew. Concrete exploded. Bug was right. This was Armageddon.

"Tell me when," Alessandro said. He stood in his circle, loose and ready. The pattern around his feet stretched to cover nearly half of the roof. I'd never seen anything like it.

I pushed my magic, trying to claim the circle faster.

The fire wall around the island sputtered and died. Either Tatyana ran out of magic or she was dead. The troops from the armored transport flooded onto the island on foot. Gunfire crackled. It had to be now.

The outer boundary of my circle shone.

Magic punched me, so much magic. I reeled, trying to absorb it. For an agonizing second it felt like trying to hold a jerking fire hose, then suddenly, the current and my power snapped together into one steady stream.

The Pit opened before my mind's eye and I saw everything in a fraction of a second: the bright magenta star of Cheryl's mind in front of me; the duller white glow of Tatyana, all but extinguished; the sharp pale radiance of Stephen behind us; the faint purple smudge that was Marat; the collection of weaker lights among Cheryl's private army; Alessandro's supernova, so powerful it took my breath away; and the glowing nebula of the Abyss, wrapping around us and stretching far back into the Pit.

The Abyss' presence brushed against me, eager. Visions of dying humans floated over my mind. I tested the circle and felt the impenetrable barrier of null space.

"Now," I said.

Orange light ran through the lines of Alessandro's design. A whirlwind of magic and orange sparks wound around Alessandro, lifting him off his feet. He leaped up and hung suspended, the magic spinning around him faster and faster, a maelstrom ready to be unleashed. The building underneath us shook.

The construct battle kept going, Arkan's people disembarking, oblivious to the breathtaking storm building up on the roof.

Alessandro raised his head. His skin glowed and his eyes overflowed with magic. It spilled out of him, radiating like a corona from the sun. He looked like an angel, a furious, majestic creature, filled with astonishing power and sent down to punish.

I forgot to breathe.

A blast wave of pure magic tore out of Alessandro and rolled through the Pit.

The constructs collapsed. Their hulking metal forms split into components and tumbled down. The tentacles still swirling through the water disintegrated, falling apart. Refuse blanketed the surface of the mire. Out of the corner of my eye, I saw Stephen fall into the water with a splash and disappear under the surface.

In my mind's eye, the area around us turned dark, as if a glowing city suddenly lost all power. A third of the Abyss vanished, and what remained crawled away from us.

All went silent.

Oh my God. He'd nullified their magic.

A hoarse high-pitched scream made me turn. Cheryl stood in the middle of the parking lot, Tatyana slumping a few feet away. Cheryl balled her fists and shrieked, wailing. It was the sound of pure panic.

We were born with magic. We felt it in ourselves and others. We used it, the way we used our eyes and ears. Every mage down below must have felt as if they had gone blind and deaf all at once. Only Alessandro's magic remained, burning like a sun.

So there it was, the true power of the antistasi.

Alessandro landed in the circle, the light of his magic suffusing him, his face beautiful and terrible all at once.

All traces of the man I knew had vanished. He wasn't the Artisan. He wasn't even human. He was a force determined to slaughter.

Alessandro raised his hands. Two blades of pure magic formed in his fingers.

He sprinted to the edge of the building and leaped out of sight.

Fear slapped me. "Bug!"

"On it."

The drone moved to me, hovering outside of my circle's boundary. On the screen Alessandro fell on Arkan's troops. His left blade carved through the first man like he wasn't even solid. A woman on his right died before she knew what was happening, her chest split in two by a magical sword.

In my mind's eye the glowing cloud that was the Abyss compacted, crested like a wave, and surged toward us. Oh, no. I spun around to face the swamp.

A horrible deep bellow tolled through the Pit. Constructs poured out of the mire, swimming through the water toward us, dozens and dozens of constructs, the hounds, the hunters, the strange creations I didn't know how to name. Tentacles slithered between packs of Razorscales, and behind it all, an enormous mass of flesh, metal, and plant surfaced, its own island in the Pit. Alessandro had hurt him, and the Abyss had unleashed his army.

On the little island, Stephen, soaked and dripping water, wrapped his arm around Marat. The summoner looked on the brink of collapse, the corpses of arcane beasts he must've summoned littering the ground around him. They were directly in the path of the Abyss' horde.

There were too many. Even if Alessandro slaughtered all of the attackers, the Abyss would overwhelm us.

It was my turn.

I sent a focused thought out. *No.*

The Abyss answered. *MINE.*

Images bombarded me. People dying, Alessandro dying, Linus dying, constructs of plant and metal rising, flooding out of the Pit onto the streets, and me, sitting in a protective bubble of magic, safe and imprisoned in the mountain of flesh now rolling toward me. The Abyss wanted to kill. He loved the power of it. It was central to his being. That's what he lived for. That's what he was made for.

Offer him what he wants, and he will bring his people to you to get it . . .

"Catalina, get out of there!" Bug screamed. "Get out!"

I thought of Nevada's baby. A tiny little baby, helpless and just drawing his first breath. I thought of my sisters and my mom. I thought of Alessandro.

No. I would stop this Armageddon. My family wasn't going to fuel the Abyss' army. Nobody else would ever end up as a brain and a spinal cord wrapped in foul magic. I would end this now.

I pulled the power from the circle. It poured into my wings and they burst out of me, huge and glowing. I opened my mouth and my song erupted, full of power, a siren's call beyond anything I had ever imagined. Power surged out of me, no longer spiraling in delicate shoots, but flowing like an ocean tide. My feet had left the ground, but I barely noticed.

Come to me. Please me.

The wave of my magic collided with the constellation of the Abyss' mind.

I sang. It was an ancient song, full of promises and whispers of bliss, the kind of song that caused seasoned sailors to hurl themselves into raging seas just to get closer.

Love me. Come to me and love me.

My magic swept through the nebula of the Abyss' mind, brushing aside his defenses, all the way to its glowing center. It wrapped around the glowing star that used to be a human mind and saturated it.

Every construct in the Pit stopped and shuddered.

Show yourself to me. Come to me. Trust me. I am happiness. I am ecstasy. I am what you desire.

The constructs charged toward me.

On the island, Stephen gripped Marat, trying to shield him. The Abyss flowed around them and hurled himself against the foot of the building I was on. The constructs piled onto each other, building a hill of squirming bodies.

Yes. That's what I want. More. Show me more.

The mire boiled. Tentacles thrust out, slapping against the hill of plant and metal growing against the building. The glowing dots of the Abyss' nodes converged on me. The shining center moved, shifting toward me. The vast mound crept to me like a colossal amoeba, rising as it neared.

Ten feet high. Twenty.

Images burst in my mind, like soap bubbles. A huge grotesque monstrosity wrapping itself around the building, begging for my touch.

I changed the pitch of my song. *No. Ugly. Clumsy. Graceless.*

The nebula that was the Abyss convulsed in pain.

I sent my own image back. Alessandro glowing with magic, moving with elegance and grace.

Strong. Fast. Beautiful. Worthy. Worthy of me.

A shudder ran through the constructs in unison. The center of the mound collapsed, sucked into itself. The tiny glowing stars of nodes surfaced from the pile by the building and rolled into the hole in the center of the mound. The constructs on the outer edges fell apart. The nebula of the Abyss' mind contracted, compacting in on itself.

Water vapor erupted on the edges of the mound. Chunks of it began to fall away. The Abyss was building something, throwing all of its energy and magic into it.

The nodes aggregated around the central light, all but merging with it. Tentacles ripped metal from random constructs and hurled it into the hole in the mound.

Yes, I sang. *Glowing. Beautiful. Yes. That's what I want.*

The mound crept forward again. Its edges decayed. Large pieces broke off and sank, inert. The nebula compacted on itself.

My vision swam. My heart fluttered in the cage of my ribs. I had channeled so much magic, and my body was giving out. I had to hold on. Almost there. Almost.

The shambling mound landed at the foot of the hill the constructs built against my building. The nebula was gone now. Only its center remained, condensed into blinding white.

The mound split. A cloud of revolting stench washed over me and dispersed.

Giant tentacles surged up in front of me and opened like the petals of a flower. A glowing man stood at their center, a giant with the body of a god made with white metal and radiant flowers, perfect and astonishingly beautiful.

I looked at his face. Nothing in the world could compare. His eyes glowed with blue light. I wanted to weep and prostrate myself, but then I would have to stop looking at him, and it was beyond me to turn away. I had never seen anything so mesmerizing. I had to keep looking at him. I could spend a lifetime staring.

Our minds touched and I saw myself standing next to him with a body that matched his. He would remake me. I would be Eve to his Adam. The Pit would be our Eden, no one would cast us out of it, and humanity would serve us forever.

He smiled. Magic radiated from him and washed over me.

My body trembled, every nerve on fire.

He was made of pure power and will. Every node he possessed was in that body. There weren't enough adjectives in any human language to describe him.

He opened his arms. His mind brushed against mine. *Join me.*

I waved my hand. The circle around me died. I sang to him, a sweet song, filled with love and longing.

Alessandro screamed my name.

The Abyss held out his hand.

In my memories, Alessandro kissed me and whispered, "I love you." It was the happiest I had ever been.

I stepped out of the circle, picked up Linus' sword, and rested my hand in the Abyss' perfect fingers.

He smiled.

I hammered a spike of magic into the sword and plunged my blade into his chest, where the once-human mind burned with magic. The null space carved through the armored body and pierced the fragile brain.

The titan fell to his knees.

I dropped my sword.

His magic blinked, pulsed with bright white, and died. He had melded all of his nodes to make this body for me. Unified into one, they were no longer capable of survival. I felt them dying one by one. The last one winked out.

The awe-inspiring body at my feet fell apart. The beautiful, murderous god of the Pit was dead, and I had killed him. The full enormity of it hit me and I screamed my grief and pain into the sky before it tore me apart, because I had murdered something indescribably beautiful and it would never exist again. The magic turned my scream into a song and once the last notes of it died, I had nothing left.

My legs gave out. I crashed onto the roof.

Alessandro would live. Everyone would live.

Behind me a loud hum announced incoming helicopters.

 Chapter 17

Alessandro came for me, covered in blood, picked me up, and we jumped off the roof while Bug screamed through his drone. I closed my eyes and clung to him, shell-shocked, my mind reeling. It felt like everything was happening to someone else.

Alessandro loaded me into a helicopter. I held on to him, afraid that he would leave, but he stayed on the seat next to me, his arm around me.

"It's over," he murmured. "It's all over."

All around us, soldiers moved with purpose, but there was nobody to kill. Alessandro had reaped a bloody harvest. None of Arkan's people survived.

Linus appeared by the helicopter and studied me, his face concerned. "Do you know who I am?"

I stared at him, blank. Making words was too hard.

He glanced at Alessandro. "Has she spoken?"

"No."

Linus turned to me, his face tense. His eyes looked . . . afraid.

"Catalina, say something. Anything at all. It's very important. Make a sound, but don't sing. Say a word."

I opened my mouth. Nothing came out.

"Just one word. You can do it. Say no. You say no so well. You've had a lot of practice."

I struggled to push words out.

"Come on," Linus prompted, his voice gentle. "Just one word. Remember, don't sing."

". . ."

"You can do it."

Something clicked in my brain. "I told my family that I'm the Deputy."

Linus exhaled and slumped against the side of the chopper. For a moment he looked old.

"Don't kill my family."

"That's fine. Don't worry. The Baylors are safe. Quite frankly, I'm surprised that it took so long. I thought you would tell them months ago. It's unrealistic to expect a Deputy Warden's family to not know their position."

It was another one of his tests. Bastard.

I looked at Alessandro. "Please hurt him for me."

"Good job," Linus said. "Carry on."

He went away. I closed my eyes and stuck my face into Alessandro's shoulder and let the world go.

I had no idea how much time had passed. At some point we were in the air and then I fell asleep again.

I woke up because the helicopter landed on a roof. Alessandro gently sat me upright.

"Where are we?" I asked.

He smiled. "Come on, there is someone who wants to meet you."

We got out and entered the building. He held my hand and we walked down a hallway, took an elevator down, walked down another hallway . . . I was just walking next to him. I didn't want to be away from him. I loved him so much, and a part of me still couldn't believe that the Abyss was dead and that this wasn't a dream. I needed convincing that I was actually here and not sitting in the bubble of the Abyss' magic, deep inside his mound.

We stopped at a nurse's station. Someone put a cap and gown on me. Someone poured sanitizer on my hands and wiped my face with some kind of wipe. It smelled like rubbing alcohol and stung. A nurse told me to follow her. I tried to stay with Alessandro, but she told me he was too bloody. I followed her down the hallway through a door with four guards outside of it.

In a large comfortable room, Nevada sat on the bed. Connor sat next to her in a chair. I saw Mom and Grandma Frida, Arabella and my cousins. Nevada was holding a bundle of blankets. I came closer, and she offered it to me.

"Congratulations. You're an aunt."

I looked at my tiny, red-faced nephew, reached out, and touched his little fist.

Everything hit me at once. I wrapped my arms around the baby, sat down on the floor, and cried.

The next morning, I sat in a plush chair in the America Tower, waiting for the start of the special session of the Texas Assembly. Cheryl had somehow escaped the Pit and thrown herself on the mercy of the Texas Houses. She must've run the moment Alessandro jumped off the roof, otherwise he would've killed her. Instead she ended up at the House of one of her well-respected friends. All of her charitable work and connections bought her a lot of goodwill and she intended to use every drop of it to shield herself from Lander's vengeance.

She still thought this was about Felix's murder.

Alessandro sat in a chair next to me. I had brought him in as my guest. He was in his full Count Sagredo persona, beautiful suit, beautiful hair, beautiful smile. You would never know that less than twenty-four hours ago he'd killed sixteen of Arkan's professional soldiers. I still remembered him smeared with soot and blood. I also remembered waking up next to him this morning. Covered with soot and blood or clean and in my bed, I didn't care. I would be with him no matter what he did.

Alessandro saw me looking, reached over, took my hand, and squeezed it.

Around us the massive chamber was slowly filling up with Primes in jet-black robes, each wearing a green stole draped over their shoulders. We were in the Upper Chamber, where only the Heads of various Texas

Houses could vote. Cheryl had demanded the judgment of her peers and only the Heads of Houses qualified.

Five rows away, in the front, Lander Morton sat in his wheelchair. A dark-haired teenage boy sat on his right and two younger girls, both with the same chocolate-brown hair, sat on his left. Lander had brought Felix's children to face their father's murderer.

I had made a report to Lander. It was carefully curated by Linus, but it outlined the version of events with enough accuracy. Cheryl had unleashed an illegal construct into the Pit. When Felix decided to seek outside assistance, she panicked, lured him to the Pit, and killed him. Then the construct ran amok, and when Cheryl realized that discovery was inevitable, she brought her House's industrial army to kill off all the witnesses.

Linus had raided Cheryl's workshop. He'd recovered the vial with traces of the Osiris serum in it. That was what remained of Cheryl's sample. She had used all of it to push the nameless telepath's mind into becoming the Abyss. She didn't know how to duplicate the serum and probably decided that bringing in someone else to replicate it was too risky.

As if on cue, Cheryl walked through the door, surrounded by Primes. I recognized a few faces, all old Houses, all respected. She saw Lander and kept walking, looking straight ahead. Her squad shielded her from Lander's gaze but not from his voice.

"Look, children," he croaked. "Look at the woman who murdered your father."

Cheryl crossed the floor and sat down in the front row on the other side.

Alessandro grimaced.

"What?"

"I should've killed her."

"You can't just murder the saint of Houston without some pomp and circumstance."

"I realize that. I just dislike leaving things unfinished. It was my last job. A shame to leave it undone."

That's right. Lander had hired him to kill his son's murderer. Wait . . .

"Last job?"

He turned to me. "I told you. I'm not leaving."

He would stay. He really meant it.

My phone chimed. A call from Bern. Odd. He almost always texted. I put it to my ear.

"Yes?"

"I finally got the footage from a gas station near Christian Ravenscroft's country club. You said the telekinetic was a Prime. Are you sure?"

"Yes. Why?"

A dark-haired man sat down in the row behind us. Alessandro went still.

I turned my head and glanced at the man. Recognition struck me.

"I'll call you back." I hung up.

There was no need to continue. I knew who Bern saw on that recording.

I skimmed his mind.

It made no sense. This man was barely a Significant the last time we met. Now, he was a Prime, a blazing powerful Prime. This was the power I had felt in the Pit.

"Long time no see." The man grinned at me, his handsome face sharp.

I kept my voice neutral. "Prime Sagredo, let me introduce Xavier Ramirez Secada. He used to be Rogan's first cousin, once removed."

"We've met," Alessandro said.

Telekinetic, silos, semi. Xavier was the one who'd knocked Alessandro off that silo, to his near death.

"It's Prime Secada now. You're probably wondering how," Xavier said, a light Spanish accent overlaying his words. "The Osiris serum is a wonderful thing."

When we raided Diatheke, Arkan's pet scientist was trying to find a way to augment one's magic with the serum. Her method warped her subjects. Apparently not all of them.

Xavier leaned his elbows on the backs of our seats and nodded toward Lander and the children. "Here's the deal. You move, they die."

Alessandro scanned the chamber.

"If it was up to me," Xavier continued, "I would kill you both." He looked at Alessandro. "You for obvious reasons." He looked at me. "And you, because you destroyed my family."

"You destroyed his family and I wasn't invited?" Alessandro said, his tone light.

"I didn't destroy anything. Xavier was under the impression he was related to Rogan. I simply found out that his mother chose to cheat on her husband." I looked at Xavier. "It's not my fault that you're a bastard."

Xavier bared his teeth at me. "When the time comes—and it will—I'll make you suffer. I have learned all sorts of wonderful ways to make the pain last and last and last."

"You were a sadistic little shit as a teenager," I told him. "I see you haven't changed."

"This is so fun," Xavier said. "But sadly, I have to take care of a bit of business."

"Please," Alessandro invited. "I'm getting bored."

"Well, we can't have that. The old man feels a sense of obligation to you for killing your father in front of you. He didn't recognize you in Montreal, but he figured it out when you came back to life like Lazarus. He's inclined to let you walk away. He feels it's fair. He killed your father, you killed three of his best, and let's not forget Cheryl."

"I'm overcome by his generosity." Alessandro's voice was light and breezy.

"You should be. As I said, I don't understand it, but he's the boss. Walk away, stop trying to kill him, stop fucking up his plans, and he'll let bygones be bygones. However, this dynamic duo you've got going is annoying, so I have orders to break the two of you up."

Xavier smiled at me. "Everything you think he is is a lie. His family is penniless. They've been drowning in debt for generations. They started borrowing money in the eighteenth century and never stopped. Now they are so deep in the hole, they will never get out. His cars? Rented. His clothes? Bought secondhand. His pictures? Staged. The magic of photoshop."

Alessandro's face was unreadable.

"You see, with his kind of magic, he's only good for two jobs, body-guard or assassin, and his grandfather wouldn't let him be either, because it's beneath a Sagredo to serve other men. Do you know what his purpose in life is? To look pretty, so they can auction him off to the highest bidder. When some idiot rich girl marries him, they will use her dowry to stave off their creditors so they can stay afloat for just a little while longer. That's how they survive. His Instagram is a billboard advertising him to his future bride. He's a prince in plastic jewels."

Alessandro's expression was still blank. He looked almost bored. How much must it have cost him? He was so proud.

"Except our boy here decided to not play by the rules. They tried to marry him off three times, and he sabotaged every single engagement beyond repair."

Xavier shook his head mockingly. "Why couldn't you be a good boy, Alessandro? Why couldn't you marry a rich girl and leech off of her, so your family could keep pretending to have some tattered dignity? Your father did it. Well, for a while anyway."

You fucking asshole. "You won't live to get old," I promised him.

"Wait, you haven't heard the best part yet." Xavier grinned. "His grandfather got so tired of dealing with him that he kicked him out of the family. He isn't a Count. He isn't even a Sagredo. He's been excised."

Oh my God.

I think your pauper prince truly loves you, poor fool. It's a shame. My grandmother knew. I thought she'd been talking about his clothes, but Victoria knew.

"All he has is what you see. He's been running around the planet, killing assassins, and sending money home to his poor mother so she can keep the lights on for his two sisters. He doesn't even keep what he earns."

So many things made sense now.

Xavier turned to Alessandro. "There is something you should know about her too. She's a gold digger like her sister. Her whole family is. Without money, a title, and a House, you're worthless to her. What's that fun American expression? She will drop you like a hot potato."

Alessandro stared at him, his expression so dark I barely recognized him.

"Go home, Alessandro. Accept what you are. Your grandfather refused to announce the excision in public, because he still hopes you will come back to the fold and earn your keep by fucking some rich heiress until she opens her bank accounts. That's your destiny."

Alessandro smiled. It chilled me to the bone.

"Well, I have done my part." Xavier rose. "Please enjoy the rest of your day."

He got up and walked away.

Alessandro looked at me. He didn't say anything, he just looked at me. They had tried to auction him. Like a horse. He must've known that's what they had planned for him. He'd spent half of his life pretending to be someone he wasn't.

Linus sat down next to me. "The show is about to start."

Slowly, deliberately, Alessandro turned away from me and looked at the dais.

The Speaker of the Assembly, Luciana Cabera, walked into the chamber. She was a Hispanic woman in her sixties who had been elected to the position after the previous Speaker retired last year. A white man in his forties walked onto the dais carrying a golden staff. He banged it on the floor. A pulse of magic burst from him.

"This special session is now open."

I didn't even care anymore. Alessandro sat next to me, still like a statue and I wanted to fix it.

Luciana walked up to her thronelike chair on the dais and sat.

"Ladies and gentlemen, thank you for joining us on such short notice. I promise this will be quick. As you all know, Cheryl Castellano, Prime and Head of House Castellano, has appealed to this body. She claims to be falsely accused of murdering Felix Morton, Prime and heir to House Morton. She believes that her business partners conspired with Lander Morton, Prime and Head of House Morton, to intentionally smear her name in an effort to remove her from the board of the Pit Reclamation Project and requests that we hear her case and render our judgment."

Cheryl had some balls. Wow.

"Normally, the Texas Assembly would be only too happy to adjudicate this matter."

A light ripple of laughter ran through the chamber. The Texas Assembly hated dealing with inter-House feuds.

Luciana raised her hand. The laughter died.

"Regretfully, we have another pressing matter, which overrides this appeal."

A burly bailiff who looked like she could stop a tank barehanded walked up onto the dais and handed the Speaker a sealed envelope. A camera projected the image of the envelope onto a huge digital screen behind Luciana. It bore the seal of the National Assembly.

Luciana opened the envelope, pulled out an old-fashioned parchment, and unrolled it.

"Cheryl Amanda Castellano of House Castellano, you are hereby remanded into the custody of the National Assembly on charges of crimes against humanity and unlawful magic experimentation."

The chamber erupted.

"Order!" the Gold Staff roared.

Cheryl jumped up. "No! No."

Chains burst out of the ground and wound around Cheryl. She fell silent, her scream cut off. Her eyes rolled back in her head and she sagged down.

Two figures stepped out from an alcove behind the dais, both wearing crimson robes with hoods that hid their faces. The shorter figure waved a hand and Cheryl rose three inches off the ground. They walked to the doorway, and Cheryl followed, gliding silently.

I leaned to Linus and whispered, "Who are they?"

"Wardens from other states," he murmured back.

Right. And everyone would see Linus sitting in the chamber, presumably having nothing at all to do with the scary hooded figures taking Cheryl away. His identity as a Warden would remain confidential.

"This is an outrage!" Lander howled, punching the arms of his chair. "She killed my son! I demand vengeance!"

The robed figures paused before Lander's wheelchair. The front figure spoke in a deep female voice.

"The National Assembly regrets the loss of your son and acknowledges the anguish of House Morton. Should she be found guilty, we invite you to join us for her execution. Be assured, Prime Morton, you won't have to wait long for that invitation."

Lander took a deep breath, then sagged in his chair. The hooded pair walked out of the chamber, Cheryl in tow.

"All is well that ends well," Linus murmured. "I'll see you both for dinner tonight. My place."

Sunshine flooded the parking lot. Heat rose from the pavement in waves. I pulled the black robe off and tucked it under my arm. Another moment, and I would bake like a pie.

Tonight, Linus would want the full report. Most likely he was working on a plan to take down Arkan. That was okay. Arkan needed to die and Xavier had to die with him. I was fine with that.

In front of us a large fountain in the shape of a giant dandelion sent mist and water into the air.

Alessandro hadn't said a word.

I held the keys out to him. "Would you like to drive?"

He turned to me, his face grim. "We need to talk."

I had expected it, but my world cracked in half anyway. I stopped.

A muscle jerked in his cheek. "What he said was true. Every word of it."

"I know."

"I grew up pretending to be the man I should've been. My job was made very clear to me after my father died. My mission in life was to attract the right kind of bride with a bank account large enough to keep our family alive. I went to the parties wearing designer clothes after listening to my mother cry on the phone with our creditors. I attended gallery openings and drank champagne while my sisters ate the same pasta with nothing but a bit of salt for three days in a row because it was all we had."

The burden of it, the shame he must've felt, had to be crushing. But he talked about it as if he were discussing the morning news over coffee.

"Every time I tried to earn money, my family spat on it. After the third time my grandfather hurled the money I brought home in my face, I realized that they would never accept it. And when I refused to be sold, they excised me. In the last decade I've earned over sixty million. All of it, except for fifty thousand dollars I keep in my account as operational expenses, went to our debt and to my mother and my sisters. Xavier is right. I'm the reason their lights are on. I have earned enough to keep the creditors off their back and to make sure that my mother and my sisters won't starve. They can afford clothes and shoes. They won't go without. I would have kept going, but my oldest sister grew up. She'd acted as my agent since she was fourteen, but now she refuses to take my blood money. She says she doesn't want the guilt of knowing I might die for it."

"I think I would like your sister."

His voice was so detached. He'd locked all his feelings into a cage of will and kept them there.

"I can offer you nothing except myself. All I can do is be an assassin or a bodyguard. I'm done being an assassin and you're the only person I want to guard. I tried to tell you this before, but I wanted you so much, it almost made me insane. I *am* a prince in plastic jewels, but I was still raised as a Prime. I know what a Prime should bring to the marriage."

"And what would that be?"

"A stable House. Political and financial connections. Alliances. Wealth. Security. I have none of it. I come to you with nothing. Right here, right now, this is all I will ever be. I can't leave you on my own, Catalina, but if you tell me to go, I will. I promise I'll never bother you again."

He waited.

His words floated from my memory. *You're beautiful, you're brilliant, and if they knew how dangerous you were, you would get buried in proposals.*

It was my turn.

"Alessandro, you're the most powerful antistasi on the planet. What you did in the Pit was beyond anything I could've imagined. You're strong, skilled, educated, and you have this incredible brain that unravels complex schemes in seconds. You walked into a building full of trained killers and eliminated everyone there to save a child you barely knew. And then you went to see Victoria Tremaine and threatened to cut her head off, and she let you go because you are charming, and your bearing is flawless. Who in this world can do that? You're kind to my relatives when you have nothing to gain. You're probably the only person aside from my family who understands me and can call me on my crap. And with all of that, you love me. You bring so much, Alessandro."

He stared at me.

"Don't you get it? Right here, right now, you are everything I ever wanted. I don't care about money, connections, or reputation. We can earn all these things, together. I just want you. You're so much more than I hoped for. If you come home with me, I'll be the luckiest person alive."

I didn't see him move. One moment he was standing by the fountain and the next he kissed me, his lips hot and desperate. He stole my breath away.

"Stay with me," I asked him.

"Always," he promised.

 # Epilogue

The hospital hallway lay shrouded in shadow. An older, distinguished man was waiting by the nurses' station, a lone nurse nervously pacing by him. An elevator chimed quietly. The doors parted and an older woman stepped out, accompanied by a young man with a sharp haircut and dressed in a black suit.

The older man by the station raised his arms. "Where have you been?" he whispered.

"Spare me," the older woman hissed. "This wasn't exactly easy."

"Hurry. We have fifteen minutes," the nurse told them. "This baby is guarded like Fort Knox."

She ushered the three of them into a room and shut the door. The young man in the suit parked himself by the door.

The older woman paced. "What if he's a dud?"

"He is not a dud. None of them have been."

She pressed her hands together and walked some more.

Hurried steps came from outside.

The door swung open and the same nurse entered, carrying a newborn, two guards behind her. The young man in a suit raised his hand and the two guards halted, their eyes blank.

The old woman rushed to the nurse and gently took the baby out of her arms. "Leave us."

The nurse glanced at the older man. He nodded. She stepped outside and closed the door.

Tenderly, the old woman peeled off the blanket revealing the baby's round face and tiny fists in pale mittens.

"What a beautiful boy. What a lovely, lovely boy."

The older man grinned.

The woman rocked the baby and smiled. "Look, Trevor, isn't he the most beautiful child you've ever seen?"

For the first time the young man in the suit spoke. "Yes, ma'am. He is."